F

L11-OM

D0416768

The Girl from Barefoot House

ALSO BY MAUREEN LEE

The Pearl Street Series:
Lights Out Liverpool
Put Out The Fires
Through The Storm

Stepping Stones
Liverpool Annie
Dancing in the Dark

The Girl from Barefoot House

Maureen Lee

ORION

Copyright © 2000 Maureen Lee

The right of Maureen Lee to be identified as the author
of this work has been asserted by her in accordance with
the Copyright, Designs and Patents Act 1988

All rights reserved. No part of this publication may be
reproduced, stored in a retrieval system, or transmitted
in any form or by any means, electronic, mechanical,
photocopying, recording or otherwise without the prior
permission of the copyright owner

First published in Great Britain in 2000 by
Orion
An imprint of Orion Books Ltd
Orion House, 5 Upper St Martin's Lane,
London WC2H 9EA

A CIP catalogue record for this book
is available from the British Library

Typeset in Great Britain by
Deltatype Ltd, Birkenhead, Merseyside
Printed and bound by
Clays Ltd, St Ives Plc

For
Deidre and David

Huskisson Street
1938–1940

'Hello, Petal. I'm home.'

'Mam!' Josie raised her arms and was lifted out of bed and hugged so hard she could scarcely breathe.

'I see you drank your milk and ate your cream crackers like a good girl.'

'Yes, Mam.' She snuggled her head against Mam's neck, into the curved space she thought of as especially hers.

'I've missed you, Petal. Now, I've got a visitor, so you sit on the stairs for a little while. Take mam's cardy, and don't forget Teddy. I'll be out to get you in the twinkling of an eye. Then I'll make us a cup of cocoa and a jam butty, like always.'

'All right, Mam.' Josie slithered obediently to the floor, and Mam gently placed the navy blue cardigan around her shoulders.

'How old is she?' The gruff voice came from a dark corner of the candlelit room, by the door. A man stepped forward, very tall, with a bent nose and black curly hair. His face was hard, but his eyes were troubled.

'Three.'

'Bit young to be left on her own all this time, isn't she? It's not safe.'

'What do you mean, it's not safe?' Mam said tartly. She removed the long pearl pin from her brown felt hat. 'There's a fireguard, and I leave something to eat. She knows I'll always come back. Anyroad, what's it to you?'

'Nowt. Just put her outside so I get what I've come for before you pass out. You're stewed rotten, and I've been waiting all night long for this.'

'It's what I was about to do before you shoved your big oar in.' The voice changed as she turned to her child. 'Go on, luv,' she said softly, shoving her through the door and on to the landing.

Josie sat at the top of the stairs and held Teddy up so that he could see the stars peeping down at them through the skylight and the filmy cobwebs floating eerily in the light of the moon. Then she wrapped the sleeves of the cardigan around her neck, and tried to tuck her bare feet inside the ribbed hem. It was cold in her nightie on the landing. Their attic was the warmest place in the house according to Mam, because heat rose, and they got the benefit of everyone's fires, as well as their own. The attic was where the maids used to live a long time ago. It had a small iron fireplace and a triangular sink in the corner. There was a tiny window just below where the roof peaked.

The stairs in the tall house in Huskisson Street, a mere stone's throw from the Protestant cathedral, had their own special smell, a mixture of all sorts of interesting things: of food – mainly boiled cabbage or fried onions – scent, smoke, dust, a peculiar smell that Mam said was dry rot. The house had once been very grand, having been owned by a man who imported rare spices from the Orient. The rooms used to be full of fine furniture; exquisite rugs and carpets had covered the floors. Everywhere, apart from the attic, had been wired for electricity, which was very up to date, as not everyone could get light at the flick of a switch. Most people still used gas.

Mam spent ages describing how she imagined the place might have looked. 'But now it's gone to rack and ruin,' she sighed. All that remained was the opulent wallpaper in the downstairs rooms. Even the bathroom had lost its grandeur: tiles had fallen off the walls, and the taps provided water at a trickle. The chain in the lavatory was just a piece of string, and no one could remember it having had a seat.

There was a party downstairs, lots of voices, music – someone was playing a mouth organ. Josie never seemed to be awake when the house was quiet. Perhaps it never was. Perhaps there were always people having parties, shouting and screaming, fighting or laughing, crying or singing. Sometimes the bobbies came, stamping through the house as if they owned the place, up and down the stairs, banging on doors, not waiting to be asked in. When this happened, Mam would sit Josie on her knee and be reading a story when a bobby barged in and demanded she come to the station.

'How dare you!' she would say in the frosty, dead posh voice she kept specially for such occasions. 'I'm just sitting here, reading me little girl a story. Since when has reading been a crime?'

'Sorry, ma'am,' the bobby would say, touching his funny big dome of a hat, followed by something like, 'I didn't realise respectable women lived here.'

Mam would toss her great mane of brown hair and say, 'Well, they do, see.'

On Sundays, after she and Mam and some of the girls had been to Mass, everyone would be in a great good humour and they would gather in one of the downstairs rooms for a cup of tea and a jangle. There were six other girls besides Mam – fat Liz, tall Kate, buck-toothed Gladys, black Rita, Irish Rose and smelly Maude. Maude was much older than the others and going bald, but was still called a girl. She smoked a lot, and the fingers of her right hand were a funny orange colour. Mam was fondest most of Maude. Josie, in her best dress, would be in her element as she was made a desperate fuss of, passed from one knee to another and petted almost to death. The girls often bought her presents – a bar of chocolate, a hairslide or a little toy. It was Maude who'd given her Teddy for her first birthday.

'They're dead envious because I've got you,' Mam would whisper. 'They'd all like a little girl like my Petal, though they'd never admit it. At nineteen, Mam was the next to youngest there, but the only one a mother. This made her very proud, as if she had one up on the others.

Josie was quite definitely not a burden or a cross to bear, as some of the girls suggested. Okay, she could have earned two or three times as much if she had been on her own, but she made enough to keep body and soul together, thanks very much. The Sunday before last, when the subject had come up again, Mam lost her temper when Kate said, 'Let's face it, Mabel, someone in our line of work would be far better off without a kiddie.'

'Cobblers!' Mam flashed angrily. 'You're only saying that because you're jealous. Our Josie's more important to me than anything in the world.'

'Why should I be jealous when I got rid of two of me own?' Kate countered. 'If you cared about your Josie all that much, you wouldn't be here. This is no place to raise a kid. You had a proper education, not like us lot. You're always on about that chemist's shop where you used to work. If you put your mind to it, you could get a decent job like a shot.'

Like much of the conversation that she overheard, this went completely over Josie's head, but she noticed Mam's rosy cheeks turn white. 'No, I couldn't,' she whispered. 'Not while I'm stuck on the booze.'

The door to the attic opened and the man with the crooked nose came out. He said kindly, 'C'mon, kid. I'll take you back in.' He scooped Josie up, carried her into the room and sat her on the bed. Mam was in her pink nightie, twisting her long hair into a plait, which made her look like a beautiful saint. She swayed and nearly fell.

'You may well be a good screw,' the man snapped, 'but you're a lousy ma. If you're not careful, one of these days the kid'll be taken off you.'

'You bugger off, you,' Mam said in a slurred, trembly voice. 'You'd go a long road before you'd find a bonnier child. And, anyroad, she'll be four in May.' She sat on the bed and put her arm around Josie's shoulders. 'You're happy, aren't you, luv?'

Josie looked up from tucking Teddy under the bedclothes so that just his head and arms showed. 'Oh, yes, Mam.'

'See!' Mam said challengingly.

'She looks fit,' the man conceded grudgingly. 'As to being happy, well, she don't know any better, does she? She probably don't know what happy means.'

After he'd gone, Mam filled the kettle from the sink in the corner and put it on the hob to boil, talking to herself all the while. 'I wonder if we should move, find somewhere else?' she muttered. 'Though I like it here, the girls are a scream, well mostly, and the landlord's more or less decent. But I'll have to start using a different pub. I don't want to come across that geezer tonight a second time, nosy-poke bugger that he was. I'll have a word with Maude, see what she thinks.' She suddenly flew across the room and seized Josie in her slim arms. 'I couldn't live without you, Petal. I'd kill us both before I'd let them take you away.'

'Yes, Mam,' Josie answered. She had no idea what Mam was on about, though she knew what being happy meant. She sat on the big bed, watching the candle send flickering shadows on to the sloping wooden rafters and the bare brick walls. Mam took some clothes off the line strung between rafters and put them over the fireguard. They began to steam and give off a warm, familiar smell. Then her mother mixed the cocoa, cut and margarined the bread, spread the jam, and Josie thought it would be impossible to be happier than she was now. In a minute, Mam would bring the butties to bed with her, leaving the cocoa on the floor for now, and they would eat them sitting up, leaning against each other.

'What is it we need, Petal?' Mam said, coming over with the butties on a cracked plate.

'A tray,' Josie said promptly. Every night without fail Mam brought up their desperate need of a tray.

'That's right. We could prop it on our knees, like a little table. Tell you what, we'll walk into town tomorrow, see if there's any trays going cheap in Blackler's bargain basement. We'll make a day of it, wear our bezzie clothes. We'll finish off with a cup of tea in Lyon's.'

'Yes, Mam,' Josie said blissfully. Mam turned every day into an adventure. Depending on the weather, they would go to the swings in Princes Park, or for a ride on the ferry to Birkenhead or Seacome – sometimes they even went as far as New Brighton, and if Mam was flush they'd go on the waltzer and the bobby horses. If it were raining, they would wander around St John's Market, or the big posh shops like George Henry Lee's and Bon Marché.

As Mam climbed into bed beside her, she said, 'We used to have a lovely black lacquered tray at home – you should have seen it, Petal.'

'Tell us about home,' Josie murmured.

'Again? You'd think I'd lived in Buckingham Palace, not an ordinary house off Penny Lane.'

''S interesting.'

Mam laughed. 'Interesting! That's a big word for a little girl not long off four.'

'Well, it is. What was the tray like?' Josie took a butty and snuggled into the crook of Mam's arm, careful not to disturb Teddy, who had gone fast asleep.

'I told you, black lacquered. It sort of shone, and had flowers, like orchids, painted on it. Orange and pink they were, with long, green leaves. Me dad brought it back from Japan, I think it was. Our house in Machin Street was full of lovely things me dad brought from all over the world. The best tray was only brought out on Sundays. Weekdays, we used the horrible wooden one. Mind you, I won't turn up me nose if wooden's all they've got in Blackler's basement tomorrow.'

'What did your dad look like, Mam?'

'You know as much about him as I know meself, and what's more, you know you know.' Mam tickled her tummy, and Josie collapsed, giggling. 'He was an Irishman from County Kildare, a captain in the merchant navy, and he died

6

in the last year of the Great War, though it was the weather, a terrible storm, that killed him, not the fighting. I was only a month old, so I never saw him, and he never saw me. Ne'er did the twain meet, as the saying goes.'

'But you saw his photo,' Josie prompted.

'So I did, Petal.' Mam grinned. 'You remember this word for word, don't you? Yes, his photo was on the mantelpiece in Machin Street.'

'And he was very handsome?'

'Very handsome indeed, my Petal. Tall, well built, with brown hair same as yours and mine and the same dark blue eyes. Not that I could tell the colours from the photo, like, but that's what me poor mam told me.'

'Poor Mam died of a broken heart,' Josie said sadly.

'More or less.' Mam shrugged. 'She was Irish, too, from the same village, and she'd known him all her life. Six years afterwards, she went to meet her maker. Our Ivy was eighteen by then, and it was her that brought me up. She was more like a mother than me real one. Until she married Vincent Adams, that is. I were twelve by then. Here's your cocoa, luv. Mind you don't spill it.' Mam's blue eyes glittered angrily. 'Three years later, she chucked me out, though she'd no right. It was a bought house, and every bit as much mine as hers. It was the only bought house in Machin Street, and the first to have electricity,' she went on grandly. 'All the rest were rented.'

'Why did she chuck you out, Mam?' Josie asked curiously. The story always got rather vague at about this time.

'She thought I'd done something wrong, but I hadn't. Someone else had done the wrong, but I was the one who got the blame. I was the one who wandered the streets, looking for a place to live, getting chucked out over and over once they realised me condition.'

'It was then you found Maude downstairs.'

'No, luv, it was Maude downstairs who found me. I'd collapsed in a back entry not far from here, and was waiting for a miracle to happen. It was Maude who brought me to her room downstairs so the miracle could happen somewhere nice and warm.'

'*Me* was the miracle,' Josie said contentedly.

'The miracle of miracles, that's my Petal, and it's "I", not "me". Now, if you've finished your cocoa, it's time we lay down and went to sleep. That party downstairs sounds as if it's going on all night. Do you want to use the po first?'

'No, ta, Mam. I used it just before you came in.'

'Well, I do.' Mam got out of bed and pulled the po from underneath. 'I hope Teddy's got his eyes closed. It's not done for a gentleman to see a lady using the chamber pot.'

'He's fast asleep, but I'll put me hand over his face, like, just to make sure.'

'Ta, Petal, but be careful not to smother him, mind.'

Mam snuffed out the candle and got into bed. 'Turn over, luv. Sit on me knee, like. It's the comfortablest way.'

They lay like that for quite a while, and Josie felt as if they'd become one person as Mam's heart beat against her own, and she could feel the warm breath on her neck. She could tell that Mam was still awake.

'Mam?' she whispered.

'Yes, luv?'

'Another miracle's going to happen one day, isn't it?'

'That's right,' Mam murmured huskily. 'Like I said, by the time you're ready for school, Mam'll be off the drink, I swear it. I'll get a proper job, and we'll get a proper little house between us. You and me will stay together nights, not like now. I'm glad it was Maude who found me in that entry, not some sanctimonious snob like our Ivy who would have had you taken away. But Maude wasn't exactly a good influence on a girl of fifteen. She got me this room and set me on a road I would never have followed otherwise, the only road she knew. Still, I'm not sorry about the way things turned out.' The voice got huskier, became a sob. Josie felt Mam's arm tighten around her waist. 'Well, not sorry much.'

★

8

Blackler's basement was an Aladdin's cave of dazzling and exceedingly tempting bargains. Mam was greatly taken with a flowered china teapot with a slightly misshapen lid and a hand-embroidered Irish linen tablecloth with nothing obviously wrong with it at all. The cheapest tray they found was brown Bakelite and rather ugly, but only elevenpence ha'penny. Mam said she'd cut a rose out of her flower book and glue it in the middle. 'Then it'll look dead pretty.' She was fond of decorating things with flowers from her book.

'You know, Petal,' she said thoughtfully as she paused in front of the cutlery, 'a new bread-knife wouldn't come amiss. Our one's so blunt it makes the bread all crumbly. They're only a tanner, 'cos the handles have got a chip out the wood.' She picked up several lethal-looking knives until she found the one with the least chipped handle. 'You can hardly count this as an extravagance.'

The shop assistant put the goods in a paper bag, and they were quickly making their way towards the exit because Mam was worried she'd spend money she hadn't got when a voice said, 'Why, if it isn't Mabel Flynn.'

Mam went very red and nearly dropped the tray. 'Mrs Kavanagh. Hello,' she said awkwardly.

'You're looking well, luv.'

'Ta,' Mam gulped.

Mrs Kavanagh seemed exceptionally nice, and Josie couldn't understand why Mam was so embarrassed. She was small and plump, with a round, kind face, pink, cushiony cheeks and brown eyes that shone with good humour. Her blue coat was extremely smart. It had a fur collar and fur buttons, and she wore a little blue veiled hat made from the same material as the coat tipped precariously over her right eye. Her hair was brown and tightly waved. Josie waited to be introduced. It was the first thing Mam did when they met someone new. 'This is Josie, me little girl,' she would say proudly. Today, though, Mam said nothing.

'How's the job going, girl?' Mrs Kavanagh asked kindly.

'The job?' Mam faltered. She was holding Josie's hand so hard it hurt. 'All right, I suppose.'

'I was surprised to hear you'd given up Bailey's Chemists – wasn't Mrs Bailey teaching you to dispense the prescriptions? – to become a live-in nanny, but according to your Ivy you love it there. Where is it over the water, luv? I forget now.'

'Er, Greasby.'

'And I suppose this is one of your little charges.' The woman beamed at Josie.

'Yes. Oh, yes. This is Josie.'

'You're very pretty, Josie.' She bent down and took Josie's hand. 'How old are you?'

'I'll be four in May.'

'I've got a little girl who'll be four next week. Her name is Lily, and she should be standing right beside me, except she's wandered off, as usual. Lily,' she called. 'Lily. Where are you?'

Mam seemed to have found her voice. 'I didn't know you'd had another baby, Mrs Kavanagh.'

'Well, five's an uneven number, luv. Me and Eddie decided to make it six, but that's our lot. I'd've thought your Ivy would've told you on one of her visits. Oh, here she is, our Lily. Come on, luv, say hello to Josie here.'

A girl came bouncing up, a mite smaller than Josie. She was very like her mam, with bright pink cheeks and sparkling eyes. Her slightly darker hair fell to her waist in a mass of tiny waves. To Josie's surprise, her coat was exactly the same as her mother's – blue with fur buttons and collar. She wore a different sort of hat, a bonnet tied under her chin.

'Hello, Josie,' the girl said obediently. Her face was alive with mischief.

'Hello.' Josie twisted her body shyly. She wasn't used to children, and had never had a friend. Mam had been the only friend she'd ever wanted, but she would have quite liked to get to know Lily Kavanagh.

However, that was not to be, because Mam said in a rush, 'We'd better be getting back to Greasby. I only came over to do a bit of shopping, seeing as it was such a nice day, like. Come on, Josie.'

Mrs Kavanagh looked disappointed. 'I thought we could have a little natter over a cup of tea and a scone. I've missed you in the street, Mabel. Everyone has.'

'That would have been the gear, Mrs Kavanagh, but I really must get back.'

'Oh, well, some other time, then. Tara, luv. Tara, Josie. Where's your manners, our Lily? Say tara.'

Lily's eyes gleamed impishly at Josie. 'Tara.'

'It's not fair. Oh, it's not fair a bit,' Mam raged as they walked quickly out of Blackler's into the bright spring sunshine. Her face was very red. Josie had to run to keep up, and kept bumping into people on the crowded pavements. A shopping basket nearly sent her flying. 'As if I'd've given up me good job in Bailey's to be a nanny, for God's sake. But I suppose our poor Ivy had to come up with something to explain why I wasn't there no more. After all, I was forced to think up all sorts of lies meself, else the truth might have killed the poor woman. Mind you, I never thought she'd turn against me the way she did. She's me sister, after all. I thought she'd stick by me.'

'Mam!' Josie panted. She had a stitch in her side, and felt confused. What on earth was Mam on about? Which poor woman might the truth have killed?

'I'm sorry, Petal. Am I going too fast for you? I'm the worst mam in the whole world.' She slowed down considerably, but remained just as angry. 'I'm glad we were all done up in our best gear and I had me beret on, not that horrible brown thing. Did you see the lovely coats they had on? Mollie will have made them, as well as them dead smart hats. She makes all the kids' clothes, including the boys'. Mr Kavanagh – Eddie, that is – owns the haberdashers by Woolworths in Penny Lane, so she gets the material cheap, like. She was ever such a good friend when I was little. I used to have me tea in their house until our Ivy came home from work. Their

Stanley's only three years younger than me.' She stopped dead in the middle of the street. 'I would have liked a cup of tea and a natter, I really would, but I was scared she'd guess what's what.'

'What is what, Mam?'

'Never mind.' Mam sighed. 'You should be wearing coats like Lily's, not other kids' cast-offs from Paddy's market. There was money left, hundreds of pounds, and half of it were mine. Mollie Kavanagh made the frock for me first Holy Communion, something you'll be needing yourself in the not too distant future, and where are we going to get *that* from, I'd like to know?'

Josie had no idea. Nor did she know why the day, which she had anticipated being so enjoyable, should have turned so sour, all because they'd met nice Mrs Kavanagh and her daughter, Lily.

Then the day became even worse. Mam noticed they were standing outside a pub. She said, 'Hang on a minute, Petal. If I don't down something quick to calm me nerves, I'm likely to bust a blood vessel. Sit on the step, luv. I'll be out again in the twinkling of an eye.'

True to her word, Mam was only a short while in the pub, and when she came out she looked much calmer. But she had claimed that drinking was a curse, that she was determined to stop altogether so she could get a job and a little house. This was the first time Josie had known her to drink during the day.

2

Josie had been at Our Lady of Mount Carmel elementary school a year when Britain declared war on Germany, and everyone began to make a desperate fuss about things. But apart from food rationing and people having to wear gas masks over their shoulders, war made little difference to their lives as far as Josie could see. All the windows had crisscross tape to protect against bomb damage – not that anyone thought there was the remotest chance that bombs would fall. Tall Kate and fat Liz had 'pulled themselves together' and gone down south to work in a factory making parts for aeroplanes. But Josie and her mam remained in Huskisson Street, where these days there was always a few bottles of stout kept in the sideboard cupboard, and the little house hadn't been mentioned in a long while.

Josie didn't mind, not very much. They still went to Princes Park and for rides on the ferry. She liked school, and could read quite well. Night-times, when Mam was out – and she was out longer and longer these days – she looked through books with Teddy and taught him the words she knew.

After the war started, Mam's visitors were mainly young men in uniform – some gave Josie a penny, or even a threepenny bit, as they were leaving. She put the money in a cocoa tin to save up for a house.

On the last day of the summer term, the children were allowed home early. They whooped out of the gates, blissfully excited at the thought of no more school for six long weeks. Josie ran all the way home, burst into the house and was halfway up the first flight of stairs when Irish Rose emerged from her ground-floor room. She was a tiny woman – 'petite' Mam called her – with lovely ginger hair, and would have been dead pretty if she hadn't had such a dreadful squint.

'Josie,' she called urgently. 'Come in with me a minute, luv. Your mam's got someone with her. She wasn't expecting you just yet.'

'Why can't I wait on the stairs, like always?' Josie hadn't realised Mam had visitors while she was at school.

'I think your mam would prefer it if you waited with me. It might take a while. Come on, luv,' Rose coaxed in her soft, lilting voice. 'The kettle's on, and I got half a pound of broken biscuits this morning – most of 'em are cream.'

At the mention of the biscuits, Josie returned downstairs. She loved Rose's big room, with its fancy net curtains and red silk tasselled lampshade. Rose had spent several days sticking tape to the tall windows in a highly complicated pattern. The linoleum was purple with a pattern of trailing vines, and the red and blue striped wallpaper, with its sprinkling of embossed gold flowers, was a relic of the importer of rare spices – faded, torn in places, but still incredibly grand. During the summer, the marble fireplace was filled, as now, with tissue flowers that Rose had made herself. A patchwork quilt covered the single bed, and the sideboard was packed with statues, holy pictures and photos of Rose's numerous sisters and brothers and other relatives back in Ireland, who would all 'drop stone dead' for some reason if they knew what their Rose was up to on the mainland.

The kettle was already simmering on the hob, the tea was quickly made and the broken biscuits emptied on to a plate.

'You can dip your bicky in your tea if you want, luv,' Rose said kindly, before proceeding daintily to dip her own. Rose was always dressed up to the nines from early morning. Today, she wore a lovely maroon crêpe dress with sequins on the bodice. Her cheeks and lips had been painted the same colour as the dress, and her lashes were two rows of stiff flies' legs. She regarded Josie searchingly with her good eye. 'And what did you get up to at school today?'

'We did games this avvy, and Catechism this morning,' Josie said importantly. 'Did you know the Pope cannot err? What does err mean, Rose?'

Rose shrugged. 'Dunno, luv. I'm a downright eejit, me. I can't even read proper.'

'Honest? Me mam reads books all the time, big thick ones,' Josie bragged. 'She gets 'em from the library.'

'Oh, we all know how clever Lady Muck is.' Rose sniffed and looked annoyed. She went on, a touch of spite in her voice, 'But she weren't clever enough to check if her chap was wearing a johnny, were she? *I* always do. The chaps hate using 'em, and only an eejit would take them at their word. Now look where it's landed her.'

'Where's that, Rose?'

14

'Up shit creek without a paddle, that's where.'

Josie was about to ask if shit creek was anywhere near the Pier Head when an agonised scream came from upstairs.

'Mam!' Josie would have recognised the sound anywhere. In her panic, she dropped a custard cream in the half-drunk tea, and almost fell in her rush towards the door.

'Wait a minute, luv,' Rose leapt to her feet. 'Oh, dear God. I should've locked the effin' door,' she groaned.

At first, Josie couldn't make out what was happening when she burst into the attic room, half expecting to find Mam being murdered and ready to defend her with her life. The terrifying scene that met her was possibly worse. The bed had been covered with a black rubber sheet on which her mother lay, legs bent and wide apart. Between them was a pool of dark red blood. Mam, her teeth bared and the whites of her eyes glinting madly, was struggling to escape from Maude, who had her pinned down by the shoulders. A strange old woman was crouched at the foot of the bed. She got to her feet as Josie rushed in.

'That should do it,' the woman said, and at the same time Mam shrieked, 'Get our Josie out of here.'

'I'll get her.' Rose arrived, breathless. 'Come on, luv.'

But a terrified Josie dodged the grasping arms. She slithered past Maude and threw herself on top of her mother who screamed again. Both began to sob loudly.

The old woman, oblivious to the commotion, said in a hoarse voice, 'That'll be a quid.'

'You should'a been a butcher, Gertie,' Maude said tersely, releasing Mam, who made no attempt to escape, but fell back on to the bed, still sobbing. 'I hope that instrument o' yours was sterilised.'

Gertie ignored her. 'I'd like me rubber sheet back if you don't mind. I'll wash it meself at home. Oh, and you'd better get the girl some Aspro. She's likely to hurt for a couple of days.'

★

Mam did more than hurt – she caught an infection. Her temperature soared, she tossed and turned, moaned in her sleep and said things that Josie couldn't make sense of.

'Don't touch me, else I'll tell our Ivy,' she would wail hysterically. Or, 'If me sister finds out, it'll break her heart.'

It was like a nightmare, Josie thought during the night as she cuddled against the hot, damp body, made worse when the air-raid siren went several times. Its unearthly wail sent shivers up and down her spine. The drone of German planes sounded in the distance, and she held her breath, praying they wouldn't get closer. Maude said bombs had dropped on Birkenhead and Wallasey. Five people had been killed.

For eight whole days, Mam stayed in bed, only getting up to use the po, which was 'like a hot knife being stuck in me guts', she said tearfully to Maude. Josie flatly refused to leave her side for more than a few minutes. She sat on the bed, making little soothing noises and gently stroking the burning cheeks.

'I don't know what I'd do without you, Petal,' Mam said when she was lucid. Several times a day she would ask, 'Would you mind taking that little glass and nipping downstairs to ask Maude for a sup of whisky? It's the only thing that helps with the pain.'

'She's drinking more than ever,' Maude said worriedly one day, after inviting Josie into her horribly smelly room – according to Mam, Maude had yet to discover the virtues of soap and water. Yesterday's make-up smudged her anxious, good-natured face, and she wore the filthy dressing-gown with both pockets hanging off that she wore all day. Because she hadn't combed her hair, the bald patch was more noticeable than usual. 'I thought she'd vowed to give it up.'

Josie tut-tutted and shook her head, very grown up. 'She vows that nearly every day, Maude.'

'She's been doing it for years.' Maude grimaced and waved her cigarette. 'It's me own fault. I was the one that got her started. I mean, you can't sit in the ale house half the night and only sup lemonade. And your mam's far too respectable to walk the streets. At least with a pub you know exactly who you're getting. But I never thought she'd take to the drink like a duck takes to water.'

'Maude?' Josie was still puzzled by the scene she had encountered the day she came home early from school. There was a question she had been dying to ask for days.

'What, luv?' Maude said absently.

'Was that old woman trying to kill me mam?'

Maude looked grave and didn't answer for a while. Then she said, 'No, luv. She wasn't trying to kill her. She was taking something away that your mam didn't want, like lancing a boil, sort o' thing.' She patted Josie's head affectionately as she poured whisky into the glass. 'Take this up to her. By the way, luv, have you had anything to eat today?'

Josie's stomach had been rumbling for hours. Mam seemed to have forgotten about food. 'Not yet.'

'Tch, tch.' Maude shook her head. 'I'll make you a brawn and piccalili sarnie. That should fill the hole for now.'

Mam got better, but for a long while her legs felt like 'a rusty pair of scissors' and her movements were stiff and painful. Walking as far as Princes Park or the Pier Head was out of the question. She preferred to rest, get her strength back, though she went to the pub at night, always bringing back a visitor, because she had no choice, her purse being completely empty.

Josie offered the one and sevenpence halfpenny out of the cocoa tin. Mam burst into tears and said she was very kind, but it wouldn't last five minutes.

During the long holiday, on sunny days, rather than seek out the friends she'd made at school, Josie preferred to wander alone down to the Pier Head where she watched children armed with buckets and spades boarding the New Brighton ferry, huge families of them, accompanied by perspiring mams and a few dads. She envied the children's carefree faces, their obvious gaiety, and on one brilliant August day, a thought she'd never had before wriggled its way into her head. Despite the heat, for some reason she felt cold as she began to wonder about the strangeness of her own existence. Why didn't Mam have a husband?

Thinking about it now, for the first time, on this gloriously sunny afternoon, there seemed something very odd, not quite right, about the never-ending visitors and what they did while Josie was out of the room. She knew that Mam got undressed, and they lay on the bed together, making dead funny noises, and afterwards she was paid. Sometimes the visitors grumbled she'd already cost them a small fortune in ale, and Mam would reply sharply she wasn't available for the price of a few drinks, thanks all the same. And since the old woman had lanced the boil, whatever the men did hurt badly. Mam was often in tears when Josie went back, and in need of a drink to ease the pain. There was whisky in the cupboard now instead of stout, and she would take a huge swig straight from the bottle and go to bed, forgetting all about their usual cocoa and jam butties.

In fact, Josie was hungry a lot of the time because Mam mostly forgot to buy food. If it hadn't been for Maude, some days she wouldn't have eaten at all.

There were children in her class at school who smelled much worse than Maude. Their bodies, their ragged clothes, were filthy. A few had no shoes, and some of the girls didn't wear knickers. Even so, Josie would have bet that these children's mams didn't get undressed for strange men. It made her feel a little bit ashamed.

She rested her arms on the rail and watched the ferry on its way to New Brighton spewing a trail of white froth. The sun glinted blindingly on the green-grey waters of the Mersey, and her eyes began to run. There was no hankie up her sleeve, so she rubbed her cheeks with the hem of her frock, and it was only then she noticed how dirty it was. It hadn't been washed since the day school finished, and in all that time she hadn't changed her knickers and vest because there hadn't been any clean ones to put on. She only had one frock that fitted, and Mam had promised ages ago to get another from the market. And she needed shoes – the ones she had on now pinched badly.

Josie didn't know why she should suddenly think of Lily Kavanagh in her lovely blue coat, but she did. The day they'd met was as clear as crystal in her mind, and she thought how nice it would be to have a mam like Mrs Kavanagh, who would remember to feed her and make her clothes, and would never allow her to wear shoes that hurt.

Mam was lying on the bed, fully dressed and fast asleep, when she got home, and Josie thought how beautiful she looked with her rich brown hair spread over the pillow. Her cheeks were pale, and she wondered if they would ever be rosy again.

As quietly as possible, she removed her clothes, then carefully took her nightie from under the pillow and put it on. She went over to the sink, where a heap of dirty clothes underneath waited to be washed, and turned on the tap. The water was cold, and she had been strictly forbidden to touch the fireguard so she couldn't warm it on the hob, and, anyroad, the fire was out. She smeared soap on the frock, and her small frame quivered as she rubbed the material together.

'What'cha doing, luv?' Mam murmured in a slurred voice.

'Just washing me frock, Mam. It's awful dirty.'

She had thought Mam would be pleased. Instead, she sat on the edge of the bed, burst out crying, and called herself every name under the sun. 'I'm the worst mam who ever lived,' she sobbed. 'I don't deserve you, Petal. I'm neglecting you something awful. There's hardly a woman in Liverpool who wouldn't look after you better than me.'

A strange feeling, a sort of painful ache, began to roll down Josie's body, starting at the top of her head and finishing at her toes. She could hardly speak for the huge lump in her throat. She didn't care what Mam did for a living, and if Mrs Kavanagh and Lily came and begged her on their bended knees to come and live with them, nothing on earth would make her go. She loved Mam, and always would, with all her heart and soul, and never more so than at that moment. They would never be parted. One day, they would get their little

19

house, even if it took all the years until she went to work herself.

She flung herself across the room on to her mother's knee and began to cover her face with kisses.

'Oh, your hands are wet, and they're all cold,' Mam shrieked, as she fell back, laughing, on to the bed.

Josie sat on her chest, looking down. She could see her own reflection in the dark blue eyes. 'I love you, Mam.'

'And I love you, Petal. I love you so much it hurts. Now, just give us a minute to sort out me head, then we'll do the washing together.'

The noise was so great, so penetrating, that Josie felt as if her brain were rattling in her head – the steady drone of the planes in the sky above, the sharp answering crackle from the ack-ack guns on the ground. Then came the bomb.

This raid was worse than any she'd known before. The others hadn't felt so close, so personal. The bomb sounded as if it had fallen right outside the house, and everywhere shook. The dishes rattled on the table, the rafters creaked and layers of dust drifted downwards. The candle went out, and the room was pitched into blackness.

Josie pulled the covers over her head and grabbed Teddy, shakily telling him that everything was going to be all right, though she had never felt so frightened and desperately wished that Mam were there to whisper the same comforting words to her. She wondered why the bed shook, then realised it was she herself who was shaking, and her teeth were chattering, and she was holding poor Teddy so tightly that he was almost being strangled.

Another bomb screamed its way to earth, and Josie screamed with it, then screamed again when a hand removed the blankets, and she couldn't see who it belonged to in the dark.

'Josie,' Mam said urgently. 'It's all right, luv. It's only me. Them Jerries have never struck so close to home before.' She lit the candle, and Josie, frozen, petrified, saw that she was alone. Mam picked her up and cradled her in her arms. 'There, there, luv. I came the minute that first bomb landed 'cos I was out of me mind with worry.'

'Don't leave me again, Mam,' Josie cried hysterically, clinging to her mother. 'Don't leave me by meself again.'

'Don't fret, luv. I won't.' Mam stroked her face tenderly. 'If we're going to go, we'll go together. I couldn't live without my little girl, my Petal.'

Mam stayed in for three nights in a row and finished off the whisky. There were no raids, but her nerves were on edge. 'This can't go on,' she kept saying. 'I'm stuck in a rut, taking the easy option.' She couldn't sit still, and talked frequently about 'getting a proper job. I might take a look around tomorrow'. They could move out to Speke or Kirkby, where she could work in a munitions factory. The wages were good. Though Josie would have to change schools. She said this in a tired way, as if it were an insurmountable problem.

'I don't mind, Mam.' Josie was thrilled at the idea of living in what she imagined was the countryside, preferably plumb in the middle of a bluebell wood, like a girl in one of her stories. At the same time she recognised with a very adult awareness that Mam was searching for ways *not* to go to Speke or Kirkby.

During that summer holiday, Josie had come to terms with several things. The oddness of her life, for instance, the peculiar thing, the precise nature of which she was still not sure of, that Mam did for a living. What hurt most was knowing that, although Mam sincerely meant it when she said she couldn't live without her and that she loved her more than anyone in the world, she didn't love her quite enough to get the proper job she was always on about, to move somewhere different. Perhaps it was the drink that had weakened her spirit, made her lose the courage she might once have had. What's more, Mam wasn't fit to work in a munitions factory unless she stopped drinking, something which Josie had given up all hope of happening. Kate had written to Maude. She worked on something complicated called a capstan lathe. It was all highly responsible, very difficult, and needed careful precision. But Mam's hands shook when she poured a cup of tea.

All this did nothing to make Josie love her mother less. In fact, she only loved her more.

There was a raid on the fourth night that Mam stayed in. The siren went early, just after seven o'clock. The hairs prickled on Josie's neck. She crawled on to her mother's knee, and they listened to the far-away hum of enemy planes. Fifteen minutes later the welcome sound of the all clear split the still, evening air.

'I think I'll nip out for a little while,' Mam said when it finished.

'*No!*' Josie seized her arm. She never wanted to stay in the room alone again. The aeroplanes might come back, the siren might go again, bombs might fall.

'I can't stay in for ever, luv.' Mam blushed and twisted her thumbs together on her knee, as if for the first time she felt uncomfortable with her daughter about whatever it was she did. 'I've got a living to make.'

'Then take me with you. *Please*, Mam.'

Her mother looked at her for a minute, frowning. 'I suppose I could,' she said eventually. 'It's still broad daylight. You could sit on the steps outside. Lots of kids do.'

The Prince Albert public house was on the corner of two short streets behind the Rialto ballroom. It was small, but impressive. The bottom half was shiny dark green tiles, separated from the plain brick upstairs by a wide band of masonry on which a row of diamond shapes had been carved and painted gold. The corner entrance was particularly grand. Five curved stone steps led to a pair of giant swing doors with fancy brass handles. Across one street, there was a small chandler's, the window a jumble of buckets and mops and tins of paint, a fish shop with an empty marble slab behind the glass, and a sweet and tobacconist's, still open. An elderly woman was sitting on a chair by the door, taking advantage of the evening sun.

When Josie and her mother arrived, a boy about her own age and a little girl who looked no more than two were sitting on the steps outside.

'I promise I won't be long, luv,' Mam said as she went through the swing doors – the glass in the doors and all the windows had been painted over for the blackout. A thick curtain hung over the entrance for when it grew dark, so that not even the slightest chink of light would show when people went in and out.

The boy on the steps was chirpy, with a monkey-like face and a shaven head full of sores. His left arm was withered. He introduced himself as Tommy. The little girl was his sister, and he was looking after her, otherwise he would be playing with his mates, which he would have much preferred. His sister's name was Nora. She couldn't talk yet, and was a pain in the bloody arse.

'I don't suppose you've got a ciggie on you?' he asked casually.

''Course not. I'm only six.'

She was amazed to learn that Tommy was ten. 'I'll be eleven at Chrimbo,' he boasted. 'I've been smoking for years.'

'Does your mam and dad know?'

'Well, no,' he conceded. 'Me dad'd batter me soft if he did.'

'It would be no more than you deserved,' Josie said primly. 'By the way, your sister wants her nose wiping.'

'Wipe your effin' nose, our Nora,' Tommy commanded, and Nora drew her arm across her face, spreading the offending green stuff over her cheek.

They played together amiably on the stone steps. Tommy was impressed when Josie jumped down from the fourth. 'Not bad for a girl,' he grudgingly conceded. Naturally, he could jump all five, landing lightly on his tiny feet, much smaller than hers.

Then Nora had a go, and screamed blue murder when she fell on all fours and grazed her hands and knees. Tommy

23

opened the pub door and yelled, 'Mam, our Nora's hurt herself.'

In view of the racket going on inside the Prince Albert – the blasts of laughter, the occasional sing-song, the thud of glasses on the tables – Josie wasn't surprised when no one came. She comforted Nora as best she could when it seemed that Tommy couldn't care less. Then her own mam appeared with a glass of lemonade and a packet of crisps, which she felt obliged to share with her new friends. Nora stopped crying, but started again as soon as the crisps had gone. Josie stamped her foot and ordered her to stop. To her surprise, Nora did.

A woman arrived carrying a baby, a scantily clad little girl trailing wearily behind holding her skirt. She plonked the baby in the girl's arms, warning, 'Drop her, and you'll be in dead trouble.'

'Hello, Shirl,' said Tommy. Shirl nodded, sat on the step with the baby and promptly fell asleep.

'She mustn't half be tired,' Josie whispered.

'Yeah.' Tommy seemed oblivious to everything except exhibiting his own athletic prowess. Despite his withered arm, he swiftly shinned up a lamppost and swung from the top. 'Look at me, Jose,' he called.

'You're nothing but a show-off,' Josie sniffed.

Tommy dropped to the ground. He seemed determined to impress her. 'Would you like to see me cock?' he offered.

'Your what?'

'Me cock, me tool, me thingummyjig. Have you never seen one before?'

'No.'

The boy undid the tweed trousers that ended just above his crab-apple knees, and proudly produced a wormlike piece of flesh. 'I'll give you a baby, if you like. I've had it off with girls before.'

Josie regarded the worm scornfully. 'Put it away. I don't want a baby, thanks all the same.' She didn't know where babies came from, only that Tommy was talking through the back of his neck.

'You're a proper ould bossy boots, Jose,' Tommy said as he fastened his trousers.

'Can I go again tomorrow?' Josie asked when they were on their way back to Huskisson Street.

Mam, flushed and bleary-eyed, was linking her arm with that of a sailor in a dead funny uniform. 'Of course, luv. Did you enjoy yourself?'

'Oh, yes, Mam. It was the gear. Tommy goes to Our Lady of Mount Carmel, same as me. I've never seen him before 'cos he's in the Juniors.'

'I'm glad. It means we've solved the problem of the air raids for now. But we can't have you hanging round once the nights grow dark. Still, we'll sort that problem out when we come to it. By the way, Petal, this is Pascal. Isn't that a lovely name? He's French, and can hardly speak a word of English.'

Pascal smiled at the sound of his name. He nuzzled Mam's cheek and said huskily, *'Je t'adore, Mabel.'*

3

Tommy had found a dog-end in the gutter. He cadged a match off a man who had paused outside the pub to light a foul-smelling pipe, and struck it between the tiles. He puffed the dog-end furiously until the end glowed red. 'That's good,' he breathed, before exhaling the smoke with the air of an expert. Nora snuffled noisily on the step beside him.

'You're showing off again,' Josie said mildly. 'Nora, wipe your nose.' She looked away when Nora wiped her nose in the usual fashion.

It was a week since she'd first come to the Prince Albert, and she had grown fond of Tommy and Nora. She felt quite touched when Nora ran to meet her and took her hand. Their father was in the army, a sergeant. Tommy said Josie was his girlfriend and had kissed her twice. Josie had told Mam, missing out the kisses. Mam laughed. 'When you're old enough for boyfriends, let's hope you can do better than *that*, Petal.'

Josie felt hurt. She was looking forward to going back to school next week and having a boyfriend in the Juniors. She watched him affectionately. He got three puffs from the dog-end, and began to look for more in the gutter. She liked him almost as much as she did Maude, and felt a motherly concern for Nora.

A small, jaunty man with a cheerful face came out of the pub. His name was Bert, and he usually exchanged a few words with the children. Tonight, he went over to the sweetshop and returned with three Mars Bars. 'Here you are, kids. It's Friday, payday, so I'm flush. Don't eat it all in one bite, now.' He winked at Josie. 'Reckon you'll be carrying your mam home tonight, luv. She's in there downing gin and tonics like nobody's business.'

Josie opened one of the swing doors as far as she dared without invoking the wrath of the landlord who didn't want children on his premises for fear he'd lose his licence. She searched with worried eyes for her mother, and saw her sitting with two khaki-clad young men in one of the wooden compartments with seats each side. All three were laughing hilariously. Mam's hat was all crooked, and when she picked up her glass, liquid spilled down the front of her frock. They all laughed again. One of the men grinned, undid the buttons and dabbed her breasts with a hankie.

'They're officers, them,' a voice said in her ear. 'You can tell by the uniform. Your mam's a tart, isn't she? She goes with men for money.'

Tommy was standing behind her. Josie let the door swing shut, conscious of the Mars Bar melting in her hand. She was too sick to eat it. She nodded miserably, and felt tears rush to her eyes. Then Tommy's shrivelled arm slid around her waist. 'Don't worry, kid. I won't tell anyone at school. And when we're grown up, you'll have me to look after you, so you won't end up like your mam.'

'Ta, Tommy,' she whispered gratefully.

26

The sky darkened early and it started to rain, only lightly. Nora cried when she finished her Mars Bar, so Josie gave her hers. She ate it greedily, and cried again after she'd licked the paper clean.

They sat in a row on the top step, four children and a baby – Shirl had just arrived, and was already fast asleep with her sister on her lap. Nora whinged. Josie couldn't stop thinking about Mam and wasn't in the mood to play. Even Tommy seemed subdued by the rain. They watched the old lady lock up the sweetshop and walk away beneath an umbrella.

A woman clattered smartly up the steps in very high heels. 'Just look at them poor kids,' she said to the man with her. 'Some parents are totally irresponsible. They don't deserve to have children.'

'Fuck off,' Tommy snarled.

The man threatened to give him a good hiding, and Tommy said if he laid a finger on him, he'd call his dad who was a heavyweight boxer.

'Oh, yeah!' sneered the man. 'And I'm Clark Gable.'

'Oh, leave them, Geoff. Poor things, they don't know any better. Let's find a different pub. I don't like the look of this place.'

'What happens if the air-raid siren goes?' Josie asked as the sky became darker. She seemed to have lost track of time.

'There's a shelter just down the street,' Tommy assured her. 'Don't worry, Jose. I'll show you where.'

'But I can't go without Mam!' The whole point of coming to the Prince Albert was so that she and Mam wouldn't be parted. A lump of fear rose in her throat at the thought of waiting outside, alone, while the bombs fell.

To her relief, the pub doors opened and Mam staggered out with the two soldiers. They wore peaked caps and neat, well-fitting uniforms.

'I told you they were officers,' Tommy murmured.

Josie's relief was followed by a feeling of horror, because it quickly became obvious that *Mam had forgotten she was there*! She shrieked with laughter when the men linked arms with her and rushed her across the street so that her feet scarcely touched the ground. They had turned the corner before Josie started to follow. Her legs felt numb, and she forgot to say tara to Tommy.

Halfway along Upper Parliament Street one of the soldiers said in a loud, posh voice, 'We seem to have acquired a shadow, an extremely pretty little shadow,' and they all turned round.

'Josie! Oh, luv. I'd forgotten all about you.' Mam's eyes were glazed, she could hardly see. She broke away from the men's supporting arms. One just managed to catch her before she fell. Two women who were passing looked at her in disgust.

Mam hiccuped loudly. 'It's our Josie. It's me little girl.'

For the second time that night, Josie's eyes filled with tears. She'd never seen Mam so drunk before – legless, Maude called it. 'This chap was legless,' she said once. 'He gave me a pound note in mistake for ten bob.'

If only she were bigger, Josie thought fiercely, bigger and stronger and older. She'd chase the men away, drag Mam home and forbid her to touch another drop of drink again.

'Come on, Josie. I'll give you a piggy-back.' Suddenly, she was lifted in the air and found herself clutching the soldier's neck. To her surprise, he smelled of scent. His hair was very fair and bristly. As they walked towards Huskisson Street, he told her his name was Roger, and he had a sister, Abigail, who wasn't much older than she was. His friend was Thomas – not Tommy or Tom, but Thomas. Thomas's hair was dark, and he had a small moustache, like a hyphen in a book. They were both quite good-looking, good-humoured and, she had to concede, boyishly nice. They were completely different to the visitors Mam usually had, and she wondered if they were just seeing her safely home.

When they reached Huskisson Street Roger put Josie down, and helped his friend half drag, half carry her mother upstairs. Mam was giggling helplessly, and by the time they got to the second floor Josie sensed the men were getting angry. They were no longer boyish, and not the least bit nice, and said horrible words like 'bitch' and 'whore'.

'This had better be fucking worth it,' Thomas swore.

They reached the attic room, Mam was roughly pushed inside and the door slammed.

Josie sat at the top of the stairs and waited. Her clothes were wet from the rain, and little needles of fear pulsed through her body. The house was very quiet for a change. She went down and knocked on Maude's door, but there was no answer. Upstairs again, she wished Teddy were there as she watched the stars, pale and unblinking, appear through the skylight. Grey clouds scudded past, concealing then revealing the tiny pricks of light.

The attic door opened. Roger emerged in his shirtsleeves and took her arm. His grip was painful. 'You'll do for a shag till Thomas has done,' he muttered.

She didn't understand. He pulled her into the room, and she went willingly because she wanted to be with her mother, make sure she was safe. She no longer trusted the men she'd thought so nice.

Through the high window, the final remains of daylight offered enough illumination to see the naked figure of her mother lying face down on the bed, moaning softly. Thomas, half-dressed, was riding her like a horse, almost galloping. Josie felt a sickly throbbing in her stomach. Still unsure what was happening, she was roughly flung on the bed and Roger crawled on top of her. She felt his hand reach underneath her frock, but she ignored it, concerned only for Mam, whose face was turned towards hers, only inches away, her eyes screwed close. Was Thomas hurting her? Josie wriggled away from Roger's groping hands and touched her mother's cheek.

'Are you all right, Mam?' she asked tenderly.

Mam's eyes slowly opened, the merest crack. Then, in quick succession, they flickered briefly, closed, snapped wide open and grew very bright and alert. Josie's blood turned to ice when a sound emerged from her mother's throat that was barely human. She growled, and the growl became a howl, and the howl became a roar. She gritted her teeth, took a deep breath and raised herself on all fours like a wild animal.

Thomas was flung off the bed on to the floor. Mam turned over, raised her feet and kicked Roger in the chest. He was thrown against the wall with a sickening thud, then slid to the floor beside his friend.

'How dare you lay a hand on me daughter?' Mam spat. 'Get out! Both of you, get *out!*'

The men were momentarily stunned. After a while, they sat up and, breathing heavily, began to adjust their clothes. Thomas got to his feet. He approached the bed, grinning. 'So, you want to play games, bitch? I know a good one.' He grabbed Mam's foot, but she shoved her other foot in his stomach, and he fell back, grunting.

Roger was up. He reached for Josie, and pulled her on to her back. 'You hold the mother while I take the kid.'

'Oh, no, you don't, not while there's breath left in me body.' Mam leapt off the bed, and suddenly she was holding the bread-knife from Blackler's bargain basement, holding it in front of her, the point aimed directly at Roger. 'Let go of her, or I'll kill you. I'll kill you both, I mean it. I don't care if I swing for it, you bastards.'

Thomas hesitated. Roger released Josie.

There were footsteps on the stairs and Irish Rose burst in, accompanied by a giant black man who was bare to the waist. Muscles rippled like dancing waves on his gleaming back. 'What's going on?' Rose demanded.

Mam said shakily, 'These men are just leaving.' She waved the knife threateningly. 'Aren't you?'

The black man stepped forward. His dark eyes swept from the frightened child to the naked woman with the knife in her hands and the handsome young Army officers crouched against the wall. He nodded his giant head towards the door, and said mildly, 'Git.'

And the two men went.

They were going back to Machin Street tomorrow, Sunday,

straight after Mass. They would turn up looking as fine as fivepence – Mam was buying Josie a new frock that afternoon.

Maude was all in favour. She came up in her dressing-gown after breakfast to see how they were. Irish Rose had told her about last night's events, and Mam announced they were leaving.

'You should have gone a long while ago, Mabel,' Maude said. 'You can't risk another night like last night, and the older Josie gets, the more likely it'll happen. She's as pretty as a picture, a real little Miss Pears, and getting more like her mam every day. It's either that, or turning professional, getting a proper flat, like, and a maid to look after Josie. I've said it before and I'll say it again, you could make a fortune on the game if you turned professional.'

'I've no intention of turning professional,' Mam said frostily. She looked surprisingly self-composed. Her face glowed and her mouth was set in a determined line. Last night, terrible though it had been, had brought her to her senses, made her see things clearly, she had said earlier. 'It was always only temporary with me,' she said to Maude. 'The trouble was, I got stuck on the booze, but only 'cos I hated what I was doing. In the end, it became a vicious circle. Now all that matters is our Josie. Isn't it, luv?' She smiled vividly at Josie who was busy emptying the drawers of their well-worn clothes.

'Yes, Mam.' Josie was still not quite sure what Roger had intended to do when he threw her on the bed. After all, she was only a little girl, six, not a grown-up woman.

'I'm chucking most of our stuff away,' Mam said. 'If there's anything decent, it can go to the pawnshop with the crockery, the cutlery and the bedding. I'll not redeem it, it's just that I want to get our Josie a frock and a pair of shoes in Paddy's market this avvy, and another few bob wouldn't come amiss. I'm not having our Ivy turn up her nose when she sees us.'

'There'll be one helluva kerfuffle, Mabel,' Maude said cautiously.

'I know, but I've already made up me mind what to say.

She'll be given two choices – either she believes me, takes us in and gives his lordship his marching orders, or she doesn't believe me, in which case I want half of everything, including the money that was left and the value of the house.' Mam folded her arms on her chest and looked extremely fierce. Her eyes sparkled angrily. 'I was fifteen when she chucked me out, up the stick and in a state. Now I'm twenty-two, and in full possession of me senses. I know what's mine by rights. What's more, I intend on having it. If necessary, I'll threaten to have the law on her.'

'Mightn't it be a good idea to leave you-know-who with me while all this is going on?' Maude suggested timidly. She appeared to be slightly in awe of Mam, who was becoming more forceful and aggressive by the minute. Even Josie found it hard to believe that this was the same woman who'd been legless in Upper Parliament Street the night before.

'No, it wouldn't,' Mam said crisply. 'I'll pop Josie in number thirty for a while. Mrs Kavanagh's bound to guess the truth, if not the whole truth, that's if she's not guessed already. Once our Ivy's been sorted, I'll collect Josie. We'll either have a home in Machin Street, or enough cash in me bag, or at least the promise of it, to take on the nice little house I've been on about for years. We'll live by one of them munitions factories, Kirkby or Speke. Kate said the pay's enough to make your eyes pop. Now, if you don't mind, Maude, I'd like to get on. Me and Josie have got a lot to do today.'

It was the best day Josie could ever remember, a day she never forgot, despite the fact it rained non-stop. It wasn't just the lovely blue velvet frock that Mam bought in the market for a shilling, or the patent leather shoes that pinched a bit – but it didn't matter because next week they'd buy a pair that fitted perfectly from Freeman, Hardy & Willis – or the three-quarter-length white socks with a curious knobbly pattern that were brand new, or the ice-cream cornet with a twirl of raspberry syrup on top that she ate in the rain on the way home. It was knowing that, as from tomorrow, there would be no more visitors and – this time she knew Mam truly meant it – no more drink. They might be living in Machin Street, or they might not. Josie didn't understand the complications. She knew there was going to be a row and that she was being left with Mrs Kavanagh – which she was quite looking forward to. All she cared about was that things were about to change out of all proportion for the better. She skipped along beside her mother, and felt she could easily have burst with happiness.

Mam felt it, too. Every now and then she had a little skip herself, and even when she realised she'd pawned the bedding and they had to spend another night in Huskisson Street, like with the shoes, it didn't matter.

'If necessary, Petal, we'll sit up all night and I'll burn the last of the nutty slack,' she laughed. 'Or we'll sleep on the bare mattress, and I'll ask Maude if she'll give us the loan of her eiderdown, and hope it don't pong too much. She only uses it in winter. Mind you, it could be winter today, it's so cold, yet we're only just into September.'

When they got home, Mam cleaned every surface of the attic room. She brushed the rafters, brushed the walls, brushed the floor, dusted the sideboard, the table and the chairs. She turned the mattress over and blackleaded the tiny grate. Then she lit the fire, borrowed an iron off Maude, put it on the hob to heat and carefully pressed the brown tweed costume, cream blouse and white beret she'd been wearing when she'd left Machin Street, and which were still her bezzie clothes after all this time. She buffed her brown suede shoes as best as she could with the hairbrush. 'We used to have a special brush for this in Machin Street,' she said. 'It were made of wire and called a suede brush. Oh, there's so many things there, Petal. Just wait till you see them.'

When the iron was cool, she turned Josie's new frock inside out and smoothed out the few creases.

'There, that's everything done.' She put her hands on her hips and glanced with satisfaction around the room, at the dust-free surfaces, at her costume and Josie's frock, hanging

33

behind the door, their shoes placed neatly under the sideboard, at Teddy who was sitting on top of their gas masks, next to the brown paper bag containing Josie's books and the money from the cocoa tin which was tied in a hankie. It amounted to two and threepence. 'All that's left is for us to wash our hair, which we'll do later and dry it by the fire.'

Josie reminded her she hadn't shaken the mat, so Mam climbed on a chair and opened the window. 'Why, the sun's come out, Petal,' she announced joyfully. 'It looks dead lovely out there. I don't know about you, but I wouldn't mind a little walk. I've got dust up me nose and in me throat, and the fresh air will clear it. Where shall we go – Princes Park? It's almost autumn, the trees might have started turning gold by now.'

'Yes, but . . .' Josie hesitated.

'Yes, but what, my fragrant, my adorable little Petal?' Mam leapt off the chair, danced across the room and caught Josie in her arms. She led them in a waltz around the bed. 'But what, luv?'

'Can I say tara to Tommy and Nora?' Otherwise, she might never see them again. Our Lady of Mount Carmel was too far from Penny Lane, and even further from Speke and Kirkby.

Mam wrinkled her nose. 'That Tommy's a right scally, luv. I can't understand how you can like him. His mam's a dead horrible woman, she batters them kids something rotten. And did he tell you his dad's in jail?'

'No, Mam. But Tommy's nice. He's . . .' Josie broke off, remembering the way Tommy had put his arm around her waist the night before, promising to look after her, the various athletic feats he'd done solely to impress her. She didn't care if his mam was horrible or his dad was in jail. She shrugged. 'He's just nice.'

'All right, luv,' Mam said resignedly. 'I suppose we could carry on into town, do a bit a window-shopping. We'll get the tram home.'

Outside, the air smelled fresh and clean, and they both sniffed appreciatively. The pavements were full of puddles, and water streamed along the gutters carrying empty fag packets and sweet papers and pouring noisily through grids down to the drains.

Nora ran to meet them when they approached the Prince Albert. She took Josie's hand, and Tommy did a perfect handstand against the wall. Mam tutted, either at Nora's runny nose or Tommy's showing off, Josie wasn't sure.

Then Mam said, 'I suppose it wouldn't hurt to go inside and say tara to me mates. They'll all wonder what happened if I just disappear.'

'*Mam!*' Josie said warningly, and suddenly wished they hadn't come anywhere near the Prince Albert.

Mam merely laughed and squeezed her shoulder. 'Don't worry, Petal. I'll just have a lemonade. I promise on me honour.'

Predictably, Nora, who cried at the drop of a hat, burst into tears when she understood she would never see Josie again. 'Want Josie stay,' she sobbed, which, Tommy said laconically, were her very first words. He'd tell his mam later, if he remembered.

It seemed Tommy couldn't have cared less that she was going. He climbed the lamppost and, turning his little monkey face away, refused to look at her. Josie didn't feel hurt. She hoped he would find another girlfriend very soon. She had come prepared to buy him and Nora a present – the hankie with the two and threepence in was clutched in her hand. She'd taken it when Mam wasn't looking because she didn't think she'd approve. She'd get Nora a Mars Bar, and ten Woodbines for Tommy.

The air-raid siren went, but outside, in the sunshine, with people around, the sound wasn't so terrifying as in the darkness of the night. It didn't seem real. Tommy, perched on the lamppost, showed no sign of having heard. Josie anxiously watched the doors of the Prince Albert, praying Mam would come. A man and two women came out and sauntered in the direction of the shelter. Then Mam opened the door and

35

shouted, 'Josie, luv. I'm going to the lavvy. I'll be out in the twinkling of an eye.'

Josie trotted across to the sweetshop. A bell rang when she opened the door. Inside it was small and dark and smelled of tobacco. The walls were tobacco-coloured. Two were lined with glass jars containing a mouth-watering array of sweets. There was no sign of cigarettes on the shelves behind the counter, and it was only then she remembered Maude saying ciggies were harder to get than gold dust.

The old woman appeared from a room at the back, putting on her coat. 'I'm off to the shelter, luv. I was just about to close up.'

'Have you got any ciggies?'

'No, and I wouldn't sell them to you if I had. You're too young.' The woman smiled at her good-naturedly.

'Can I have some sweets, then?'

The woman smiled again as she buttoned up her coat. 'Sorry, luv, but I'm not prepared to weigh them out, not while there's a raid about to start. I'm rather anxious to get to the shelter.' She cocked her head and listened. 'In fact, I think I can hear a plane now – it sounds like more than one.' She came from behind the counter and began to push Josie towards the door. 'Come with me, luv. Hold me hand. You can come back for the sweets later.'

'But I wanted . . .' Josie turned to look at the bars of chocolate at the front of the counter behind a sheet of glass '. . . three Mars bars.' One for herself, one for Nora and one for Tommy, though he would have preferred ten Woodies.

Suddenly, there was a high-pitched whine, which got louder and louder, and higher and higher, and the old woman, instead of pushing her out, was pulling her back, and she was shoved behind the counter, where she fell full length. The old woman landed on top of her, nearly knocking her out.

Then the whole world erupted with a dull rumbling sound, the floor shook, the windows shattered, a mighty wind raged through the shop and the bottles flew from the shelves. Something big and heavy thudded against the counter, wood broke, glass broke, the counter fell backwards with a creak and a groan, and propped itself against the shelves where the ciggies should have been. Josie and her protecter were showered with shards of glass.

The rumbling stopped, the world stood still. There was, for a moment, silence. In that brief ensuing silence, Josie was sure she could have heard a pin drop. Then someone screamed, someone shouted, a child cried.

Nora! She prayed the child was Nora. If Nora was all right, then so was Mam. Surely. Please, God, *Please, God, make Mam be all right.*

She tried to scramble to her feet, but the old woman said with bewildering calm, 'Don't move, luv. Let me edge out first. Careful you don't cut yourself, mind. There's glass everywhere.'

Mam, Mam, Mam! The word hammered through her head.

The woman was gradually crawling backwards, oh, but so slowly, too slowly. Josie felt the weight on her body ease. A minute later, ignoring the advice to take it easy, be careful where she put her hands, 'Oh, mind out, luv!', she was free to shuffle through the glass and the dozens of bars of chocolate that had slid off the counter. Her hands and arms were bleeding, she could feel glass in her hair. Her dress was torn. She didn't care.

The first thing she noticed when she stood upright was that it was so bright. When she'd entered the shop it had been dark. Now it was bright, because there was no window, no door, no front to the shop at all, and no building opposite to shut out the light.

No Prince Albert!

The shop was full of chunks of masonry. Dark green tiles glittered like emeralds in the rubble. Grey dust hung in the air. The Prince Albert lay in ruins before her. It lay in the shop and in the street outside, blown into a million pieces.

The crying child was Shirl. She cried still, across the street, standing in the rubble, holding her baby sister and crying for her mam.

Josie regarded the destruction with dull, uncomprehending eyes. A bell clanged. A fire engine was approaching, or it might have been an ambulance, she didn't know. People appeared, their faces fierce and angry, and began to pull at the debris with their bare hands.

And as it slowly began to make sense, Josie felt curiously empty, withered, like Tommy's arm, as if her heart and soul, her spirit, had flown up to heaven to be with Mam.

Machin Street
1940–1951

I

After the explosion, Josie was taken to a still, silent place where there were nuns. She refused to give her name. Either she couldn't speak, or she wouldn't speak. No one was sure, not even Josie.

The sisters were very kind. They blessed her, fed her, put her to bed, dabbed her cut hands with iodine and said hundreds of Hail Marys, rosary beads threaded through their worn fingers. They provided her with a red gingham frock much too small, and a cardigan much too big, because the clothes she had arrived in were dirty and badly torn. Josie had no idea how long she stayed in the silent place. She knew she was alive, but she felt dead.

One morning, Sister Bernadette, who looked about a hundred, came to Josie's tiny white room, with its iron bed and wooden crucifix on the wall. Maude was with her. She wore a dreadful felt hat shaped like a tin helmet, and a moth-eaten fur coat which Mam had said privately looked as if it was made from rats.

'That's her!' Maude exclaimed. 'That's Josie Flynn.' She fell upon Josie with open arms. 'Oh, luv!'

'I'm afraid she has lost the power of speech,' Sister Bernadette murmured.

At this, Maude gave a little shriek, seized Josie's shoulders and violently shook her, as if the power of speech could be restored if she was rattled hard enough. Then she burst into

39

tears. 'She's the spitting image of her poor mam, you know, Mabel – may the good Lord rest her soul.' She bowed her head and made the sign of the cross.

According to the whispered conversation that took place between Maude and Sister Bernadette in the corridor, not everyone had died in the Prince Albert. Most customers had been pulled out of the wreckage alive. But Mam, in the lavatory, in the yard where the bomb had fallen, had taken the full blast. Josie had known the very second it happened. She had felt it in her heart.

Two children had been killed. Well, the building had virtually landed on top of them. One a boy of ten, the other his sister, only two. And, would you believe, their mam, who had suffered only a few scratches, had been seen in another pub the next night, laughing fit to bust.

Sister Bernadette said that, no, she wouldn't have believed it, ever, had she not heard it directly from Maude's lips. But she would remember the woman in her prayers, for she was obviously more in need of God's love than most.

'Huh!' Maude said disgustedly, and went on to inform the sister that the bobbies had been round to Huskisson Street looking for Josie because they'd found her identity card in her poor mam's handbag. That was when they'd learned that Mabel was dead. The whole house was stunned. 'The house is flats,' Maude went on, as if it needed an explanation. 'Quite superior flats.'

But where *was* Josie? Nobody knew. Lines of communication had become all tangled between the bobbies and the rescue services. The woman from the sweetshop was somehow involved.

'Is there someone who will take the child – a relative?' Sister Bernadette enquired gently.

'Well, Mabel had a sister living in Machin Street off Penny Lane. I don't know what number. Mind you, I'm not sure if she's fit . . . her husband's a . . .' Maude was becoming as tangled as the lines of communication. 'Knowing Ivy, not that I do, mind, but from what I've heard, she might not take her.'

She began to sob again. 'She's such a lovely kid, I'd take her meself, like a shot I would. But me job wouldn't allow it. I work these dead funny hours, see.'

'The authorities will find her, this Ivy. They will sort everything out,' Sister Bernadette said with quiet confidence.

The voices grew fainter as the women walked away. Josie crept over to the door and listened, because she wanted to know everything there was to know about Mam.

'The remains . . . hardly recognisable. Well, you can imagine, can't you, Sister? The girls . . . the other residents, that is . . . making a collection . . . couldn't abide the thought of Mabel going to a pauper's grave . . . only four and sixpence in her purse . . .'

Then the voices faded altogether and Josie heard no more.

Aunt Ivy was as nice as could be, almost fawning, with the woman in a green uniform who took Josie to Machin Street by car two days later. Josie had been told the woman's name, but forgot it immediately. The sky was heavy with dark grey clouds and it was drizzling. The windscreen wipers weren't working properly, and the woman kept tut-tutting when she pressed buttons and nothing happened. She crouched over the wheel, trying to see through water-streaked glass.

They were expected at precisely half past two. The woman had been to see Aunt Ivy the day before to discuss Josie's future. 'She's looking forward to having her pretty little niece to live with her,' the woman said on the way. 'She hasn't any children of her own, so you're all the more welcome. You'll like her, dear. She's very nice.'

Josie didn't answer. Her throat felt as tight as a fist. Perhaps she would never talk again.

'We're turning into Machin Street, Josie. This is where you're going to live.'

I don't want to! She didn't want to live anywhere if it wasn't with Mam, particularly not in one of these red brick houses with square bay windows and sentry-box porches that made the street look like a fortress.

41

The car stopped. 'Here we are.' The woman got out. She came round and opened Josie's door, saying kindly, 'Don't look so frightened, dear. I'm sure you're going to be very happy with your auntie.'

Aunt Ivy must have been watching through the window as the door opened and she came out and waited for them on the step, clapping her hands and laughing aloud as they approached. 'You're right,' she cried. 'She's just like our Mabel.'

'I never met your sister, Mrs Adams, but one of her friends remarked on the fact to Sister Bernadette.'

'Come in, darling.' Aunt Ivy took Josie's hand. 'I'm sure you're going to be very happy in your new home.'

'That's what I just told her,' the woman smiled.

The woman stayed only a few minutes to hand over Mam's handbag, which looked remarkably undamaged. 'Josie's ration book and identity card are in there. The rest of your sister's possessions are in Huskisson Street. You can collect them any time. Ask for Miss Maude Connelly.'

'Thank you,' Aunt Ivy said, 'but I shan't bother.'

Teddy! She'd forgotten all about him. Josie thought about Teddy sitting on top of the gas masks. She remembered her new velvet frock, Mam's bezzie costume, all ready to come to this very house last Sunday after Mass. Her heart threatened to burst with sadness. If only she hadn't gone to buy sweets that night. If only she'd stayed outside the Prince Albert with Tommy and Nora, then she would be dead. More than anything in the world she wished she were dead so she could be with Mam.

The woman was going, she had a dozen things to do that afternoon. She kissed Josie's cheek and wished her every happiness, and shook Aunt Ivy's hand. 'She's such a sweet little girl. With a bit of love and kindness, I'm sure her voice will soon come back. It was almost certainly the shock that did it, the shock of the explosion, then losing her mother. I've known it happen before. If you have any problems, do get in touch. You have my card. Goodbye, Mrs Adams. Goodbye, Josie.'

'Tara,' Aunt Ivy called as she closed the door.

Josie shrank against the row of coats hanging in the hall, because in the space of the few seconds it took to shut the door and turn around Aunt Ivy had become a completely different person. No longer smiling, her eyes glittered alarmingly as she swooped upon her niece, grabbed her arm and led her none too gently into a room at the back of the house. Four chairs with backs like ladders were set around a table covered with a dark green chenille cloth. The sideboard was twice the size of the one in Huskisson Street, with shelves almost reaching the ceiling, full of darkly patterned dishes. Through the window, overlooking a small garden, she could see that a corrugated-iron air raid shelter had been built.

'Sit down,' Aunt Ivy said curtly.

'I want it understood right from the start,' Aunt Ivy went on in the same curt voice when they were seated at the table, a voice nothing like the one she'd used when the woman was there, 'that I'm only having you because it's me Christian duty. Seeing as how you're me sister's child, to do otherwise would be a sin. You'll have a roof over your head, I'll feed and clothe you, but that's as far as it goes. Have you got that, miss?'

Josie nodded. Her head was throbbing. A ball of black fear rolled around her stomach, and she was worried she might vomit all over the posh cloth. It was horrible here, she hated it. And she hated Aunt Ivy most of all.

There was nothing about Aunt Ivy to remind her of Mam. It was hard to believe they had been sisters. Neither tall nor short, thin nor fat, her aunt's eyes were the colour of dirty water. She had yellow, mottled skin and a very low hairline, rigidly straight. When she frowned, as she did now, the black hair and thick black eyebrows almost met. Her hair was neatly parted, neatly waved, and a hairclip secured the longer side. She wore a purple costume with a mauve lacy jumper underneath, high-heeled black shoes and a surprising amount of make-up – almost as much as Irish Rose, though she didn't use mascara. Her nails were very long and painted scarlet.

'Don't you nod at me, miss,' she snapped. 'I want a proper answer, using the voice that the good God gave you. You can't fool me with your silly histrionics. I said, *have you got that?*'

The fist in Josie's throat tightened further. She tried to swallow, but it wouldn't go down. Aunt Ivy pinched her wrist, the scarlet nails dug into her flesh, and her throat felt even tighter. Her eyes smarted with the pain, and she knew that she had to answer to make the pain go away. She swallowed again, almost choking on the fist, and a sound like a grunt was expelled from her mouth. 'Yes,' she croaked.

Aunt Ivy released her wrist and her face twisted in an unpleasant smile. 'I thought as much. It was all put on. Your mam was the same, always putting on an act, full of airs and graces, making eyes at people.' She placed her arms on the table and leaned forward, so that her face was only inches from Josie's own. Her breath smelled worse than Maude's. 'Now, miss, we've got matters to discuss. I've taken you in, but I'm not having the neighbours knowing me sister gave birth to a bastard, so we've got to make up a story. I want you to listen very carefully. From now on, you're only five, not six. Understand?'

Josie opened her mouth to argue, but stopped when her aunt reached for her wrist.

'You're only five, otherwise they'll guess why our Mabel left home. A year later, she was old enough to get married, and that makes you legitimate. Her husband, your dad, was killed in the Battle of Britain.'

'But Mam didn't have a husband, and I didn't have a dad,' Josie protested.

Aunt Ivy impatiently pursed her red lips. 'I know that, and you know that, but we want the neighbours knowing something different. I told you, this is a story. We're making it up. Your dad was a rear gunner in the RAF. His name was – John Smith! Mabel met him when she was working as a

44

nanny. I'll say I didn't tell anyone because I disapproved, thought she was too young to get married. You stayed living over the water, anywhere will do – Ellesmere Port. Repeat that, miss – Ellesmere Port.'

'Ellesmere Port,' Josie said reluctantly. Mam had taught her never to tell lies.

'And what was your dad?'

'A rear gunner in the RAF. He died in the Battle of Britain.'

'And his name?' Her aunt raised her thick, black brows.

'John Smith.' It was all very difficult to take in. 'Does it mean I'm not Josie Flynn any more?'

'It most certainly does, miss. From now on, you're Josephine Smith, and you're only five.' Aunt Ivy leaned back in the chair, looking pleased. 'Good. You've got a good memory, like your mam. She could tell me things I'd said years ago, repeat them word for word. It means you should do well at school, like she did. You'll be starting Monday, it's all arranged. Sat'day, we'll go to Penny Lane and get you some clothes.'

She looked through the window at the yard and said thoughtfully, 'It's got Flynn on your ration book, so I'll have to register you with shops that don't know me, somewhere in town. I'll go in me dinner hour. It'll be a nuisance, but the shops round here know everyone's business.' She got to her feet.

'Well, miss, I'm going back to work now. I had to take two hours off because of you, and I've got a very responsible job. I'm secretary to the head of Claims at the Mersey Insurance Company. Mr Roberts can't cope if I'm not there.' She smirked. 'I'm never home before six, so someone's coming round at four to make your tea, but you can learn to do it yourself in future so that we don't have to bother people. My Vince is on afternoons – it'll be half ten at least by the time he puts in an appearance.' She looked keenly at the child crouched over the table. 'Did you know you've got an Uncle Vincent?'

45

'Mam talked about him sometimes.'

'I bet she did, the sly bitch.' She picked up a crocodile handbag off the sideboard. 'I'm off. You be good, and if you stay good, behave yourself and keep out me way, we'll get on just fine. You should be grateful you've got a nice, respectable home.' Her lips twisted in a sneer. 'I know what your mam was up to. If you'd stayed in Huskisson Street with that crowd of slags, you'd have ended up on the streets in time with your slag of a mam. That's right, isn't it, miss?'

Josie was pleating and unpleating the chenille cloth between her fingers, because her hands couldn't keep still. Her aunt's words, horrible words, beat against her brain, like tiny nails being tapped into her head. She felt as old as Sister Bernadette, a hundred, as memories returned, scenes flashed before her eyes and she recalled things that Mam had said.

I couldn't live without my little girl, my Petal.

Hello, Petal. I'm home.

She visualised her beautiful mother standing at the foot of the bed, arms outstretched. She used to think Mam was weak, but last Friday she'd been ready to defend her daughter with her life. Josie firmly believed she would have killed the two men if Irish Rose and the black man hadn't come. *I'll swing for you*, she'd said. Mam was strong. And *she* would be strong. No one would insult her and get away with it. *No one.* She wouldn't be sneered at or called names. And the same applied to her mother – she had no idea what a slag was, but it sounded horrible.

Aunt Ivy was still waiting for a reply. She returned to the table and tapped her foot. Josie, boosted by her newly found confidence, decided that if her wrist was pinched again, then her hand could drop off before she'd admit her aunt was right. She looked up at her, and felt hate burning in her eyes.

'Don't you *dare* call me mam a slag,' she said slowly in a voice so deep it surprised herself. 'You're the one who's horrible. You chucked her out, she told me. And I'd sooner be living in Huskisson Street any day than here.'

'Oh, Oh, I see.' Aunt Ivy was momentarily taken aback,

but quickly recovered. Her face darkened. 'Oh, so now we know where we stand. You know, all I have to do when I get to work is pick up the phone and you'll be in an orphanage by tomorrow. Don't imagine I *want* you here.'

'I don't want to be here.'

There was silence. A clock ticked loudly on the wall. It was an extremely grand clock, with peculiar letters instead of numbers on its pearly face.

Aunt Ivy's face turned dark with anger. She said abruptly, 'I haven't time to argue. I'll see you later, miss.' Her heels clicked down the hall. She called, 'We'll soon see who's boss.' The front door closed.

Josie was shaking. She realised she'd won something that she hadn't wanted to win: a minor battle. But she didn't want to be at war with Aunt Ivy. Suddenly, all the hideousness, the misery, of the last few days came washing over her and she began to cry. It was the first time she'd cried since her mother died, and the sobs racked her body till it hurt. Her chest was sore, her throat was sore, hot tears scalded her eyes. She couldn't believe that she would never see Mam again, or hear her voice, touch her, live with her in the attic room. It seemed she was destined to live in Machin Street with Aunt Ivy for ever. The future, so bright a few days ago, stretched ahead of her, black, miserable and lonely. Everything had changed in the twinkling of an eye. She put her hands to her ears, to block out the future, to block out the fact that Mam was dead.

Why, then, could she hear screaming? Not so much screaming as a thin, pathetic wail, as if a small animal were caught in a trap, pleading to be rescued.

The screaming, the wail, came from herself, and she was running round the house, running upstairs, slamming doors, kicking furniture, beating the walls with her fists. And screaming. She pulled at curtains, threw pillows and cushions on the floor. In the bathroom she stopped to vomit in the sink, then rested her forehead on the cool, white porcelain rim.

47

After a while she lifted her eyes, and noticed the lavatory. It didn't just have a wooden seat, but a lid as well. She sat on the lid, feeling calmer. Mam would be dead ashamed if she knew the way she'd just behaved. She'd been determined to make a good impression on Aunt Ivy. 'I'm not having her turning up her nose at us,' she'd said.

Josie slid off the lavatory, cleaned the sink and went around the house straightening the curtains, putting the cushions and pillows back in place. This time she noticed the lovely things that Mam had told her about. The ornaments and little items of fancy furniture, the pictures and mats that her very own grandad had brought back from foreign countries like Japan – elaborate brass candlesticks, mosaic bowls, statues, vases. She sat briefly on the puffy green settee in the parlour and admired the carved elephant with ivory horns with a table on its back. In the big main bedroom, two lamps with shades made from little bits of coloured glass glittered on each side of the double bed, which was covered with a mountainous maroon eiderdown.

There were two bedrooms at the back, one full of cardboard boxes. The other must have been Mam's and, she assumed, would be hers. A pretty white mat with raised flowers lay beside the single bed which had a dark blue embroidered coverlet. Another brightly coloured mat hung from a pole on the wall, which seemed a most peculiar thing to do with a mat, though perhaps it was a picture: a man, a shepherd because he had a crook, was standing at the foot of a mountain, a hand shading his eyes as he stared at a rainbow.

Josie threw herself on the bed, exhausted, and stared at the ceiling. In its much smaller way, this house was as grand as the one in Huskisson Street when it had been owned by the importer of rare spices. Even so, she didn't want to live there, not with Aunt Ivy.

But where else could she go? Even if Maude was willing to have her, Josie knew that Mam, up in heaven, would strongly disapprove. And Mam would be as miserable as sin if she knew her Josie was in an orphanage. She supposed that she had no alternative but to stay with Aunt Ivy, pretend her name was Smith and that she'd once had a dad called John. Most of all, she resented having to say that she was five, because she was proud of being six.

She closed her eyes. If only she could sleep and never wake up! Sleep, however, refused to come, and she remained stubbornly awake, reliving last Saturday, hearing the bomb, the explosion, over and over. She'd *known* Mam was dead, she'd just *known*.

When someone knocked on the front door at first she considered taking no notice. But the knock came again. It was almost certainly the person to make her tea. If she didn't answer, it would be reported back to Aunt Ivy, and she'd have another black mark against her.

She trudged downstairs, wishing she'd had time to wash her face because it was probably all swollen, and her eyes felt as if they were glued together. She wished it even more when she opened the door and found a smiling Mrs Kavanagh and Lily on the doorstep, both looking extremely smart. Mrs Kavanagh wore a pink linen costume and matching hat, and Lily a grey pleated skirt and a white jersey. She had a leather satchel over her shoulder. Her long brown hair rippled, like a cloak, around her shoulders.

'Hello, Josie, luv. We've met before, remember?' Mrs Kavanagh said warmly.

'Have you been crying?' Lily demanded.

'No,' Josie said pugnaciously. 'I never cry.'

'Me, I'd cry buckets if me ma died.' Lily tossed her head and looked superior.

'Oh, do be quiet, Lily,' her mother said crossly. 'We all know you have to do the opposite of everyone else.' She turned to Josie. 'I promised Ivy I'd pop in and make your tea, but that seems a bit daft when you can have it with us. We're only just down the street. I'm surprised Ivy didn't take the afternoon off, 'stead of leaving you by yourself on your first day. Are you okay, luv? You look a bit rough.'

'I'm fine, ta.'

'Why is your frock too short?' Lily asked rudely.

'Because a bomb tore me old one,' Josie explained, thinking this would make Lily sorry for her rudeness.

Instead, Lily said smugly, '*We've* never been bombed.'

'Oh, shut up, Lily,' her mother said. 'Come on, Josie. All the kids are home, 'cept Stanley who's at work. And I've made scouse, everyone's favourite. There's treacle pud for afters.'

At the mention of scouse, Josie realised she was starving. She loved scouse – Mam made it all the time because there was a limit to the meals you could do on a hob over the fire.

The Kavanaghs' house wasn't remotely as posh as Aunt Ivy's, but she much preferred its untidy clutter. A fire burned in the parlour, where the flowered three-piece was faded and well worn. Books and toys littered the floor, and the sideboard was piled high with more toys, a pair of football boots and some ravelled knitting. A doll squinted at her from the mantelpiece, reminding her of Irish Rose. In the square bay window, a treadle sewing machine was draped with yards of bright red tulle. A wireless was on, and a woman was singing very loudly, 'Wish me luck as you wave me goodbye.'

Two very sunburnt boys with green eyes and hair the colour of butter wrestled each other on the floor. The biggest, who looked about twelve, was clearly winning, and a girl, a slightly older version of Lily, oblivious to the din, was reading a book, her legs draped over the arm of the chair. She looked up, said, 'Hello,' and returned to the book.

'H-hello,' Josie stammered. The change from the tomb-like atmosphere of her aunt's house to the noisy chaos of the Kavanaghs' was welcome, but slightly daunting. She stood in the middle of the room, not sure what to do. Should she sit down? Mrs Kavanagh and Lily had disappeared into the kitchen, and she wondered if she should follow, offer to help set the table or something.

The boys had noticed she was there. They stopped wrestling. The older one held his brother down by the throat, and asked curiously, 'Who are you?'

'I'm Josie Flynn, I mean Smith.'

The boy grinned. 'Josie Flynn-I-mean-Smith. That's a dead funny name.'

Josie drew herself to her full height and said haughtily, 'It's Josie Smith.'

'All right, you don't need to bite me head off, Josie Smith. I'm Robert, and this is our Benjamin on the floor. We call him Ben. He's only eight. Us boys are called after prime ministers, Conservative ones, natch.' His green eyes sparkled mischievously. 'The girls are only flowers. That's our Daisy over there. She's ten, and you won't get a word out of her till she's finished that book.'

'Oh, shut up, Robert,' Daisy snapped. 'I'm not likely to finish me book while there's such a racket going on.'

'So why don't you read in the bedroom?'

'Because our Marigold's trying on frocks. She's going to the pictures tonight with Gabrielle McGillivray.'

'What to see?'

Daisy sniffed. 'I dunno, do I? I haven't been invited.'

Josie was doing her best to remember the names – Marigold, Daisy and Lily, Robert, Ben, and who was the boy at work? Stanley, she remembered. She wondered if Mr and Mrs Kavanagh ever got confused when their children were all there together.

Throughout the noisy meal that followed, Mrs Kavanagh got confused all the time. 'Pass us the bread, Mar-, Dais-, *Lily*,' she would finish triumphantly when she got it right. Or, 'Our Robert's late. He should be home by now.'

The children grinned at each other. 'Robert's here, Ma. It's our Stanley who's late.'

The six Kavanaghs had been born neatly, a boy and a girl alternately, all two years apart. The girls were slightly plump like their mother, with the same dark brown eyes and the same brown hair which they wore long and parted in the middle. They looked like a set of Victorian dolls, with their pink, glowing faces, pert noses and tiny rosebud mouths.

Lily might well be the youngest, but she had more to say

than the others put together. She talked in a firm, opiniated voice, to be met with, 'Oh, shut up, Lily,' from various members of the family.

At half past five, Stanley arrived home from his boring job in a bank, followed by Mr Kavanagh a few minutes later. He was very tall, very thin, very sunburnt, with pale, creamy hair like his sons. His dark suit was covered with threads, and Josie remembered Mam saying he owned a haberdasher's in Penny Lane. He had the air of a man who was seriously moidered, but smiled benignly on his large family, who were still around the table where they'd been for almost an hour, because everyone was too busy talking to leave. Only eight-year-old Ben, next to Josie, hadn't said a word.

Mrs Kavanagh went into the kitchen and fetched a plate of scouse. 'There's treacle pud for afters, Eddie.'

'Goodo,' he said, winking at Josie, and she thought it mightn't be so bad living in Machin Street, with the Kavanaghs only a few doors away.

At half past six, Mrs Kavanagh suggested she go home. 'Only because Ivy should be back by now and she'll be worried where you are. Tell her it's my fault you're late. Oh, and luv.' Josie was led into the hall, where it wasn't exactly quiet but at least they were alone. Mrs Kavanagh sat on the stairs and pulled her down beside her. 'That time we met in Blackler's basement, luv, I guessed straight away that Mabel was your mam – you're too alike to pretend otherwise. Anyroad, I never told your auntie that I'd seen you. Poor Ivy, she's not a bad woman, but she's a stickler for appearances. It means I know darn well you didn't have a dad who died in the Battle of Britain – Mabel would have been bound to mention she was married the day we met. And I remember you telling me then you were nearly four, so you can't be only five like Ivy ses. I didn't argue when she told me all that rubbish the other night. Even so, her secret's safe with me. And, Josie, whatever happens, remember you're always welcome in this house. Mabel was one of the nicest girls I've ever known, as well as the prettiest. I don't give a damn what she got up to, and she'd have wanted me to be your friend.'

'Ta.' It was a relief to know that another person knew the truth.

'Oh, and another thing, luv. You won't have met your Uncle Vince yet, but you'll find he's a real Prince Charming.'

'Will I?' Josie felt even more relieved. Mam hadn't talked much about Uncle Vince, but she'd had the feeling he'd done something bad. If Mrs Kavanagh thought so highly of him, then she must have got the wrong end of the stick. Who, she wondered was 'His Lordship', the person who had to be given his marching before Mam moved back in?

Lily offered to come with her when she realised she was leaving. 'In case you've forgotten your house, like.'

''Course I haven't forgotten,' Josie said scornfully. 'It's seventy-six.'

'Still, I'll come with you all the same.'

To her surprise, when they were outside Lily linked arms, and Josie didn't know whether to be pleased or annoyed. Since she'd got to know her, she wasn't sure if she liked Lily all that much. She was far too bossy and sure of herself.

'Ma said you're starting St Joseph's on Monday. Our Marigold left last term – she's gone to commercial college – but there's still four of us Kavanaghs left. I'll call for you, shall I?'

'If you like.'

'Pity we won't be in the same class, else I'd have told Tommy Atherton to shove off and you could have sat beside me.'

Josie wriggled her shoulders and didn't answer. Aunt Ivy had been in touch with the school and would have told them she was five, which meant she'd have to go through the whole first year again, learn to read and write and do sums when she could already do them. She was wondering how this could be avoided when Lily said, 'I think our Ben's stuck on you.'

'What?'

'Our Ben, he's got a crush on you. He didn't say a word

during tea, just kept looking at you sideways, sort'a thing. Mind you, he's a soppy lad, our Ben. I wouldn't be all that flattered if I were you.'

'Don't worry, I'm not,' Josie snapped.

They had arrived at Aunt Ivy's, who opened the door to Josie's knock, her face like thunder. 'And where the hell d'you think you've been, miss? I've . . .' Her voice became a simper and she gave a sickly smile when she saw Lily. 'Oh, hello, luv. I should have known she'd be in your house. Your mam, she's all heart.'

'She's a living saint, Mrs Adams,' Lily said in sepulchral tones. Josie realised she was making fun of her aunt, and warmed to her new friend. 'And she said Josie can come to ours for tea every night. "Another mouth at the table won't make much difference," as she said to me da'.'

Josie couldn't remember Mrs Kavanagh saying any such thing, but didn't argue. Aunt Ivy began to mutter something about if she was being fed regularly she'd have to take along some rations, and Lily said, 'God bless you, Mrs Adams.' She nudged Josie playfully in the ribs, and went home.

It was hard not to think of the Kavanaghs' happy, noisy house when the door closed and she was left alone with Aunt Ivy, who remarked spitefully, 'If you hadn't been at the Kavanaghs', miss, you'd have gone to bed early. I was dead worried when I got in and you weren't here.'

'I'd like to go to bed early, please.'

Her aunt shrugged. 'Suit yourself. You'll find a nightie on the bed. I got it in Lewis's on me way home from work.'

'Ta.' She was halfway upstairs, already feeling tearful, longing to be alone so she could think about Mam which she'd hardly done at all over the last few hours, when Aunt Ivy called, 'Don't forget to draw the blackout curtains.'

'No.'

'Are you all right?'

Josie turned, taken aback by this unexpected expression of concern. 'I'm okay, ta.' Her aunt was standing at the bottom of the stairs, looking up. Her face was odd, all screwed up, as if she were about to cry.

'I suppose, well, as that woman said this morning, you've had a shock. It'll take a while to get over that business with your mam. I was dead upset when me own mam died, but I got over it eventually. You'll find the same.'

'Ta,' Josie said again. Perhaps Aunt Ivy was sorry about the way she'd behaved earlier and would be nicer in future, but this turned out not to be the case.

2

It wasn't until Saturday, at breakfast, that Josie met Uncle Vince. When she went into the dining room he was tucking into a plate of bacon and fried bread, a small, slight figure wearing a shirt without a collar and a hand-knitted Fair Isle waistcoat. Aunt Ivy, her back to Josie, was pouring tea. She glanced at her niece and didn't speak.

'Hello there, luv.' Uncle Vince turned round and chucked her under the chin. He smiled. 'You're a lovely big girl for six.'

'Five,' Aunt Ivy snapped.

'Oh, yes, five.' He winked at Josie from behind his wife's back, and she risked a little smile back.

As Mrs Kavanagh had said, he was a genuine Prince Charming, with thick, straight hair a lovely golden colour, blue eyes as pale as a misty sky at dawn, and a dead straight nose. Had his chin been firmer, he would have been perfect, but it sloped away under his mouth, making him look weak. He must have been weak, Josie thought, the way he let Aunt Ivy boss him around. Yet the funny thing was, she was mad about him.

She had still been awake last night at half ten when Uncle Vince came home from his job as a quality control inspector at the Royal Ordnance factory in Fazakerley. As he ate his tea, she could hear Aunt Ivy telling him to sit up straight, not put his elbows on the table and eat up quickly before the food got cold, but all said in a fond, dopey voice, as if Vince were a little boy, not her husband.

'My Vince' was how her aunt referred to him when she spoke to the neighbours who'd called to see 'Mabel's little girl' for themselves, and remark in amazement at how incredibly tall she was for five.

'My Vince is on afternoons this week,' Aunt Ivy would say in the same dopey voice, and with an equally dopey smile, or, 'My Vince can't stand that awful dried milk.' 'My Vince would have joined the army like a shot if it hadn't been for his dicky heart.'

When Lily called, Josie was not long home from a shopping trip to Penny Lane where Aunt Ivy had sourly bought her a grey pleated skirt, two white blouses, a navy blue cardigan, shoes, socks, underwear and a drab brown frock with long sleeves that was dead cheap but would do for church and to wear around the house until Mrs Kavanagh ran up something nicer.

'You can chuck that rag away when we get home.' Aunt Ivy nodded at the red gingham frock. 'I'd have thought Mabel would have decked up her kid a bit smarter. I made sure she was dressed nice when she was your age.'

Josie thought about the blue velvet frock from Paddy's market. A picture flashed through her mind, of Mam ironing the frock. It seemed like an eternity ago. 'There, that's everything done,' she'd said. Later, they'd waltzed around the room.

'Come *on*.' Her reverie was rudely interrupted by Aunt Ivy pinching her arm. 'It's time we made tracks. My Vince will be dying for a cuppa.'

They hadn't been in five minutes when Lily knocked. 'Me ma thought Josie would like to see the fairy glen in Sefton Park,' she said sweetly to Aunt Ivy.

Josie was upstairs, changing into the brown frock. 'I'm sure she would, luv,' Aunt Ivy said in a grovelling voice.

When she came down, Lily was in the parlour chattering

away to Uncle Vince about football. He had a pools coupon on his knee, the wireless was on and he was waiting for the results.

'You won't win much.' Lily warned. 'Even if you get eight draws, you'll only get about fifteen hundred pounds, least so me da' says. Since the war, people have stopped doing the pools.'

'Fifteen hundred quid would do me fine, luv,' Uncle Vince replied.

Aunt Ivy ruffled his golden hair. 'I thought I told you to put your collar on, Vince,' she said fondly. 'It looks bad when people come.'

'Oh, sorry, luv. I forgot. I'll do it in a minute.'

'You better had.'

'That's a horrible dress,' Lily said the minute they were outside. 'It's the sort of thing they wear in the workhouse.' Before Josie could think of an equally rude reply, Lily put her arm through Josie's and said, 'I see you've met My Vince.'

'He's very nice,' Josie said defensively. She was convinced Vince would be even friendlier if it wasn't for his wife.

'Oh, he's dead lovely, My Vince.' Lily giggled. 'Our Marigold's madly in love with him, but me da' said Ivy would kill her stone dead if she found out. He doesn't like either of 'em.'

'Your da' doesn't like your Marigold?' Josie gasped.

'No, silly. He can't stand My Vince or your Auntie Ivy. He said *she's* besotted, though I don't know what that means, and *he's* a ponce. I don't know what that means either. Me da' thinks he only married her 'cos she had a house. It's usually the fella that supplies the house. And, according to me da', your auntie's not short of a few bob. She *bought* his services, he said. When I asked for an explanation, I was told to mind me own business. He wasn't talking to me, but to me ma.

'"Look at the clothes she's always buying him," he said before he realised I was listening. "He's got four suits." Me poor da's only got two, one for best and one for every day.

57

Ma says he's jealous, because she doesn't wait on him hand and foot, like Ivy does My Vince, and he's not nearly so good-looking.'

They had reached Sefton Park, and Lily showed her the fairy glen, a small clearing where the surrounding trees were turning bronze, and a few leathery leaves had already fallen on to the emerald grass, dotted with buttercups and daisies. The sun shone through the trees, making yellow patterns underneath. A slight breeze shook the branches, and the patterns shivered.

Josie was instantly enraptured. They were the only ones there, and the atmosphere was magical, like something out of a book. She half expected a fairy or an elf to come dancing towards her as she wandered down the sloping bank towards a stream, where goldfish, all different sizes, swam lazily in the tinkling, silvery water. If only she could stay for ever, never see Aunt Ivy again, but hide herself in the dark, rocky place where the stream disappeared and the trees joined thickly together to make an arch.

Two ducks came paddling towards her in their ungainly way, quacking angrily. Josie backed away. Perhaps living here wasn't such a good idea.

'They won't hurt you.' Lily was standing beside her. She must have sensed that Josie was awesomely impressed by the fairy glen. Her expression was smug, as if she owned the place, had planted the trees herself and had supplied the fish and the ducks and the frog that suddenly leapt from the water on to the bank.

'Have you seen trees before?' she asked patronisingly.

"Course I have,' Josie snapped. 'Mam used to take me to Princes Park.'

'What was your mam like?'

'Beautiful.'

'I bet she wasn't as beautiful as mine.'

It seemed a futile argument. Josie didn't bother to reply. She watched the frog, which kept leaping and pausing, leaping and pausing, until it disappeared from sight.

There was silence, which she already realised was unusual when in the company of Lily Kavanagh. Then Lily said in a careful voice, 'Do you like me?'

'I'm not sure,' Josie said honestly.

'I'd like you to like me.'

'We'll just have to see.'

'You can come to the pics with us tonight,' Lily said in a coaxing voice, as if this might help Josie make up her mind.

'The pics?'

'The pictures, to see a film. Me ma's taking me and our Ben to see Deanna Durbin in *Spring Parade*. Have you never been to the pictures, Josie?'

'No. But me Auntie Ivy mightn't let me.'

'She will if I ask. She'll do anything to keep in with the Kavanaghs.' Lily puffed out her chest conceitedly. 'We're the most important family in the street. Me da's a councillor on the corpy, as well as chairman of the Conservative Party, and me ma runs the Townswomen's Guild. Our Stanley and Marigold are the Amateur Junior Waltz Champions of the North East of England.'

Lily hesitated and looked less sure of herself. 'Or it might be the North West. They don't do it so much nowadays. They used to go with a crowd in a big charabanc to places like Manchester and Blackpool, but now there isn't the petrol. You can come with us to the Grafton ballroom next time there's an exhibition. Our Stanley's got an evening suit, a proper one, and Marigold's got seven spangly frocks me ma made. You should be dead pleased that I like you and want you for a friend.'

'Oh, I am,' Josie said sarcastically. Privately, she was impressed, particularly with the waltzing bit. The sarcasm was wasted on Lily, who greeted the reply with a complacent smile.

'Anyroad,' she said, 'your auntie will be pleased if you go out tonight. Sat'days, her and My Vince go to the pics in town. She wears her fur coat, and he gets dolled up to the nines. Me da' ses he looks like one of them dummies in Burton's shop window.'

St Joseph's was already three days into the autumn term when Josie started on Monday. She noticed she was taller than all the girls in class 1 and most of the boys. When the teacher, Miss Simms, called the register, she answered clearly in a loud voice. Not normally given to pushing herself forward, she showed off outrageously, putting up her hand at every opportunity when the class was asked a question. At break time, Miss Simms asked her to remain behind.

'Would you like to read this page for me, Josie?'

The page was composed of short sentences of mostly three-letter words. The cat sat on the mat. The man had a gun. The dog lay by the log.

Josie read the entire page without a pause. Miss Simms was impressed. 'Who taught you to read, dear?'

'Me mam,' Josie said in a rush. After all, Aunt Ivy considered it all right to tell lies. 'She taught me to do sums, an' all. I can do add up and take away. *And* I've learnt some of the Catechism. I know the Pope cannot err, but I don't know what err means. Do you, miss?'

Miss Simms laughed. 'It means he can't make a mistake, and it's clever of you to ask. But I think *I* might be erring if I kept you in this class. I'd better have a word with Mr Leonard, the headmaster.'

On Tuesday morning she was moved up to class 2, which had been her objective all along. It was annoying when Mr Leonard took her into the new classroom, and Lily Kavanagh leapt to her feet and screeched, 'Can she sit beside me, sir? I'm the only friend she has in the world.'

Josie was woken at half-past eleven that night by Aunt Ivy shaking her arm. 'The siren's gone. Come on, miss, stir yourself. My Vince is working. He's on nights.'

'Where are we going?' Josie stumbled out of bed, half-asleep.

'The shelter, of course. Get a move on.'

The air-raid shelter was small, with a narrow bunk each side. Aunt Ivy lit a portable fire, and the shelter immediately stank of burning oil. The light from the fire revealed a dead spider suspended from a single thread. Josie lay on a bunk, and the dead spider sprang to life, raced up the thread and disappeared behind one of the wooden struts supporting the roof. She kept her eyes firmly on the spot where it had disappeared, knowing she'd never sleep a wink while it was there. The bombs didn't bother her. She didn't care if she was killed.

A thought occurred to her. She was reluctant to speak to her aunt unless she absolutely had to, but this seemed one of those times. 'Where will I sleep if there's a raid when Uncle Vince is home?'

Aunt Ivy was adjusting a thick, flesh-coloured net over her metal curlers. She tied the net under her chin. Her head was curiously at odds with the rest of her, as she wore a glamorous black satin dressing-gown and lace nightie. She only wore the curlers when Vince was at work. Other times, she waved her hair with metal tongues which she heated on the fire. She plumped the pillow. 'I suppose you'll have to curl up with me.'

Never! Never in a million years.

Two days later, when the siren went, Josie clung to the headboard and refused to get up. 'I'm not scared, I'd sooner stay.'

'But you can't!' Aunt Ivy raged. 'It's dangerous. You might be killed.'

'I'm not going,' Josie said flatly. 'You'll have to drag me there.'

The buzz of planes could be heard, getting closer. For a few seconds, Aunt Ivy glanced wildly from her niece to the door, before giving up. 'On your own head be it, miss,' she said in clipped tones, and closed the bedroom door.

As the weeks went by the raids got worse, but the worse they got, the closer Josie felt to Mam. She could almost *feel*

Mam's warm body in the bed with her as the bombs screamed to earth and exploded with deafening thuds. The house would rock.

After a while, she decided she didn't want to die after all. She would never stop missing her mother, but even though Mam was dead, incredibly, it seemed possible to be happy, at least for some of the time.

'Shove off, our Ben,' Lily said cruelly when her brother tried to sit by them in the school canteen. They were just finishing their dinner.

'Don't speak to him like that,' Josie admonished when a downcast Ben loped away, shoulders hunched. With his thin face, big, brown eyes and shaggy blond hair, he reminded her of a defenceless puppy. She felt sorry for him, and was fed up with the way he was treated by his sister. Most people quickly got fed up with Lily and her bossy ways. It seemed to Josie that *she* was the only friend Lily had in the world, not the other way round.

'He's a drip,' Lily sneered as they wandered into the playground.

'No, he's not. Cissie O'Neill said the other day he's very clever. He's expected to pass the scholarship when he's ten, and go to grammar school.'

Lily's eyes narrowed. 'Since when have you been friends with Cissie O'Neill?'

'I'm not, we were just talking. Though I wouldn't mind us being friends, she's very nice.'

'Hmm.' Lily considered this seriously and must have decided it wasn't a line of conversation she wished to continue because she said, 'Only drips pass scholarships.'

'Only thickos fail them,' Josie replied smartly. Perhaps the reason she didn't mind Lily so much was because she gave as good as she got. She wasn't prepared be told what to do, or what not to do, by someone who was shorter than she was and only a month older, not that Lily knew that.

Lily took offence at this, and marched off with her little

nose in the air, but quickly returned when she could find no one else to play with. She took Josie's arm, and they smiled warmly at each other.

'Josie.'

Josie turned, and saw Ben Kavanagh galloping towards her on his long, thin legs. She was on her way home from school, by herself for a change because Lily was off with a cold and driving her mother to distraction with her non-stop demands.

Ben blushed scarlet, and mumbled something which at first she didn't catch. He licked his lips nervously and repeated the words. 'Can I carry your satchel?'

'If you like.' She gave it to him, and thought he looked a bit daft with a satchel on each arm.

'Are you coming to ours for tea?'

'Well, yes.' It was a silly question, but she reckoned he was embarrassed. She had tea with the Kavanaghs every day. 'But I've got to call home first for a pound of self-raising flour.' Last week it had been margarine, and the week before a tin of cocoa, because Aunt Ivy insisted on providing rations to make up for what Josie ate.

Ben seemed useless at conversation. His Adam's apple kept wobbling as he cleared his throat to speak, but nothing came. Josie felt desperately sorry for him, and searched her mind for something to say, but Ben's awkward silence seemed to have affected her too. 'It's a nice warm day for December,' was all she could manage.

'Yes,' Ben croaked. After an awkward pause, he went on, 'They say it will stay warm over Christmas. Not like last year. Remember last year, Josie?'

She nodded. Last year it had snowed and snowed, and the whole world had been muffled in white. The attic had felt particularly warm and cosy. Her face grew sad at the memory.

'You're very brave,' Ben said boldly.

'Brave?' Josie stared at him. He was still very pink.

He cleared his throat again. 'Ma told us about your mam

63

and dad, both dying, like. Your face is often sad, like it was just now, but you never cry.'

'Oh!' She felt touched. He was much more perceptive than his sister. She said impulsively, 'But I do cry, Ben. I cry every night with me head under the bedclothes so no one'll hear.'

Ben's face crumpled, as if he was about to cry himself. 'That's awful,' he gulped.

Josie smiled cheerfully. 'I'll just have to get along with it, won't I? Promise you won't tell your Lily about me crying. She'd never understand.'

He looked chuffed at the idea of them sharing a secret. 'Don't worry, I won't say a word.'

There were times when Josie felt very odd, like two completely different little girls living in two completely different worlds. In one world, the outside one, lived the Josie who liked school, Lily's best friend. In the other, darker world, a silent, surly Josie lived with Aunt Ivy, and cried for her mam every night.

She never told anyone how horrid it was at home because she didn't want them feeling sorry for her, particularly Lily.

Aunt Ivy was impossible to please. If Josie put something down, it should have been put somewhere else, and she would be told so in an awful sneering voice, as if she were dead stupid. To be the object of such derision made her feel less than human.

'You're as bad as Mabel. She was never much of a one for housework. I bet that place you lived was filthy.'

Remembering how Mam had usually kept their attic spotless, Josie wanted to shout that this wasn't true, but she had given up arguing. It wasn't lack of courage, or that answering back made things worse, but her sullen silences, sullen eyes, drove her aunt wilder than words would ever do.

'Cat got your tongue?' she would scream hysterically, and shake her till her head was spinning.

For the slightest of reasons she would be sent to bed early, and sometimes for no reason at all, which she didn't mind because it was better than sitting in the parlour with Aunt Ivy and My Vince, and being picked on all the time.

Not that Uncle Vince said anything nasty. When his wife wasn't looking, he'd wink at Josie, and throw her a big smile.

And soon they were to share another secret, Josie and her Uncle Vince.

Christmas week, and the air raids were the heaviest Liverpool had known. They continued throughout the night, night after night, lasting ten hours, eleven, twelve.

The night before Christmas Eve, Josie listened to the sound of her city being blown to smithereens by Hitler's bombs. It was like hell on earth, impossible not to be frightened. Fire engines clanged, fires crackled, glass shattered, people screamed, the earth shuddered. She put her arms around the pillow and tried to pretend it was Mam.

During a lull, her aunt came in and called upstairs for her to come to the shelter, but Josie refused. She yearned for company, but not her aunt's. She wanted Maude, or Lily – any one of the Kavanaghs would have done. Most of all she wanted her mother. It didn't seem fair, she thought fretfully. Cissie O'Neill sat under the stairs with her little brother when there was a raid, and their mam read stories until they went to sleep. The Kavanaghs went to Hughes's cellar, the bakery on the corner, because their shelter wasn't big enough for eight people, and they played I Spy and the Churchwarden's Cat. Other children went to public shelters with flasks of tea and sandwiches, and sang 'Bless 'Em All' or 'We're Going to Hang Out the Washing on the Siegfried Line'.

The all clear went at a quarter past five. Her aunt and uncle came indoors, the kettle was put on, dishes rattled. After a while they came upstairs, and she could hear them talking. Eventually, the bed creaked, as they lay down to catch a few hours' sleep.

But Josie couldn't sleep. She lay, tossing and turning, wondering if any other girls and boys had lost their mams during the night. War was wicked. She couldn't understand it.

Some time later, the front door closed. Aunt Ivy had gone to work, but was finishing early, at lunchtime. My Vince must still be in bed. She almost wished it were a schoolday, that Lily would call any minute. They liked to get to school before everyone else and play ball in the empty playground.

She slid out of bed and opened the blackout curtains. A pall of black smoke hung low in the sky, which was otherwise bright and clear. The houses behind were still standing, and a woman cleaning an upstairs window gave her a little wave. Josie waved back. No matter how bad the raids, people very quickly returned to normal. She got dressed and washed her face in the bathroom. Her eyes were sticky, her knees shaky, as if they might give way any minute. She hoped they wouldn't, because she and Lily were going to Penny Lane this avvy – if Penny Lane still existed – to buy Christmas presents for each other.

Apart from the ticking of the various clocks, the house was quiet. Josie made her bed, and a feeling of terrible loneliness swept over her. She groaned, determined not to cry.

'Is that you, Josie? Are you all right, luv? That was a raid and a half, that was.'

Uncle Vince! 'I'm all right, ta,' she called.

'Why don't you come and say hello?'

Josie hesitated, then slowly crept along the landing. Uncle Vince was sitting up with the maroon eiderdown tucked around him. He wore blue and grey striped pyjamas buttoned to the neck and his bright golden hair was tousled. There was a tray of tea things on the bedside table. He smiled, and patted the space beside him. 'Come on, luv. I heard that groan. Come and tell your Uncle Vince all about it. What's up, luv?'

She sat on the bed. Uncle Vince slid an arm around her shoulders. 'We've never had a little tête-à-tête before.'

'What's that?'

'A little talk, a chinwag. Either you're in, or I'm out, or Ivy's here.' Josie assumed from this that her aunt wouldn't approve of the little talk. 'I've wanted to ask about Mabel.'

'About me mam?' Josie was startled.

66

'I wondered what she got up to after she left, that's all. I miss her terrible. She was like a ray of sunshine, Mabel.' He shifted in the bed and scratched his perfect nose. 'Did she ever talk about me?' he asked casually.

'Sometimes.'

His arm tensed around her shoulders. 'I hope she only said nice things.'

'I can't remember. Did someone used to live here called His Lordship? She didn't like him much.'

Uncle Vince gave a funny little gasp. 'Not since I've been here, luv.' He looked down at her with his kind, blue eyes. 'I expect you still miss Mabel, your mam.'

'Oh, *yes!*' Perhaps it was the arm on her shoulders, the kind eyes, the wistful, understanding expression on his face, as if he knew exactly how she felt, that made her cry – not the despairing, hopeless way she cried at night, her head under the clothes, but sad, gentle tears, more to do with the fact that she hadn't slept a wink and had been frightened out of her wits during the raid.

'There, there, luv.' Uncle Vince stroked her face and kissed her cheek, and it was so nice to think that someone actually *cared* that Josie cried for ages and ages, until she fell asleep.

'Josie, luv.' She woke up to find Vince, fully dressed, beside the bed. 'Your friend's here, Lily.' He lifted her up and sat her on his knee. 'Let's not tell anyone about our little tête-à-tête, eh? Ivy, well she's inclined to be jealous, like, and she'd only take it out on you. We'll keep it a secret, luv, just between you and me.'

The bombing of Liverpool continued for another year. It wasn't until after the following Christmas that it stopped altogether, and everyone gave a collective sigh of relief.

After that, it was easy to believe there was no such thing as war. Josie and Lily went regularly to the pictures, and Josie fell in love with Humphrey Bogart, who was, Lily said scathingly, hideously ugly. She far preferred Alan Ladd, who was a little bit like My Vince. If the film was a U certificate, they were allowed to go by themselves, otherwise Mr and Mrs Kavanagh would take them, or Stanley and his girlfriend, Beryl. The minute they got inside, Stanley and Beryl would make for the back row, where they would kiss each other extravagantly and entirely ignore the film, which Josie and Lily thought daft. Why didn't they do it outside for free?

It came as a shock when, twelve months later, Stanley received his call-up papers. He was nearly eighteen.

All the Kavanaghs, Josie and Beryl, went to the Pier Head to wave goodbye to the thin young man about to sail to North Africa, looking so vulnerable in his khaki uniform. Beryl burst into tears when the ship's horn went, and soon everyone was crying, including Josie. It was like losing a big brother. She turned, without thinking, and buried her head in Ben's shoulder.

'Don't worry, Josie. You've got me.'

She looked up in surprise, remembering Tommy, who'd once said the same thing. Ben was blushing but, then, he rarely spoke without going red. 'I'll take you to the pictures from now on.' He went even redder, and looked as if he were about to curl up and die with embarrassment.

'It would have to be a U certificate, or we wouldn't be let in,' Josie said practically. He was only ten.

Two weeks later, they went to see Will Hay in *The Ghost of St Michael's*. Josie had assumed Lily would be coming, but Ben made it plain his sister wasn't welcome. A furiously jealous Lily hardly spoke to Josie for a week.

In the cinema, they sat in the front row where the seats only cost threepence, and he gave her two warm, melting lumps of Cadbury's milk chocolate wrapped in silver paper. She felt a little thrill. This was her first date. She had one up on Lily for a change.

She peeled the silver paper off the chocolate. 'Would you like some?' she enquired, and was a bit put out when he took half.

During the interval, he told her he was going to be a scientist when he grew up, and discover something vital that

68

would change the world, like penicillin, which she'd never heard of, or radium, which she hadn't heard of either, or electricity, which fortunately she had.

The film was dead funny, but frightening when the ghost appeared. Josie hid her head in Ben's shoulder during the scariest bits. She heard him swallow nervously, then reach for her hand, and they managed to remain hand in hand throughout the remainder of the film and all the way back to Aunt Ivy's.

'Shall we go again next Friday?' Ben gulped.

'I wouldn't mind, ta.'

'I think we should get married when we grow up.' He stood before her, suddenly not the least bit red, not at all nervous, very manful for ten.

'If you like.'

Ben nodded seriously. 'I would, very much.'

3

They pretended Uncle Vince was her dad. It wasn't often they were alone. Only in the school holidays, when he was on late shift and Ivy had gone to work, did they have the house to themselves.

'Josie,' he would call as soon as Ivy closed the front door, and she would run along the landing in her nightie. They would roll around the bed, and he would tickle her, cuddle her, kiss her, just like a dad.

'Aren't we the perfect couple,' Uncle Vince would say afterwards, looking at their flushed faces in the dressing-table mirror.

But she had learnt, a long time ago, that things could never be relied on to stay the same. Within the twinkling of an eye, everything could alter – sometimes for the better, sometimes for the worse.

She was nine, and it was just after Christmas. They were looking at themselves in the mirror and, as she watched, she saw his expression change. He seemed abstracted and vague, not very pleased about something. Josie thought she'd done something wrong. She fell silent, hunched her knees and stared at her toes.

Suddenly, Uncle Vince grabbed her, roughly turned her on her side, away from him, and held her so tightly that she could hardly breathe. She felt something stiff and hard pressed against her bottom, and Vince started to make dead funny noises, like gasps. It made her feel frightened, but she daren't ask him to stop in case he got annoyed, something best avoided. Uncle Vince rarely got annoyed, but when he did he was like a child, worse than Lily. He would jump up and down, wave his fists and shout in a funny, squeaky voice, like the day Aunt Ivy scorched his best shirt, or the time he lost one of his gold cuff links. Even his wife was struck dumb when My Vince lost his temper. Josie had a feeling that telling her uncle to stop when he was making the funny noises was something that would make him very annoyed indeed.

She couldn't stop thinking about it all day and next morning pretended to be asleep when he called. After a few minutes, she gave a sigh of relief – he must have given up. Instead, the door opened and he came in.

'Who's a little sleepyhead this morning?' He smiled, but behind the smile his eyes looked strange. 'It's going to be a bit of a squash in a single bed, but never mind, eh?' Josie turned away, feeling trapped, helpless, when he climbed in. She kept her eyes shut until he finished making the funny noises.

'Don't forget, luv,' Vince whispered, 'this is our secret. It's just between you and me. Don't think of telling Ivy, 'cos she'd never believe you. She'd think you were making it up, like, and there'd be hell to pay. She might even send you to one of them orphanage places, and you'd never see your friend Lily again. And that'd be a shame, wouldn't it, luv?'

At St Joseph's, class 5 was being prepared to sit the scholarship in June. Miss Simms had left long ago to get married, and Mr Leonard had been called up, although he was forty-one. Other teachers had gone, either to join the forces or take up important war work. Their replacements were retired teachers, glad to return and do their bit.

As there was no one to know better, Josie was assumed to be nine and entered for the scholarship along with Lily. Lily had convinced herself she would pass with flying colours.

Their form teacher, Mrs Barrett, was eighty if a day. Mr Crocker, the headmaster, was even older. They had worked together before and disliked each other intensely.

Everyone had been working hard and was looking forward to the Easter holidays. Lily would be ten on Good Friday, and was having a party the next day. Mrs Kavanagh had made them a new frock each. Lily's was a genuine party frock – green taffeta with short sleeves, a heart-shaped neck and a gathered skirt. Aunt Ivy didn't believe in party frocks, they were a waste of money. 'You don't get enough wear out of them,' she said thinly, so Josie's frock was more sensible – cream Viyella, with long sleeves, a navy blue collar and matching buttons – and would do for less salubrious occasions, like church. Even so, Josie was delighted. She was having a final fitting after school. It was her own birthday in May, six weeks off. There wouldn't be a party. Josie's age was something her aunt preferred to ignore.

She sighed happily, ignored Mrs Barrett, who was enthusing about fractions, and thought instead about Ben, who'd passed the scholarship two years ago and was now at Quarry Bank Grammar School. He'd kissed her for the first time last week, but only on the cheek. They'd discussed where they would live when they were married. Would she mind leaving Liverpool? he wanted to know. Josie said she wasn't sure.

In desperation, because she felt left out, Lily had more or less forced Jimmy Atherton to be her boyfriend, and they went out in a foursome, to the Pier Head or the pictures, to the fairy glen in Sefton Park or for a cup of tea in Lyon's in Lime Street. Jimmy insisted Lily pay for herself. He was prepared to be her boyfriend, reluctantly, but not if it meant being out of pocket. Mr Kavanagh had doubled Ben's pocket money for passing the scholarship and also, he said, chuckling, 'Because he's got a woman to support.'

The Easter holiday would be the gear. There was only one fly in the ointment, an enormous one: Uncle Vince, who was part of that other, inside world, where nothing had ever been the gear.

Josie's stomach churned. She gnawed her lip and wondered how she could avoid him. If she got dressed and sneaked out of the house as soon as Aunt Ivy left, it would mean wandering around for ages until it was time to meet Lily, which she wouldn't mind. But she'd have to return home eventually, see Uncle Vince, meet his eyes, feel as if she'd let him down.

'Josie Smith! I have asked you twice what four over four equals.' Mrs Barrett's voice was sharp with annoyance. 'Your body is present, but your mind clearly somewhere else. If you could bring mind and body together for a moment, you might come up with an answer.'

'Sixteen?'

Mrs Barrett sighed. 'No, dear. I think you'll find the answer's one. I expect you're all tired, I certainly am. Thank goodness we break up tomorrow.' The class uttered a huge groan of relief, and Mrs Barrett smiled wearily. 'It might be nice to dispense with lessons on the last day, do something less taxing – a quiz, for instance. I'll see what his lordship has to say.'

'*Who*, Miss?' Josie's hand shot up.

'His lordship, dear. In other words, Mr Crocker, our esteemed headmaster.'

'Why did she call him that?' Josie whispered hoarsely to Lily, sitting beside her.

Lily looked puzzled. 'It's not rude or anything, Jose. Me ma sometimes says, "Where's his lordship?" when she wants me da', or "What's his lordship up to?"'

'Lily Kavanagh, stop talking, *please*!'

'Sorry, miss.'

'It was my fault, miss.'

'In that case, Josie, you must be an expert ventriloquist. I could have sworn the words I heard came from Lily's mouth.'

His lordship!

Either she believes me, takes us in, and gives his lordship his marching orders, or . . .

Had Uncle Vince been doing the same thing to Mam, pressing against her, making funny noises? Was that why Mam had left?

No, Aunt Ivy had chucked Mam out because she was in some sort of condition.

It was very confusing. Josie's head ached with the effort of trying to make sense of it all. She began to dread the Easter holiday even more. Vince would be home as he was on nights.

Aunt Ivy got up at six. Josie heard her pottering around the kitchen. The smell of frying bacon wafted upstairs. Her aunt came up and went straight down again. She must have put the hot-water bottle in the bed. Shortly afterwards, Vince came home.

'Oh, he*llo*, luv,' Aunt Ivy said in a warm, thrilling voice, as if she hadn't seen him in years. Vince's light voice was inaudible. Josie wondered if they were kissing, or was Aunt Ivy patting his shoulders, stroking his cheek with the back of her finger, caressing his hair, like she did all the time?

'She can't keep her hands off him,' Lily had said, who'd noticed. 'She finds him irresistible, like I find Alan Ladd.'

'Come on, luv. Your breakfast's ready. Put your slippers on, they're warming by the fire.'

The truth might have killed the poor woman.

Josie sat up. Gradually, things were falling into place. Uncle Vince must have done something bad, but Ivy was Mam's sister. Mam didn't want to hurt her by telling the truth. Ivy was 'besotted' with Vince. Lily had looked it up in the dictionary. It meant 'to be blindly infatuated'. Then she'd had to look up 'infatuated'. 'To be inspired with foolish passion', it

73

said. If Mam had told her sister the truth about Vince, it might have killed her.

Her aunt and uncle were coming upstairs! Josie quickly got dressed. She sat on the edge of the bed and heard the springs creak as Vince lay down. Aunt Ivy went to and from the bathroom several times. Instead of bacon, the house was full of her powerful scent.

At a quarter past eight, dead on time, her aunt's heels clattered downstairs. She paused in the hall to put on her coat, the front door closed.

Josie was dying to use the lavatory. She reached the bathroom just in time, and went back to collect a cardy. She felt the hairs prickle on her neck when she turned to leave. Uncle Vince, in his pyjamas, was smiling at her from the door.

'Here's me, looking forward to the holidays so we can have our little *tête-à-têtes*, and you're about to run out on me. Are you deserting your Uncle Vince, Josie?'

'No, me and Lily are going to Mass, the nine o'clock one. It's Holy Week, see. She'll be here in a minute.'

'No, she won't, luv,' he said mildly. 'That's three quarters of an hour off. There's still time for a cuddle.' He came into the room. 'Come on, luv, let Uncle Vince give you a nice big kiss.'

'*No!*'

He frowned, hurt. 'No?'

Backing away, Josie furiously shook her head. 'No!'

'Why not, luv?' He shrugged, mystified.

'I don't like what you do, the other thing.'

'There's no harm in it, luv.' He came closer. Josie took another step back and found she'd reached the bed. She sat down, though she hadn't meant to. Uncle Vince sat beside her and laid his arm across her knees. She was trapped. He idly played with her hair, making curls around his finger. 'You know, luv,' he said softly, 'if you're not nice to me, I might tell Ivy one or two things, not very nice things. A word from me, and you'll go shooting out the door faster than a bullet. You'll end up on the streets like Mabel, or in one of them orphanage places I mentioned before. You'll never see your friends again.'

'But I haven't done anything.' Her voice trembled. She tried to push his arm away, but it felt like a rod of iron. He was stronger than she'd thought.

'I know, luv, but it wouldn't stop me saying I caught you nicking a quid out me wallet, or I saw you up to no good with that little boyfriend o' yours. What's his name, Robert?'

'Ben, and I don't know what you're talking about.' He was being dead horrible, worse than Aunt Ivy because he spoke so kindly and reasonably and smiled the whole time. 'Anyroad, Ben's not little,' she said heatedly. 'He's bigger than you.' She threw caution to the winds. 'You're only a little sprat, Lily ses.'

His pale eyes narrowed angrily. He shoved her back on to the bed, and began to untie the cord of his pyjamas, watching her all the while. Then his face seemed to melt. 'You're a lovely girl,' he said huskily. 'Almost a woman, almost ten, double figures. You get more like Mabel every day. Take your clothes off, there's a good girl. It's time we were a proper couple.'

'*No!*' She tried to push him away, but when this had no effect she remembered the way Mam had got rid of Roger and Thomas. She planted her feet forcefully in his stomach, and pushed with all her might. His blue eyes popped, he gave a funny little hiccup, folded his arms over his stomach and fell back against the wardrobe with a soft thud.

She flew downstairs. Outside the house, she panicked. Which way to go? If she didn't get a move on, Uncle Vince might come out and drag her back. No one would stop him, they'd consider he had a perfect right. She began to run towards St Joseph's. By the time she reached it she had a stitch in her side. The iron gate was padlocked, as expected, and she wondered why she'd come. A few boys had managed to climb over the high, spiked wall and were playing football in the playground. She watched them through the gate, envious. They seemed without a care in the world.

Where now? She needed somewhere quiet, to think. More slowly now, she walked towards Sefton Park, to the fairy glen.

The gently sloping banks were a carpet of yellow daffodils, and the trees looked as if they had been sprinkled with pale green confetti as buds sprouted into tiny leaves. Josie watched two squirrels chase each other up and down the branches, leaping skilfully from one tree to the next. There was a fresh, invigorating smell, springy. Could you smell the spring?

A pale sun shone weakly through a veil of light grey cloud, and it made the dew glisten like little diamonds on the grass. It was too wet to sit on, and the only bench was already occupied by a girl in a yellow frock, her face buried in a newspaper. Josie went down to the stream and watched the large goldfish moving ponderously through the water and the smaller ones dart aimlessly this way, that way, backwards and forwards.

She knelt beside the stream, and it was only then that the events of the morning caught up with her and she began to tremble. Uncle Vince had been about to rape her, she realised that now. She knew about rape because less than a month ago a friend of a friend of Marigold Kavanagh had been raped by a soldier on the way home from a dance. Lily had told her about it. She shouldn't have been listening, but Lily spent half her life listening to conversations she wasn't meant to hear. She knew all sorts of things. How babies were made, for instance – men put their John Thomas in the place where women did a wee, and nine months later a baby was born. 'It's as easy as that!' Lily had said, wide-eyed and a bit dismayed.

What had happened that morning, however, dreadful though it was, seemed less important than what was to happen now. Where was she to live? How could she possibly *tell* people what Uncle Vince had tried to do? If she could get over the embarrassment of putting it into words, they'd say she led him on. Josie had the squirmy, uncomfortable feeling that it was all her fault. She felt sick, remembering the way she'd let him touch her, press against her, make funny noises.

She shivered. The grass was cold and she hadn't got a cardy.

She longed for a drink, a cup of tea. Something plopped on to her bare knees – tears. She was crying.

'Josie, is that you? I thought I recognised you from the back.'

She turned. Daisy Kavanagh was coming towards her through the wet grass, folding a newspaper. She held it up. It was called *The Daily Worker*. 'Me da' won't allow this in the house. They get *The Times*, which is dead stuffy, full of letters from retired colonels.' She lifted the skirt of her yellow frock, which went perfectly with the background of daffodils, and knelt beside the younger girl. Daisy always looked as if she were posing for the cover of a romantic novel. Her long hair was tied back with a big yellow bow. The Kavanagh girls always had matching bows, headbands, dolly bags and even hankies to go with their frocks, which their mam made from bits of leftover material. 'What's up, Jose? You don't half look sad.'

Daisy was the quietest of the girls, and spent all her spare time reading. She had just left St Josephs, and was due to start work next week in the local library, putting books away, keeping the shelves tidy, while she trained to be a proper librarian.

'Has your Auntie Ivy been horrid? You know, I've never liked that woman.'

Josie wished that were the case. It was something she was used to. She shook her head.

'Something's wrong, Jose. I can tell by your face. Have you had a fight with our Lily?'

'No.' She quite enjoyed her fights with Lily.

'You know, a trouble shared is a trouble halved, so Ma always ses,' Daisy said wisely. 'If you tell me, I promise, on my honour, to keep it in total confidence. I won't tell a soul.'

'It's something dead awful.' Josie picked up a clump of grass and pulled it to pieces. 'You'll be disgusted.'

Daisy gave a tinkling little laugh. 'Nothing disgusts me, Jose. I've read hundreds of books, and you wouldn't believe some of the things that happen. But let's sit on that bench first before me knees freeze solid. Come on, Jose.'

'Well,' Josie began hesitantly when they were seated. Daisy seemed the ideal person to talk to, not quite an adult, not quite a child, worldly wise and not easily shocked. 'It all started last Christmas, no, four Christmases ago, when I was six . . .' It was a relief to let it all pour out. She kept making excuses for herself. 'I know it's me own fault. I shouldn't have encouraged him. But we were pretending he was me dad, see,' she finished.

'Some dad!' Daisy's face was blank. She had always seemed very grown up but now she looked a bit lost, as if Josie's story was nothing like she'd read in books. Perhaps it was too dreadful to have told someone who was only fourteen.

There was a long silence. 'Oh, I knew you'd be disgusted,' Josie wailed. 'I wish I'd never told you. Now you hate me.'

'Oh, Jose. I don't hate you. I just don't know what to say.' Daisy reached for her hand. 'Let's go home. You've had nothing to eat. You must be starving.'

'You won't tell your ma, will you?' Josie said anxiously. 'I'd hate anyone else to know.' She felt a bit worried when Daisy didn't answer.

Apart from the clink of dishes from the kitchen, the Kavanaghs' house was unusually quiet. Quarry Bank didn't break up until tomorrow so Ben was still at school. Marigold had gone to work in the solicitor's office where she was a junior secretary, and Robert to the factory where he was a trainee draughtsman – Mrs Kavanagh was praying the war would be over before he reached eighteen. Lily, still in her nightie, was in the parlour with her head buried in an exercise book. Josie thought she had started on her homework, until Daisy angrily snatched the book away.

'That's mine,' she snapped. 'How dare you? It's my novel.'

'It's very good.' Lily had no shame. 'I don't think much of the hero, though. And what's a mousetachy?'

'It's moustache, idiot. I can't see you passing the scholarship. And you should have been called Deadly Nightshade, or Garlic Mustard, instead of Lily. You're dead horrible.' She turned to Josie. 'I'll ask Ma to make us a cup of tea.'

'What are you doing out so early?' Lily enquired when her sister had gone. 'And you haven't combed your hair. It doesn't half look untidy.'

'Oh, shut up, Lily.' Josie sank into a chair. Her head was throbbing. She glanced around the untidy room. There were hardly any toys nowadays, but the typewriter Marigold had used to practise on, and now Daisy, was on the sideboard, alongside a pile of *Girl's Crystals*, which she'd borrowed and avidly read. Pieces of grey flannel were draped over the sewing machine, waiting to be turned into a pair of trousers, and there were books everywhere, dozens of them. How wonderful it would be to live here, be part of this family, she thought.

'You're very lucky,' she said.

Lily misinterpreted this completely. She tossed back her wavy hair. 'Oh, I know. I'm pretty and clever, and I'm going to pass the scholarship and be a great success. When I grow up, I shall be a famous film star or a singer or a dancer. The whole world will know who I am. Have you ever heard me sing?'

'Of course I have. It was dead awful.'

'It was not.'

'It was.'

'It was not.'

'Josie,' Mrs Kavanagh said from the door, 'would you come here a minute, luv?'

Daisy appeared behind her, looking slightly shamefaced. 'I'm sorry, Jose. I've never betrayed a confidence before, but I couldn't have kept what you told me to meself. Something's got to be done, and I'm afraid I haven't a clue.'

'What?' Lily leapt to her feet and nearly fell over her nightie. 'What's she told you? She's *my* friend – why didn't she tell me?'

'Oh, calm down, Lily,' her mother said irritably. 'This is nothing to do with you. Go upstairs and get dressed this minute, or I shall be very cross.' Lily flounced out of the room, and Mrs Kavanagh led Josie into the kitchen. 'I can keep an eye on the stairs from here, case that little madam creeps down to listen.' Her plump, good-natured face became grave. 'Now, luv, Daisy's told me everything, so you don't have to go through it again. There's just one thing I want to say – *it's not your fault*. None of it's your fault.' She gave Josie's shoulders a little shake. 'Understand?'

'Yes, Mrs Kavanagh.'

'Now, we've got to tell Ivy as soon as possible, because you can't go home the way things are.' She thoughtfully bit her lip. 'I'll meet her off the bus tonight. She's going to have to give his lordship his marching orders, I'm afraid.'

'That's exactly what me mam said!' Josie exclaimed. 'There was something Mam had wanted to tell Aunt Ivy a long time ago, but she couldn't because it would have killed her. Then something happened, and we were coming back to Machin Street, but the night before Mam was . . .' She stopped, unable to go on.

Mrs Kavanagh had gone as white as a sheet. She gave Josie another little shake. 'Try not to think about it, luv.' She turned away and took the cosy off the teapot. 'Oh, Lord,' she muttered. 'This is worse than I thought. Much worse.'

Over the next two days, Josie felt as if there was a little black cloud hanging over her. She stayed with the Kavanaghs, sleeping on the settee in the parlour, and would have enjoyed herself had it not been for the cloud. And there was another worry lurking in the corner of her mind, too awful to think about.

Lily oozed curiosity from every pore. She had been forbidden to ask questions, but Josie could tell she ached to know what was going on.

Ben took her to the pictures to see *Pinocchio*, which helped a bit. She'd never seen a picture in Technicolor before. On the way home, he said seriously, 'When we're married, everything's going to be dead fine. You'll never have a single thing to worry about again.'

On Thursday evening after tea, Mrs Kavanagh suggested

gently that she go home. 'I'll take you, luv. It's been lovely having you, but you can't stay for ever.'

'But Vince'll be there, and Auntie Ivy's still at work!'

'You'll find Vince has gone, luv, and Ivy hasn't been to work in days.'

Josie hung back. 'She'll *hate* me,' she said fearfully.

'No, luv. She doesn't hate you, not the least little bit.'

Outside number seventy-six, Josie said shyly, 'Ta, very much. You've been dead kind.'

Mrs Kavanagh's eyes were watering for some reason. 'It's one of the reasons we're put on this earth for, to help each other. Least, so I've always thought. One of these days, when you're grown up, maybe you can give me a hand if I need it.' She smiled. 'The way things are going with you and our Ben, I reckon you'll be one of the family by then. Go on, luv.'

Mrs Kavanagh gave her a little shove, and Josie returned to the house she thought she had left for ever.

4

It was still light outside, but the parlour was in semi-darkness because Aunt Ivy never parted the thick, green curtains by more than a few inches in case the sun faded the carpet. Even so, Josie was able to see the numerous framed photos of Mam which were scattered around the room.

'Ooh!' she whispered. She picked up one of Mam when she was a little girl making her first Holy Communion. She wore a white frock with puffed sleeves and smocking on the bodice, white shoes and socks. Most of her hair was hidden beneath a short, triangular veil, and she was holding a white prayer book and grinning broadly. A sprinkling of snow lay on the ground outside the church, and the trees were tipped with frost.

Josie pressed the photo against her breast. 'She must have felt cold,' she said to Aunt Ivy.

'She never felt the cold, not much,' her aunt replied. 'You might have noticed. She took a lot of persuading into a vest when winter came, and I could never get her to wear a liberty bodice. I've still got that prayer book and the veil put away. You can have them if you like.'

'I'd like them very much, ta.'

Aunt Ivy was wearing the navy blue coat overall she only wore on Saturdays to clean in. Since Josie had last seen her a few days ago, she seemed to have aged twenty, thirty years. Her yellow face was wizened, she looked smaller and was hunched in the corner of the big settee, as if she'd like to disappear inside it. Josie was shocked to see the naked misery evident in the small grey eyes.

'I loved her, you know.' She nodded at the photo. 'She was six then. Same age as you the day you came. I hated you for looking so much like her. I felt she'd come back to haunt me. Every time I looked at you I felt guilty. I'd put them away, the pictures, hid them in the spare room. But I couldn't put you away, could I? You were always here, reminding me of what I'd done. Oh, God!' She put her head in her hands and began to cry.

'What did you do?' Josie felt as if they had swopped places, that she was the aunt, Ivy the child.

'I chucked her out, didn't I?' Ivy cried wildly. 'I threw me own sister on the streets, when all the time I knew it wasn't her fault. I *knew* Mabel as well as I knew meself. I'd brought her up. I knew damn well she'd never go with a fella, particularly her own sister's husband. She wasn't that sort of girl. But I put the whole thing to the back of me mind, out of sight, and whenever it came to the surface I pushed it back again, because although I loved Mabel I loved my Vince more. I refused to let meself *think* he could have done such a thing.' She raised her burning eyes. 'You know he was your father, don't you?'

Josie sat down. She held Mam's photo tight against her breast. 'I've wondered, over the last few days, but I did me best not to think about it.'

'Like me, eh?' Ivy chuckled, but it came out more like a sob. 'There's some thoughts best kept hidden, otherwise they'll drive you doolally in the end.' She gave a bitter smile. 'I met him, Vince, outside church. I was with our Mabel. She was twelve, and I was twenty-four.' She glanced at her niece, and it was the first time Josie had known a look from Aunt Ivy that wasn't filled with hatred.

'You'll never know what it's like to be plain. I don't know where me looks came from – some throwback in the family, an ugly little leprechaun. It didn't help when I caught yellow jaundice when I was a kid. Me dad, he was a fine-looking man – Mabel took after him – and Mam was dead pretty. Mind you, I assumed I'd find a husband one day, but I never thought it would be someone like Vince. He was so handsome, Josie,' she said dreamily, as if Vince were dead and Josie had never met him. Then she sighed. 'But perhaps it was Mabel he was after all along. I think that crossed me mind right from the start, but I kept it hidden in a dark cellar in me brain, like all them other things.'

She suddenly reached behind the arm of the settee and brought up a glass and an almost empty bottle of whisky. 'I think I might be just a bit sozzled. I've been drinking all day and yesterday.' She emptied the remains of the whisky into the glass, and waved the bottle. 'It's five years old, this, so you can see I don't normally indulge. Make yourself a cup of tea if you fancy one. As from tomorrow, I'll start looking after you proper. Right now, I'm not fit to walk as far as the kitchen.'

'I will in a minute, ta.' The loathing Josie had always felt for her aunt had gone. It was impossible not to feel sympathy for the poor, pathetic woman huddled on the settee. And, young though she was, she understood the need to make excuses, apologise, explain. She must have felt gutted when Mrs Kavanagh told her what her husband had been up to.

'Oh, and another thing, luv.' Her aunt drained the glass. Her voice was thick and slurred, the way Mam's used to be. 'I'd never have left you alone with *him* if I'd thought there was a chance he'd lay a finger on you. Not on his own *daughter*. He must be sick in the head. It's a crime, that is. It's called something, I can't remember what right now. That's how I got him to leave. I threatened to fetch the bobbies to him.' Her face seemed to shiver. 'Oh, I wonder where he is, if he's got a place to sleep, like?'

Josie felt her blood turn to ice. *She still loves him!* In her heart, perhaps Ivy still longed to convince herself that My Vince had done no wrong.

She made tea and took it to the lounge, where she drew the blackout curtains, discreetly hidden behind the green silk, and switched on the lamp.

Aunt Ivy was sobbing wretchedly. 'She let me put her out rather than tell the truth about Vince.'

'She thought the truth would kill you,' Josie said.

'Oh, dear God,' her aunt shrieked, and crossed herself. 'Dear God, forgive me.'

Not long afterwards Ivy fell asleep. Josie fetched the maroon eiderdown to lay over her, then went to bed herself.

Neither Josie nor Lily passed the scholarship. 'I suppose we're just not clever enough,' Josie said when the letters with the results arrived. St Joseph's had broken up two weeks ago for the summer holiday.

'I would've passed if I hadn't had such an awful headache,' Lily claimed. 'And my nib was crooked, and I'm sure Mrs Barrett hadn't taught us some of them sums.'

Josie grinned. 'And the chair was uncomfortable, the sun was shining right in your eyes and the desk kept wobbling.'

'I don't know what you're talking about. Anyroad, if our Ben can pass, then so should I.'

'Oh, Lil. Didn't you read your Ben's end–of–term report? He got top marks for everything except art.'

'If they'd had art in the scholarship, then I'm certain to have passed,' Lily grumbled. 'Mr Crocker said that picture I did of a tiger was dead brilliant.'

Mr Crocker had said all their pictures were brilliant, but sometimes it wasn't worth arguing with Lily.

★

Like thousands of streets all over the country, Machin Street was throwing a party. It was 8 May 1945, VE Day, and the war was finally over. Hastily made bunting fluttered in the warm breeze. Union Jacks hung from the windows, blackout curtains were taken down, the ugly crisscross tape removed. Tables groaned with food, and there was a bar of chocolate for every child.

The day was a national holiday and everyone went completely mad. Several pianos were dragged outside to accompany the singing and dancing. Neighbours who'd never spoken to each other before, or who had sworn never to speak again, shook hands and promised to be the best of friends.

There were sing-songs and dancing, and everyone got extremely emotional when they sang, 'We'll Meet Again' and 'Land of Hope and Glory'. Josie danced with Lily. She clung to Mr Kavanagh's waist when the entire street did the conga, Aunt Ivy holding on behind. They made circles and did the hokey cokey and Knees up Mother Brown. Later, when it grew quieter, Ben took her in his arms for the waltz, Who's Taking You Home Tonight?

'We'll always remember this day, Josie,' Ben whispered. 'We'll talk about it when we're very old – the day the worst war the world has ever known came to an end.' His eyes glistened with emotion. 'I love you, Josie,' he gulped.

'I love you,' she replied in a small voice.

The celebrations continued late into the night. When it grew dark, the lights in every room in every house were switched on, and the whole street sang 'When the Lights Go On Again' followed by a tremendous cheer and a chorus of 'God Save The King'.

Next morning, before she went to work, Aunt Ivy offered her one and only piece of motherly advice. 'I saw you dancing with Ben Kavanagh last night, luv. You want to be careful there.'

'But he's ever so nice,' Josie protested.

'Oh, he's a lovely lad, from a lovely family. I'd be dead chuffed if you became a Kavanagh.' She closed her eyes, as if imagining herself sharing the limelight with Mrs Kavanagh at the wedding. 'But you're far too young for boyfriends, luv. Ben's obviously smitten, and if you're not careful you'll find yourself walking blindfold into marriage with a chap you don't love because you've never known anyone else. All the love will be on *his* side, and although he might think that's enough for both of you it's not true.' She pursed her lips sadly. 'It's something I know from bitter experience. I loved my Vince enough for ten women, and look at what he did.'

'I'm sorry, Auntie,' Josie sighed.

'Oh, Lord, luv, don't apologise. He tried to ruin your life, as well as mine. But at least we're still alive to tell the tale, eh, not like our poor Mabel.'

5

'Of course, we're middle class, stupid,' Lily said furiously. 'Me da' owns his own shop, our Stanley's a sergeant in the army in Berlin, Marigold's married to a solicitor, Daisy's a qualified librarian, well, almost, our Robert manages something or other down in London, I work in an office and look at our Ben, off to Oxford or Cambridge next October.' She finished her litany with a superior sneer.

'I've got exams to take first,' Ben reminded her.

Lily tossed her waist-length hair. 'Oh, don't be silly, Ben. We all know you'll come top in everything.'

Francie O'Leary, the prime target of Lily's wrath, looked at Ben with his small, mean eyes. Lily was madly in love with him. She found him attractive in a small, mean way, like a handsome rat. Francie talked out of the corner of his mouth like Humphrey Bogart. Even though they were inside, he wore a trilby hat on the back of his head that made him look a bit of a rogue. 'What have you got to say about this, Ben?' he enquired lazily.

'Me!' Ben laughed. 'I don't believe in the class system. As John Ball said, "Ye came as helpless infants to the world, Ye feel alike the infirmities of nature, Why then these vague distinctions?"'

'Who the hell's John Ball?' Lily interceded.

'Leader of the Peasants' Revolt.'

'I thought that was Wat Tyler.' Francie had been Ben's friend at Quarry Bank. His father had been killed in the war, and he'd left at sixteen to provide for his mother and two young sisters. Josie wondered if he resented his friend going to university. It seemed very unfair that the son of a man who'd given his life for his country had been denied higher education.

Ben said, 'Wat Tyler was the brawn, John Ball the brains.'

'He can't have had much in the way of brains,' Francie said drily. 'The whole bloody revolt was a wash-out. The peasants were routed, if I remember right.'

'They were betrayed. John Ball was hung, drawn and quartered. I don't know why we're arguing, Francie. We're both on the same side. Our Lily's the only one out of line.'

'Do you mind?' Josie broke in. 'I've no idea whose side I'm on, thanks all the same. I don't know what class I am either, and, quite frankly, I don't care.' Months ago, the four of them had got into the habit of coming to town on Saturday mornings, sitting for hours in a restaurant and arguing – about politics, life, religion, the headlines in that morning's newspapers.

'You're what's called a "white-collar" worker, Jose, so you're definitely middle class,' Lily said firmly. '*And* you live in Machin Street, which is in a middle-class area. There's already five families with cars, me da' amongst them.'

'Bollocks!' Francie snorted. 'If it were middle class, it'd be a road, Machin Road – or Machin Avenue. Streets are only for us poor, working-class fodder.'

'What about Downing Street?' said Josie. 'And Harley Street, where the posh doctors live?'

Lily threw her a grateful smile, and Francie clutched his brow and pretended to look devastated. 'You got me there, Jose. That was a knock-out blow.'

Ben squeezed Josie's shoulders. 'Clever girl,' he whispered.

She thought it obvious, not clever. He was being a bit patronising, but she daren't say anything because he got disproportionately upset if she criticised him. She could never truly be herself with Ben.

The manageress glared at them from behind the till. They'd been there two hours and had bought only a single coffee each, and she was expecting an influx of lunchtime customers any minute.

They took the hint, drained the dregs of the coffee, now stone cold, and wandered into Bold Street. Josie pulled on a woolly hat that covered her ears, buttoned her coat against the bitter February wind and wrapped a scarf twice around her neck. Francie took Lily in his arms and they kissed passionately.

'Young love!' Ben rolled his eyes and took Josie's hand. He disapproved of such demonstrations, which he considered showy and insincere. Lily had kissed previous boyfriends with equal passion, though she swore things were dead serious between her and Francie. They hadn't yet gone all the way, but it was likely to happen any minute. Lily couldn't wait.

Ben had never tried to go all the way with Josie. He respected her too much. Although he had never discussed it, she took it for granted that they would wait until they were married, which would be after he'd got his degree and found a job. Josie felt relieved, as she wasn't particularly looking forward to it. She quite enjoyed Ben kissing her and touching her naked breasts, which he'd never properly seen because she was always fully clothed, and he merely slid his hand inside her frock or under her jumper. Pleasant though these occasions were, she had the feeling she wasn't enjoying herself remotely as much as Lily when she did the same thing with Francie, but, then, Lily was always prone to exaggeration.

'It was heaven,' Lily gushed the first time. 'I went all woozy. I completely lost control, and so did Francie. We might well have gone all the way if it hadn't been raining.'

Lily and Francie paused for another kiss. Ben said, 'Hey, folks, where are we going?'

'The Pier Head?' Francie suggested.

'It's bloody freezing.' Lily shivered. She looked up at the bleak, grey sky. 'It looks as if it might snow. Can't we go somewhere inside? Has anyone got any money?'

'I'm skint,' Francie announced. 'You gave a penny towards me coffee, remember?'

'I've only got three bob, but I need half that for next week's fares to work. Then there's tonight . . .' Josie's finances were a mess. She'd only been paid the day before, but by then she had owed Aunt Ivy her entire wages. The same thing happened nearly every week. She couldn't resist the clothes she saw as she wandered around town during the dinner hour. Last week, she'd seen a lovely black frock with embroidery on the bodice that looked like a waistcoat. Aunt Ivy had loaned her a pound towards it, and she'd had to borrow her fares for the rest of the week.

Lily was rooting through her purse. 'I've got nearly eight bob, but I need stockings and a Max Factor panstick. If there's enough over, I'll treat everyone to another coffee, as long as someone does the same for me next week.'

Ben, who had to exist on five shillings a week pocket money, took no part in this debate. Josie paid for herself at the pictures nowadays, and sometimes for Ben, though he claimed it made him feel like a kept man.

They went to Owen Owen's department store. After Lily had bought the stockings and the panstick, they decided to tour the shop for something to do. In the furniture department, Francie pushed Lily down on a fully made-up bed and kissed her again.

'Do you mind?' an elderly assistant said frostily.

'We were just trying it out, like, seeing if it felt comfortable.' Francie pulled Lily up, and patted the bed. 'What do you think, darling? Shall we buy it or not? We're getting married soon,' he explained to the assistant.

'I'd like to look around other shops first.'

All four exploded into giggles and made for the stairs.

'Would you say that was a proposal?' Lily gasped as they raced to the ground floor, the boys ahead.

'He was only joking, Lil.'

'I'll sue him for breach of promise, take him to court. You and Ben can be me witnesses.'

'I doubt if that would work.' If Lily was set on capturing Francie O'Leary, she needed to be a bit more agreeable. He wasn't the sort of chap who appreciated being called an idiot, or told he was dead stupid if they happened to disagree.

'I suppose not,' Lily sighed. 'But I'm determined to get Francie to the altar one way or another. I could get pregnant – that might do the trick.'

'The baby will look like a little rat.'

'Yes, but a very handsome little rat.'

'What are you two laughing at?' Ben enquired when they caught up.

Josie and Lily looked at each other and started to laugh again. 'Nothing,' they said together.

'Let's go to Lyon's,' said Lily. 'I've enough left for a pot of tea for four.'

Outside, Ben said, 'Where shall we go tonight?'

'Where else but the pictures.' Josie shrugged. 'It's the only place that's cheap, particularly if we sit at the front and go somewhere outside town. Oh, Ben, I wish I weren't so extravagant. Auntie Ivy takes hardly anything for me keep, and I spend a small fortune on clothes. Me new frock cost almost two pounds. But it's dead pretty. You'll love it. I'll wear it tonight, shall I?'

Ben stopped and looked down at her shining face. He glanced round to see if anyone was looking, then kissed her. 'I love *you*, Josie. I'd love you even if you wore rags.'

Josie noticed two girls about her own age eyeing her enviously from across the road. They were envious of Ben – blond, six feet two inches tall, no longer all elbows, slim instead of gawky, graceful and self-assured. He clearly didn't feel the cold. He wore flannels, a green tweed jacket and an open-necked shirt. His school scarf was draped casually around his neck. Even Lily conceded her soppy brother had become a handsome young man.

She nestled against him. 'And I love you.' She was immensely lucky. She had never had to suffer, as other girls did, the torture of praying a boy she liked would ask her out, or the awkwardness of a first date, wondering if she'd be asked again, or hoping she wouldn't because the chap had picked his nose non-stop throughout a picture you'd been dying to see for ages, as had happened with Lily during *Blood on the Moon*, with Robert Mitchum. She didn't have to worry if she would get married, because it had all been decided a long time ago. As Mrs Kavanagh had said, they were 'made for each other'.

Two years ago, when they had left school, after much discussion between Mrs Kavanagh and Aunt Ivy, Josie and Lily had been sent to the same commercial college Marigold had attended. They practised on the same typewriter. College was dead boring, but what else could girls do except work in a shop, a factory or an office? There were no vacancies in the *Liverpool Echo* for actresses or dancers or singers. No one advertised for fourteen-year-old girls to climb mountains, go to Timbuktu, drive trains or fly aeroplanes, any one of which Josie and Lily would have done like a shot.

If college had been boring, work was even worse. Lily worked for a stationery suppliers in Edge Hill. She spent her days processing orders for copy paper, bank paper, boxes of carbon, bottles of ink, pencils, all the rubbish people needed to work in other offices. Worst of all, not a single man worked there she fancied marrying, though it didn't matter since she'd met Francie two months ago.

'Sometimes I feel as if me brain's gone dead,' she moaned to Josie.

'It can't be as bad as insurance,' Josie grumbled. '*Car* insurance. Nothing but policies and premiums. The letters are as dull as ditchwater. It wouldn't be so bad in Claims. At least they have accidents to deal with.'

They yearned for adventure. One day they would get married, settle down, have children, but in the meantime it would be marvellous if only something *exciting* would happen.

Josie had already tried on the new dress several times. It fitted perfectly. She put it on again that night, twisting and turning in front of the full-length mirror in Aunt Ivy's bedroom. Sometimes it was uncanny, looking at herself. She would feel pins and needles all over because it was as if she were looking at Mam. The same eyes, dark blue and wide apart, the same over-generous mouth. The nose that had looked dead perfect on Mam, because everything about her had seemed perfect, was actually a mite too long. She wore her thick brown hair shoulder-length, and brushed it frequently, as Mam had done, to make it shine.

Only the other day, Ivy said in a puzzled voice, 'You know, when I look at you, it feels like our Mabel's never been away. She was fifteen when I last saw her. Now you're a year older, and it's almost like you've taken over and there's never been a break.'

Ivy was in the bathroom humming as she made herself up for a night on the town with her friend, Ellen. Josie walked towards the figure in the mirror and held out her arms. 'Hello, Petal. I'm home,' she whispered. She put her hands, palms facing, on the glass and pressed her mouth against the cold, reflected one. When she stepped back the glass was clouded, and it was even more spooky, watching the face of her mother reappear as the cloud began to fade. 'I love you, Mam.'

'I'm off now, luv,' Aunt Ivy shouted from the landing.

Josie jumped. She went to the bedroom door. Her aunt was wearing her fur coat and an unusual amount of diamanté jewellery. 'Which picture are you going to see?'

'I'm going to the theatre, luv, for a change. Margaret Lockwood's on at the Royal Court in *Pygmalion*.'

'I thought Ellen didn't like the theatre?'

'Ellen got herself a new fella a long while ago. I'm going

with another, er, friend. That frock looks lovely. Take care, luv. Have a nice time.'

'You, too.' She wondered if Ivy's new friend was a fella, and she was too embarrassed to say.

Ben came minutes after Ivy had gone. He thought the frock was well worth the inconvenience of being broke for a whole week.

'You look gorgeous.' He slid his arms around her waist and kissed her soundly. 'Ma's loaned Lily and Francie five bob,' he said when they came up for air. 'It was only to get them out of the way while she and me da' got ready for a dinner dance, so they're coming with us. You don't mind, do you?'

'Of course not.'

They went to the Grand in Smithdown Road to see *Samson and Delilah*, which Josie and Lily thought very moving. It was annoying when the boys laughed when Samson grew his hair and pulled the temple down on top of the entire cast.

'Let's go for a drink,' Francie suggested when they came out. Tiny particles of ice were being blown about in the freezing wind, like fireflies against the yellow streetlights.

'A proper drink?' Lily squeaked. 'In a proper pub?'

'A proper drink in a proper pub,' Francie confirmed. 'We can just afford two pints of ale between us.' He grinned. 'I'll ask for four straws.'

Lily wrinkled her small nose. Josie knew she had planned on getting Francie back to the house while it was empty. 'Me and Josie aren't old enough.'

'You *look* old enough. Ben and I will get the drinks. You two sit in the corner. What do you say, Josie?'

'I don't mind.' It would bring back memories of the Prince Albert, but she couldn't avoid pubs for the rest of her life. It was only nine o'clock, too early to go home and consider the night over. She shivered, and stamped her feet on the icy pavement. 'Can we go somewhere before we all freeze to death?'

'We'll go to the first pub we come to,' Francie promised.

A welcoming fire burned brightly in the grate of the first

pub. Whoever was playing the piano had their foot pressed firmly on the loud pedal as they banged out 'Bless 'em All', but perhaps the pianist was determined to be heard above the deafening singing. Inside, the air was warm and full of smoke. They looked for somewhere to sit, but every seat was taken and there were crowds standing round the bar. Lily immediately began to complain. The smoke got in her eyes, the singing hurt her ears, she was tired and wanted to sit down. And she hated war songs, she added, as if further confirmation of her discomfiture was necessary.

'Let's find somewhere else, then,' Francie said patiently.

'I bet all the pubs around here are just as rough. It's that sort of area. Every single man here is probably a crook, and the women look no better than they ought to be. This is a dead stupid idea, Francie.' She fluttered her eyelashes and put her hand on his shoulder. 'I'd sooner go home.'

The fluttering eyelashes and the hand had come too late for Francie. He lost his temper. 'Me dad used to come here.' His small eyes flashed and he gestured angrily around the room. 'These people are the salt of the earth. Who the hell d'you think you are, calling them criminals and whores?'

Lily's jaw sagged. 'But I didn't . . .' she began.

'Yes, you did,' Francie said curtly. 'You know what you are, Lily Kavanagh? A snob! A petty, mean-minded, prejudiced snob. You and I have got nothing in common, and we never will. Quite frankly, you get on me fucking nerves. Oh, and it's about time you got your hair cut. It looks daft on someone your age.'

'Eh, hold on a minute, Francie.' Ben touched his friend's arm. He and Josie had been watching the proceedings, stunned. Francie shook the arm away.

'I'm off, Ben. Enjoy your drink.'

'I haven't bought one yet. Anyroad, you've got the money.'

'So I have.' He shoved a handful of coins in Ben's pocket. 'That's the change from what your mam loaned us. Forget the drink. Take your sister home to that nice, middle-class house in Machin Street.'

'But it's *you* I want to go home with, Francie,' Lily cried. 'It's what I've wanted all along.'

'Well, you picked a bloody funny way of showing it. Tara, Ben, tara, Josie.'

Francie pushed his way out the door. 'Well, he certainly had a hump and a half,' someone said admiringly.

'What's a whore?' Lily asked, then burst into tears. 'Oh, what did I do wrong?'

Ben put his arm around his sister's heaving shoulders. 'You were dead tactless, Sis. You should think before you speak. Every time you open your mouth, you put your foot in it.'

Lily didn't listen, she rarely did. 'I'm going after him. I'll tell him I didn't mean it, that I love him.' She looked at them tearfully. 'I do, you know.'

She rushed out, and Josie and Ben looked at each other. 'What shall we do now?' he asked. 'Would you like a drink?'

'No, ta. It's not our money, it's your mam's. Anyroad, I think we should go back to yours. I doubt if Francie's in the mood for making up. Lily's quite likely to turn up any minute in a terrible state and there's no one in.'

They strolled back to Machin Street, talking quietly and feeling sorry for everyone in the world except themselves.

Lily was still in a state next morning. She cried, she screamed, she threatened to kill herself, she refused to go to Mass. Mr Kavanagh found it necessary to go to the shop and do a bit of stocktaking. Daisy remembered she'd promised to see a friend. Ben was despatched to fetch Josie in the hope she could help.

'Well, I wasn't much use last night, was I?' Lily had managed to catch up with Francie, who'd repeated the pub diatribe, along with a few more home truths.

'He likes *you* better than me,' Lily raged. Ben had made himself scarce. 'He thinks you're a far nicer person. If Ben wasn't his friend, he'd ask you out. What do you think of *that?*'

Josie thought of that, and felt a surprising – and most unwelcome – little thrill at the notion of Francie kissing her, touching her breasts. 'He was only saying it to get at you.'

'Have you been making eyes at him?'

'Of course not.' She decided to get angry. 'How dare you suggest such a thing?'

'Thank goodness you're here, Josie,' Mrs Kavanagh said on Sunday morning. 'I don't know what to do with her. She's in the bedroom. Our poor Daisy hardly got a wink of sleep. Lily wept and wailed the whole night long. See if you can talk some sense into her, there's a good girl. Oh, Lord,' she moaned. 'She's only sixteen. I hope we don't have to go through this performance every time she's jilted by a boyfriend.'

Lily was sitting up in bed when Josie went in. Her eyes were bloodshot and swollen, but she had a strange, beatific smile on her puffy face. 'I've decided to become a nun,' she announced grandly. 'I'm going to dedicate the rest of me life to God.'

'Don't be daft, you haven't even been to Mass.'

'I'll go later, the twelve o'clock. Oh, Jose, just imagine, the quiet of a convent, the peace.' Lily put her hands together, as if in prayer. 'No more boyfriends, no more having to be nice to someone so they'll ask you out. No more *men*! Just priests, *holy* men. All you have to do is kiss their rings, not . . . well, that thing Francie once suggested.'

'Since when have you ever been nice to anyone?' Josie was unimpressed by this desire for a quiet life. 'You'd have to shave your head, and never wear make-up again or buy pretty clothes or wear nylons. You'd be bored out your skull within a week.'

Lily looked at her kindly and a touch disdainfully. 'You don't under*stand*, Jose. Those sorts of things wouldn't matter any more. I wouldn't even *think* about them while I was communing with God. My mind would be on a different plane. I never realised I had a vocation. I'm looking forward to shaving me head. I'd better go downstairs and tell Ma.'

'The silly girl is driving us up the wall,' Mrs Kavanagh complained a few weeks later. 'She goes around with this stupid grin on her face, as if butter wouldn't melt in her mouth, and wakes us up every morning with a hymn. If I hear "Faith of Our Fathers" once more, I think I'll scream. She can't get this idea of a convent out of her head. Have you seen her hair? She's had it cut, makes her look like Shirley Temple.'

That was Monday. On Tuesday Lily decided she liked her hair too much to have it shaved off. Instead, she was going to join the Army and spend the rest of her life serving King and Country.

'You're too young,' Josie said. 'You have to be eighteen.'

'I've already thought of that,' Lily said complacently. 'I shall pretend I'm our Daisy – she's twenty.'

'Does Daisy know?'

'No, but I'm sure she won't mind.'

'Your legs will look dead fat in khaki stockings.'

'Oh, don't be such an old misery guts, Josie Smith. Stop trying to put me off.' She preened herself. 'I'm officer material, me. I bet I'm promoted in no time.'

Josie nearly fell off the chair laughing. 'The Army won't have a cap to fit a head as big as yours, Lily Kavanagh.'

An outraged Daisy flatly refused to allow her identity to be used by her sister so she could join the Army, and Lily was forced to abandon the idea, though she claimed her heart had been broken for ever by Francie O'Leary.

It was Lily who saw the poster in Hewitt's sweetshop window. She dragged Josie round to see it the same night.

The poster was printed in bright red on yellow foolscap.

STAFF REQUIRED

KITCHEN HANDS, PORTERS, CHALET MAIDS

MAY TO OCTOBER, GOOD RATES OF PAY

ACCOMMODATION AVAILABLE IF REQUIRED

APPLY IN WRITING TO:

HAYLANDS HOLIDAY CAMP, PRIMROSE MEADOW, COLWYN BAY

Josie's eyes sparkled. 'Adventure!' she breathed.

'And boys,' Lily said in an awed voice. 'Stacks and stacks of boys, different ones every week. I'd be over Francie O'Leary in a jiffy. Oh, Jose, it's only two months off. We'll apply to be chalet maids the minute we get home.'

Over the next few weeks, they changed their minds a dozen times. They almost didn't fill in the application forms when they came, but Josie persuaded Lily to do it, or it might have been the other way round.

Mr Kavanagh was dead set against the whole idea, 'But when did anyone ever give a fig for my opinion?' he said with a martyred air.

'I wish I'd done something like that when I was a girl,' Mrs Kavanagh said wistfully. 'I think you're showing a great deal of enterprise. You'll easily get other jobs when you come back. And it'll be nice to get rid of our Lily for a while. Anyroad, she'll only make our lives a misery if she's thwarted.'

'Oh, I will!' Lily said sweetly.

'You'll keep an eye on her, won't you, Josie, luv?'

'Yes, Mrs Kavanagh,' Josie assured her. She had no intention of doing any such thing.

'What do you think?' Josie asked Aunt Ivy several times. Ivy still saw the mysterious friend, but he or she had never been invited to the house.

Her aunt was always encouraging, so much so that Josie had the oddest feeling that she actually wanted her to go. 'As I said before, luv, it seems a good idea. I'm sure you and Lily will have a lovely time.'

'Will you be all right on your own?' Josie asked anxiously, the day the letters arrived confirming their employment.

'Of course, I will, luv.'

'I can still change me mind. It's three days before I need to give in me notice at work,' Josie assured her.

'I'll be all right,' her aunt said irritably. 'I don't know how many times I have to tell you.'

Josie turned away, hurt. Since Vince had gone, she had got

on well with Ivy. It came as a shock to find her aunt so willing to see her leave. She felt very unwanted. Even Ben hasn't tried to persuade me to stay, she thought miserably.

She couldn't have been more wrong about Ben.

Josie and Ben were sitting on the same bench on which she'd told Daisy about Uncle Vince eight years ago. It was Friday, and the girls had handed in their notices that afternoon, which meant there was no going back. They would leave for Haylands a week tomorrow.

'Mr Short, me boss, said he was dead sorry to see me go. He made me promise to contact him when I get back. If there's a vacancy, he'll take me on again like a shot. I thanked him nicely, but there's no way I'd work for an insurance company again. I'd love to work for the *Echo*. It would be dead interesting, hearing the news before any one else. What do you think?'

'Since when have you been interested in my opinion?' Ben said coldly.

'I'm always interested in your opinion,' she replied. For the first time, she noticed they were sitting several inches apart, that he hadn't automatically put his arm around her shoulder when they had sat down.

'That's not true. You haven't asked what I think about you working in that camp, not once.'

'But I've discussed it with you every day,' she said indignantly.

'No, you've *told* me about it every day.' He leaned forward and folded his arms on his knees. His voice was stiff with hurt. 'You haven't asked if I *care* that you're leaving, if I *mind*.'

'But I'm not leaving for ever,' she protested. 'I'll only be gone five months. It never entered me head you'd mind. I mean, you're going away for three whole years in October. Have you asked if I mind about that?'

He gave her a curt glance. 'That's entirely different. I'm going away to learn, get a degree, so one day I'll get a well-paid job. I'm doing it for *you*, so we can have a nice house, and a nice life, and you'll never want for anything. Your only motive is to have a fine old time.'

'What's wrong with that? I bet you'll have a fine old time at university.' Josie laughed, but there was a prickly sensation in her stomach. They had never fought before, but she felt she had right on her side and wasn't prepared to give in. He was being totally unreasonable. 'And don't pretend you're doing it for me, Ben. You're doing it for yourself, you know you are.'

'No, I'm not.' His lips twisted sadly. 'I would have still gone, even if I'd never met you. But, you see, one day, I was only eight, I was wrestling on the floor with our Robert, and when I looked up there was this girl, younger than me. Oh, if only you knew how sad you looked, Josie, how frightened. I felt myself go limp. I suppose I must have fallen in love then, but I was too young to know. I just knew I wanted to be with you for the rest of me life.' He sat back in the seat, not looking at her, but at a couple with two small children by the stream.

'So, you see, I am doing it for you. I do everything for you. Whenever I sit an exam, I think to meself, I'm doing this for Josie. You're never out of me mind.' He turned and put his arm around her. He kissed her hair, her forehead, her cheeks. Then he gently kissed her lips. 'I love you, darling.'

He had never called her darling before. She saw his eyes were wet with tears, and felt ashamed of being the cause, because he was probably the best young man in the whole world. He put his other hand on her neck, and she could feel his thumb hard on her cheek. 'I love you, Ben,' she whispered.

They kissed again, and a kiss had never felt so sweet before, so loving and so tender.

'Please, don't go, Josie. If you truly loved me, you'd stay.' His voice was hoarse with passion and pleading. But Josie couldn't see the *harm*. Five months, that's all, for just five months she wanted a bit of adventure. Once it was over she'd settle down, get another job, commit herself to him entirely. She'd even try to save up for the wedding, start a bottom drawer.

But she had hesitated too long. Ben stood. His face was bleak and raw with hurt. Josie was shocked to think she could cause such hurt to another human being. With a further shock, she realised that he wasn't meant for her. No matter what Ben did, he couldn't possibly hurt *her* so deeply.

'I'm sorry, Ben.' She touched his arm, and they stared at each other. They both knew it was over.

'I'm thinking of the day I first saw you.' He almost smiled.

'And me of that day we went to the pictures. You gave me some chocolate and took half back. Ben?'

He was already walking away. He turned. 'Yes, Jose?'

'If I asked you not to go to university, what would you say?'

'I've sometimes hoped you would. Tara, Josie. I might not see you before you go, so have a nice time.'

She watched him walk away, a tall, loping, extremely nice young man with a broken heart. There was lump in her throat when she returned to the seat and watched Ben until he disappeared into the trees. She suddenly felt so lonely that it made her body ache. One minute she'd had a boyfriend, now she hadn't. And it had all happened so quickly, the way the most profoundly important things always did.

The girls were very quiet on the bus that took them from the Pier Head to Colwyn Bay. Lily kept sniffing and burying her face in a hankie. They perked up when the coach stopped outside the camp, and they saw the gaudily painted 'Haylands Holiday Camp' sign on an arch above the gates.

'You know what, Jose?'

'What, Lil?'

'Over the next few months, I'm determined to go all the way with a bloke.'

Josie smiled. 'Good luck.' She wasn't considering *looking* at a man, let alone sleeping with one. She couldn't stop thinking about Ben.

Haylands

I

'Oh, what pretty chalets.' Lily's voice throbbed with excitement. 'Can we pick our own?'

The driver of the long open trolley carrying them and their luggage looked at her drily. 'No, luv. You're in the staff quarters behind the theatre.'

'There's a theatre!' Lily nudged Josie in the ribs. 'I wonder if there'll be any famous stars.'

The pebble-dashed chalets had been built back to back, the fronts facing each other across a wide concrete path, with a strip of grass in the middle. Wooden tubs, each with an identical green shrub, had been placed neatly, about twelve feet apart. There were five long rows of chalets altogether. Like all the buildings in the camp, the chalets had been freshly painted cream.

They had already passed two bars, the Coconut and the Palm Court, a fish-and-chip shop called Charlie's Plaice, a ballroom called the Arcadia, an amusement arcade, a parade of shops, a small fairground, a children's nursery with swings and a see-saw outside, though there wasn't a child in sight. In fact, there were few campers around and they were mainly elderly. Signs pointed to tennis courts and crazy golf. A few hundred yards in front, the Irish Sea glimmered dully, like pewter, the waves as unnaturally stiff as freshly permed hair. The sky was dark and getting darker, and there was a touch of rain in the air. Despite all the gaudy entertainment on offer, the camp had a desolate, deserted air.

'I love crazy golf,' Lily remarked.

The man steered the trolley towards a large cream building with 'The Prince of Wales Theatre' over the entrance in unlit neon. A poster announced that night's play was *Strip Jack Naked*.

'I wonder who it's by?' Lily mused aloud as the trolley veered violently to the left and they clung on for dear life.

'I don't know, luv,' the driver said, 'but it ain't Shakespeare.' He veered to the right and stopped. 'This is youse lot here.'

Josie stepped off the trolley and hauled her suitcases after her. 'Oh, dear.'

'Bloody hell.' Lily went pale. 'Is this what they meant by "Accommodation Available if Required"? It looks like a concrete bunker left over from the war.'

Hidden from view, no one had bothered to paint the grey slabs of the long, single-storey building, badly joined together with lumps of cement. The windows were slits, presumably for guns, now fortunately glazed. A thin woman in a white overall came out of a door marked 'Women' and marched towards them. She regarded them sternly. 'Are you Kavanagh and Smith?'

'We're Lily Kavanagh and Josie Smith,' Josie said icily. She wasn't prepared to live in a concrete bunker *and* be treated like a second-class citizen. She vaguely hoped the woman would take offence and they'd be sent back to Liverpool on the spot. 'I didn't think we'd joined the Army.'

'Good for you, Jose,' Lily said under her breath.

To their surprise, the woman laughed. 'I'm Mrs Baxter, the women's supervisor. I *was* in the Army, so I suppose surnames have become a habit I must get out of. Come on, Misses Kavanagh and Smith, and I'll show you where you'll live for the next five months. I hope you didn't expect the Ritz, because you'll be sadly disappointed.'

'We already are.' Josie picked up her cases and followed

Mrs Baxter into a badly lit corridor with numbered doors each side. She opened number five, and entered a small room in which two double bunks and four green-painted lockers had somehow been crammed. A small mirror was screwed to the wall. Josie was immediately put in mind of a prison cell.

'I told you not to expect the Ritz,' said Mrs Baxter. 'Your two companions won't be joining you till next week when the camp will be busier. There's not many people here at the moment, and you'll find they're all very old. *Very* old,' she added with a grin. 'This is the cheapest time, you see. So if you were hoping to cop off with a fella tonight, girls, you've got another disappointment in store, I'm afraid.'

'There's no sink,' Lily complained, 'and no lavatory.'

'You'll find plenty of sinks and lavatories behind the door marked "Ablutions".'

'You mean we have to get washed *in public?*'

'I'm afraid so – are you Kavanagh or Smith?'

'I'm *Miss* Kavanagh.'

'Well, *Miss* Kavanagh, I suppose it is like the Army in a way, though you won't be put on a charge. You will, however, be ordered to leave immediately if you're found with a man in your room, or you consistently fail to turn up promptly at eight o'clock for work. I don't care if you've got a hangover, as long as you turn up.'

'What's a hangover?'

'I think I'll let you find that out for yourself, Miss Kavanagh. You must be the first chalet maid I've ever met who didn't know. It's rather refreshing.' Mrs Baxter rubbed her thin hands together. 'Well, girls, the rest of today is yours to do with as you please. The staff have their tea in the dining room after the campers, around seven. Tomorrow, being Sunday, you can have a nice lie-in, otherwise breakfast's at seven, but I shall expect you in the laundry at twelve to show you round and tell you what you have to do. You'll find overalls in the lockers. Always keep the key on your person, or you might have your valuables nicked. Oh, and I'd like your ration books, please.'

'What about Mass?' Lily enquired.

'You'll find a list of church services in Reception. I think the Catholic Mass is ten o'clock.'

'Ta.' Josie made a face as soon as Mrs Baxter left the room. 'I might pray to be released. We'll never get all our clothes in them lockers, Lil. I've brought virtually everything I own.'

Lily was climbing the ladder of one of the bunks. 'Bagsy me sleep on top.' She burst out laughing. 'Oh, Jose. This isn't a bit like I imagined. What have we let ourselves in for?'

'I dunno. I'd sooner be working in car insurance any day.' To think she'd let Ben go for *this!* She banged her head throwing herself on to the bottom bunk. 'Ouch! It's worse than prison. Actually, Lil, I feel like a good cry.'

Lily's head appeared upside down. 'Never mind, Jose. We'll have a fine old time. I can feel it in me water. Let's unpack, and we'll explore.'

It was, Lily said later, the most miserable day of her life. To cheer themselves up, they bought lipsticks in the chemist's, and decided to have a go on the fairground, but found it unmanned. By now it was raining heavily, so they couldn't play tennis or crazy golf. The bars were virtually deserted. At seven they turned up in the dining room, where several tables were packed with staff who all seemed to know each other. Some had worked at the camp before, and were comparing notes on what had happened since last year. Others were locals, about to go home for the night.

'Help yourself to fish and chips, dearies,' a woman shouted. They collected the food and took it to an empty table.

'They're wearing dead funny uniforms,' Lily murmured. 'On the table next but one. And they don't half talk dead posh.'

Josie had already noticed the dozen or so attractive young people dressed in black and yellow striped blazers, the men in bright yellow trousers, the women with yellow sun-ray pleated skirts. They made everyone else look very drab, and seemed to be blessed with enviable self-assurance, talking loudly and dramatically throwing their arms about. The meal finished, the group made a great show of leaving.

'See you later, Jeremy. Have a good show.'

'So long, Barbara. Try not to kill any poor souls at bingo.'

'I loathe bloody bingo,' Barbara yawned.

'Darling Sadie, if you haven't organised an olde-time dance, you haven't lived.'

'I wish we wore uniforms like that,' Lily said inevitably. 'They've got more class than an overall.'

For something to do, they went to the theatre where, with about twenty other people, they saw *Strip Jack Naked*, in which half a dozen actors, dressed only in their underwear, rushed in and out of bedrooms that weren't their own. Lily was disgusted, but refused Josie's suggestion that they leave in the interval.

'Now, as we're here, we may as well stay till the end,' she said primly. 'Did you recognise some of the cast, Jose? They're the ones we just saw in the dining room. I'd have applied to be an actress if I'd known.'

Over the next few days, the weather improved, and they slowly got used to the camp and the concrete bunker. At eight they reported for duty at the laundry, and helped sort the dirty linen. They went round the chalets, making beds, cleaning sinks, collecting rubbish, brushing floors, and were aghast to find they had to clean the communal lavatories at the end of each block. Lily worked with one hand, held her nose with the other and wished they'd never come.

By the end of the week, though, they were looking forward to July and August when, according to staff who'd been before, the atmosphere would be somewhat similar to Las Vegas, and it was humanly impossible *not* to have the time of your life. The camp would be full, the ballroom and bars crowded, and there would actually be queues for crazy golf and tennis.

The extrovert young people in the black and yellow uniforms were called Wasps. Most were in show business, and organised the dances, beauty competitions and games, or could be seen nightly on stage at the Prince of Wales. It was Josie's and Lily's job to clean their chalets – they lived in pairs in a row set aside from the main camp. Lily considered it degrading to clean up after people who were merely staff like themselves.

'Yes, but very superior staff,' Josie reminded her with a grin. Lily was insanely jealous of the Wasps.

Their room-mates turned out to be two intimidatingly tough-looking, leather-faced sisters in their thirties. Rene and Winnie ran a market stall selling second-hand clothes in Bermondsey. They were married, but their husbands had 'taken a hike' years ago, and their seven children had been left with their nan because Rene and Winnie were 'sick to death of the bleedin' sight of them, if you must know'. They'd come for a break, and another sister was looking after their stall. Over the next few months, they intended to get 'as drunk as pipers every bleedin' night, and shag every man who looks at us twice'.

It seemed strange to the girls, coming from women old enough to be their mothers. At first, they found Rene and Winnie faintly menacing, but their tough exteriors hid hearts of gold. It was rather comforting to be told, in a motherly sort of way, 'If you ever have trouble with a bloke, darlin', just tell me or Winnie here and we'll lay the bugger flat.'

A great heap of post awaited Josie when she called in Reception on her second Tuesday at Haylands. 'Is it your birthday, dear?' the woman behind the counter enquired.

'Yes, I'm seventeen.'

'Many happy returns of the day,' the woman smiled.

'Ta.' She opened the cards there and then. Her boss and two of the girls from the insurance company had remembered it was her birthday. Aunt Ivy enclosed a pretty georgette scarf with her card. There were cards from most of the Kavanaghs, but none from the person she most wanted one from – Ben. Josie turned away, knowing it was unreasonable to feel so disappointed. Since leaving Liverpool, she had missed Ben far more than she had expected. She had grown used to him just *being* there.

She was walking away when the woman cried, 'Oh, Josie – it is Josie, isn't it? Look, I've just found this little parcel on the floor. It's addressed to you. It must have been in the middle of the cards and I dropped it. Sorry, dear.'

The brown paper parcel was no more than three inches square. Inside was a velvet box containing a tiny silver locket, hardly bigger than a sixpence, with a curly, engraved 'J'. 'For my one and only girl', Ben had written in his admirably neat hand, and underneath in brackets, 'I bought this months ago. It seems a shame to let it go to waste.'

Weeks passed, and more and more people, from the very young to the very old, descended on the tight, self-contained, over-heated little oasis of pleasure that was Haylands. Only one thought was in their heads: to have the best possible time during their stay. For the young and single, this meant throwing conventional morality aside. The men hoped to copulate frequently with a member, or members, of the opposite sex. The girls looked forward to romance, passion, to meeting the man of their dreams. Many tearful goodbyes were witnessed on Saturday mornings. Whether any of the prom-ised letters were ever written, or the fervent vows to meet again were kept, no one knew.

Lily could have gone all the way with half a dozen blokes a day, but hadn't met a single one that appealed. 'I'm too picky,' she moaned. 'They've always got something wrong with them. If it's not their looks, then they're too pushy. I want the first time to be extra-special, not some ten-minute, fumbly thing in return for a few drinks. I quite enjoy a good old necking session, but some boys don't find that enough.' Still, she lived in hope that one day the ideal bloke would turn up, and waiting didn't stop her from having a marvellous time.

Josie felt very much a wet blanket. Already, she was tired of the dances, of being asked the same old questions over and over again. 'What's your name?' 'What do you do?' 'Where do you come from?' 'Can I walk you to the chalet?' And if she let a boy take her back to the concrete bunker, she felt traitorous. They would pass rows of heaving couples lined up outside the ballroom, the chalets, in every dark corner. But after a single kiss she would flee, convinced that Ben was watching with his sad, hurt eyes. She preferred to go home alone. Lily would usually arrive about an hour later, and Rene and Winnie even later, or sometimes not at all. It was July but so far she hadn't particularly enjoyed herself. She liked playing tennis or crazy golf with Lily, but the inevitable boys would arrive, wanting to make a foursome and a date for that night. The same thing happened on the fairground or in the theatre. You weren't even safe from male attention in a shop, and she felt obliged to play along for Lily's sake. She began to wonder why they'd come. For adventure, she recalled. Lily had come for the boys, of which there'd been plenty. She herself had wanted adventure but so far there had been no sign of it.

One day Josie returned to their room after work to find a parcel the size of a small shoe box on her bed. 'I noticed it in Reception,' Winnie said. She was lounging on the bunk, drinking gin and orange. 'So I thought I'd bring it.'

'Ta. I wonder who it's from?' She didn't recognise the writing, but her name and address had been printed in large, anonymous capitals.

'Open it, darlin', and find out.'

Josie undid the string, opened the box and stared at the contents, mystified. She removed them one by one, and found a note at the bottom. 'Dear Josie, You forgot to take these with you. Love, Ivy.'

It hadn't crossed her mind to bring the photo of Mam making her first Holy Communion. Even less would she have thought to bring Mam's veil and the white prayer book, which she considered her most precious possessions. And she had deliberately left behind the watch Aunt Ivy had given her as a leaving school/starting work/fourteenth birthday present, in case it got damaged or even lost.

Winnie nodded at the photo. 'Who's that, darlin'? Let's have a decko.'

'It's me mother, me mam,' Josie said. 'She died ages ago. I can't think why me auntie sent it.'

'She's pretty, just like you.'

'Ta.' The parcel made Josie feel uneasy. It seemed such an extraordinarily strange thing for Aunt Ivy to do. Hardly a day went by when she didn't think of Mam, but seeing her picture, holding the things that Mam herself had once held, brought everything flooding back, as if Mam had died only yesterday.

Next morning, Lily received a letter from her mother which she read over breakfast. 'Our Marigold's in the club again,' she gurgled, loud enough for everyone to hear. 'And our Stanley's getting married in Berlin to someone called Freya.' Her voice rose to a shriek. 'And we're *buying* our own house. It's a semi-detached in Childwall with a big garden and a garage for me da's car. Our Daisy's staying in Machin Street with her friend, Eunice. And me brother, Ben, is going to Cambridge University. Look, Jose, Ma's sent you a note an' all.' She handed Josie an envelope. 'She's marked it "Private" – as if I'd have opened it,' she said in a hurt voice.

Mrs Kavanagh had written:

My dear Josie,

I have no idea whether Ivy has told you her news. Somehow, I suspect not, which is why I am writing this, though I hate to spoil what I hope is a happy time in the camp. I worry you might hear from someone else, and thought you should be forewarned.

Anyroad, I'll stop beating about the bush. The thing is, dear, Vincent Adams is back in Machin Street. I heard a rumour months ago that Ivy had been seen with him in town, but couldn't believe my eyes when I saw them walk by our parlour, arm in arm and as bold as brass. I can't help but wonder what she's told the neighbours.

It means you have some thinking to do about your future, Josie. Whether to go back to Machin Street in October, with all that entails, or find yourself somewhere to live, a little flat or a bedsitting-room. Or perhaps a job with accommodation would be a good idea, a hotel, for instance, or some sort of boarding school. You can stay with us in the new house while you sort yourself out – Ben will have gone by then. But he is still shattered over the break with you, and I know he misses you dreadfully. We're hoping he'll feel better about things by Christmas, so it would be best if he didn't find you here. (Are you QUITE sure it's over between you? Eddie and I still have hopes you'll be our daughter-in-law one day.)

I know this will have come as a shock, dear. My thoughts will be with you over the next few days.

Your loving friend, Mollie Kavanagh.

Aunt Ivy knew someone would tell her. She'd sent those things, her most precious things, as a sign she didn't want her back. Not that she would dream of going back, not with Vince there, but just in case, in desperation, with nowhere else to go, she returned to the only flesh and blood she had on earth.

Perhaps the penny had yet to drop, because the only feeling Josie had was pity for her aunt. Poor Ivy. Fancy loving someone so much that you excused every single thing they did, no matter how wicked. Besotted, that was the word Lily had used. Ivy was besotted with Vince. He must have been the friend she'd been meeting. Haylands had come up at an opportune time. No wonder she'd been anxious for Josie to leave.

'What did Ma have to say that's so private?' Lily sniffed.

'Nothing,' Josie said abruptly. She stuffed the letter in her overall pocket and quickly left the dining room before her friend could follow. She wanted to be by herself to think.

Outside, the camp was virtually deserted. A few hardy

campers had risen early to savour the lovely July morning. The fresh, salty air was rent with the harsh cry of seagulls as they swooped on the remains of last night's fish and chips which would shortly be swept up.

She wandered over to the fairground. Without the bright lights and loud, jangly music, the rides looked rather shabby, she thought, in need of a lick of paint. She climbed on a bobby horse and found the Irish Sea within her sight – vivid, sparkling, green, the waves tipped with creamy foam.

'One day I'll sail across there, to America.' In a way, Mrs Kavanagh's letter was a ticket to freedom. She had no responsibilities, no dependants. She could go anywhere in the world.

'The world is my oyster,' she said aloud.

Climbing down from the bobby horse, she made her way to the big wheel, which was only small as big wheels went. She sat in the bottom seat, pushed her foot against the platform to make it swing and thought about the letter again. What was she going to do? Did she really want to be totally independent at seventeen?

At that moment, on such a beautiful morning, with the sun shining warmly on her back and the sea glittering in the distance, the problem didn't seem that acute. But Josie knew that with each day that passed, October growing nearer, the problem would get bigger and bigger.

She read Mrs Kavanagh's letter again. There wouldn't be enough to pay rent out of a seventeen-year-old's wages, though she'd quite like to work in a hotel. But she would feel vulnerable, living there, as well. If things went wrong, she would lose her home as well as her job. The same thing went for a boarding school, and everyone would go home in the holidays except her.

A gull had perched on the back of the seat in front, and was watching her curiously with bright, black eyes.

'No,' she said, and the gull flew away. No, she didn't want to live and work in either of those places.

'You can stay with us until you sort yourself out,' Mrs

Kavanagh had written. But she mustn't be there at Christmas when Ben came home. It wouldn't be fair. 'Eddie and I still have hopes you'll be our daughter-in-law one day.'

Reading it again, Josie saw a simple way out her problem. She would write to Ben, tell him she missed him as much as he missed her, that she was sorry she'd gone away. It was true. His shadow had haunted her ever since she'd come to the camp. Just dancing with another boy made her feel guilty, because it wasn't *him*. There was no need to wait to get married. Circumstances had changed. They could get married next year, as soon as she was eighteen, and live in Cambridge. She would find a job and support him until he was ready to work himself.

She smiled. Why hadn't she thought of it before?

Josie wondered why, despite having sorted everything out so satisfactorily in her head, she felt more confused than ever.

She was cleaning the chalets that housed the Wasps. So far, she had managed to avoid Lily, who was unbearable if she knew something was being kept from her. Josie wasn't in the mood for her friend's remorseless probing, followed by the predictable oohs and ahs and shrill expressions of disbelief that Vince Adams was back in Machin Street.

'And after what he did an' all!' Lily would say, having guessed a skeleton of the truth. 'What exactly *did* he do, Josie?'

Most Wasps lived in a terrible state of untidiness. A few women kept their chalets neat, their clothes hung up. Some even made their own beds. It wasn't Josie's job to tidy, so she ignored the mess, merely straightening the beds beneath the heaps of clothes on top. She brushed floors, took mats to the door to shake. She worked automatically, her mind on other things.

The next chalet she entered, Barbara's and Sadie's, was a little home from home, kept scrupulously clean. There was a teddy bear on Barbara's pillow, film posters on the walls, dried flowers and photographs on the dressing-table.

Josie bent to pick up the mat to shake it. Her eyes became

level with one of the photographs. She'd never once looked at them before, though Lily took everything in, even read letters if they'd been left around.

The photo had been taken in a garden – a couple standing under trees, the man with his arm around the woman, both middle-aged, both smiling. Josie picked it up to study it more closely. The couple looked complacently happy – the woman must be Sadie's mother, she had the same dark, pretty eyes. She looked at the back. 'Mummy and Daddy's Silver Wedding' was scrawled in purple ink. There was another photo, an ordinary wedding, about twenty adults and half a dozen children grouped around the bride and groom. She recognised Sadie as a bridesmaid and noticed the middle-aged couple in the group. On the back she read, 'Jenny and Peter, 1949.'

'Aah!' Josie breathed. How lovely to have a family, a mam and dad, brothers, sisters, uncles, aunts – to *belong*.

Mrs Kavanagh's letter was stiff in her pocket, reminding her that, as from now, she was entirely alone. She had no one – unless she wrote to Ben.

There were typical mounds of clutter in the next chalet, Jeremy's and Griff's. Both beds were heaped with clothes, and the floor was full of empty beer bottles. There must have been a party the night before, as Jeremy and Griff couldn't have drunk so much between them. The sight depressed her for some reason. It seemed that with each chalet she went into she grew more and more aware of her situation and the future seemed more stark, more bleak. Unless she wrote to Ben, she reminded herself again, and wondered why she kept forgetting such an obvious way out.

'Mam,' she whispered. 'What am I going to do? Oh, why did you have to go and die on me?' She sat heavily on a bed, and began to cry.

There was a shriek. Josie screamed, leapt off the bed and a man's head appeared from beneath the pile of clothes. 'You sat on me,' he said accusingly.

'I'm sorry.' Josie, limp with fright, sat on the other bed, then quickly jumped off in case there was someone in it.

'It's all right, it's empty.'

She sat down again. 'You scared me.'

'Not half as much as you scared me. I thought the Russians had dropped the dreaded atom bomb or something.' He sat up. It was Griff Reynolds, a Jack-of-all-trades who played the piano and the double base, acted a bit, sang a bit and told terrible jokes. He was the handsomest of the Wasps, with a face like a Greek god, lovely blue eyes surrounded by enviably long lashes and brown curly hair that was a mite too long, trailing rakishly around his perfect ears. Winnie said he was a fag, a pansy. You could tell by the way he walked and talked – the prissy little steps he took, the limp way he waved his hands, the high-pitched, effeminate voice. Winnie was then obliged to explain to the girls what being a pansy entailed. Lily had gone on about it for days.

This was the first time Josie had spoken to a Wasp, other than saying 'Hello' or 'Good morning'. They normally kept very much to themselves.

Griff rolled up his pyjamas and examined his perfectly shaped legs. 'I think you've broken one. Or at least an ankle.' He wore a white pyjama jacket with black spots, and black bottoms with white spots. 'If I have to go on stage tonight in crutches, then it'll be your fault, darling.'

'I'm sorry,' Josie said again. 'Anyroad, shouldn't you be on duty? It's half eleven.'

'I'm ill, angel,' Griff said mournfully.

Josie glanced at the bottles. 'I'm not surprised.'

He caught her glance. 'It was Jeremy's birthday, sweet. We had friends in.' He rooted through the clothes, found a pillow and propped it behind him. 'How dare you come in crying, muttering about someone having died, then have the cheek to actually sit on me?'

'You were awake? You should have said something.'

'I was only half-awake, darling. And I wasn't expecting to be used as a chair. Why were you crying? Who has died?'

Josie sensed that behind the jokey remarks, he seemed genuinely to care that she'd been crying.

'The person died a long time ago,' she explained. 'It was me mam, and I still miss her. I just think about her whenever I feel miserable, that's all.'

'And why should such an adorable young woman have reason to feel miserable when it's such a glorious day outside?' He squinted at the window where the curtains were still closed. 'I assume it *is* a glorious day?'

'It's lovely.'

'Are you homesick, poppet, is that it?'

Josie smiled. 'I haven't got a home to feel sick about.'

'You poor little homeless orphan,' he cried. 'Tell your Uncle Griff all about it.'

She got to her feet. 'I can't. I'll get in trouble if I don't finish by twelve o'clock. I'm already a bit behind.'

Griff sprang out of bed – too quickly. He clutched his head and winced. 'I'll help, sweet. Where do the bottles go?'

'In the trolley outside. Ta.'

Between them, they disposed of the bottles. Griff threw the clothes off his bed, straightened the bedding, then threw the clothes back, while Josie made the other. He shook the mat while she brushed the floor.

He giggled. 'I might come back next year as a chalet maid.'

'You'd be wasted. I've seen your shows. You're very good, particularly when you sing and play the piano at the same time.'

'What a perfectly sweet thing to say. You know, I've seen you around, but I don't know your name. I can't very well call you Little Orphan Annie, it's a bit of a mouthful.'

'It's Josie.'

'I'm Griff.'

'I already knew that.' She stared up at him. He wasn't as tall as Ben, about five feet eleven, but much broader. His shoulders and arms were heavily muscled. She remembered he was very good at tennis. For the first time since leaving Liverpool she felt a flicker of interest in the opposite sex, but if

Winnie was right, Griff wasn't attracted to women. Yet there was something in his eyes . . .

'Why don't we meet up for a drink tonight after *Hit For Sex*?' he suggested.

'What?'

'The play, my love.'

Her heart beat a fraction faster. 'I'd like that, ta.'

'The curtain comes down about five past ten, then I have to change and remove my disgusting make-up, so I'll see you at about twenty past in the Palm Court?'

She nodded. 'Okay.'

For the rest of the morning, she mostly forgot about Mrs Kavanagh's letter, and thought about Griff instead.

That night, she took great pains with her appearance, brushing her hair vigorously and applying make-up with particular care. After staring at the contents of her crammed locker for several minutes, she reached for a white linen skirt with an inverted pleat at the back, a lemon silky jumper with short sleeves and a V-neck, and white sandals that showed off her tanned legs to perfection.

'You look nice,' Rene remarked. 'Lovely and fresh, like a pineapple. Are you meeting someone special tonight?'

'Not really.' She couldn't tell anyone, not even Lily, about Griff. They'd only make fun.

The girls usually caused a stir when they entered the ballroom. Lily was small and plump, with Shirley Temple hair and cheeks rosier than ever from the sun. Her brown eyes sparkled, as if she was determined the evening ahead was going to be fun. Josie was taller, slimmer, her dark blue eyes more wary than her friend's, her expression withdrawn, almost cold. She was beautiful, or so she'd been told a score of times, and supposed it was true. People who'd known them both said she was the spitting image of her mother, the most beautiful person Josie had ever known.

They were asked to dance immediately, and it continued that way for the next two hours. Josie was glad when Lily became attached to a nice young man called Harry, but unfortunately Harry had a friend, Bill, and Josie was forced to claim a headache and leave early, otherwise she would have found herself landed with Bill.

It was only ten to ten. She went for a walk around the tennis courts, entered the Palm Court at a quarter past, found an empty table and waited for Griff.

He arrived a few minutes later with his room-mate, Jeremy, who led communal sing-songs in a fine baritone voice. They stood by the door, laughing, nudging each other, as if sharing a private joke. Griff wore a blue shirt with an open neck and dark trousers. A belt encircled his narrow waist. His eyes searched the room. Josie waved, and they came towards her, Griff with his funny, wiggly walk. She noticed the campers grin and wink at each other when he passed their tables.

'*There* you are, darling,' Griff gushed. 'Josie, this is my pal, Jeremy. Jeremy, Josie. What are you drinking, precious? Lemonade! Jeremy, fetch this young lady a lemonade, and a pink gin for yours truly.' He threw himself on to the next chair, and gave her a searching look. 'Feeling better, poppet?'

'Yes, ta,' she gulped. 'How did the show go?'

'Like a dream, dear heart. The audience loved it.' He told her about his career so far, 'which wouldn't fill the back of a postage stamp. I've yet to find my niche.' He'd had a few small parts in West End revues and had played the piano on the wireless a few times. 'But the vile producer wouldn't let me sing.'

Jeremy arrived with the drinks. There was no sign of a pink gin. Instead, he put a tankard of beer in front of his friend.

As the night wore on, more and more Wasps joined their table. Josie didn't open her mouth during the fascinating conversation that went on. What on earth could she contribute of the faintest interest to people who said things like, 'Larry Olivier actually kissed me on the lips, darling. Poor Vivien, she was *livid*!'

'Tommy said – Tommy *Handley*, that is, darling, "I just *know* we'll see your name in lights one day, Stella." Such a pity he died, poor man.'

'Who's got a pantomime at Christmas?'

There was a groan and a chorus of, '*I* have!'

The strains of the last waltz drifted from the ballroom, 'When We Sound The Last All Clear'. The orchestra played the same tune every night. 'We're going to the beach, sweetheart,' Griff said. 'Like to come?'

'Oh, *yes*.' She didn't want to miss a single thing.

'Good grief,' Griff shrieked when he saw the dozens of writhing couples on the sand. 'This place is becoming more and more like Sodom and Gomorrah every day. Don't look, my pet. You're far too young.' He put a casual arm around her shoulder, and she felt a stupid little thrill.

Then Jeremy said something very strange. 'Calm down, mate. There's no need to keep up the act. We're amongst friends.'

'Phew!' Griff said in a deep, perfectly normal voice. 'One of these days, I'll forget who I really am.' He squeezed Josie's shoulders. 'That other guy is merely a performance put on to entertain the campers. You guessed, didn't you, Josie? Otherwise you'd never have come.'

'Yes,' Josie said weakly. Perhaps she had!

'We come here most nights. It's peaceful after a hectic day acting so bloody cheerful.'

'It's lovely,' she breathed, suddenly extraordinarily happy.

The midnight sky was perfect – a dark, luminous blue, cloudless, strewn with a million twinkling stars and a few dusty patches of gold. The waning moon was a tangerine segment, and the sea gleamed as if it were illuminated from underneath. She removed her shoes and the sand felt warm and powdery beneath her feet. Ahead, a bonfire burned merrily, and Josie could hear music and the crackle of flames.

The music came from a portable wireless. Half a dozen Wasps were lying around the fire and heralded their arrival with subdued murmurs. Josie didn't know where to look when four of the newcomers, three men and a girl, stripped off and ran *stark naked* into the sea. They began to kick water at each other.

Griff sank down on to the sand, and pulled her down so she was sitting in front of him, his arms around her waist. It seemed only natural to lean back, relax against him.

Little was said over the next hour as they watched the flames, watched the wood turn to brilliant red ash, watched the red ash crumble and become grey. They hummed occasionally to the music, and Josie lay contentedly in Griff's arms. Then someone yawned. Soon everyone was yawning and stretching. Jeremy said, 'One last swim for me.' He began to remove his clothes.

'I love this song,' Josie murmured. The haunting strains of 'Goodnight, Sweetheart' came from the wireless.

'Let's dance.' Griff lifted her up, and slid his arms around her waist. There was nothing to do with her arms except put them around his neck, which she willingly did. He pressed his cheek against hers as they shuffled over the sand.

She closed her eyes, and when she opened them Jeremy was entering the water without a stitch on, holding the hand of a girl as naked as himself. Sand was being kicked on the fire, parts of which still glowed dullish red. The sky looked even more beautiful, as if more stars had appeared, and the moon had got bigger and more orange.

Josie caught her breath. It was an enchanting scene, and she was part of the enchantment. Not everyone might regard the last few hours as an adventure, but it would do.

2

Next morning, Lily's eyebrows narrowed in a frown when Heidi and Barbara passed their breakfast table. 'Morning, Josie,' they called. The frown deepened when Jeremy said, 'Enjoy yourself last night?' Before she could open her mouth to demand an explanation, Griff came up. 'See you tonight, darling. Same time, same place.'

'Okay,' Josie replied weakly.

'Did you enjoy yourself *where?*' Lily looked about to burst a blood vessel. 'And you haven't got a date with *him*, surely?'

'Griff was in the chalet yesterday when I cleaned it,' Josie said haughtily. 'We had a little chat. He's very nice. I met him again last night on me way home from the dance, and he asked me for a drink. Then a big pile of us went to the sands.'

'You went to the sands with a pile of *Wasps?*' Lily's eyes gleamed jealously. 'I *crept* in last night, so as not to disturb you because you said you had a headache. I didn't even turn on the light. I thought you were in bed, but all the time you were cavorting on the sands with piles of *Wasps*.'

'We weren't cavorting. We were merely talking and listening to music. We danced a bit and some of them swam.' She didn't mention they swam in the nude, as Lily was likely to choke.

'That sounds like cavorting to me.'

'Well, it isn't,' Josie snapped. 'And quite frankly, Lily, it isn't any of your business if we were cavorting or not. Nor is it anything to do with you who I go out with. I never offer a word of criticism of your various boyfriends.'

'You said Frank from Manchester was ugly.'

'No, *you* said Frank from Manchester was ugly. I just agreed that he was as ugly as sin.'

Lily's bottom lip quivered with rage. 'Another thing, you still haven't told me what was in the letter from me ma.'

'She wouldn't have marked it "Private" if she'd wanted you to know. It's another thing that's none of your business, Lily Kavanagh.'

'You're a fine friend, Josie Smith.'

Josie wasn't sure what came over her, other than a wish to remove the wind from Lily's sails completely. She said airily, 'Me name's not Josie Smith any more, it's Josie Flynn.' With Aunt Ivy out of her life, there was no need to keep up the pretence.

Lily's face collapsed. She floundered, 'What? *what?* What on earth are you talking about?'

Josie smiled mysteriously. 'Wouldn't you like to know?'

It was the first row they'd had since they'd come to Haylands and they were both quite happy with it. They linked arms on the way to the laundry to fetch their trolleys.

'Actually,' Lily mused, 'I wouldn't mind a platonic relationship. It makes things so much easier, no wondering how far a bloke's hands are going to roam and if you should let him if they do. And I must admit that Griff is dead gorgeous.'

'Who said it was platonic relationship?'

Lily's face collapsed for the second time that morning. 'But I thought, I thought . . .'

'Well, you thought wrong.' Josie felt smug. 'It's just an act he puts on to entertain the campers.'

'Did – did he *kiss* you?'

'Only me ear.'

'Oh, Jose. It sounds dead romantic.' Lily sighed. Later, as they pushed their trolleys towards the chalets, she said, 'You know that business of your name being Flynn, not Smith. I take it you weren't having me on, so you will tell me one day, won't you, Jose? And whatever it was me ma had to say in her letter. After all, we're *friends*.'

The tide had not long gone out, and the sand was moist beneath Josie's feet as Griff twirled her round and round in an old-fashioned waltz. They were getting further and further away from the group around the bonfire who lay uncaringly on the damp sand. There was no moon, and the only illumination came from the leaping flames and a strange, grey light that hung over the sea. The horizon was a dark, silvery blur.

Josie trod on something and yelped, and Griff led her back to where the sand was dry. They sat down and he examined her foot. 'Nothing there, darling,' he said after a while. Suddenly, he kissed her toes, he kissed her legs and her knees. He put his arms around her waist, pushed her down on to the sand and kissed her lips. Josie felt a wild, fluttery sensation in her stomach that she'd never had with Ben. She kissed him back, and willingly opened her mouth when he tried to force it with his tongue, a habit she'd previously thought disgusting. Nor did she mind when his hand crept under her jumper, under her bra, pulling it away, and he bent and kissed her breasts. In fact, it was so nice, so incredibly nice, that she wanted to scream how nice it was, and that she didn't want him to stop, not ever. There was a throbbing between her legs, and she longed for him to touch her *there*.

'Griff. Josie. We're going.' The shouts sounded far away.

Griff raised his head. 'Coming.' He looked down at Josie and lightly touched her left nipple. 'Have you done this before?'

'Well – almost.' She felt disappointed that he'd stopped. There seemed something daringly wicked about lying in the open air with her breasts bare. She stretched voluptuously.

'I thought as much.' He pulled down her jumper. 'That's enough for tonight, my darling. And don't tease.'

She thought about him the second she woke. He was on her mind all day, as she counted down the hours and the minutes before she would see him again.

That night, they wandered far away from the bonfire to the place they'd lain the night before, where they fell on the sand in each other's arms and began to kiss eagerly. Josie felt as if her body were on fire as it began to respond to Griff's touch, his hands or his lips exploring every secret part of her. Suddenly, he sat back on his haunches. She was surprised to see that he was naked – and so was she, though she couldn't remember either of them having removed their clothes. He was the handsomest man she had ever known. Her head was whirling, and she felt as if a spell had been cast upon her. Making love had been far from her mind when she'd come to the camp. She had thought it would be years away, when she was married. But now it was about to happen, on an enchanted Welsh beach under a dark sky, to the sound of the rippling tide and the faint, tinny music from the wireless.

'What are you doing?' she asked impatiently. Griff was feeling in the pockets of his trousers. She wanted him *back*.

'Looking for this.' He held up something very small. 'We don't want a little memento of Haylands arriving in nine months' time.' He straddled her, then tenderly cupped her face in his hands. 'Are you sure you're ready for this?' he said gently. 'I won't be cross if you change your mind. Well, not very.'

Josie clasped her arms around his neck. 'You'll have to put me in the mood again.'

'Willingly,' murmured Griff.

Lily was irritable next day, and it was all Josie's fault. She wasn't concentrating, she wasn't listening, she was in another world. 'You're bloody miles away,' Lily said accusingly.

'Am I?' Josie dreamily shook a mat.

'You're supposed to shake it *outside*, not in. I've just brushed that floor.'

'Sorry, Lil.' Josie shook the mat outside.

'You've already done that. I'm just brushing the muck up.'

'Sorry, Lil. What shall I do now?'

'Empty the bin, make the beds, clean the sink, same as we do every day. What on earth's got into you, Josie?' Lily said acidly. She looked at her friend intently. 'What's happened? I've never known you so vague before.'

'Something wonderful, Lil,' Josie said in a husky voice. She had to tell someone, and there was no one else but Lily. 'Something truly incredible and . . . and, oh, *wonderful*.' She could almost hear the ticking of Lily's brain as she tried to think what the something was. Her eyes grew wide and her jaw fell as enlightenment dawned.

'You've gone all the way!' she cried. 'Did it hurt, Jose?'

'Only a bit, only at first.'

Lily's face twisted ferociously as she tried to adjust to the news. She pouted. 'I'm the oldest. I should have done it before you.'

'Oh, Lil. It's not a race.'

'Are you in love? You *look* like you're in love.'

'I'm not. It's purely sexual.' Josie sighed rapturously. 'We can't keep our hands off each other.'

'You lucky bugger!' Lily's expression changed from one of envy to concern. 'Our poor Ben, though. Does this mean you'll never get back together? Ma keeps hoping you will.'

'I'm afraid it does, Lil. I never felt with Ben the way I do with Griff.' She had forgotten the letter she'd meant to write.

Lily said wistfully, 'I love being here. It won't half seem dull when we're back in Liverpool, working in an office.'

Josie reluctantly came down to earth. She decided it was time she dropped her bombshell. 'I'm not sure if I'm going back to Liverpool, Lil.'

'Why ever not?' Lily's face was a picture of bewilderment.

'Because Vince Adams is back with Auntie Ivy. That's what the letter from your ma was about. I've got to find somewhere to live, as well as a job.' In order to get everything out of the way in one go, she explained that her mother hadn't been married and that Ivy had insisted that Josie change her surname to Smith so no one would know. 'But from now on, I'm Josie Flynn.'

The *Liverpool Echo* was on sale in the camp. Josie bought a copy every day. By the end of August, the only live-in job even vaguely suitable was as a cook in a men's hostel, which she didn't fancy, mainly because she couldn't boil an egg. Most rented accommodation was way beyond her means. Even the few affordable places meant she'd be left with scarcely anything to live on.

Lily was desperate for her friend to stay in Liverpool. 'We've got to stick together, Jose. I don't know what I'd do if you weren't around. I'd miss you far more than I would our Daisy or Marigold.'

Even Griff became involved in the search of a job for Josie. 'You could join the forces,' he suggested one night after they had finished making love. They were in his chalet because it was raining. Jeremy had been ordered not to come back for an hour. 'Become a Wren or a Wraf. Or you could marry me.'

She looked at him in surprise. 'Do you mean that?'

He appeared a tiny bit shocked. 'I'm not sure. It just sort of slipped out.'

'*I'm* sure. It wouldn't work. We hardly know each other.'

'I would have thought we knew each other better than anyone else on earth. I'm familiar with every single part of your body, and you with mine.'

Josie's stomach lurched. 'Yes, but we still don't *know* each other. We don't know what goes on inside each other's heads. I mean, we never *talk*.' She began to touch him. There was still time to make love again before Jeremy came back. 'Oh, but I'm so glad you were the first,' she cried. 'I'm so lucky it was you.' She would never see him again after October, but she would remember him all her life.

It was Lily who saw the job that might possibly do. 'Secretary/companion required by elderly gentlewoman to commence mid-October. Own large room. No cooking/cleaning/nursing. Formby area. References required. Salary: £10 per month.'

'There's a box number,' Lily announced when she read the advertisement aloud. 'It sounds perfect, Jose.'

'Would you fancy being companion to an elderly gentlewoman?' Josie said huffily.

'I'd hate it. But I don't need to find a live-in job, do I?'

'Thanks for reminding me. What's a *gentle*woman when she's at home, anyroad?'

Lily shrugged. 'Same as a gentle*man*, I suppose. In other words, dead posh. But ten pounds a month, Jose, and you wouldn't have to buy food. You wouldn't need fares.'

'Hmm, I dunno.' Josie chewed her lip. 'I couldn't very well write from Haylands, could I? It wouldn't look good to say I was a chalet maid.'

'Put our new address in Childwall, and I'll send it to Ma to post. She'll send the answer here.'

'I don't suppose it would hurt.'

A fortnight later, Mrs Kavanagh sent the reply with a short note to say the job sounded ideal, and she hoped the letter contained good news.

The letter was signed by a Marian Moorcroft and was short and to the point. 'Dear Miss Flynn, In regard to your application as secretary-companion to my mother, kindly present yourself for interview at the above address on Wednesday, 2nd September at 2 p.m. Please telephone if you are unable to keep the appointment.'

'Oh, well, that's that.' Josie threw the letter at Lily. 'I can't possibly go all the way to Liverpool for an interview.'

'Someone's not going to take you on as companion to her dear old ma on the strength of a letter,' Lily argued. 'It stands to reason she'll want to see you. You can easily get there and back in a day. Wednesday's our afternoon off, and I'm sure Mrs Baxter would you let you have the morning off as well. We've both been reliable workers. Oh, look at the address – Barefoot House, Sandy Steps, Formby. It sounds lovely. Come on, Jose,' she coaxed. 'Formby's only the other side of Liverpool. We could go out together nights and weekends. At least you'll have *friends*, which won't be the case if you move away.'

'I'll think about it,' said Josie.

It was a bright, sunny day, and Liverpool seemed incredibly *loud* when Josie got off the bus at the Pier Head, loud and very crowded. Trams clattered noisily along the metal lines. They, and the buses, seemed much bigger than she remembered, and she almost gagged when a car passed exuding clouds of black fumes. The New Brighton ferry had just docked, and people were hurrying to board down the big, floating gangway – families, mainly, the children carrying buckets and spades.

Josie paused for a second on the very spot where she'd stood once before and watched the same scene. It seemed a lifetime ago, and she found it hard to connect the small, mixed-up child with the person she was now. Yet they were the same. And she was still mixed up, but in a different way. And then she'd had Mam.

She walked to Exchange station, where the Southport train was waiting. It left almost immediately. After the wide open spaces of the camp, with its small cream buildings, the landscape she passed through seemed claustrophobic, the houses small and dark, crammed together in narrow streets. There were still bomb sites to be cleared, and the air was full of smoke. But when they reached Formby, the scenery became more countrified, the houses spaced widely apart with big gardens. Cows grazed in a field.

It wasn't quite half past one when she got off the train at Formby station. There was plenty of time to find Barefoot House – Mrs Kavanagh had been unable to find Sandy Steps on the map.

Unfortunately, the few shops were closed and wouldn't be opening again because it was half-day closing, and there wasn't a soul about. She walked along a road of large, detached houses, and approached a man working in his garden.

'Sandy Steps? Sorry, dear, I've never heard of it, or Barefoot House. Try the post office.'

'It's closed.'

Two girls on bikes couldn't help either, or a woman walking her dog, or the man about to get in his car. By then it was almost two, and the idea of having come all the way from Colwyn Bay and not being able to find the house added desperation to her search. It wasn't hot, but her hair felt damp against her neck and her armpits were wet, although she'd rubbed them with deodorant that morning. Worst of all, the canvas shoes which had always felt so comfortable, began to rub her heels.

At last! 'That's where Louisa Chalcott lives, isn't it?' exclaimed an elderly lady in conversation with another over a garden gate. 'It's at the bottom of Nelson Road, on the beach. Go back down this road, turn left, then second right. It's quite a walk,' she chuckled, 'but it won't take long on your young legs.'

As Josie limped away, she heard the other woman say, 'I thought Louisa Chalcott was dead?'

Nelson Road was lined with bungalows, and led directly to the shore, beyond which flowed the greeny-brown waters of the Mersey. At the point where the bungalows ended, the road sloped down to meet the sand, and on the right a series of steps, attached to a brick wall, led to a tall iron gate with a name on a metal plate: BAREFOOT HOUSE.

With a feeling of relief mixed with annoyance at the lack of directions, Josie hurried down the steps, through the gate, up more steps and into a small garden of withered bushes, bent reeds and long-dead trees, separated from the sand by a low wall. She almost ran towards a large, windswept, sandstone house with curved bay windows upstairs and down. The window frames had more paint off than on, and the front door, which might have once been grey, was pitted, as if gravel had been thrown against it.

She knocked, and the door was opened by a smiling woman in a flowered wrap-round pinny, a scarf tied turban-wise around her head.

'I'm so sorry I'm late,' Josie began, 'but—'

'There's no need to apologise to me, luv,' the woman said cheerfully. 'Save it for the terrible twins in the parlour. What's your name, luv? I'm supposed to announce you. Stupid bitches,' she said under her breath.

'Josephine Flynn, er, Miss Flynn.' Josie was a bit put out by the reception. She ached to go to the lavatory, and would have liked to comb her hair, see if her lipstick had smudged, have a wash. As she followed the woman across a square, spacious hall, she tried to straighten herself up as much as possible.

'Miss Josephine Flynn,' the overalled woman said regally when she opened a door without knocking. She jerked her head at Josie. 'Go on in, luv.'

Josie entered a massive, sparsely furnished room overlooking the river, where two women in pastel twinsets and pearls were seated officiously behind a table. They would have been identical, except that one wore glasses and the other didn't. Their round, narrowly set eyes regarded the newcomer with disapproval. She saw her letter on the table.

'You're late,' the woman with glasses snapped. She looked at her watch. 'It's a quarter to three. In another fifteen minutes we have to interview somebody else.'

'I'm sorry, but—' Josie began, but the other woman interrupted. 'It hardly seems worth our whiles interviewing this person, Marian. Not only was she very late, but she's far too young for Mother.'

'I agree with you there, Hilary.'

Josie plonked herself in a chair without being asked. She was seething. 'If you'd bothered to put the proper address on your letter, I wouldn't have been late,' she said spiritedly.

The women gave each other an outraged look. 'Everyone knows where Barefoot House is,' Marian said curtly. 'Our mother, Louisa Chalcott, is very well known.'

'Well, I asked loads of people who'd never heard of Barefoot House, and the only one who had thought Louisa Chalcott was dead.' Josie tossed her head. 'As to me being too young, I put me date of birth on me letter. All you had to do was work it out.' She rose to her feet, knowing that the job would never be hers, but she wasn't leaving without tearing the women off a strip. 'You're both very irresponsible and rude. I don't appreciate having me time wasted by the likes of you.'

Their faces sagged in stupefaction. Josie went to the door and opened it. 'Tara,' she said loudly, and they both jumped.

'Stay!' an imperious voice thundered.

It was Josie's turn to jump. Outside the door stood a very old, very tall, painfully thin woman with jet black hair, lightly sprinkled with grey, and black, bushy eyebrows. She had a walking stick in one hand. The other, trembling slightly, she held in front of Josie's face. She wore baggy tweed trousers, a man's shirt worn loose and carpet slippers. Her dark eyes, large and very beautiful, flashed angrily in her deeply wrinkled face. She gave a terse nod, which Josie took as an indication to return. The woman followed, leaning heavily on the stick, and sat down with difficulty, waving aside Josie's attempt to help. 'If I need a hand, I'll ask for it,' she snapped.

'Please yourself,' Josie snapped back. She wasn't in the mood to be nice to people, even if they were old and walked with a stick.

'Really!' Hilary gasped.

The older woman smiled. She took cigarettes, a holder and a silver lighter from her breast pocket, lit a cigarette and inhaled deeply. Puffs of smoke emerged from her nostrils, reminding Josie of a dragon. 'I want *her*,' she said emphatically. 'I don't want another retired schoolteacher fawning over me, or a retired nurse, or a widow with nothing to do. I want someone young for a change, someone with a bit of spirit who'll answer back. I want someone like *her*.' She nodded at a dazed Josie, then chuckled spitefully. 'I enjoyed the way she wiped the floor with you two.'

'Have you been eavesdropping, Mother?'

'I most certainly have.' The woman – presumably Louisa Chalcott – had a deep, hoarse, attractive voice, and spoke with an accent Josie couldn't identify. 'I was amused to hear some people think me dead. I am, however, very much alive, and, despite your insistence to the contrary, I am not an invalid. I am also still in possession of all my faculties, and quite able to choose a secretary for myself.'

'But, Mother, you *are* an invalid,' Marian cried. 'We were only trying to help. This . . .' She waved her hand at a still-dazed Josie. 'This person is entirely unsuitable.'

'She isn't to me.' Louisa Chalcott banged her stick on the floor and yelled, 'Phoebe.'

The woman in the flowered overall must have been indulging in a spot of eavesdropping herself, because the door opened immediately. 'What, Lou?' Hilary and Marian winced.

'Show this young lady to the room that would be hers should she deign to live with us. She is quite likely to subject you to the third degree, and I'd like you to be brutally honest so she'll know what to expect. Oh, and, Phoebe, show her the lavatory on the way. She looks desperate for a pee.'

The upstairs room was the same size as the one below, and just as sparsely furnished. There was a double bed with a white cotton cover, a wardrobe and chest of drawers, both urgently in need of varnish. Two faded rugs graced the polished wooden floor, and faded cretonne curtains the big bay window. The view, overlooking a vast expanse of the Mersey, was breathtaking. Josie knelt on the window-seat to watch a liner, making its stately way along the gleaming river, and several other smaller ships – tugboats and coasters. There was a single yacht, poised like a bird on the water. Fluffy clouds raced across the blue sky, much faster than the ships. Fancy waking up every morning to this!

Phoebe was standing inside the door, arms folded. 'I must say you put the twins in their place,' she said with a complacent smile. 'Me and Lou laughed like drains.'

Josie climbed off the window-seat, sat on the bed and bounced a few times. It felt nice and soft. 'Who exactly is she, Louisa Chalcott? I've never heard of her meself.'

'Not many people have, luv, only intellectual types. She writes poetry, used to be quite famous in her day. Before the war this house was full of people, parties most weekends. But then poor Lou had a stroke. That's when I came to work here. She was only sixty-two, but it left her paralysed one side. She's much better than she used to be, though she never goes out and there's scarcely been a visitor since, apart from the twins. Lou doesn't want people knowing the state she's in.'

'Why does she need a companion if you're here?'

Phoebe came and sat beside her on the bed. 'I'm only the cleaner, luv. I come a few hours a day, make Lou's meals – she eats like a bird. She wasn't always so thin. She needs someone to do her typing and live here full time, case she falls, like. She has to sleep downstairs because she can't manage the stairs.' She patted Josie's hand. 'I hope you decide to take the job, luv. You're just what she needs, young and full of life. As long as you answer back, stand up for yourself, like, you and Lou will get on fine. She can't abide what she calls lickspittles or toadies. Her last companion walked out in tears. Marian and Hilary will be here till October, and they need someone to take over then.' Phoebe made a face. 'I can't wait to see the back of them, interfering pair of bitches.'

'What happened to Louisa's husband?' Josie enquired. She had, after all, been more or less authorised to ask questions.

Phoebe winked. 'Never had one!'

Josie gasped. 'But she's got two daughters!'

'Lou's never been what you'd call conventional. And she never does things by halves. She didn't just have one baby on the wrong side of the blanket, she had twins.' Phoebe shook her head. 'Lord knows what people said at the time. It must have caused a terrible scandal – she was forty an' all. Mind you, she's a Yank. Perhaps they do things different in America.'

Louisa Chalcott was waiting in the same chair, smoking a fresh cigarette. There was no sign of her daughters. Or, Josie noted with amusement, the woman who'd been expected at three o'clock. 'Well, young lady,' she said with a grin. 'I expect Phoebe has just washed all my dirty linen in front of you. Can I expect you in October or not?'

'Yes.' She didn't have much choice. 'I've got a name, you know. It's Josie Flynn.'

'And I'm Louisa Chalcott. Thrilled to meet you, Josie. You can call me Lou or Louisa. I don't mind which.'

The children had gone back to school, and with each week fewer and fewer campers came to Haylands. Once again the camp was almost deserted, the bars hardly used. The ballroom was a miserable place with so few people there, nearly all couples. Staff left, and Josie and Lily bade a tearful goodbye to their room-mates. Rene and Winnie had enjoyed themselves. The break had done them good, they were looking forward to seeing their kids. They took each other's addresses and promised to write.

The summer too had ended. September was a cold,

blustery month, unsuitable for midnight sojourns on the sands. Half the Wasps had gone, back on the dole or to menial jobs in London where they could keep in touch with their agents and hope for better things. A lucky few had tiny walk-on parts in far-flung theatres throughout the country, which they hoped would lead to something better. They left, praying they *wouldn't* meet up again in Haylands, a certain sign of failure.

Griff had the chalet to himself, so they could make love whenever they pleased. But something was missing – the enchantment, the company, the moonlit beach, the music. Josie knew she had been right to dismiss the idea of them getting married.

On the final night at Haylands, she and Griff talked for a long time. They said things to each other that they'd never said before. She hadn't known he'd been a soldier in the war and that he'd hated every minute. She told him she was dreading being stuck in Formby with a horrible old woman.

They made love for the last time. It was sweet, tender, devoid of passion, like an old married couple who'd done the same thing a thousand times before.

'I'd better be going,' Josie sighed. She detached herself from his arms. 'We're catching the ten o'clock bus in the morning, and I haven't packed a thing.'

'I'll walk you back.'

'No, ta. I'd sooner go by meself.' She could feel tears behind her eyes. If he touched her again, she would only cry. She dressed quickly and went to the door. 'Tara, Griff,' she whispered. His handsome face was just visible in the faint light that filtered through the curtains from the lamp outside. He looked devastated.

'Bye, Josie, my darling. Have a nice life.'

'You, too.' She closed the door. That night, she cried herself to sleep. She was still crying next morning. Lily, who had no one to cry for and was leaving with her virginity still intact, was irritated when her friend cried most of the way home on the bus to Liverpool.

★

The Kavanaghs' new house in Childwall was light and roomy. It had a sunshine lounge, a breakfast room, a large, modern kitchen and four bedrooms. Josie was staying for a few days before going to Barefoot House.

The first thing Lily did was inspect her room, where she immediately found fault with the wallpaper. The flowers were too big – she'd wanted smaller ones. 'And couldn't you have found net curtains with a frillier frill, Ma?'

'Lily, luv. We did the best we could,' Mrs Kavanagh said in a hurt voice.

'Oh, I suppose it'll *do*.'

Josie knew her friend had been jealous of her relationship with Griff. Now, as if she was trying to get her own back, even things out, over the next few days she felt convinced Lily was doing her utmost to emphasise Josie's aloneness when compared to her own comfortable place within a large, loving family. As soon as Mr Kavanagh sank into his armchair, Lily would drape herself all over him and demand a cuddle. She apologised to her mother for criticising the room. 'After you'd gone to so much trouble for your little girl.'

Perhaps I'm just imagining it, Josie thought. But Lily had always wanted to be on top. It rather spoiled her stay at the Kavanaghs', which she'd been looking forward to.

One day she went into Ben's room. He had a bookcase of his own now, and a desk. She noticed that the books had been placed alphabetically on the shelves, and the desk was bare, a chair neatly placed in front. The only ornaments were the various cups he'd won at school over the years placed neatly on the window-sill. The room had a stark, monk-like air.

'This is the way he left it,' Mrs Kavanagh said from the door. 'I never needed to tidy up after our Ben.'

'I suppose you miss him.'

'More than I can say.' Mrs Kavanagh came into the room. 'I miss all me kids. Lily's the only one left. I've got two grandchildren and another on the way, but they're not the same as your own.' She smiled ruefully. 'You know, luv, Ben's still heartbroken. Is it definitely over between you two?'

135

Josie nodded. 'I'm afraid so. I nearly did something awful, though. When I heard Vince Adams was back, I thought about making up with Ben. I was feeling desperate, you see.' She squared her shoulders. 'I'm glad I didn't. It would have been dead unfair. It was the Kavanaghs I wanted to marry, not Ben.'

'I understand, luv.' The older woman gave her a hug. 'Anyroad, I'm a realist. Our Ben will make some girl a good husband, but not a very exciting one.' She picked up one of the cups and tenderly polished it with her sleeve. 'Children,' she sighed. She looked at Josie. 'I'm sorry about Lily, luv, the way she's behaving. I know she's me daughter and I love her to death, but always remember this – you've got more character in your little finger than our Lily's got in her whole silly body.'

Next day, Josie left for Barefoot House. She telephoned first, and Phoebe said to come at five o'clock. 'Lou's expecting the doctor around four, and she hates anyone being there.'

With each portion of the journey, her heart sank lower and lower. By the time she reached Barefoot House and entered the bleak, petrified garden, she felt totally detached from the real world of ordinary people leading ordinary lives. She had no one: no Mam, no Aunt Ivy, no Kavanaghs just along the street.

From now on, she was truly on her own.

Barefoot House

1951–1954

I

It had originally been called Burford House, Louisa said, built for someone called Clarence Burford in 1858. In those days, it had stood entirely alone on the sands. Louisa had lived there for almost thirty years.

'We landed in Liverpool from New York, and decided to spend a few days here, take a look round one of the most famous ports in the world. Chuck managed to borrow a car. He was actually driving the damn thing along the beach when we saw the house. I fell in love with it straight away, though I didn't spend much time here. I was for ever flitting off to London or New York.' The twins had called it Barefoot House, and the name had stuck. Phoebe said they were ten years old before their mother sent for them from America.

Nelson Road hadn't existed when Louisa had bought her house, and she loathed the new properties. 'Moronic,' she called them. 'Moronic little houses for moronic little people.' Fortunately, they were only visible from the back, and then from the upstairs rooms which were only used when Marian and Hilary came to stay. It was still easy to believe that Barefoot House, surrounded as it was on three sides by ten-foot-high walls, and only sand and the river visible from the front, stood entirely alone.

The doctor was just leaving the day Josie arrived. He tipped his hat. 'If you're the new companion, then you have my every sympathy, young lady. Her ladyship's in a foul mood.'

Josie went inside, deposited her suitcase at the bottom of the stairs and shouted, 'Hello, it's me.' There was no reply.

There was a rattling sound coming from somewhere at the back. Josie found Louisa Chalcott, clad in tweed slacks and a short-sleeved shirt, her black hair wild and uncombed, in the kitchen trying to support herself with her stick. At the same time she was struggling with a strange metal contraption, a sort of pan, trying to get the top off.

'Hello,' Josie said again.

Louisa, startled, dropped the metal contraption on the floor. 'Fuck!' she spat. She glared at Josie. 'Don't tell me you're a creeper. I can't stand fucking creepers. I had someone once, Miss Twizzlewit or something, who crept around like a fucking mouse.'

'I didn't mean to frighten you, but I walked in quite normally, and I shouted, too.'

Louisa ignored her. 'That stupid doctor's just told me there's something wrong with my heart. A creepy-crawly companion is the last thing I need. Since you're here, you can make some coffee. I like it black and very strong, no sugar.' She kicked the pan. 'The percolator's on the floor.'

Josie picked up the contraption. She'd never seen the likes of it before. 'What am I supposed to do with this?'

'Make coffee, stupid. You'll find it in the cupboard, and you'll find water in the tap. The coffee goes there.' She pointed to a round part with holes that seemed to fit on top. 'Fill the bottom with water and put it on the stove. I'll tell you when it should be ready.'

'Thank you.'

'I'll be in my room, and when you bring it, *don't creep*.'

'I didn't creep,' Josie said pleasantly. 'And another thing, if you ever call me stupid again, I shall leave on the spot.' She thought this might evoke an apology, but Louisa merely gave a contemptuous snort and limped heavily away.

I'll start getting the *Echo* again, look for another job, a shaken Josie vowed as she watched the pot boil and the delicious aroma of coffee filled the small, old-fashioned kitchen, with its stone floor and deep brown sink. The stove and boiler looked as if they'd come out of the ark. A grille over the small window made the room very dark. And there were draughts. It would be freezing in winter.

Her bottom lip trembled. This time last week she'd been at Haylands, but the camp, and everything that had happened there, was already beginning to feel like a lovely dream that she'd woken up from a long, long while ago.

There was a bang and a shout. 'It should be ready now.'

Louisa's room appeared to have been a study. There was a large desk and the shelves on the walls were crammed with books. A double bed was dumped uncompromisingly in the middle. She was sitting in a rocking chair, smoking, and staring out of the window at the river. She didn't look round when Josie went in.

'Getting old's a bitch,' she said gruffly. 'You'll find that out for yourself one day. When I first came here, I used to imagine myself striding along the beach at eighty. I was always very fit, you see, used to swim every morning.' She laughed bitterly. 'Now I can't even manage the stairs. The doctor comes once a month, and always finds something new wrong with me. If it's not my ears, then it's my joints or my eyes. This time it was my heart. It's beating too fast, or too slow. I can't remember which. I try not to listen. I don't want to know. If I think about it too much, I get upset, and I can't abide people who feel sorry for themselves.' She turned round and regarded Josie with her large, brilliant eyes. 'Are you a virgin?'

The question was so unexpected that Josie nearly dropped the coffee. She put it on the window-seat beside her strange new employer. 'Mind your own business,' she gasped.

'That means you're not, or you would have said something like, "Of course I am," in the same outraged voice.' Louisa stretched her gaunt arms, the backs riddled with bright blue veins. 'How old are you? Seventeen? I had my first man at thirteen – he was a friend of my father's. Oh, tell me some gossip, Josie,' she cried. 'What is your young man like? What's his name? Are you still seeing him? Is he likely to come to Barefoot House courting you with flowers?' She leaned forward and said slyly, 'Or has there been more than one? Titillate me. What is going on in the world outside these four walls?'

'Have you never heard of newspapers?'

'Reading about it isn't the same. Oh, I know all about Ingrid Bergman's affair with Roberto Rosselini and her two little bastard sons. But I prefer my gossip face to face. It's juicier that way.'

'Well, you're not getting anything juicy out of me.'

Next day, Phoebe showed her the office. It had a desk and chair, a typewriter so old it could have been the first ever made, and a small shelf of books, mainly reference works. The desk drawers were full of curling, yellow paper and odd sheets of well-used carbon. The room was as small, cold and dark as the kitchen opposite, and just as draughty.

Louisa only needed two or three letters a day to be typed, which was just as well as the keys on the typewriter took all Josie's strength to press, and then there was no tail on the 'p', no top on the 'b' and the 'e' was hardly visible. She had to fill them in with a pen afterwards. Sometimes the letters were to Louisa's agents – there was Cy Marks in New York, and Leonard McGill in London – usually to do with one of her poems being used in an anthology or a magazine, or acknowledging a cheque, always very small. All her books were out of print, Phoebe said, though she still received letters from students and admirers, for which there was a standard reply.

The worst, most nerve-racking times were when she wrote to old friends. She would stand over Josie, breathing heavily and refusing to sit down, and rattle off a stream of lies. She felt fine. She was writing furiously. There'd been a house party last weekend. She'd been to the theatre. 'Have you brought last night's paper, Phoebe,' she would bawl, 'so I can check what's on? Where had I got to?' she would demand of Josie.

'I've no idea. I've only reached the bit about you writing furiously. You're dictating much too fast. I can do shorthand, you know. It would be much easier.'

'It wouldn't be so spontaneous.'

'I don't see anything spontaneous about having to repeat yourself half a dozen times. The fastest typist in the world couldn't keep up on *this* damn thing. Josie typed 'furiously' ponderously. The 'y' seemed to have disappeared altogether.

As the weeks passed, Josie gradually got used to Louisa Chalcott's rude and demanding ways. It was hard sometimes to be rude back. She wasn't always in the mood, and would have preferred to disappear into her room for a good cry, but it would have been fatal to show any sign of weakness in front of her employer.

She quickly got into a routine. As soon as she got up, if the weather was even faintly reasonable, she would go for a walk on the shore. On her return, she would make breakfast – Louisa's a boiled egg with a single round of bread and butter, cornflakes for herself. At around ten, Phoebe arrived with the groceries, and Josie would retreat to the office and attend to that day's mail. Phoebe made dinner at noon, and all three would eat together in the parlour, the cheeriest time of the day as far as Josie was concerned as Phoebe would regale them with hilarious stories about her family – she had five children, all married, and twelve grandchildren, always getting into scrapes. Louisa would become deeply involved in the rather trivial tales, and ask numerous questions.

'It's pathetic, really,' Phoebe said privately. 'She don't half miss the outside world. She wouldn't be seen dead in a wheelchair, else you could've taken her for walks. What she needs is a companion who can drive. There's a car in the garage she used to drive herself. She'd enjoy being taken shopping.'

Josie investigated the garage behind the house, where high double gates, now firmly padlocked, opened on to Nelson Road. There was indeed a car inside, a dusty little black box on wheels. One of these days, she might suggest to Louisa that she take driving lessons.

Afternoon and evenings, Josie found herself with little to do, except make sandwiches at teatime and numerous cups of coffee. Louisa spent most of the time in her room, in bed or the rocking chair, lost in thought or scribbling away in her large, wild, execrable writing in a shiny red notebook, which she would close if anyone went near. When Josie took her in a drink, she would talk, usually about her lovers, of which there seemed to have been hundreds – poets, actors, writers, politicians and notorious playboys – or so she claimed.

Otherwise, a bored Josie sat in the parlour, reading, teaching herself to knit, staring at the view. But she was fed up with the sight of only sea, ships and sand – only a few hardy souls took to the beach in winter. She longed for company, noise, traffic, a wireless, and would have offered to do the shopping and the cooking if it hadn't meant treading on Phoebe's toes. It was actually a treat when Louisa ran out of cigarettes, and she had to walk as far as the shops, where she usually bought a newspaper to look for another job, so far without success. Marian and Hilary often telephoned, wanting to know how their mother was, but Louisa flatly refused to speak to her daughters and it was left to Josie to explain stiffly that she was fine. Louisa only came to the phone in the hall if it was an agent or her friend, Thumbelina, from New York, when she would chatter away for ages. Every month, Thumbelina would send a pile of American newspapers, which Louisa eagerly read from cover to cover.

'That's a dead funny name to give someone,' Josie said.

'I call her Thumbelina because she's so tiny,' Lousia explained with a fond smile. 'Only four feet ten. Her real name is Albertine. She's had six husbands, each one richer than the one before. I expect any day to hear she's about to marry Mr Seven, who is bound to be a multi-multi-million-aire.'

Tuesday evening and all day Saturday, Josie had off. With a feeling of exhilaration, she caught the train to Exchange station to meet Lily. Mid-week, they went to the pictures. On Saturdays they went shopping, then to the Kavanaghs' for tea and to get changed for a dance at the Locarno or the Grafton. But tea would have to stop soon because it was December, and Ben was due home any day. Mrs Kavanagh didn't want him upset.

When she got back, Louisa would ply her with questions. 'Did you meet any nice young men? What picture did you see? Did you go to George Henry Lee's? Y'know, I used to buy a lot of my clothes there once.'

And Josie would answer every question, even down to a physical description of Richard Widmark, whom she'd just seen in *Night and the City*, and display every item of her shopping for Louisa to examine, usually critically. 'I used to buy Helena Rubinstein cosmetics. The lipsticks came in big gold cases, not piddling little Bakelite tubes like that.'

'If you double me wages, I'll buy Helena Rubinstein, too.'

At Louisa's suggestion, she brought Lily to see her. At first Lily was plainly terrified of the forceful old woman, who immediately began to pry into her private life, but softened when told she had flirtatious eyes. 'I bet you have scores of young men after you,' Louisa said slyly.

'Well, quite a few,' Lily conceded, although there wasn't a single man on the horizon at the moment.

'And I bet you give them a good run for their money.'

'Oh, I do,' Lily concurred.

'Don't run too fast, though.' Louisa nodded wisely. 'You must pause and let them catch you once in a while.'

'Oh, I do,' Lily said again.

'What the hell was she on about, Jose?' Lily asked when Josie walked her to the station. 'All that talk about sex. It's peculiar coming from an old woman. Is she round the bend?'

'Possibly,' Josie said.

'Do you think I've got flirtatious eyes?'

'Possibly.'

On Christmas Day, Josie woke up with a heavy heart and a

143

sense of gloom, knowing the day was going to be thuddingly boring – like Sundays, only worse. The weather didn't help. The sky was the colour of wet slates, threatening rain, the river brown and murky. She went early to Mass. On the way back the skies opened and she got soaked, despite her heavy mack and umbrella. Once home, she changed her clothes, hung the mack in the bathroom and lit the parlour fire. Louisa was still in bed, and the cold, dark house felt very still and quiet. All that could be heard was the sound of the rain against the windows.

What am I doing here?

Josie had an hysterical urge to scream. After Christmas, she'd seriously start looking for something else. She quickly went round the house, turning on every light – in the hall, on the landing, in the parlour – before going in to the kitchen to make tea. Phoebe had left a chicken, already stuffed and roasted, in the meat safe, and a pudding she'd made herself. All Josie had to do was prepare the potatoes and the Brussels sprouts, and make the gravy and custard.

She thought about the Kavanaghs, and how different their day would be. Marigold, her husband, Jonathan, and their three children were coming to dinner, as well as Daisy and her friend, Eunice. Robert was travelling up from London. Ben was already home. Stanley would probably telephone from Germany – Freya, his wife, was expecting their first baby. She visualised the ritual exchange of presents after breakfast, and remembered Lily's present to her was in her room, but couldn't be bothered to go upstairs and open it.

The telephone rang. It was Hilary, wanting to wish her mother a merry Christmas. 'She's still in bed. I'll wake her.'

There was no answer when Josie knocked. She went in. Louisa was lying face down under the clothes. 'Hilary's on the phone. She wants to speak to you.'

Still no answer. With a feeling of alarm, Josie shook the still figure. 'Fuck off,' Louisa snarled without moving. 'Tell Hilary I'm spending the day in bed.'

'But it's Christmas Day, you can't.'

'I know full well what day it is, and I'll do anything I want. Tell my idiot daughter to go screw herself.'

'She's still a bit sleepy,' Josie told Hilary. 'Perhaps you could call later, this afternoon.' Her gloom deepened. She wasn't in the mood to cope with Louisa in one of her fouler moods. With a sigh, she returned to the room. 'What's the matter?'

'I told you to fuck off.' Louisa hadn't moved. All that could be seen was the top of her black hair under the clothes.

'I've no intention of, of doing what you say. Would you like a cup of coffee?'

'No! Why don't you go to your friends in Childwall? Have dinner there, pull your crackers, drink your sherry, open your presents. Have a lovely time.'

'I can't,' Josie said flatly. 'I'm not welcome there today.'

At last Louisa raised her head. Her old face was full of creases from the pillow. Her eyes looked suspiciously red, as if she'd been crying. 'Why not?'

'Because me old boyfriend's there – Ben. He's home from university, and they're worried I'll upset him.' Josie knew this trite piece of information would be of interest, and she was right. She didn't offer assistance as Louisa struggled to a sitting position, knowing it would be churlishly rejected.

'Is he the one you slept with?' she asked eagerly.

'I've never said I've slept with anyone, have I?'

'No, but you have. I can see it in your eyes. You're a woman, not a girl. Oh, please, Josie,' she implored, her dark eyes glowing, 'tell me about it. These days I live through other people. I'm starved of sex, starved of romance. I'm a parasite. I feed off other people to stay alive.'

'All right,' Josie said brusquely, 'but not until you're up, dressed and in the parlour with a cup of coffee.'

Louisa thought the episode with Griff desperately romantic. 'And he actually pretended to be homosexual!'

'No, he just gave the impression. After all, he's an actor.'

'I slept with a homo once. He was okay, I managed to teach

145

him a few things. Have you ever done it with a woman? Now, that's *really* interesting.'

'*No*. There are times, Louisa, when I suspect you only say things to shock.'

'My dear, I have never told you anything even faintly shocking.' She laughed coarsely. 'I was regarded as a nymphomaniac in my day. I could tell you things to make your blood run cold.' She glanced out of the window, and said in a voice full of envy and longing, 'I wonder where that liner's off to?'

Josie watched the large, brightly lit ship sailing past. She would have given anything to be on it herself, on her way to somewhere dead exciting, instead of pandering to a selfish, bad-tempered old woman on Christmas Day.

'I spent Christmas on a ship once.' Louisa sighed. 'We had a party that lasted three whole days. I slept with three stewards and the purser.'

'Is that all you ever thought of – sex?'

'Yes,' Louisa said flatly. 'I still do. It's the only thing that's ever mattered to me.'

'What about love?' Josie asked curiously. 'Didn't you ever fall for the men you had this never-ending sex with?'

'Occasionally, but love gets in the way. Love brings jealousy in its wake, and things quickly get nasty.' She groaned, and wrapped her arms around her sagging breasts, hugging herself. 'I still miss it, the sex. I *ache* for it. My body's grown old, but my mind hasn't. I'm still a young girl inside my head.'

Josie turned away, embarrassed. Once again, she thought about the Kavanaghs' bright, cheerful house. 'I'll go and peel the potatoes,' she said dully.

'Get some wine from the cellar,' Louisa called. 'Fetch two bottles. I think I shall get intoxicated today.'

'I was about to take a sleeping tablet this morning when you came in,' Louisa said over dinner. 'I thought of all the Christmases that had gone before, the gay times we had, the games we used to play, the flirtations, the silly presents we gave each other. I couldn't abide the thought of another Christmas in this house – so fucking *dull*. The best thing was to sleep through it. You know,' she said brightly, 'I once spent Christmas with Virginia Woolf.'

'Did you really?' Josie had never heard of Virginia Woolf. She wondered if Louisa ever had the faintest regard for anyone's feelings but her own. Had she not thought that taking a sleeping tablet would make her companion's day even more depressing than it already was?

Louisa was on her fourth glass of wine. Her cheeks were flushed. Josie collected the plates, took them to the kitchen and made custard for the pudding that was steaming on the stove. She took the bowls into the parlour, and said, 'If only I could drive, we could have gone to the Adelphi for dinner, or some posh hotel in Southport. We could even go shopping now and then.'

'I'm not prepared to be driven about like an invalid.' Louisa's cheeks flushed a deeper red.

'In that case, I'm handing in a month's notice.' She'd get an ordinary job, find a bedsit, even if she was only left with a few bob a week. 'Frankly, Louisa,' she said in a shaky voice, 'I'm bored out of me skull. You're not the only one who finds this house dull. As for Christmas, this is the worst I've ever known. It's so bloody miserable, I could *scream*.'

'Oh.' There was a long silence, broken by the shrill ring of the telephone. Marian this time, asking for her mother.

'Tell her Merry Christmas,' Louisa snapped. 'Say I'm too ill to talk.'

'That would be cruel. There's nothing wrong with you. She's just coming,' Josie said into the receiver. She watched Louisa make deliberately heavy weather of limping towards the hall.

That night, Louisa said shortly, 'I'll pay for you to take driving lessons. Whether I'll come out with you, we'll just have to see. If you're bored, take more time off. I like to hear about the dances and the films. And bring Lily round more. I

147

like her.' For the very first time since Josie had known her, there was the suggestion of a quiver in the harsh, gruff voice. 'You're my connection to life, Josie. I don't want you to leave.'

Josie felt uneasy at the end of December when she found her wages had gone up from ten pounds a month to fifteen. 'When I gave me notice in, I wasn't trying to blackmail you,' she said hesitantly. 'You don't have to do this.'

'Don't look a gift horse in the mouth,' Louisa snarled. 'And if I'd thought you were blackmailing me, you'd have been out the door like a shot.'

2

Josie passed her driving test just after her eighteenth birthday. The same night, with a mixture of pride and nervousness, she drove all the way to Childwall in the little black Austin Seven, as it was apparently called, to tell the Kavanaghs.

They were duly impressed. Lily decided to take driving lessons herself. 'I'll save up and buy meself a car. Something more modern than that. It looks like an antique.'

'I thought I'd get a bit of practice in. Louisa said I can use it whenever I like. And she's condescended to go shopping. I'm taking her to Southport on Friday.'

It took several hours to get Louisa ready to go shopping. Her clothes were in her old bedroom, and Josie's legs ached from running up and downstairs, fetching things for her to choose from – lovely, expensive outfits, silk-lined, hand-stitched, intricately embroidered – all terribly old-fashioned, but it didn't matter when they were going shopping and she could buy more up-to-date things. There was a search upstairs for stockings, a suspender belt, underwear, jewellery. 'There's a three-strand pearl necklace and earrings in the little dressing-table drawer,' Louisa called. 'And don't forget face powder and lipstick. And scent. Oh, and shoes.'

'You look dead beautiful,' Josie said admiringly when Louisa emerged from her room – she'd insisted on dressing herself. She wore a navy blue silk suit patterned with large white orchids, white court shoes and a white toque. Despite her age and her infirmities, she looked extremely smart. She must have been outstanding in her day.

'Don't patronise me. I look ghastly. These shoes are too big, and I need a safety pin in the skirt. I tried, but I can't fasten it.' She frowned peevishly; she loathed asking for help.

Phoebe, who was also taking part in the exercise, fastened the pin. She and Josie trailed behind, making faces at each other as Louisa made her own slow, determined way out of the back door into the balmy sunshine of a late May day. They watched, longing to offer a hand, as she struggled into the passenger seat of the small black car. Phoebe picked up her shoes when they fell off.

'I don't envy you today, Josie,' she whispered.

Josie drove cautiously, never exceeding twenty miles an hour, all the way to Southport, ignoring the queue of impatient traffic that gathered behind. She managed to park in Lord Street, a wide, elegant thoroughfare with a tree-lined central reservation, full of exclusive and outrageously expensive shops. Louisa, who had been very quiet during the journey, deigned to take her hand when she alighted from the car.

She stood on the pavement, supported by her stick, and took several deep breaths, her dark, brilliant eyes raking the shop fronts, the pedestrians, the passing traffic. 'Why haven't I done this before?' she said in a dazed voice. 'So near, yet so far. I should have come years ago. Suddenly, the world feels so much bigger. We must go to dinner one night. And the movies, the theatre.' She put her arm in Josie's, crying, 'How pleased I am you came to work for me. Come, my dear, we'll do some shopping.'

Over the next few hours, Louisa went quite mad with her cheque-book. She bought a striking scarlet dressing-gown and slippers to match, two glamorous nighties, a yellow linen costume, an amber pendant on a fine, gold chain, two pairs of narrow-fitting shoes – she put on a pair straight away – a straw picture hat, kid gloves, a lizard handbag and two colourful scarves.

'There's stacks of gloves and scarves upstairs,' Josie protested, 'and at least a dozen handbags.'

'Oh, yes, but these are *new*,' Louisa said with childish glee, 'and a woman can't have too many handbags. Oh, isn't this— what is it you say in Liverpool? Isn't this the *gear*?'

'Don't overtax yourself, Louisa.'

'And don't you nag. I feel like Sleeping Beauty, just awoken from a very long sleep.' She chuckled. 'Except with me the years have taken their toll. By the way, this is for you.' She pushed the box with the amber pendant into Josie's hand.

Josie tried to push it back. 'I didn't expect a present.' But Louisa was implacable. 'I bought it with you in mind. You said how pretty it was. I wouldn't be seen dead in such an anaemic piece of jewellery.'

'Ta, Louisa. But you mustn't do this sort of thing again.'

'I shall do whatever I like with my money, dear,' Louisa said loftily.

They paused for coffee in a charming, glass-roofed arcade of tiny shops. Halfway through a cheese scone, Louisa said, 'There was a quaint little bookshop around here where I used to order books from the States. I flirted quite madly with the owner, Mr Bernstein, but he probably retired years ago. I wonder if the shop's still in business? I'd like to order that book they're making such a fuss about back home, *Catcher in the Rye*.'

The shop was three blocks away, according to the waitress, too far for Louisa to walk. They returned to the car, stowed the shopping in the boot and Josie drove the three blocks.

There was no need to order *Catcher in the Rye*. The attractive young man behind the counter of the long, narrow shop said it had been published in this country, and they had several copies in stock. Louisa was writing a cheque when an astonished voice cried, 'Miss Chalcott! Miss Louisa Chalcott?'

A small, extremely elderly man was coming towards them, arms clasped dramatically across his chest. The lack of hair on his pink head was made up for by a lustrous silver beard.

'Mr Bernstein!' Louisa said emotionally. 'Why, how lovely to see you.'

Mr Bernstein snapped his fingers. 'Ronald, fetch a chair for Miss Chalcott.' He beamed. 'This beautiful lady is a famous poet. Sit down, sit down, Miss Chalcott. Would you like a sherry?'

Josie might as well not have existed during the fulsome and mutually flattering conversation that ensued. She retreated to the counter, where Ronald whispered, 'Who's Louisa Chalcott? I've never heard of her.'

His favourite authors were Dashiell Hammett and Raymond Chandler. 'I was put off poetry at school,' he confessed. 'I never want to hear "The Boy Stood on the Burning Deck" again.'

Josie said she felt the same about Wordsworth's 'The Daffodils', and she liked Agatha Christie and Dorothy L. Sayers. She told him she'd tried to read Louisa's poems once, but couldn't make head nor tail of them.

The conversation turned to pictures. Ronald's favourite films were thrillers, too, and Josie said that she also liked them best. 'When I was young, I had a crush on Humphrey Bogart.'

'You're not exactly old now.' Ronald had a quirky smile and lovely dark green eyes. Josie, who hadn't met a man she considered even remotely attractive since she'd said goodbye to Griff, regarded him with interest. He leaned on the counter. '*Key Largo*'s on across the road, starring your old hearthrob. Perhaps I could take you tomorrow night? I could pick you up,' he added nonchalantly. 'I've got a car.'

'So've I,' Josie said, equally nonchalantly. 'The thing is, I'm seeing me friend tomorrow, but I'm free Monday.'

'That would be even better. *Key Largo* will have finished, but they're showing the latest Hitchcock film, *Strangers on a Train*. We could meet outside at seven o'clock. If it's too early, we'll go for a coffee.'

Across the shop, Mr Bernstein was presenting Louisa with a copy of Robert Frost's *Complete Poems*. 'A little gift, dear lady. Hot off the press. It only came in this morning.'

'I always thought Robert Frost a trifle overrated, but thank you very much, Mr Bernstein. Now, don't forget, I'm expecting you on Wednesday on the dot of half past seven. We shall have a lovely little talk about literature.'

'I am already looking forward to it, Miss Chalcott.' With a flamboyant gesture, Mr Bernstein kissed her hand.

'I think that was a most satisfactory shopping expedition,' Louisa said on the way home. 'Fancy Mr Bernstein recognising me after all this time! He's become a widower since we last met. I think I might seduce him. Wives never stopped me in the past, but I think one might have stopped Mr Bernstein.'

'Oh, Louisa!'

'Take no notice of me, dear. I can dream, can't I? Now, where shall we go tomorrow in the car?'

It was summer. Josie woke up to the warm sun shining through her window, the squawk of the gulls, the tide lapping on the beach. She would leap out of bed and walk down to the water in her bare feet, glad to be alive on such a lovely day, thinking how incredibly lucky she was compared to Lily and all the other people who worked in boring, stuffy offices and factories. Being Louisa's companion no longer felt like a job. She felt slightly guilty when she took her wages.

Back in the house, she would make two cups of coffee and drink hers with Louisa, sitting cross-legged at the foot of the bed, and they would look through last night's *Echo* to see what pictures were on, or discuss a play they'd just seen, which reminded Louisa of an affair she'd once had, or several affairs.

She saw Ronald twice a week. He was a perfect boyfriend. They had plenty to talk about, and he seemed quite satisfied with a few enjoyable and passionate kisses at the end of the evening. Lily was green with envy. 'How do you do it, Jose? I only go out with a bloke once, and he never wants to see me again.' Lily had given up all hope of getting married, and was prepared for a life on the shelf.

It would have been easy to feel smug about how fortunately things had turned out, but Josie had already experienced how quickly life could change. When Lily casually announced that she and her mother were going to Germany to stay with Stanley, Freya and the new baby, Josie, who'd been expecting to go on holiday with her friend, found herself with nowhere to go and no one to go with. Once again she felt conscious of her solitariness. She would just have to spend the time at Barefoot House, carry on as normal. When Marian and Hilary came in September for their annual holiday, she would take a few days off.

It was difficult to believe that the twins, with their plain looks and severe clothes, were the daughters of passionate, extrovert Louisa. They appeared slightly aggrieved that their mother looked so well, had put on weight and was obviously much happier than when they'd visited a year ago. As if to prove she'd been right in her choice of companion, Louisa exaggerated the visits to the theatre and the cinema and the shopping trips, making it seem as if they led the life of Reilly and went out every day.

The two women did their utmost to sideline Josie. They made Louisa's meals, took in her morning coffee, fussed over her in a way Josie knew she'd hate. Phoebe said it was always the same. 'They call the doctor if she so much as sneezes, and keep telling her how ill she is, how old, reminding her she's an invalid. Oh, I won't half be glad when the pair of them have gone.'

It would have been nice to have gone away, be out of it for a whole fortnight, but all Josie could do was take time off. She went into town nearly every day and met Lily in the dinner hour.

One day Lily emerged from her office looking unusually grave. She grabbed Josie's arm. 'Ma telephoned this morning,

Jose. She tried to call you, but you'd already gone. She ses to tell you that Vince Adams died yesterday of a heart attack.'

The news left Josie cold. 'I wonder if I should write to Auntie Ivy?'

'I wouldn't if I were you.'

'I'll think about it. Where shall we go for dinner? I'm starving.'

'Let's try that new place in Whitechapel. They take luncheon vouchers. Are you all right, Jose? You look a bit peculiar.'

'I'm fine.' But she wasn't fine. For some reason, when they reached the restaurant, she no longer felt hungry. Her head was full of thoughts that didn't make sense. Vincent Adams had been her *father*. It was her *father* who had died the day before. If it hadn't been for Vince, she wouldn't have been born. How could your father die and leave you feeling cold and completely unmoved? Her life had been so strange, so different to everyone else's, that she had no warm feelings for the man responsible for bringing her into the world.

She said goodbye to Lily, but didn't walk back with her to Victoria Street as she usually did. Instead, she set off in the opposite direction. All of a sudden, she felt a strong desire to see Huskisson Street, take a look at the house in which she'd lived with Mam. She hadn't seen it since the night of the bomb. Their final conversation came back as clearly as if it had taken place only yesterday.

Why, the sun's come out, Petal, Mam had cried joyfully during their last minutes in the attic room. *It looks dead lovely out there . . . I wouldn't mind a little walk.*

If only they'd gone to Princes Park as Mam had suggested!

Yes, but . . . Josie had said.

Yes, but what, my fragrant, my adorable little Petal? Mam had leapt off the chair, danced across the room, caught Josie in her arms. They had waltzed around the bed.

Josie bit her lip. 'Oh, Mam,' she breathed.

She had walked so fast that she reached Huskisson Street sooner than expected. The house had been done up. The window-frames had been painted and the front door, which was open, was bottle green.

Dare she go in? Could it possibly be that Maude, or any of the other girls, still lived there? Just now, if there was one thing she'd like to do more than any other, it was to talk to Maude, tell her about Uncle Vince.

She climbed the steps into the wide hall, which had pale cream walls and a biscuit-coloured carpet. 'Can I help you?' a woman's voice demanded sharply.

The voice came from a window in the wall, the wall of Irish Rose's room. A woman had slid back the glass and was regarding Josie balefully.

'I'm sorry to bother you, but I was wondering, who lives here now.'

'No one. It's a solicitors'. It should be obvious from the plate on the door.'

'What's upstairs?' Josie glanced at the carpeted staircase.

'Rooms. Now, if you don't mind, I'd like to get on.' The window was snapped shut.

'Thank you,' Josie said to no one at all.

If you sat on the window-seat facing westwards – at least, she'd worked out it was westwards, but she could be wrong – you could see the lights of Birkenhead and Wallasey gradually being switched on.

Josie had no idea how long she'd been there, but at first it had been daylight and the shore had been crowded. Then people had begun to pick up their blankets, their sunshades, their toys and go home. Now the sands were empty and it was dark, and the lights across the Mersey twinkled brightly in the distance.

She had been reliving her childhood, every single scene, something which she had never done before. She felt immeasurably sad for all the things she had missed: going on holiday with her mother, for instance, like Lily; telling Mam about her boyfriends. What would Mam think of Ronald? Of Griff? Would she have thought it a bad idea to have married

Ben? Josie remembered that she hadn't liked Tommy. She'd thought her daughter too good for him, that she deserved something better.

Apart from the creaks and groans of the old house, and the rustle of the tide, everywhere was quiet. Marian and Hilary kept very early hours. She vaguely remembered hearing them come upstairs a while ago. Louisa, so different from her daughters, usually stayed up till all hours, scribbling away in the red notebook, or they would talk – Josie hated going to bed early. On top of the usual sounds, she became aware of a faint shuffling and a tapping noise.

Rats, Josie thought, but she didn't care if the house was invaded by rats. The twins could get rid of them. She thought about making herself a cup of tea. Louisa, if she was awake, might like some coffee.

In a minute, she told herself.

The tapping and shuffling was getting closer. She was feeling a touch alarmed when the door opened and Louisa came puffing in.

'Why are you sitting in the dark?' She switched on the light. She was wearing her red dressing-gown and slippers and looked pleased with herself. 'Those stairs! That's the first time I've climbed them in ten years. What an achievement. Oh, but if I don't sit down soon, I'll collapse.' She shuffled over to the bed and eased herself down with an exaggerated sigh of relief.

Josie didn't move. 'I thought you were a rat,' she said.

'Oh, I am, I am,' Louisa panted. 'It's an insult usually reserved for men. People seem to forget there are female rats. I wonder why that is? And why are only women described as kittenish?'

'I've no idea. You can explore the contradiction in your next poem.'

Louisa clapped her hands delightedly. 'Josie! How glad I am to see you. You treat me like a normal human being. I'm sick of those silly girls fussing round. I'm openly crossing off the days before they go home on my calendar, but they refuse to take the hint. Now.' She looked at Josie sternly. 'I heard you come in. It was half past four. There's been dead silence ever since. What's wrong, dear? Is it something to do with that phone call? Phoebe said someone rang after you'd gone.'

It was no use beating about the bush with Louisa. 'It was Mrs Kavanagh, Lily's mam, to say me father died yesterday.'

'Oh, my dear! But . . .' the heavy brows puckered '. . . I could have sworn you told me your father was already dead.'

'I did. I told everyone he was dead. Mrs Kavanagh is the only one who knows the truth.' Josie swung her legs off the window-seat and rested her head in her hands. 'It's funny, but it's only today, now that he's dead, that I've thought about him as me father. He was also me Uncle Vince, you see, Auntie Ivy's husband. I told you a bit about them, too. Me father and me uncle were the same person.'

'How extraordinarily interesting,' Louisa remarked. She lit a cigarette. 'Tell me more. For instance, was your mother a willing accomplice in the deceit?'

Josie smiled. It was just the sort of reply she would have expected from Louisa who, unlike most people, would never come out with expressions of sympathy and shock. 'No, he forced himself on her. He tried to do the same with me, but I kicked him in the stomach.'

'Good for you. You should have aimed for the balls, much more painful.' She flicked ash on the floor. 'So, why are you mooning around because this despicable individual has died? I would have thought it a cause for celebration.'

'Oh, I dunno.' Josie turned to stare at the lights across the water. Louisa was reflected in the window, watching her with interest. 'It just feels unnatural not to *care* that your father's dead. I feel as if I'm missing out on something.'

'I can never understand why we are automatically expected to love our relatives,' Louisa said irritably. 'I respected my father, but I never loved him. I felt sad when he died, that's all. Mom, now, I miss her still.' Her face creased tenderly. 'She was my best friend. I was an only child, so I have no idea how I would have felt about siblings. As for my children, I expected to love them – I *wanted* to love them – but when they were born they were such an ugly little pair I asked the nurse to take them away.' She smiled ruefully as she attempted to get off the bed. 'I've rather missed being a doting mother. Come, let's go downstairs and you can make us some coffee. We can continue this conversation there.'

Eighteen months later Louisa suffered another stroke, only a mild one but she had to stay in bed for weeks. She was a fearsome patient, browbeating mercilessly the private nurse, Miss Viney, who came to see her twice a day – the only person she would allow to give her the bedpan. At other times Josie was ordered from the room, while she dragged herself to the commode, which only Miss Viney was allowed to empty.

Mr Bernstein and Lily were forbidden to visit. On Saturdays Phoebe and her husband, Alf, spent the day at Barefoot House, so Josie could have time off, to go dancing or to the pictures with Lily. The rest of the time she stayed in because Louisa couldn't be left on her own.

'I'll be all right,' Louisa growled awkwardly, the stroke having slightly impaired her speech. 'Ask that stupid nurse in.'

'I'll do no such thing. The poor woman's terrified of you. I don't want to add to her misery. Do you feel better now that you've got the telephone next to the bed?' Josie had arranged for the telephone company to move it.

'As long as you continue to answer it. I don't want to be stuck with one of my girls. But it's nice talking to Mr Bernstein or Thumbelina. Did I tell you she's just married husband number seven? He collects oil wells the way some people collect stamps.'

For something to do, Josie attacked the front garden. She dug up the dead bushes and the dried yellow grass, and broke down the crusty, clay-like soil. Alf removed the trees, sawed the dead wood into logs and stacked them in the garage.

'They should keep the fire going a treat,' he said. He was a tall, robust man with the strength of an ox. 'See you through the winter, that lot.'

Josie knew nothing about gardens. She'd assumed everything had to be grown from seed, and was thrilled to discover you could buy plants partially grown, and a ready-made lawn in the form of turfs, from a place called a nursery. Alf said there was one of these magic places not far away.

She spent her twentieth birthday pushing and pulling the rusty garden roller she'd found in the garage over the hard earth to make it smooth enough for a lawn, nearly dislocating her arms in the process. As soon as it was done, she drove to the nursery, bought dozens of hardy plants which she put in the car, and ordered turfs and a wooden bench for Louisa to sit on when the garden was finished, to be delivered next day.

That afternoon she planted the border, putting a handful of bonemeal in the hole with each plant as the woman in the nursery had suggested. The day was hot and the sun burned down on her back, so she was exhausted by the time she finished. Despite this, she was outside early next morning, impatiently waiting for the lorry to arrive, and had already begun to lay the turfs before the driver had finished unloading. At eight o'clock that night, Barefoot House could boast a neatly laid lawn, surrounded by a border of bushes and tiny flower plants. There was a bench beneath the window of Louisa's room. Josie went inside to tell her the garden was finished. 'You can come and look now.'

'Do you think I haven't looked already? You've been bobbing up and down outside my window for weeks.' Louisa had only been allowed out of bed a few days and was in a dreadful temper. She longed to go shopping or to the pictures, but was too weak to walk more than a few yards. She flatly refused to go merely for a drive. 'It would be too fucking boring.'

Josie took her arm, noticing how thin it was again, and how bent her back had become, and how slowly she shuffled from the house, barely able to lift her feet between each step. She led her to the bench and helped her sit. 'What am I supposed to do now?' Louisa asked acidly. Her tongue was as sharp as ever.

'Look at the view, smell the fresh air, enjoy the atmosphere. It's a beautiful evening, Louisa.' Josie sniffed appreciatively. Apart from two boys some distance away, playing football, the beach was deserted. The tide was receding in a ruff of creamy-white froth, and the gleaming ribbon of wet sand left in its wake was getting wider and wider. Gulls rode the waves as lightly as bubbles.

'Would you like a coffee?'

'No, thank you. I'd like my cigarettes, though.'

'I thought it would be nice for you to sit here early in the morning,' Josie said when she returned. 'Or late at night, when it's dark, round September, like. If I put the bench by the other window, you can see the lights across the water.'

'Is that all you've got to think about?' Louisa said in a cold voice. 'Where I am to sit come September?' She lit a cigarette. 'At your age, you should be concentrating on young men, clothes, movies, having a good time. I thought of little else when I was sixty, let alone twenty. As for gardening, it was furthest from my mind, along with similar stultifyingly boring pursuits.'

'I thought you'd be pleased.'

Louisa gave her a contemptuous look. 'Oh, I am. And Marian and Hilary will be delighted. You've increased the value of the house no end. What shall you do next to get rid of your excess energy? Paint the windows, the door, decorate inside? Everywhere could do with a lick of paint, and we can both sit and watch it dry. Where's Ronald?' she asked unexpectedly, and peered around the garden, as if expecting Ronald to pop up from behind a newly planted bush.

'I gave him up.'

'Why?'

Josie squirmed. 'We didn't get on.'

'Liar! You gave him up shortly after I had my stroke. You told him you couldn't see him again because of me. He was heartbroken, according to Mr Bernstein. He had hoped one day you would get married.'

'I would never have married Ronald,' Josie said truthfully. 'Why are you getting so ratty, anyroad? I'd have thought you'd be pleased about that, too.'

'Your loyalty and devotion do you credit, Josie, but they are entirely misplaced. I am not worth it.' She stared at the river. 'You know, I can hardly see.'

'You should wear—'

'I know,' Louisa interrupted testily. 'I should wear my long-distance glasses. Or is it the short-distance ones? I can never remember. Any minute now, I'll need a hearing-aid, too. I'm finding it increasingly difficult to hear. I'm breaking down, Josie. I can scarcely walk. I hardly sleep. The only thing that works perfectly is my brain.'

'Louisa,' Josie said gently.

'Oh, take your sympathy, girl, and stuff it where the monkey stuffed its nuts,' Louisa said so nastily that Josie flushed. 'Fetch me my lizard handbag. It's on the floor beside the bed.'

The large handbag having been brought, Louisa rooted inside and took out a large brown envelope and two small white ones. She handed Josie a white one. 'I had intended giving you that on your twenty-first birthday, but circumstances have changed.'

It was a letter, addressed to her, written in Louisa's hardly discernible scrawl. Josie read it with difficulty. Her jaw dropped when she understood the message it contained. 'You're giving me a month's notice!' she said, completely taken aback.

'Got it in one,' Louisa chuckled. She handed Josie the other white envelope. 'Now read this.'

At first the typed enclosure, full of meaningless figures, was equally difficult to make sense of. 'It's a plane ticket to America,' Josie said after a while. 'To New York. Louisa, what on earth is this all about?'

Louisa was staring at the river again. Now it was almost

dark, the boys had gone and the water shone a greeny-silver. The moon had appeared, not quite full, and there was a sprinkling of early stars. Except for the rustling tide, the silence was total. 'When I first came to live here, we used to go skinny-dipping in the moonlight. Do you know what that means?'

'I can guess, but, Louisa, this ticket. And why do I have to leave?' Her voice trembled.

'I've always been a very selfish person,' Louisa continued as if Josie hadn't spoken. 'I've used people all my life, men in particular, women if I felt in the mood. I dropped them the minute they'd served their purpose, satisfied my need.' She shifted irritably on the bench. 'I shall need a cushion for this. Not now, dear. Some other time will do,' she said when Josie made to get up. 'I shall only have you one more month, so sit down and hold my hand.' Josie did, and the skin on the hand felt soft and shiny, like old silk.

'I should never have taken you on,' Louisa sighed. 'The girls were right, but for all the wrong reasons. They thought you couldn't cope. I knew you could, but that's not why I insisted. I wanted you for your bright face, your fresh blood, your young soul. I hoped they might rub off on me.' She smiled ruefully. 'I'm like a fucking vampire. I should have let the girls show you the door. You would have eventually found something better to do than dance round after an egotistical old woman for three years. No, don't argue.' She wagged a gnarled finger.

'For the first time in my life, I am making a sacrifice, so consider yourself lucky because I don't want you to leave. I want you to stay so much it hurts.' Josie felt the frail hand tighten on her own. 'But leave you must,' Louisa said firmly. 'It's time you started to live, my dear. I've had you far too long. As for me, I'm dying.' She laughed a touch bitterly. 'But I'm a stubborn bitch. I shall put up a fight. I could last for years, getting blinder, deafer, more and more impossible and ill-humoured with each day. There is no way, Josie, that I will allow you to sacrifice yet more years of your young life to watch me die.'

'But I want to stay, Louisa,' Josie wailed, and was rewarded with a look of utter contempt.

'Well, you can't,' Louisa snapped. 'You have just been given your marching orders, and I want you out of this house by the end of June. The plane ticket is a leaving present. You can get a refund if you want, use it as a deposit on a flat. Otherwise, Thumbelina is off on a belated honeymoon early in July, and you can stay in her grand house in New York. You won't be alone, the staff will be there.' She chuckled. 'I promised her you're not the sort who'll take off with the silver. There is a heap of American currency somewhere upstairs. I always thought I'd go back one day, but that's not likely now.' She removed her hand. 'I would appreciate a cup of coffee, dear, though inside, I think. It's getting chilly out here.'

As she helped Louisa to her feet, Josie felt a flood of gratitude mixed with sadness and something else, possibly love, for the impossible, cantankerous, surprisingly kind old woman. 'But who'll look after you?'

'That, dear girl, is no longer any of your business,' Louisa said brusquely, and refused to discuss the matter further.

'What's this?' Josie picked up the large brown envelope, surprisingly sealed with red wax.

'Nothing much, just a few notes I've made.' Louisa looked at her enigmatically. 'You're not to open it until nineteen seventy-four.'

'Why then?' Josie asked, surprised.

'It will be obvious at the time.' She grasped the window-sill and began to make her way inside. 'Do you know, my dear, I can already smell the flowers in my new garden.'

'There aren't any yet, just leaves. They need a good watering. I'll do it in a minute.' The plants looked rather sad, she thought, as if they realised she would soon be going.

'Then I can smell the leaves.' Louisa squeezed her hand.

163

'I'll come and see you the minute I get back,' Josie promised as they went into the house.

'You will do no such thing,' Louisa barked. 'I don't want to see or hear from you in a long while. If you must know, it would upset me. Perhaps this time next year.' She laughed gaily. 'Yes, this time next year. Come and see how your garden grows, Josie dear.'

3

'Oh, Jose. I won't half miss you,' Lily said sadly. 'I wish I could come with you, but they'd never let me off work a whole month. Anyroad, I couldn't afford the fare.'

'I wish you could come, too, Lil. Still, I'll only be gone a month, and you've made new friends over the last few years. You had to, didn't you? You haven't seen much of me.'

'Yes, but you're me *best* friend, Jose.' They were sitting together on Lily's bed in the house in Childwall. Josie was spending two days with the Kavanaghs before flying to New York, having left Barefoot House for ever.

Louisa hadn't even turned round when she went to say goodbye. She was in her rocking chair facing the window, and said gruffly, 'Bye, dear. Have a nice time.' Josie wanted to fling her arms around her, have a good cry, but Louisa waved a dismissive arm, which Josie took as a sign she didn't want an emotional farewell. Closing the door quietly behind her, she cried on the train instead. The new companion, a retired headmistress, seemed very nice, very firm. Louisa would be safe with her, but she didn't doubt the poor woman would be reduced to a nervous wreck in no time.

Mixed with the sorrow was a feeling of relief, a sense of freedom, the awareness that Louisa had been right to let her go. Somewhere, buried deep within her mind, there'd been a dread of remaining in Barefoot House for years while she watched Louisa die.

Tomorrow, she would leave Lime Street station for

London, where she would stay the night – she'd booked into a little hotel right by Euston – then make her way to Heathrow early next morning to catch the plane to New York. Thumbelina was picking her up from Idelwild airport. Josie had a passport with a horrible photo inside that made her look like a criminal, and over three hundred yellowing American dollars that had been found in an old handbag in Louisa's wardrobe upstairs. Since Louisa's second stroke, there hadn't been much opportunity for Josie to indulge her weakness for new clothes, and she'd managed to save up over fifty pounds. This she was keeping for when she came back from America. She'd have to start again then, find somewhere to live, another job.

A new beginning! It made her feel almost as excited as the holiday.

That afternoon, Marigold and her family were coming for a farewell tea, as well as Daisy and Eunice. Daisy had telephoned earlier with a message from Aunt Ivy. 'I told her about your trip to America. She'd love to see you, Jose.'

Mrs Kavanagh shook her head when asked for her advice. 'I don't think it's such a good idea, luv,' she said. 'That part of your life is well behind you. Don't rake it up.'

'I promised meself I'd never go back to Machin Street again,' Josie said, relieved. Mrs Kavanagh had promised to look after Louisa's brown envelope and Mam's Holy Communion veil and prayer book, because it seemed silly to take them all the way to America.

The front door opened, and a man's deep voice shouted, 'It's only us, Ma. I've been showing Imelda the fairy glen.'

Lily made a face. 'I wonder what she thought of *that?*'

Imelda was Ben's fiancée, who'd come for the weekend to meet her prospective in-laws for the first time. They were getting married at Christmas because Imelda had always wanted a winter wedding. She and Ben had just left Cambridge, Imelda with a first class (hons) degree in English, and Ben with the same in physics. He was due in Portsmouth in a few weeks' time to start his national service in the Navy, and would be made an officer straight away because of his degree.

The Kavanaghs had been expecting to meet a studious-looking girl with glasses, a blue-stocking. Instead, Imelda was dainty, with delicate white skin and china blue eyes. Her hair was black, shiny and very straight, and she wore it parted in the middle and tucked behind her ears, which really did resemble two little pink shells.

It went without saying that Lily couldn't stand her soon-to-be sister-in-law, who was everything Lily wanted herself to be; thin, with manageable hair and make-up that seemed willing to stay on for ever. 'And she's all over our Ben. She keeps kissing him in front of everyone. I'm sure he's dead embarrassed.'

'He doesn't seem embarrassed to me.' Last night, when Josie had first arrived, also expecting to meet someone plain, possibly with plaits and flat, lace-up shoes – how else would you expect a woman with a degree to look? – she had felt a totally unreasonable stab of jealousy when she saw an exquisite creature wearing strappy, high-heeled sandals and a stiff petticoat under her white sundress, making her look like a fairy off the top of a Christmas tree. Ben didn't seem to mind at all when she snuggled close, tucking his arm in hers as they sat together on the settee and occasionally nuzzling his ear.

'Hello, Josie.' Ben had leapt to his feet when she went in. 'It's good to see you.' He had kissed her cheek, in the friendly way you'd kiss a cousin or an aunt.

'You've changed. Oh, you've got a moustache!' She had to stop herself from reaching up and touching the pale hairs on his upper lip.

'Imelda persuaded me to grow it.'

'But he won't grow a beard,' Imelda pouted.

Ben grinned. 'One day.'

Why did I go to Haylands? Josie wondered wildly. Why did I give him up? The moustache made him look dashing and sophisticated – and older, more like twenty-five than twenty-two. He wore khaki cotton trousers and a white shirt

166

with the sleeves rolled up, revealing tanned, surprisingly muscular arms. The mere fact that someone like Imelda found him attractive only increased his appeal in Josie's eyes.

It could have been *me* marrying him at Christmas!

She was relieved when Ben took Imelda out that night to see a play at the Royal Court, because she was worried he would guess how unsettled she felt, full of doubts and uncertainties. Had she made a terrible mistake?

During the night, as she tossed and turned in the uncomfortable camp bed in Lily's room – naturally, Imelda had been given the spare – she could have sworn she heard someone on the landing. Ben creeping into Imelda's room, or perhaps it was the other way around.

I'm being stupid, she told herself. If Imelda had been as ugly as sin, I wouldn't have felt like this – at least, I don't think so. Anyroad, if Imelda didn't exist, and Ben asked again if I would marry him, he'd be dead set against me going to New York, and we'd be right back where we started. I'd have to tell him, no.

Phew! Josie snuggled her face in the pillow and fell asleep.

New York
1954–1955

I

She fell in love with him at first sight, something she hadn't thought possible, not in real life. It was her last night in New York. In Thumbelina's magnificent house, her case was packed, and Matthew had been alerted to drive her to the airport in time to catch the ten o'clock flight to Heathrow. She had bought him and Estelle a little present each for looking after her so well. She was sorry to be leaving New York, yet looked forward to going home.

Then she met Jack Coltrane and everything changed.

Four weeks previously, just as the sun was setting, Thumbelina, tiny, dazzling, seventy-five years old but looking more like fifty, with improbable golden hair and five-inch heels, had picked Josie up from the airport in a chauffeur-driven car. Josie was introduced to the chauffeur, Matthew, a handsome, grizzled black man, then to Henry Stafford Nightingale the third, known as Chuckles, who was in the back, a mild, tubby man with a bright red face who reminded Josie of a robin. They were leaving early next morning on a round-the-world cruise, Thumbelina explained, a belated honeymoon. 'Aren't we, hon?' She gazed adoringly at her new husband, who gazed adoringly back but didn't speak.

Josie felt shaken after a bumpy flight. Her legs were like jelly, and she had never felt so hot before. She tried to concentrate while she was bombarded with questions about

Louisa, about herself and about Liverpool, which Thumbelina knew well, having stayed many times many years ago at Barefoot House. It was difficult to answer when her brain was still halfway across the Atlantic, and had yet to catch up with her body.

They were driving through an area called Queens, she was told, which had a look of Liverpool about it, but then the car crossed a bridge over a shimmering green river, reaching the other side through a vast arch flanked by colonnades, and Thumbelina said, 'We're on the island of Manhattan, hon. This is Chinatown.'

All Josie's tiredness, her feeling of disorientation, vanished in a flash, and she blinked in disbelief at the brilliantly lit shops, the pagoda-topped telephone boxes, restaurants with the names written in Chinese, tiny cramped arcades hung with banners and bunting. All the shops were open, although it was late, and the pavements were packed. Some people wore genuine Chinese clothes, long, gaudy silk robes with frogging and embroidery.

'Oh!' she murmured, and Chuckles glanced at her awe-struck face, smiled and opened the window of the air-conditioned car to allow in hot, spicy smells, mixed with wafts of musky perfume, as well as gentle tinkly music that sounded slightly off key, and the buzz of a hundred voices speaking a hundred different tongues. Or so thought an open-mouthed Josie as she listened to the strange sounds and breathed in the strange smells. The world seemed to have got lighter and brighter, noisier, busier, more colourful, larger than life. She was captivated instantly. New York was undoubtedly the most fascinating, the most exciting city in the world.

Louisa had said the Upper East Side was the poshest place to live in Manhattan. The house in which Josie stayed for the next four weeks was palatial – a double-fronted brownstone off Fifth Avenue, solidly built, with a row of pillars supporting a balcony that ran the width of the front. Josie was impressed, but wouldn't have wanted to live there permanently. It was more like a museum than a place to live. Even the house in

Huskisson Street in its glory days couldn't have looked so grand. 'I'm not exaggerating, Lil,' she wrote in the first letter to her friend, 'but you could live in one of the wardrobes. They're *huge*. Downstairs, the floors are marble-tiled, but the carpets upstairs are so thick my feet almost disappear. You should see my room, it's a parlour as well as a bedroom.'

Her room was about forty feet square, with an oyster silk three-piece, a four-poster bed with matching drapes, a red carpet and lots of heavy black furniture decorated with gold.

When Matthew's wife, Estelle, the matronly housekeeper, took her upstairs on the first day, insisting on carrying her case – which made Josie feel uncomfortable because she was so much older – she did a little jig when the door closed, because she had rarely felt so happy. She began to unpack her case. 'If only you could see me now, Mam,' she crowed.

Dinner was served in a room that reminded Josie of Liverpool Town Hall, where she'd once gone with Lily to hear Mr Kavanagh make a speech. After a five-course meal that was more like a banquet, Thumbelina and Chuckles, who were leaving early in the morning, bade her goodnight and goodbye. She kissed them both, and wished them a lovely holiday, and they kissed her and wished her the same. Thumbelina said she must come back one day and they'd show her a real good time. Josie felt as if she'd known them for years. She went to bed immediately and slept like a log for twelve hours.

'I looked in earlier,' Estelle said next morning when she brought in a cup of coffee, 'but you were sleeping as soundly as the sweet Baby Jesus, so I decided not to wake you. It's ten o'clock. Now, honey, do you want breakfast in that mausoleum of a dining room or in the kitchen? Me and Matthew have already eaten, but we'll share a cup of coffee with you.'

'The kitchen, please,' Josie said promptly. While she ate scrambled eggs, followed by delicious pancakes with maple syrup, Matthew explained where to find the nearest bus stop and subway station.

'You're welcome to eat with us whenever you want,

honey,' Estelle said, 'but if you decide to eat out, you'll find delis and diners are the cheapest. Oh, and Macy's is the place for clothes. It's the biggest department store in the world,' she finished proudly.

Matthew gave her the key to the door and said she was to come and go as she pleased. Josie went upstairs to collect her handbag and guide book, give her hair a final brush and renew her lipstick, before setting off to explore the glorious wonders of New York.

Time flashed by. Days merged, became weeks. She went up the Statue of Liberty and the Empire State Building, sampled the gaudy, clanking delights of Coney Island, wandered along Fifth Avenue. She gaped at the prices of the clothes in the windows of the opulent shops, nipped into Bloomingdale's, sprayed herself with Chanel No 5, then nipped out again, which Estelle had done when she first came to New York. She went to Mass in St Patrick's Cathedral, to Chinatown and Little Italy, the garment district, and so many museums she forgot which was which. She stood in the sharp, black shadows and gazed up in awe at the towering skyscrapers – it was like being in the middle of a giant pincushion – gorged on hamburgers, bagels, pancakes, pizzas and exotic ice creams, discovered a penchant for peanut butter and a passion for Coca-Cola with ice, not just because the weather was so hot.

And it *was* hot, as if a furious fire raged beneath the streets of this unique, fantastic city, and the heat could be felt through the thin soles of her sandals. Her feet hurt, her legs hurt, her head hurt from the noise, the crowds, the stifling atmosphere.

But Josie loved every minute. She rode buses and the sweltering subway, and sat on the grass in Central Park where she saw *As You Like It* and *The Merchant of Venice* for nothing. She spent far too long in Macy's, where there were four floors of mouth-watering women's clothes, and bought two sunfrocks and a lovely linen jacket.

The place she liked best of all was Greenwich Village, bohemian, unconventional, with quaint, tangled little streets that made a pleasant change from the rigid block system in the rest of the city. She wondered if anyone in Greenwich Village ever slept, because no matter how late it was the shops were still open, the bars and restaurants full, the streets buzzing with an almost anarchic excitement. It was possible to enter one of the dark little coffee-bars and find a play or poetry reading in progress, or a meeting going on, usually something political, to do with banning the bomb or stopping the McCarthy witch-hunts, whatever they were. Josie would sit in a corner and listen, savouring every little thing, no matter how trivial, because it was like nothing she had ever known before.

Suddenly it was her last week, her last few days, then the final day of the most wonderful holiday anyone could possibly have had. She had bought presents for everyone at home: a pretty necklace and earring set from Chinatown for Estelle, and for Matthew a leather tobacco pouch because the one he had was wearing thin.

'What are you going to do with yourself today, honey?' Estelle asked over breakfast.

Josie had the day all worked out. 'See all my favourite places one last time – Chinatown and Fifth Avenue, St Patrick's Cathedral, then Macy's because I've got a few dollars left and it would be a shame not to spend them. Tonight, I'm going to see *A Midsummer Night's Dream* in Central Park, then have a coffee in Greenwich Village.' She sighed. 'I can't believe I'm going home tomorrow.'

'We'll miss you, honey. It's been a pleasure having you here.' Matthew vigorously nodded his assent. 'But don't forget,' Estelle went on, 'you've been invited back. We might see you again some time.'

'It would be worth coming back if only for your lovely pancakes.'

She felt sad, walking round the vivid, noisy streets of Chinatown, not sure if she would ever see them again. She could promise herself she'd come back until she was blue in the face, but fate might not allow the promise to be kept. In life, nothing could be relied on – she'd learnt that a long time ago.

She stayed quite some time in the cathedral, savouring the calm, the aroma of incense just discernible in the cool air, and prayed she would find a nice place to live when she got home, a nice job, that she would be happy. She prayed for Louisa, for Lily and everyone she could think of.

It was time for lunch when she came out, so she ate in the nearest diner – hamburger, a banana split, Coca-Cola. Afterwards, she set off for Macy's, where she roamed the aisles of clothes for hours before buying a long narrow black skirt and a baggy cerise jumper. There were just enough dollars left for a dead cheap evening meal and a final coffee in Greenwich Village.

He was at the next table, a slim young man with straight, coal black hair falling in a careless quiff on his forehead. Dark eyes sparkled in his lively, mobile face, which had a slightly dusky hue. He looked Italian, Josie thought, or Spanish, something foreign. The table he was at was crowded, and the young man was clearly the centre of attention. Everyone seemed to want his opinion, vying to make him notice them, clutching his arm, shouting each other down.

His name was Jack. Or perhaps it was Jacques. He might be French. He wore black pants and a dark blue shirt with the top button undone. His check tie was pulled loose. Every now and then he would throw back his head and laugh, and there was something joyous and uninhibited about the laugh, as if it came from deep inside him.

The coffee-bar was called Best Cellar, reached down a poky stairway on Bleecker Street. She'd been there twice before. The young man – she couldn't take her eyes off him – was animatedly sounding off about something to do with politics, waving his arms about. His listeners regarded him silently, with respect.

Josie glanced at her watch. Half past eleven. It was time she was getting back, she had a plane to catch tomorrow. But she was reluctant to leave while the young man was there, which was crazy. He hadn't even glanced in her direction. Did she intend to sit there in the hope that everyone would go except him, leaving *her* to be the object of his undivided attention?

She was already feeling dead peculiar, anyroad. *A Midsummer Night's Dream* had been a magical experience. Dusk had fallen over Central Park halfway through the performance, then night came, stars appeared. The grass on which the audience sprawled, mostly couples, felt cooler, and the scent of a million flowers was almost overpowering. As the sky grew dark the stage became brighter, the actors' voices louder, more resonant, the audience more rapt. Something stirred in Josie, an acute awareness of the beauty and the clarity of her surroundings and the sheer brilliance of the lines the actors spoke. Then came something else, a longing to have someone with her. Not Lily, a man, a boyfriend, in whose arms she could lie as she watched the play draw to a close, and they would experience the beauty of the magical night together. Would she ever meet a man like that?

Then she'd come to Best Cellar, and there he was.

Suddenly, the young man leapt to his feet and removed himself from her life for ever. He raced up the stairs two at a time. The occupants of the next table seemed to droop, as if his leaving had removed a vital element from their lives, though after a while they began to talk quietly amongst themselves.

'Oh, well.' Josie gave a wistful shrug, drained her third cup of coffee, picked up her bag and made for the stairs. Halfway up, she met the young man hurtling down. 'Forgot my jacket,' he muttered. He smiled, but she could tell he wasn't actually *seeing* her.

'Some people'd lose their heads if they weren't screwed on,' Josie remarked, which, given the circumstances, was probably the most stupid thing she could have said but was all she could think of when they had to stop on the stairs to squeeze past each other.

They were standing sideways, facing, touching, and the

young man was looking at her, astounded. 'Was that a Liverpool accent I just heard?'

Josie's heart thudded, unnaturally fast, unnaturally loud, as the dark eyes smiled into hers. 'Yes.'

'Oh, then please can I kiss you? I haven't kissed a girl from Liverpool in almost fifteen years. What's your name? Where are you from? I mean, what part of Liverpool?'

'Penny Lane,' she stammered. 'I'm Josie Flynn.'

'And I'm Jack Coltrane from Old Swan.' He kissed her on both cheeks. 'Pleased to meet you, Josie Flynn.'

She could hardly breathe. There was a weird sensation in her stomach, as if everything had collapsed inside. He was looking at her with a slightly puzzled expression. Suddenly he laughed. 'You're very beautiful, Josie Flynn. Can I kiss you again?'

Next day, instead of going back to Liverpool, she moved in with Jack Coltrane.

2

It was like a dream, or a film, or a book. No, it was like none of those things, but something else, impossible to describe. She had become another person, quite literally lost her senses.

He had invited her to dinner. She was about to explain that she was leaving tomorrow when she realised he meant have dinner *now*, at midnight. On the way to the restaurant the ground felt different where she walked, and the things she touched weren't real, and when she looked at people they were slightly askew. It didn't help her surreal state to be faced with spaghetti Bolognese and a bottle of wine at a time when she would normally have been in bed, or at least thinking about it.

She also seemed to have lost her voice, which didn't matter because Jack didn't stop talking. Before the war, he told her between mouthfuls of spaghetti, his father had been a doctor in Old Swan. In 1939, with war threatening, the family had upped roots and moved to America, where an uncle on his mother's side already lived. They settled on the coast of Maine. At first, it was only supposed to be temporary, but his father started practising again, his mother, a trained nurse, returned to work, and by the time the war was over there was no question of going back to England. They applied for American citizenship.

'And Dad thought the new National Health Service was the work of Communists. Free health care for the masses? No way. I realised me and my family hadn't much in common. I left home at nineteen. I've hardly seen my folks since.' He grinned. 'So, that's how I ended up a Yank instead of a scouse.'

Josie listened, only half taking it in, wondering if he was as fascinated with her as she was with him. Had he only asked her for a meal because they had Liverpool in common? Would she see him again after the meal had finished?

Apparently she would. 'Let's dance,' he said, when the wine had gone and their plates were empty.

'Here?' she glanced around the crowded bistro. There wasn't a soul dancing.

He laughed. 'No, sweetheart, on a dance floor. There's a club just around the corner.'

She could easily have fainted, at the 'sweetheart' and the pressure of his thin arm around her waist when he led her out to the still busy street. He stopped on the pavement and took her in his arms and she could feel his heart beating against her own. She slid her arms around his neck, and rested her head on his shoulder, knowing this was the place where God had intended her to be. His hand moved to the small of her back, to her neck, to her face. He stroked her hair, as if he was trying to make sure she was real. Then, regardless of the passers-by, he kissed her. As she stood within the shelter of his arms, Josie had the oddest feeling that nothing real, nothing of importance, nothing that mattered, had ever happened before, that she had crossed a bridge and entered another world, a magic, brilliantly lit other world, inhabited by Jack Coltrane.

Their lips parted. Jack's dark eyes were moist. They stared deep into hers, and she felt as if he were seeing into her soul. He sighed. 'So, this is it, then?' he whispered. 'Shall we forget about dancing and go home?'

Josie nodded. But, despite his words, Josie was never truly sure if Jack had entered the other world with her.

His apartment was over a dry-cleaner's in a busy street in Little Italy. Opposite was a greengrocer's with a green and white striped awning, a tiny cinema that screened only Italian films – *Stromboli*, with Ingrid Bergman, was showing the day Josie collected her suitcase from Thumbelina's and moved in – and an ice-cream parlour with window-boxes upstairs full of bright flowers and trailing ivy.

Matthew had expressed concern when she told him she wasn't going back to Liverpool. 'Are you sure you're doing the right thing, girl?'

'Course she is. Just look at her face.' Estelle had hugged her hard. 'Be happy, honey. You'll never have that look again.'

The apartment consisted of two largish, badly furnished rooms, a bathroom and a kitchen that was only used to make coffee as Jack usually ate out or had food delivered. The gloomily patterned wallpaper looked as if it had been up for decades but, as with the awful furniture, it didn't seem to matter. It wasn't just because Jack was there, with personality enough to totally eclipse his surroundings, but the place had a warm, well-lived-in feel, full of evidence of his active life. Books and papers were piled on the floor and political posters covered the walls, as well as several paintings done by his friends. More friends had showered him with objects they had sculpted, chiselled, moulded or carved – a lovely hand-woven rug hung over the unused fireplace. The front room was a cross between a second-hand shop and a small art gallery.

'Let's christen the bed,' Jack said the very second Josie had plonked her suitcase on the floor.

'We christened it last night, oh, half a dozen times.'

He pulled her into his arms and kissed her chastely on the brow. 'Yes, but now you're permanent. It'll feel different.'

Permanent! The word gave her a thrill, yet at the same time made her feel uncomfortable. She was a good Catholic girl, who had never faintly envisaged living in sin with a man. It just wasn't *done*, at least not in Liverpool where people got married first. What on earth would she tell Lily when she wrote to say she was staying in America for good? And she must let Louisa know she was in love.

'Hey, you having second thoughts?' Jack kissed her again, this time on the lips, this time more urgently.

'Gosh, no.' She'd probably go to hell, but it was worth it. She relaxed against him. 'What are we waiting for? Let's christen the bed.'

Jack Coltrane was a playwright – there were eight scripts on a shelf to prove it. With the first six, he'd got nowhere but the next, *The Disciples*, had been taken up by an off-Broadway theatre and received excellent reviews.

'I thought I'd made it until Joe McCarthy stuck his big nose in.' Jack glowered darkly. He rarely lost his temper, but could never control his anger when he spoke about the way his play had been treated. 'I was small fry, not important enough to be called before his damn committee, but it didn't stop one of his goons having a word with the theatre, and my play was pulled. The manager was very apologetic, but a play with a socialist message wasn't appropriate in the present climate. Arthur Miller could get away with it, but not someone like me.'

Senator Joseph McCarthy was a hate figure in the eyes of every liberal-minded person in America, Josie learned. His Anti-American Activities Committee had ruined the careers of hundreds of illustrious figures from all walks of life, including many from the theatre and cinema.

Jack had since written another play. He was writing one now, sitting solidly in front of the typewriter for four hours every morning because he was a driven man with a head full of dreams, ideas, plots, that simply had to be put down on paper. But there was no point in submitting them, he said with a sigh. 'I'm only trying to say the same thing as in *The Disciples*.' He laughed bitterly. 'I'd have to send it under a different name, and I'm not prepared to hide behind a pseudonym. There isn't a theatre in America that would even *read* a play by Jack Coltrane, let alone stage it. Word gets around. I'm a bit of a pariah.'

'Only for now,' Josie said stoutly. 'Things might change.' Had it been someone else, she would have suggested they forget the politics and write a thriller or something funny, but she had quickly learned that Jack had too much integrity to write about what he didn't strongly feel. He was, he explained once, trying to get across man's inhumanity to man, the social injustice in the world, trying to fathom out why some people had so much and others had so little, yet most folk didn't seem to care.

Josie remembered reading once that couples were never equal, that one loved more than the other. There was a giver and a taker. She suspected from the start that she gave and Jack took. There was nothing selfish about it – he hadn't a selfish bone in his body – but it was the way the dice had fallen, or how the cookie had crumbled, as they said in America. Only in bed where, time after time, they brought each other to a rapturous, scarcely bearable climax did she feel totally certain that he was committed to her and her alone, that she was *extra* special.

It was an undeniable fact that Jack had the knack of making the whole world feel special. His warm smile was free to anyone, his normally sunny disposition shared with everyone he met. Josie watched his numerous friends, men and women alike, watching him, waiting for Jack to notice *them*, to smile his all-embracing smile just for *them*, to shake their hand, give them a hug, a kiss, a friendly slap on the back. They adored him.

There'd been women before her. She found hairclips and

an earring under the bed, a pink jumper in the wardrobe, a half-full bottle of scent in the bathroom cabinet. Josie tortured herself with the thought that, like these other women, she was only temporary, that one day Jack would meet someone else and she would be dispensed with. Once they were in bed and he told her how much he loved her, that he'd been waiting all his life for a girl like her, the thought would vanish, then slither its poisonous way into her head next morning. She hadn't known it was possible to be so deliriously happy one minute and so abjectly miserable the next.

She got a job in Luigi's, the dry-cleaner's downstairs, where she worked from two till ten, the same hours as Jack worked in a local bar. To her horror, she discovered she was classed as an illegal immigrant, but Luigi didn't give a damn that she didn't have a green card allowing her to work legally in the States. Anyroad, she'd have been useless in an office, where she could have earned more, because they never went to bed before dawn.

For Jack Coltrane, the good times started late. New York was a sleepless city, with plenty of all-night clubs and all-night bars. All-night parties were the norm. He always knew where a party was being held, and there was never a more welcome guest. Within seconds he would be surrounded by people, wanting to touch him, wanting to know his opinion on this or that, hanging on to his every word, and Josie would be left with mixed feelings. This slight, not very tall, delightful, handsome man, this man in a million, loved *her*. She would feel a glow of possession, particularly when Jack put his arm around her shoulders and drew her into the crowd.

What she wanted more than anything was for them to get married, for him to be truly hers in the eyes of God and the law. She was careful never to drop the slightest hint. Marriage might be the furthest thing from Jack's mind.

When, one Sunday in October, Miranda Marshall arrived at Jack's apartment Josie pretended not to care. Every Sunday from midday on, people began to drop by, armed with a bottle of wine. They came to talk, to argue, to sort out the world. Around teatime, Jack would send for a Chinese or an order of pizzas.

Miranda, though, was different. She hadn't come to talk, she'd come for Jack.

She was a sleekly attractive woman with a feline, sharply angled face. Glossy maroon lipstick made her lips look wet, and gold shadow adorned her almond-shaped eyes. Her dark brown hair was tied in a ponytail, not at the back of her head but over to one side, giving a jaunty and slightly eccentric impression.

Miranda was an actress, and had appeared in Jack's off-Broadway play. They had been great friends for years, and she was just back from Hollywood after an unsuccessful attempt to get into movies.

'I'm going back, I'm not giving up, but I just felt like a few days in New York to see my friends. I thought I'd lay claim to your couch for a few days, Jack.' The almond eyes rested fleetingly on Josie. 'I didn't know you had company. I'll find somewhere else.'

'You'll do no such thing,' Jack said. He looked at Josie. 'You don't mind, do you, sweetheart?'

'No,' Josie lied.

She minded terribly. She minded so much she wanted to cry, particularly when Miranda went to the bathroom and came back waving the scent from the cabinet. 'So *this* is where I left it,' she crowed.

They must have been lovers! Miranda had been hoping to take up with Jack where they'd left off. Laying claim to the couch had been a lie. It was Jack she wanted. Josie burned with inner fury.

That afternoon a whole crowd of them went to a political rally in Central Park to protest against the Chinese occupation of Tibet. Miranda came with them. She accompanied them to Pogo's, a blues club in SoHo, then to a party in Canal Street, where she seemed to know everyone. Josie watched closely, sensing that no one liked Miranda much. They made faces behind her back, which pleased Josie so much she felt ashamed.

By the time all three returned to the apartment, her head was spinning and she felt sick, imagining Jack creeping out of bed in the middle of the night to make love to Miranda on the couch. Wouldn't most women protest if their lover invited his old lover to stay? They'd never had a row before, but she'd have it out with him that night.

When they went to bed Jack immediately reached for her, but she gripped his hands. 'I want to ask you something.'

He nuzzled her neck. 'Ask away.'

Josie took a deep breath. 'Have you had an affair with Miranda?'

'Yes,' he said lightly. 'It didn't mean anything but, yes, I have.'

'Would you mind if one of my old lovers turned up and I let them sleep on the couch?'

'Sweetheart, you're *jealous*.' He laughed and tickled her waist. Josie squealed and put her hand over her mouth in case Miranda heard. Their guest was in the bathroom getting washed.

'I didn't say I was jealous.' Josie pushed his hands away and did her best to sound reasonable. 'I asked a direct question. How would you feel if the situation were reversed?'

'I'm not sure.' There was a long silence, during which he rested his face against hers. 'How many lovers have you had?' he said eventually.

'Only one. I had a fiancé, too, Ben. We were going to get married when he finished university, but I gave him up.'

'What was the lover's name?'

'Griff. He was an actor. Still is, I expect.'

Jack lay on his back, staring at the ceiling. 'I don't know why, I thought you were a virgin, that I was the first.'

'I hope you're not going to say you're disappointed.' She adopted a slightly amused tone. 'I was probably the twenty-first for you, or the hundred and first, for all I know.'

He turned and grabbed her by the shoulders. 'I know it's

unreasonable, but I can't stand the thought of another man touching you,' he said gruffly. 'I want to ask stupid questions, like how was it with this Griff – was he better than me?'

'He wasn't. It was just a holiday romance. Was Miranda better than me?' she asked, more flippantly than she felt.

'Don't joke.' He shook her and said urgently, 'There's never been anyone better than you, and there never will. I love you with all my heart and soul. I've told you that a million times.'

'But I've told you the same,' she cried as she clung to him. 'It didn't stop you getting cross about Griff. I think I've a right to worry about Miranda. I can't stand the thought of you having slept with her. I can't stand the thought of you having slept with *any* woman. I don't want you to so much as *touch* another woman again, only me.'

'As if I would,' he said softly, kissing her. 'You're for me, and I'm for you, and that's the way it's going to be till the end of time.'

They made love, and it was as if they'd never made love before and were discovering each other's bodies for the first time. When it was over, and she nestled in his arms, he said, 'I'll tell Miranda to go in the morning.'

'There's no need,' Josie said contentedly. From now on she would never feel insecure again.

Of course, she did. Even when she discovered the couch was empty, and Miranda had done a midnight flit, the doubts had already begun their stealthy return. It seemed she would never feel fully happy with Jack Coltrane unless they spent the rest of their lives in bed!

Autumn had arrived in New York. The trees in Central Park shed their leaves to make a crisp, golden carpet. The air became fresher, cooler, with a hint of champagne. The endless hooting of the traffic sounded slightly muted. People had begun to wear coats, scarves, boots.

When Josie bought a fur coat for five dollars from a thrift shop, she thought longingly of the smart winter clothes she'd left in Lily Kavanagh's wardrobe. She bought a pair of dead cheap boots, one a slightly darker grey than the other, but at least they hadn't been on some other woman's feet. Luigi paid peanuts in the dry-cleaner's, and she was always short of money.

On 25 November Jack abandoned his precious play, and took her to see the Thanksgiving Day parade. The entire length of Broadway appeared to be covered in balloons, thousands of them, millions, of every conceivable colour. Josie watched, entranced, as float after float drove by, each more glorious, more eye-catching and inventive than the one before. This was the day Santa Claus arrived in New York, and he finished off the parade in a white fur coach, clanging his bell, already wishing everyone a Merry Christmas.

'That was wonderful,' she breathed when everything was over and the crowds began to disperse. Jack was standing behind her, his arms around her waist, his chin resting on her shoulder. He kissed her neck.

'How about a coffee?'

'I'd love one.'

'Then a coffee it is.'

They linked arms. Jack began to walk quickly, his step slightly ahead of hers so she had to hurry to keep up. He did everything quickly combed his hair, washed, dressed, undressed, typed, ate – as if worried the world might end before he'd finished. She had something to tell him. Perhaps over coffee? But should she tell him yet that she was pregnant?

She hadn't taken much notice when she'd missed her August period. Although she'd always been as regular as clockwork, one missed period wasn't worth getting worked up about. But two! When nothing happened in September she began to worry, but convinced herself she couldn't possibly be pregnant because she felt so well. There'd been no morning sickness. She didn't go off her food, or get a hankering for peculiar things like treacle butties, as Marigold Kavanagh had. Then she'd missed October, and yesterday another period had been due ...

There was no doubt about it – she was four months pregnant. Her waist was starting to thicken. She was expecting Jack's baby, and didn't know whether to be glad or not.

It must have happened the night they met on the steps of Best Cellar, because since then he'd always taken precautions – he was so careful that she took it for granted he didn't want a child. Their lifestyle would have to change drastically. She had tried, but she couldn't see Jack content to stay home at night, happy to relinquish the parties, the clubs, the politics. The apartment wasn't big enough for a baby, and she'd have to leave work. Jack's wages weren't much. He made as much again in tips, but not enough to pay the rent and support a wife and child.

She imagined telling him, imagined his face lighting up. 'I've always wanted a child, a son.' Men always seemed to want a son. That was the best scenario. But he might be horrified, might even suggest an abortion. He was a Catholic, but didn't go to church. Perhaps that's why she hadn't told him. She was leaving it until it was too late even to discuss getting rid of her child, *their* child, because it was something she would have flatly refused to do, even for Jack.

Josie sighed. 'The bar will be busy today,' Jack said. 'The parade's over, but not the celebrations. Hey, this place looks interesting.' He steered her inside a diner with a real skeleton in the window. It was called Bones. 'What was that big sigh for, sweetheart? I felt it shudder right through me.'

'Nothing.'

Josie's waist was becoming thicker, her stomach bulged slightly. Hardly anything fitted. She tried to avoid Jack seeing her naked, reaching for something to put on before getting out of bed, because she still hadn't told him. Though he was bound to notice soon . . .

'Sweetheart . . .' he said one morning. It was a week after the Thanksgiving Day parade, and he was seated at the table, typing like a madman. She emerged from the bedroom, having only just got up. 'Sweetheart, I think you should cut down on the spaghetti. You're getting quite a tummy on you.'

Josie didn't answer. She looked down at the baggy cerise jumper she'd bought in Macy's on what she'd thought would be her last day in New York. It wasn't baggy enough to hide the ever-growing bump. 'If I didn't know better, I'd say you were in the club, girl,' Jack went on in the pretend Liverpool accent he occasionally used as a joke.

'I *am* in the club, Jack,' Josie said softly. 'That's the reason for the tummy.' She sat on the other side of the table and watched his thin, expressive face.

He looked stunned, then he frowned and opened his mouth to speak, but nothing came out at first except a groan. Then he said, 'Of course, that first night!' He tried to smile. 'You must be very fertile, sweetheart,' he said lightly. 'If we're not careful, we could end up with twenty kids.'

'Do you mind?' It was a silly question, because he obviously minded very much.

'To be honest, I'm not sure.' He laughed, not his usual, wholehearted laugh. 'I'm twenty-six. I suppose it's about time I settled down.'

'But you weren't planning on settling down just yet?' He didn't want the baby. She felt her veins turn to ice, and cursed herself when two solitary tears trickled down her cheeks.

'Sweetheart! Come here.' He patted his knee, and she crept into his arms. 'This is my fault. I should have been more careful. How far gone are you?'

'A bit over four months.' She began to cry properly.

'Aw, shit, Josie,' he said angrily. 'Why didn't you tell me before?'

Because I was worried you'd react in exactly the way you're reacting now, she wanted to say. Instead, she whispered, 'I don't know.'

Suddenly he grinned. Nothing could keep Jack down for long, not even an unwanted baby. 'Will you marry me, Miss Josephine Flynn?' He tipped up her chin with his finger. 'Please say yes.'

Josie nodded. 'Yes.' But she felt sure he would never have asked if she hadn't been pregnant. She would never be sure of anything with Jack Coltrane.

So that the priest wouldn't be shocked by a bride on the verge of motherhood, the wedding was arranged to take place as soon as possible.

The bride's outfit came from a thrift shop – a pink, silkily soft velvet skirt with a long, matching jacket to hide her swollen stomach.

On the morning of the wedding a letter came from Lily, enclosing a cutting from the *Echo*. Louisa Chalcott, the American poet, who had lived in obscurity in Liverpool for more than thirty years, had died peacefully in her sleep a few days before.

'Miss Chalcott's cerebral writing was well before its time. The day may well come when she will be recognised as one of this century's major poets . . .'

There was more, about Louisa's unconventional lifestyle, her legendary lovers, that she had never married but had borne twin daughters to a man she refused to name.

'That's because she didn't know who it was,' Josie said, showing the cutting to Jack. She felt incredibly sad, but at the same time relieved that Louisa had departed from this world painlessly, and in her sleep.

'Try not to let it worry you, sweetheart. She's gone to a better place, as my mother would say.'

'Louisa would do her nut if she thought I'd let it spoil me wedding day. As regards her being in a better place, I doubt it. She's probably in hell, trying to seduce Old Nick as we speak.'

The ceremony was held at midday in a little Italian church off Hester Street, only a short walk from where they lived. Jack had borrowed a respectable suit, black and white pinstriped. He looked like a member of the Mafia. The church crowded with his friends, whom Josie had never come to regard as hers. She had always felt very much in his shadow,

187

and sensed they resented her, as they would have resented any woman their hero had chosen to fall in love with.

Now they would resent her even more. Not only was she marrying him, but she was taking him to England, to London, though it was Jack's idea, not hers.

He had come bursting into the apartment days ago, his dark eyes alight with excitement. 'Hey, I've had a brainwave. Let's go live in England. That's what two of the blacklisted directors did – Joseph Losey and Carl Foreman. No one there gives a shit about your politics. I can start again, submit my plays – and boast of a Broadway production under my belt.'

'Off-Broadway,' Josie reminded him, at the same time trying to get her brain to adjust to the idea of them living somewhere else. Jack, she felt, was *part* of New York. He belonged here, every bit as much as the Empire State Building and the Statue of Liberty. Would he be happy in a place that was so utterly different? She reminded herself that he'd been born in Liverpool. England was his country as much as hers.

'Don't be a wet blanket. Off-Broadway, on-Broadway, it still sounds impressive.' He began to pace the floor, his excitement growing. Josie sometimes wondered if electricity rather than blood flowed through his veins. 'Oh, God, Josie. Why didn't I think of it before?' he whooped. 'It makes even more sense now with the baby – no medical fees, for one. I don't want some makeshift midwife delivering the little chap in here, and we couldn't afford a hospital.' He came over and kissed her tenderly. 'We'll live in London, where the contacts are – the agents, the actors, most of the theatres. I'll get a job, and you'll be a lady of leisure in our little apartment in Mayfair overlooking Park Lane.'

'A lady of leisure – with a baby!' she spluttered.

'You know what I mean. What do you say, sweetheart? It makes perfect sense, don't you think?'

She would have gone anywhere in the world with Jack Coltrane even if it made no sense at all. 'Of course it does.' She smiled. 'As soon as we're married, we'll go to England.'

The sun was shining brightly enough to crack the

pavements, but inside the church it was dark. Light struggled unsuccessfully to penetrate the gloomy stained-glass windows, probably thick with dust and too high to clean.

The young priest looked very serious as he went through the motions of joining Josephine Flynn and Jack Frederick Coltrane together in holy matrimony.

'For richer, for poorer . . .'

'In sickness and in health . . .'

'Do you take this woman . . .?'

'I do,' Jack said gravely.

'Do you take this man . . .?'

'I do.' Josie's voice was little more than a whisper.

'I now pronounce you man and wife. You may kiss the bride.'

'Hi, there, Mrs Coltrane.' Jack kissed her warmly on the lips. He looked happy enough, she thought, as if the day had been inevitable since they met. He didn't *have* to marry her. But he had, whether out of a sense of honour or because he loved her as much as she loved him. The baby chose that moment to give its first, extremely violent kick. She rested her hands on her stomach. She was married. She was Mrs Jack Coltrane, and with that she would have to be content.

From Cypress Terrace . . .
1955–1957

I

As usual, the hall was awash with leaflets and old letters. A few weeks ago, not for the first time, she'd collected everything together, thrown the leaflets away and put the letters in a neat pile on the window-sill in case old tenants returned to see if there'd been any mail, which happened occasionally. Since then the letters had managed to get back on to the floor, and there were more leaflets, dozens of them. No one else living there seemed to give a damn about the state of the hall. There was a notice on the battered pay phone. OUT OF ORDER.

Josie plodded wearily up to the second floor. The office had been exceptionally busy today. Peter Schofield had wanted an urgent quotation to catch the post, and she'd had no alternative but to stay till half past six because two girls in the typing pool were off.

'Don't worry, darling. You'll find an extra few quid in your wage packet on Friday,' Peter said. He was very generous. 'Now you go home to that nice hubby of yours. I'll post this.'

'Ta.' Josie managed to squeeze her face into a tired smile. Peter didn't know about Laura.

The couple in the first-floor back room were having a fight, screaming at each other at the tops of their voices. Thank God we don't live over them, she thought. The man in the room below them made hardly a sound, unlike the young man on the ground floor who had friends round every night and played music till the early hours. The woman in the basement seemed quite respectable, but there was something wrong with her. More than once Josie had heard the sound of desperate weeping coming from the flat. She might have investigated had she not felt much like weeping herself. Jack said the woman's name was Elsie Forrest. She was a retired nanny, and often admired Laura. There were other tenants she didn't know – they kept changing all the time.

It was time Mr Browning got someone in to give this place a good scrub. She scowled at the dirt encrusted in the corners of each linoleum-covered stair. And a few repairs wouldn't have gone amiss. Several bannisters were missing, the light in the hall didn't work and there was a cracked window in the communal bathroom, where hot water was just a far-off dream. But all Mr Browning was interested in was collecting the rent. Still, he hadn't turned them away when she was obviously pregnant, like so many other landlords and landladies had done. But, then, Mr Browning didn't live on the premises, and probably didn't give a damn if a crying baby disturbed the other residents.

Josie reached the second floor. Before opening the poorly fitting door with gaps top and bottom, she threw back her shoulders and fixed a bright smile on her face. She turned the knob, and went in. 'Hi,' she sang out. 'How's things been?'

Jack was pounding away at the typewriter, and Laura was fast asleep in her cot at the foot of the bed. Josie bent over her beautiful six-month-old daughter, half resentful, half thankful she was asleep. She longed to give her a cuddle, yet ached to sit down and relax with a cup of tea.

'Everything's fine, sweetheart.' Jack abandoned his typing to give her a hug. 'You're late. I was getting worried.'

'I had this quotation to do. I tried to phone, but it's out of order again.'

'You can't hear this far up, anyway, particularly if I'm typing. The kettle's boiled. Fancy a cuppa?'

'I'm *dying* for a cuppa.' She sank thankfully on to the lumpy settee, her head swimming. 'How's the play going?'

Jack made a face. 'Okay, but two came back this morning,

one from the Liverpool Playhouse.' He grinned. 'Bastards! No loyalty to a fellow scouse.'

She knew the grin was fake, like her smile. Every play he had submitted had been returned – even *The Disciples*, in which he'd had such faith – usually with unfavourable comments. 'Not tense enough.' 'The characters have no depth.' 'Where is the plot?' one director had rudely demanded.

'Perhaps you're before your time,' Josie had suggested once. 'Like Van Gogh, for example.'

'Well,' Jack drawled, 'let's hope I don't have to wait as long as he did, like long after I'm dead.'

He was unhappy in London. He missed his friends and the buzz and excitement of New York. Instead of looking out over a row of busy shops and a cinema, their large, dingy bedsitting-room in a Fulham cul-de-sac was opposite an abandoned factory with smashed windows and graffiti on the walls. Unlike New York, where Jack's radiance made everything around him seem pale in comparison this ugly room with its bits and pieces of well-used furniture and faded, fraying lino diminished him. He seemed smaller, slighter, less important, just an ordinary man struggling, unsuccessfully, to make something of himself. Moving to London had been a disastrous mistake.

He brought a mug of tea. 'I thought I'd send a play to the BBC,' he said. 'Bob knows someone who knows someone there. He said they're always looking for new writers.'

'It wouldn't hurt,' Josie said encouragingly. She didn't say it would hurt their finances. With ten plays constantly in circulation, the cost of postage both ways, and envelopes and paper, bit deeply into her wages. But the whole point of this very unsatisfactory way of life was so Jack could concentrate on nothing but writing.

During her pregnancy, and for two months after Laura was born, he had worked for a pittance in a pub in Fulham. There had been scarcely enough to pay the rent and buy basic food. Josie didn't know how she would have managed if Mrs Kavanagh hadn't sent a huge parcel of baby clothes from

Marigold, with a tactful note to say, 'It seems a shame to let these go to waste. Some haven't even been worn.'

'I could kick myself for not staying at college, getting a degree,' Jack complained frequently. He was completely unskilled. All he knew was bar work.

Josie was the one with a trade, but she hadn't worked as a shorthand-typist since leaving the insurance company four years ago. When Jack was out, she sharpened her skills by retyping his plays, with the excuse that the manuscripts had got shabby during their constant journeys in the post. As she typed, she had the worrying thought that the plays weren't very good. They seemed too wordy, rather dull, a bit preachy. Even *The Disciples*, of which he was so proud, had copies of the reviews clipped to the cover, and they weren't all *that* marvellous. Only two, from badly printed magazines she'd never heard of, had flattering things to say. When a play was returned with the comment, 'Where is the plot?' she couldn't help but agree.

She brought her shorthand back to speed by taking down the news from the wireless. As soon as she felt up to it, she suggested Jack give up the pub. *She* would work so *he* could write.

'I can earn more than you. It seems the sensible thing to do.' It was the hardest decision she had ever made in her life, to desert her lovely baby.

Jack's reaction still upset her when she thought about it four months later. He had gazed at her wretchedly. His body seemed to shrink before her eyes. 'Oh, Christ!' The sound, a mixture of a groan and a cry, seemed to come from the very depths of his being. 'I'm no good at this.'

Josie felt as if she were shrinking herself, melting away to nothing in the face of his despair. 'At what?' she asked shakily.

He gestured round the room. 'At looking after a wife and kid. It's not *me*. It's not what I had planned, at least not until I was *someone*. Back home I was a playwright who worked in a bar to make a few dollars. Now, I'm a fucking *barman*! Sometimes I feel too damn dispirited to write.'

'I'm sorry,' Josie said tightly. The doubts she'd had on her wedding day had been confirmed. He hadn't wanted to marry her. He didn't want to be a father. He may well love her, and he adored Laura, but both were burdens to this rather splendid, rather immature, intensely good-humoured man. She remembered the first time she'd seen him in the coffee-bar in New York, without a care in the world. That man no longer existed, though he still put up a front, but now, with his guard down, he looked destroyed.

'It's not your fault, sweetheart.' He dropped his head in his hands and didn't speak for several seconds. Then he looked at her dully. 'Look, why don't I find something else? One of those smart West End places might well snap up a Yankee barman, and if I smile nicely at the customers, I'll make a load in tips.'

'You're not a barman, Jack. You're a playwright.' Her voice was sharp. 'You expected to take London by storm, but maybe the storm's a long time coming. Oh, does that sound stupid?'

He smiled. 'A bit.'

'Anyroad,' she said seriously, 'our best plan is for you to concentrate on writing, and *I'll* work. It shouldn't be for long. Laura won't give you any bother. You'll just need to take her a little walk around lunchtime, that's all.'

She would have to stop breast-feeding. That would be the hardest part. She had so much milk, gallons of it, and breast milk was so much healthier for a child. The best times of the day were when she watched her daughter suck furiously on her white, overlarge breasts, sometimes grabbing the flesh with her tiny hands, squeezing it. It was the oddest sensation, almost sensual and at the same time totally natural. Mother and child, joined together, one nourishing the other.

Everything about leaving Laura was hard. On her first day as a secretary with Ashbury Buxton, a civil engineering company in Chelsea, she cried the whole way on the bus. She couldn't stop thinking about her little daughter.

She'd told all sorts of lies to get the job, apart from the

glaring omission that she had a child. She'd been working as a secretary in New York, she told Peter Schofield, and tried to look confident, at the same time praying he wouldn't suggest sending for a reference to the mythical company she'd invented. He'd been impressed, didn't mention a reference and employed her on the spot. There was a good atmosphere in the office, though the work was hard, and there was never time to stop for a chat with the other women.

Four months later, Josie still hadn't got used to leaving her child. When she got home Laura was usually asleep. She'd always been a perfect baby, and rarely woke during the night.

I'm missing so much, she thought as she watched Jack move the typewriter to the floor, then take the casserole she'd made the night before from the oven and put it on the table. She'd been at work while Laura had spent a whole hour trying to pull her fingers off one by one, and when she'd sat up unaided for the first time and held out her arms to be picked up. At weekends, when she nursed her, she noticed Laura's eyes turn to Jack. Who is this stranger? Josie imagined her thinking. Who the hell is this funny woman whose knee I'm sitting on? In another few months Laura would start talking, and her first word wasn't likely to be 'Mummy'.

The graffiti-covered factory served as a background to their meal. If there had ever been cypress trees in Cypress Terrace, there was no sign of them now. 'I was wondering,' Jack said, 'if we could run to a television? Not buy one,' he added hastily. 'I mean get one on hire. It only costs about a dollar a week. It's just that, if I'm to approach the BBC, I'd like to see a few plays first. Bob said they have on at least two a week. You might enjoy having a set, sweetheart.' Bob was someone he'd met in the corner pub, his only social outlet and so utterly pathetic when compared to the frantic clubbing and partying in New York.

She would never have time to watch TV. There was always ironing to do, Laura's nappies to wash and soak before they went to the launderette, things to mend, next day's meal to prepare – the inevitable casserole or stew – tidying, cleaning.

She was lucky if she managed to snatch an hour with a book before it was time for bed, where Jack always wanted to make love, and she had to pretend it was wonderful when all she wanted to do was sleep.

He was looking at her pleadingly, and she couldn't stand it. She hated being the breadwinner and her husband asking for money.

'Of course we can afford it,' she said cheerfully.

'I'll arrange it tomorrow.'

She took her empty plate over to the sink, and noticed a canvas holdall on the floor. 'Jack, did you take the washing to the laundrette?'

'Christ, I forgot.' He jumped to his feet. 'I'll take it now – they're open till ten.'

'You might as well have a drink while you're waiting.'

He planted a kiss on her cheek. 'I suppose I might. Bye, sweetheart. See you later.'

'Bye.' Josie let out a long, slow breath when the door closed. She put the dishes in to soak and sat at the foot of the bed beside the cot. Laura was on her back, her hands raised in a position of surrender. Josie lifted the quilt. Her knees were spread, feet together, making a perfect diamond.

'I love you,' she whispered. Laura uttered a tiny cry, opened her brown eyes – Jack's eyes – stared unseeingly at her mother, then closed them. She was Jack's child, with his eyes, his fine nose, fine eyebrows, the same coal black hair.

The nurses had exclaimed in surprise at the amount of hair she'd had when she was born. 'This baby already needs a haircut,' the midwife said. The birth had been as easy as the pregnancy – no complications, no stitches, hardly any pain.

'You're a dream baby,' Josie told her, 'which is just as well. If you were like some babies I've heard of, your dad would hardly get any writing done. Mind you, I wouldn't mind if you had a little cry in the middle of the night, so I could pick you up and give you a bit of a cuddle, like. But then, frankly, luv, I feel more than a bit worn out, so ignore that.'

★

196

Two months later, Josie came home to find Laura standing up in her cot, clutching the bars and grinning fiendishly. 'She did that herself,' Jack said proudly. 'You should have seen the look of determination on her face. She was going to stand up or die in the attempt. She's enormously pleased with herself.'

'I wish I'd been here,' Josie said wistfully.

'So do I.' His expression changed to one of mild irritation. 'Lately, her favourite game is throwing her toys out the cot, and expecting them back straight away so she can throw them out again. I must have got up at least twenty times.'

'She can't stay in her cot for ever. She'll be crawling soon.' Josie knelt beside the cot. 'Won't you, darling?'

Laura did a little jig. 'Bah!' she cried.

'Would you like a rusk?'

'Bah!'

'I've already fed her,' Jack broke in. 'Don't give her any more. She'll get fat.'

Josie stroked her daughter's plump arm. 'She's already fat. Shall I change her nappy?'

'She had a fresh diaper about half an hour ago.' He put the kettle on. 'Hey, despite the trials and tribulations of the day, I finished that play for the BBC. It took some discipline, trying to fit the whole thing into an hour and a half.'

'Good.' Josie picked Laura up out of the cot and carried her to the settee, half expecting Jack to tell her not to. The baby immediately made a grab for her necklace of multicoloured beads. 'What's it about, the play?' He was unwilling to discuss plots until he'd finished.

She only half listened as he explained that it was about a pit disaster somewhere, followed by a famous strike, aware only that it sounded dead dull, as Jack's plays usually did. It was strange because he was basically a happy soul, yet everything he wrote was as miserable as sin.

How much longer would this go on? she wondered as Laura tried to strangle her with the beads. They'd been in London fourteen months, yet Jack was no nearer success than the day they'd arrived.

Suddenly, the beads broke. They fell on the cushions of the settee and rolled on to the floor.

'Damn!' Jack exclaimed.

'It doesn't matter, they're only cheap ones.'

'I don't give a shit about the necklace,' he said irritably. 'I'm worried Laura's got one in her mouth. You should have stopped her chewing it.'

'I didn't notice she was,' Josie said in a small voice.

Laura, conscious that something was happening she didn't understand, raised her arms and looked nervously at Jack. He came over and plucked her off Josie's knee. 'It's all right, honey. Open your mouth for Daddy. Let's see what you've got in there. Good girl, four perfect little teeth, another two on the way and not a bead in sight.'

It was all Josie could do not to burst into tears.

It was Friday. Josie came out of the office, and saw Jack waiting on the other side of the road. He smiled, waved and came striding across, lightly dodging the traffic. For the first time in ages she felt a tiny thrill. There was something about the confident, bouncing walk that reminded her of the Jack of old.

'Where's Laura?' she demanded as soon as he arrived.

'I left her with Elsie Forrest,' he said easily. 'I've got some great news.'

'Elsie Forrest, the woman in the basement?' Josie hurried towards the bus stop. 'She's not quite right in the head, Jack. Haven't you heard the way she cries?'

Jack laid a restraining hand on her arm. 'Josie, I told you ages ago, she used to be a nanny. She's looked after dozens of children. Laura's completely safe. Elsie only cries because she's lonely, that's all.'

'But, Jack . . .' Entirely against her will, she found herself being steered into a pub. 'I'm worried about Laura.'

'I've told you, she'll be fine. 'What do you want to drink?'

'I don't want a drink.'

'Well, you're having one, so sit down. We've got

something to celebrate.' He brought her a sherry and a beer for himself.

'What have we got to celebrate?'

His dark eyes danced. 'This morning, I was leaving the apartment to take Laura for her walk when the phone rang. It was a woman from the BBC, wanting to talk about my play. The long and short of it was, she asked if I was free for lunch. It was too good an opportunity to miss, so I said yes. I was going to call your office, ask you to come home, but thought about Elsie Forrest. She was only too pleased to oblige. I've been home since,' he said quickly when Josie opened her mouth to speak. 'Laura didn't want to know me. She's fine with Elsie. Anyway, back to this afternoon. Matty took me to a very smart restaurant in Mayfair.'

'Mattie?'

'Mathilda Garr, Mattie, the woman from the BBC.' He waved a dismissive hand. 'She's old. Although she didn't think much of the play, she reckons I've got a way with dialogue. She wants me to write a pilot for a series she has planned. My play arrived quite fortuitously while she was casting around for a writer.'

'What sort of series?' She was doing her best to relax. Surely Laura wasn't likely to come to harm with an ex-nanny?

'A crime thing. An American cop, a detective, joins the Metropolitan Police. There's all sorts of resentment until he becomes accepted.' He put his hand over hers. 'Oh, sweetheart, I've a feeling this is it. By this time next year we'll have that flat in Mayfair that I promised.'

'But, Jack, it doesn't sound your sort of thing,' Josie said cautiously.

His lip curled. He leaned back in the chair and shook his head. There was a hard look on his face she'd never seen before. It made her feel very sad. 'I don't think anyone's interested in my sort of thing, sweetheart. If Mattie likes my script, there'll be a four-figure advance for seven episodes. I say, fuck plays, I'd sooner have the cash.'

Josie felt even sadder. If they had never met, he would be in

New York, still full of ideals, writing plays that *meant* something. What would his old friends say if they knew the noble Jack Coltrane had sunk to writing for money?

Still, it would be more than welcome, the money. She felt guilty that she'd been so preoccupied with Laura that she wasn't as excited as she should have been at his news which, now she thought about it, was dead marvellous. He looked a bit let down, she thought. He'd have expected her to be as thrilled as he was.

She put her hand over his and squeezed it warmly. 'Congratulations, luv. Let's buy some wine on the way home. We'll drink to your success tonight.'

Josie was relieved to find her daughter sitting contentedly on Elsie Forrest's floor, surrounded by her toys and scribbling furiously in a pad. She completely ignored their arrival.

Elsie, a small, neat woman with lovely silver hair, wore a navy blue pinafore dress and a white starched blouse and apron, almost a uniform. The basement flat was clean, probably cleaner than the Coltranes', and Elsie was smiling radiantly. 'That's Mummy she's drawing.' She looked fondly at Laura. 'I never thought I'd care for a baby again. I'm so happy.'

Jack gave Josie a challenging look. There! I told you it would be all right, it seemed to say.

'Why don't you leave her a little longer and have a nice dinner to celebrate?' Elsie suggested. 'She'll fall asleep soon. She's been too busy all afternoon to take a nap.'

They went to a small Italian restaurant in Soho with red gingham cloths and candles on the tables. The owner, Marco, was the brother of someone Jack had known in New York, and it was almost like old times when he introduced himself. Marco slapped him on the shoulder and shook his hand for a good five minutes.

'Course I hearda Jack Coltrane. Frankie tolda me you come to London. You Mrs Coltrane? Sit down, sit down, here, nice, private corner.' He produced a menu and waved his arms expansively. 'Meal's on the house for Frankie's best 'a friend.'

Josie couldn't remember having met anyone called Frankie, but in New York everyone regarded themselves as Jack's best friend. The wine arrived, and with it some of the old magic. She knew it would never return completely, not after the hard look she'd seen on Jack's face. Circumstances had changed him, as they had probably changed her. She had never been a happy, carefree person, not like Jack, she had too many painful memories. She was too introverted, she took everything too seriously, but over the last eighteen months she'd felt as if she was carrying the weight of the whole world on her shoulders.

... to Bingham Mews, Chelsea
1957–1960

They had moved less than a mile, to another cul-de-sac of tall
terraced houses, but it was like moving to the other side of the
world. The yellow brick residences were brand new, and the
estate agent described them as 'town' houses, not terraced.
There were twelve altogether, six each side, built on the site
of an unused church off the Kings Road, Chelsea. They were
mostly occupied by young couples like the Coltranes.

It was an area that reminded Josie a little bit of New York.
She loved the boutiques with their outrageous clothes, and the
coffee-bars and pubs where she frequently glimpsed faces she'd
seen in films or on television.

The ground floor was a garage in which they kept the blue
Austin Healey convertible. There was a small room at the
back that Jack used as a study. The living-cum-dining room
was on the first floor, with a window that took up the entire
wall. Behind, overlooking a paved courtyard, was a kitchen,
with matching units, a refrigerator, a Hoover twin-tub
washing machine and an alcove with padded seats and a table,
where they ate if they didn't have guests. Three bedrooms and
a bathroom were on the floor above.

Everyone in Bingham Mews was friendly. In summer, they
held cocktail parties in the open, drifting in and out of each
other's houses in search of snacks and drinks – Jack was an
expert at mixing cocktails. There was sometimes a drinks party
on Sunday afternoons, and they invited each other in small

groups to dinner, gravely discussing the Suez crisis, the enforced desegregation of schools in America, the revolution in Cuba led by a man called Fidel Castro.

Josie didn't care that she was the only woman in the mews who did her own cleaning, but found it nerve-racking having to make meals for half a dozen dead posh people – her previous culinary experience extended no further than casseroles and shepherd's pie from the cheapest mince. But she had no intention of letting down the working classes. She bought a 'Good Housekeeping' recipe book and learnt how to make chicken marengo, turkey blanquette, venison and all sorts of gateaux and meringues, as well as discovering thirty different ways to use an orange.

Elsie Forrest, now their regular babysitter, usually came to help. Elsie was frequently 'borrowed' by other residents with children. She had moved to a much nicer flat in Fulham, and considered Jack entirely responsible for her change in fortune. 'If he hadn't trusted me with your darling Laura, I'd still be wasting away in Cypress Terrace.'

Josie had made a friend in Charlotte Ward-Pierce, a gaunt woman with large, sick eyes, who had two small children and lived next door but one. She came for coffee on Monday mornings, and Josie went to her on Fridays. Charlotte's father was Lord Lieutenant of somewhere, and her husband, Neville, managed an Arabian bank. The two young women were grateful for each other's company at the various social functions held in Bingham Mews.

Josie waited until all the carpets and curtains had been fitted, and every item of furniture bought, before inviting Lily Kavanagh to stay. It was December 1957, three and a half years since she'd last seen Lily, and although they corresponded regularly it felt more like a hundred.

Lily had wanted to come before, and couldn't understand why Josie didn't visit Liverpool. Josie had felt obliged to tell her the truth. 'Because I don't want you to see the dead awful place where we live.' She had tried to make it sound bohemian. 'Quite frankly, Lil, I'm too exhausted to travel. I'm supporting an artist, remember? I'm working full time.'

She had had to work another six months before Jack's pilot script had been deemed suitable for production by the BBC and a series had been commissioned. With a sense of overwhelming relief, Josie handed in her notice. Laura quickly got used to being looked after by her mother, though she retained an especially close relationship with Jack.

Her little girl was a joy to be with. Laura had an impish sense of humour, and kept her mother entertained during the long hours Jack was downstairs in his study, at meetings, at script conferences or lunching with Mattie Garr.

After living in one room for almost two years, the new house felt incredibly spacious. For the first few weeks Josie used to go for walks, in and out of rooms, up and down stairs, hardly able to believe it was *theirs*.

They weren't rich, not yet, but no expense had been spared when it came to furnishing their new home – a beige leather three-piece, a walnut table with six matching chairs, two of them carvers, a maple bedroom suite. Nearly everything came from Peter Jones in Sloane Square, one of the poshest shops in London.

What would Mam say if she could see me now? Josie wondered as she ordered furniture costing hundreds of pounds. She found the change from being dead poor to seriously well off somewhat daunting. People came to measure for curtains and carpets, and she had swatches of material and samples of carpet to choose from.

Laura's room was painted pink, and had a glossy white junior bed, wardrobe and chest of drawers. Josie stuck transfers on the walls, and bought a fairy castle nightlight to keep her little girl company in the dark.

It was lovely, splashing money around like there was no tomorrow, but it was accompanied by the scary knowledge that the more successful Jack became, the further apart they grew.

Jack Coltrane was now a name to be reckoned with at the

BBC. A second series of *DiMarco of the Met* had been commissioned and would start in the new year. They'd bought his play, *The Disciples*, though Mattie Garr had insisted on numerous alterations, and it was due to be shown at Easter. Now there was talk of a completely new series, and Jack was spending a lot of time in discussions with Mattie before he wrote the pilot.

There was nothing Josie could put a finger on. They made love almost as often as they used to, with almost the old fervour. It was just a feeling in her bones that something was wrong. She would catch a far-away expression on his face, as if he were thinking, What the hell am I *doing* here? She'd had the same disturbing thought herself that first Christmas at Louisa's. Despite everything, Josie suspected he would sooner be living in the apartment opposite an Italian cinema and an ice-cream parlour, working in a bar and writing plays with a message that no one wanted to hear. Having a wife and child had led to a lifestyle the old Jack would have despised.

On the day she was due to meet Lily at Euston station, Josie got dressed up to the nines in a green suede coat and matching high-heeled shoes she'd bought in the Kings Road. Underneath, she wore an orange polo-necked jumper and a slightly flared tweed skirt with orange flecks nestling in the green. She dressed Laura in her white hooded fur coat and tied her black hair in bunches with white ribbons.

'Me take Blue Bunny,' Laura said as they were leaving. It was a statement, not a question.

'Mind you don't lose him.' Laura and Blue Bunny were inseparable. Josie had felt the same about Teddy.

'Look for your Auntie Lily, luv,' Josie said later when the Liverpool train drew in. 'She's small and plump with short curly hair. Oh, look! She's grown it long again. She's got a bun.'

Lily was walking towards them in a black fitted coat and long boots, smiling and waving. Outside the barrier, Josie waved frantically back, and Laura waved Blue Bunny's paw. It was so lovely to see a familiar face that the long gap shrank rapidly, and it was as if she'd only seen Lily's pert, pretty face yesterday. The two girls embraced warmly. Not to be outdone, Laura curled a fur-clad arm around her new aunt's neck.

'You suit a bun, Lil,' Josie said. 'It looks nice.'

Lily took a long, deep breath, and smiled rapturously. 'Oh, it's good to see you, Jose. You look dead smart. And you . . .' She chucked Laura under the chin. 'You're beautiful, you are. Can I hold her?'

'Bootiful,' Laura agreed as she was passed from one set of arms to another. 'Kiss Blue Bunny,' she commanded, and Lily duly complied.

Josie took her friend's arm. 'You haven't changed a bit, Lil.'

'You've aged, Jose. You look older than twenty-three.'

It was quite like old times. 'I've had a baby,' Josie remarked tartly. 'And things haven't exactly been easy over the last few years.'

They arrived at Bingham Mews, and Lily had never seen such funny-shaped houses before. 'Fancy living over the garage! Were the builders short of space? I bet these were dead cheap.'

Josie assured her they were three times the cost of a house in Liverpool, which Lily found hard to believe.

'If you don't believe me, there's a famous model living opposite. Her name's Maya, and she's in all the posh magazines. There's an actor next door, and there's stock-brokers and bankers.' She tossed her head. 'And there's us!'

They went up to the lounge. 'Where's that famous husband of yours?' Lily enquired. 'I'm dying to meet him.'

'At lunch, which can go on for hours. He probably won't be home till six.' The lunch was usually accompanied by several bottles of wine, and Jack was likely to come home ever so slightly drunk.

She went to make tea, leaving Laura with a badly smitten Lily. Like father, like daughter, Josie thought ruefully. Laura, with her all-embracing smiles and beguiling ways, could charm the birds off the trees.

'I don't look all *that* much older.' She regarded her reflection in the little mirror behind the kitchen door. There were no wrinkles – not that you'd expect them at twenty-three – but she didn't look *young*. It was something to do with the expression in her blue eyes, as if she'd seen too much, known too much that she would have preferred not to. Perhaps it had been there since the day the bomb had fallen on the Prince Albert, and she'd never noticed before.

Trust Lily to point it out!

'Tell me all the news,' she demanded, returning to the living room with a tray of tea-things. Laura was dozing off on Lily's knee.

'I've told you everything there is to know in me letters. Oh, except this. I only heard it yesterday.' Lily's eyes gleamed and her voice rose to a squeak, a sure sign she was about to impart something of remarkable significance. 'Your Auntie Ivy's got married again. He's a policeman, Alfred Lawrence, and really huge, about six feet six.'

Josie grimaced. 'I hope he turns out a better bet than Vincent Adams.' She didn't want to talk about Aunt Ivy. 'What's the girl like your Robert's engaged to? Is there any sign of your Daisy getting married? Is Imelda still as horrible? How's your Ben? It must be awful, being married to someone no one likes.' Josie snuggled into a leather armchair. 'This is nice. I haven't had a gossip in years.'

'Imelda's pregnant again, and she's completely round the bend,' Lily said flatly. 'You should hear the way she nags Ben something rotten when they come to visit. Did I tell you they're living in Manchester? Ben's got a job there in a laboratory. Poor lad, he can't do a thing right. Ma daren't say a word in case Imelda won't come again, and it's Ben who'd suffer most. At least Sunday dinner at ours gives him a break – he goes for a drink with me da'. Anyroad, we're all dead fond of Peter. He's a super little boy, only a few months younger than this little one.' She removed a lock of hair from Laura's eyes. 'Imelda doesn't hesitate to have a go at him as well.'

Poor Peter. And poor Ben, so nice, so polite, so innocent, always anxious to do the right thing. It wasn't fair that he should end up with someone like Imelda.

'As for our Robert,' Lily was saying, 'Julia seems okay but, then, so did Imelda. Ma said she'll give her judgement in another five years. And our Daisy shows no sign of getting married.' Her voice fell, as if she might be overheard. 'Frankly, Josie, I'm beginning to wonder if she's a lesbian. She and that Eunice seem awfully close. They're always off on holiday together, and neither has ever had a fella.'

'She's only twenty-seven.' Josie laughed. 'Your Daisy's a career woman. She's bent on being chief librarian of Liverpool. There's plenty of time for her to get married.'

Lily sniffed. 'It was you that asked. Actually, Jose, would you mind taking Laura? I'm desperate to go to the lavatory.'

Josie carried Laura up to her pink and white bedroom, then went down to the ground floor, through the little door at the bottom of the stairs which led to the garage. She rolled up the garage door for when Jack came home so he could drive straight in. When she returned, Lily was coming out of the bathroom, full of admiration for a change. 'I've never seen a blue suite before, it looks dead pretty.'

'I'm glad we've got something you like.'

'Everywhere's nice.' Lily flushed. 'The house is lovely.' She sighed as they returned to the lounge. 'I'm jealous, that's all. When I saw you waiting by the barrier with Laura, I wanted to kill you stone dead, I envied you so much. Our Ben wanted to marry you, and that chap you met at Haylands, Griff. Now you're married to someone who had his picture in the *Radio Times*. He's *gorgeous*, Josie. I took it to show the girls at work.' Lily hunched her shoulders. 'I want a husband and children so much I can't think of anything else most of the time.'

'Haven't you met anyone you fancy, luv?'

'Oh, loads,' Lily said promptly. 'The trouble is, they don't fancy me. Remember Francie O'Leary? I would have married him like a shot.' Her eyes grew frightened. 'I'll be twenty-four next April, Jose. I'm worried I'll be left on the shelf.' She sort of smiled. 'I'm still a virgin, you know.'

Josie poured more tea. She said slowly, 'If only you knew how much I envied *you* over the years. I would have given anything for a mam and dad, a family.' She smiled. 'I even envied your coat the first time we met in Blackler's basement before the war. It was exactly the same as your ma's, blue with a fur collar, though I wasn't exactly crazy about your hat.'

'I suppose the grass is always greener . . .'

'On the other side of the fence.'

A car drove into the mews, and she recognised the harsh roar of the Austin Healey. The garage door was pulled down, and a few minutes later Jack came in to the room.

'You're fatter than I expected,' Lily told him plainly when they were introduced. 'You looked much thinner in your photo in the *Radio Times*.'

Josie glanced at her husband. Lily was right. She hadn't noticed, but his once-lean cheeks were fuller, and he was becoming jowly. He looked well fed, a touch prosperous. When he removed the jacket of his expensive suit, the black trousers were tight around his waist. She had a moment of fear. He looked a stranger.

He seemed slightly taken aback. 'I like a woman who speaks her mind,' he said, politely shaking Lily's hand, though Josie sensed he was annoyed. But no one liked to be told they're growing fat, particularly by someone they'd only just met. Lily was incorrigible.

She herself felt annoyed with Lily, then with Jack, who announced he had work to do and went down to his study. She was even more annoyed when Lily said, 'He's not quite as gorgeous as I thought. Is he a bit pissed, Jose? His hands were shaking.' It would have been easy to have had one of their famous rows, but Josie resisted the temptation. They were older, and it might not pass off as easily as their frequent childish ones.

★

Lily stayed for five days. With Laura in tow, Josie took her to see the sights, most of which she hadn't had time to see herself – the Tower of London, the Houses of Parliament, Madame Tussaud's. They lunched in Lyon's Corner House, went for walks through Hyde Park, along Oxford Street, Regent Street, Piccadilly, all decorated for Christmas.

They took the opportunity to buy each other presents, and Josie searched for something expensive and unique for Mrs Kavanagh, who had been the nearest thing she'd had to a mam over the years. She decided on an antique cameo brooch in a gold setting which cost twenty-five pounds. 'It's second hand but, then, you can't buy a new antique, can you?' Lily promised to give it to her mother on Christmas morning.

What should she buy Jack? Last Christmas and the one before they'd been poor. They'd bought each other things like chocolates and scarves. She'd knitted him gloves, but the fingers were all the wrong size. This year she could afford to buy something dead expensive.

'What about one of those?' They were in Selfridge's menswear department. Lily pointed to a rack of pure silk dressing-gowns in dark colours – maroon, navy blue, bottle green.

'Hmm! I'll keep them in mind.' The Jack Coltrane she'd met in Greenwich Village three years ago hadn't owned pyjamas, let alone a dressing-gown, and he would have laughed at the idea of silk. It shocked her that Lily considered such a *poncy* garment suitable for the Jack of today.

Later, as they walked through the art department, looking for the lift, she noticed a large framed picture of New York. Close up, she saw it was a photograph, taken at night. The sky was dark, the soaring buildings black, the river oily. But every light in every window was switched on, and the effect was dazzling. As Josie stared, the yellow lights seemed to be winking back at her, as if she were *there*.

She bought it immediately, and arranged for it to be delivered. Jack would love it. He could hang it in his study.

Jack managed to remain invisible during most of Lily's stay.

In the privacy of their bedroom, he confided he couldn't stand her. 'In spite of what I said, I *don't* like people who speak their minds, not if it's hurtful.'

Josie was sitting up in bed. 'In Liverpool, it's called not being polished. It was one of me Auntie Ivy's favourite sayings. "You know me, I'm not polished." Were you hurt?'

He made a face as he climbed in beside her. 'I suspected I was putting on weight, but not so that you'd notice. Since your unpolished friend pointed it out I've tried a few exercises. I must be out of condition. I can hardly touch my toes.'

'It's all those lunches, Jack, and all the wine. Lily noticed you were drunk.'

'Bitch!' Jack said savagely, and Josie wondered why she kept comparing one Jack with the other, as if they were two entirely different people. The other Jack would have merely laughed. This one swore.

She would have liked to have continued the conversation. Having spent the first six years of her life with an alcoholic, Jack's drinking worried her. She thought it wrong that he should drive. But he switched off the bedside lamp, wished her an abrupt goodnight and pulled the bedclothes around his shoulders. He lay with his back to her. Josie stayed sitting up. For some reason, she wanted to cry.

The Liverpool train was packed. Lily raced ahead, peering through windows for a seat. Josie followed with a reluctant Laura, who dragged her feet because she didn't want Aunt Lily to leave and seemed to think if she made her miss the train Aunt Lily might stay for ever.

Lily must have spied a seat. She hoisted her suitcase on board, and by the time Josie arrived a slender young man with a sweet face could be seen through the window, helping to put the case on the overhead rack. He smiled, and put a book in the place where she was to sit. Lily appeared in the corridor and leaned out of the window.

'He looks nice,' Josie remarked. 'He's keeping you a seat.'

'He's a bag of bones,' Lily said dismissively, 'and you should see his Adam's apple. It don't half wobble. I hope he doesn't talk to me. I want to read my book.'

Laura had begun to cry. 'Want Auntie Lily stay,' she sobbed.

Josie picked her up to be kissed by a suddenly tearful Lily. 'You will come at Easter, like you promised, Jose? Everyone will be thrilled to see you, particularly Ma.'

'I promise absolutely.'

The guard's whistle sounded. A few seconds later the train began to move, and Laura's sobs increased. 'Have a lovely Christmas,' Josie shouted.

'The same to you, Jose.' Lily blew kisses with both hands until the train disappeared.

The young man Lily sat next to on the train was called Neil Baxter. When Josie went to Liverpool at Easter, she was matron of honour at their wedding.

'I don't love him,' Lily said flatly the day before the wedding, 'but he loves me, and I like him *ever* so much, Jose. He's got a good job with the post office, and we have loads to talk about and never argue. Oh, and we're both mad about Elvis Presley. We want a family, two kids at least, a boy and girl. We'll call them Troy and Samantha, but we're leaving children until we've moved up a notch in the housing market. The place we're buying in Orrell Park is nice, but there's no garden. And it's a bit run-down. We're going to do it up and sell it at a profit in a year or so's time. I'll keep on working, natch, so there'll be two wages coming in.'

'You've got everything worked out for years.' Josie thought it sounded very hard-headed, not at all romantic. Yet for a woman who claimed not to be in love, Lily looked radiant the following morning when she walked down the aisle of the church of Christ the King in the brocade Victorian-style wedding dress her mother had made. Her shoulder-length veil was secured, somewhat appropriately, by a wreath of lilies of the valley, and the delicate flowers mingled with the white roses and trailing ferns in her bouquet.

Neil Baxter's eyes glowed tenderly as he watched his bride come towards him on the arm of her da'. Mr Kavanagh looked quite emotional, though the night before he'd claimed to be as pleased as Punch to be finally shot of his loud, argumentative daughter.

Josie was the sole attendant, as Lily wanted to avoid the expense of bridesmaids. She wore a plain yellow costume and a black straw picture hat with a circle of yellow flowers on the crown, both from Harrods, black shoes and gloves, and carried a posy of yellow roses. Her only jewellery was the amber pendant that Louisa Chalcott had bought in Southport, nestling within the deep V of her collar.

All the Kavanaghs had turned up for the wedding of their baby sister. Stanley and Freya had flown from Berlin with their two children. Stanley was going bald, Josie noticed when they were outside and the photographs were being taken – Lily had got someone from the office to do them on the cheap. She'd last seen Stanley the year the war ended, and supposed it was silly to expect him to look the same thirteen years later. And Marigold cut a rather matronly figure in the severe navy costume she hoped would make her look slim. She was only thirty-one but, then, she'd had four children since they'd first met when Josie had gone to Machin Street to live with Aunt Ivy.

Robert still lived in London doing something in the City, and it was impossible to imagine him aged twelve, wrestling on the parlour floor with his little brother. His fiancée, Julia, was dressed smartly in a grey costume and a little pillbox hat with a pink veil. She'd been impressed to learn that Jack was responsible for *DiMarco of the Met*. 'We must meet up in London some time, go to dinner,' she gushed earlier. Jack had greeted the suggestion with a charming smile that Josie knew was false. He was here under sufferance and hating every minute.

Only Daisy Kavanagh hadn't changed at all. In a glorious

213

cream and purple frock and a dramatic picture hat, she looked no different from the girl in the fairy glen who'd asked what the matter was. Perhaps being single isn't such a bad thing, Josie thought. No husband to worry about, no kids, no money problems. Daisy's face was smoothly serene, contented. Her friend, Eunice, seemed equally content.

Her eyes searched for Laura and Jack. Of Jack there was no sign, but Laura was playing with Heidi, Stanley's and Freya's youngest, who couldn't speak a word of English, yet somehow they seemed to understand each other. Her three-quarter-length white socks were filthy, and Josie was wondering if she could get back to the house for a clean pair before they went to the reception when a voice said in her ear, 'She's beautiful.'

She turned. Ben was looking down at her. He nodded towards Laura. 'Quite beautiful.' His lips twisted in a wry smile. 'And so are you.' He took her hands. 'You look stunning, Josie.'

'You're not so bad yourself.' She gave a small, lying laugh. He looked *terrible*. His brow was creased like an old man's, his eyes were tragic. He was stooped, yet he used to hold himself so very straight, so erect. 'How's things, Ben?' she asked, which was a silly question, because she knew things were dead awful. There was something inherently wrong with Imelda.

He shrugged. 'Oh, you know, okay, I suppose. I like my job. Manchester's a nice place to live. Imelda, well, Imelda's . . .' His voice trailed away. 'Have you seen Peter?' His face suddenly brightened. 'He's about the same age as your little girl. He's around somewhere . . .' He stopped again, and she felt his hands tighten on hers. 'Oh, Josie,' he said in an anguished voice. 'If only you hadn't decided to go to that damn holiday camp.'

She wanted to say, if only you hadn't tried to stop me. But that would only be rubbing it in, and he was miserable enough already. He had seemed to regard it as a test of his manhood to make her stay. And if she had stayed, or if he had let her go, how would things have turned out?

He continued to hold her hands, more loosely now, like two old friends together. 'Where's this famous husband of yours?'

'Around somewhere.' She'd had a terrible job persuading Jack to come. They'd fought for days. 'What's the point of having a husband,' she angrily demanded, 'if he won't come with you to important things like your best friend's wedding?'

'You know I can't stand Lily,' Jack said reasonably. 'I feel sorry for the poor guy she's managed to drag to the altar.'

In the end, he had agreed to come just for the day. He was returning to London straight after the reception. Josie was staying with the Kavanaghs until Wednesday.

'There you are!' A very pregnant Imelda came out of the church, dragging a small boy by the hand. Her pretty face was screwed in a scowl, and the child's bottom lip was trembling, as if he was about to cry. 'He's your child as well as mine,' she said acidly to Ben, completely ignoring Josie. 'I just caught him at the candles. He could have burnt himself.' She virtually flung the little boy in the direction of his father. 'It's your turn for a while.'

Ben released Josie's hands and she felt his body droop beside her. He lifted up his son. 'Have you been a naughty boy, Peter?'

'He was being curious, not naughty,' Josie said. 'Come and introduce him to Laura.' Seeing Ben, she was almost sorry herself she'd come to the wedding.

Jack must have been watching for them. When the taxi stopped, he came out while Josie was paying the driver.

'Daddy!' Laura launched herself upon him. She squealed in delight when he swung her small, squirming body above his head.

'Did you miss me?'

'Oh, *yes*, Daddy,' Laura confirmed.

Jack propped her in the crook of his arm and put his other arm around Josie. He kissed her, and it was more than just a welcoming kiss. There was something hungry about it. 'And

I've missed you, both of you. It's been very quiet and lonely here by myself.'

In the lounge, all three sank together on to the settee, which squeaked in protest. 'Did you enjoy yourselves after I'd gone?' Jack asked.

'We had a lovely time. I took Laura to New Brighton and Southport. There was a party last night for Stanley and Freya – they left the same time as us.'

'I won a game, Daddy. I got a prize, a box of chocolates.'

'Only because you cheated. It was musical chairs,' Josie explained. 'She couldn't quite get the hang of it.'

'Did you eat them, the chocolates?'

'No, Daddy. Blue Bunny ate every single one.'

Josie went to put the kettle on. It had been nice, meeting everyone again, but sad, seeing how much older they were. Mrs Kavanagh's hair had turned completely grey over the last three years, and she was wearing glasses, quite thick ones. She thought about Ben and his tragic eyes. She hadn't realised how much she missed Liverpool till she'd gone back. It was where she fitted in, felt at ease, which she would never do in Bingham Mews if she stayed for the rest of her life.

She returned to the lounge. 'I think the wedding went off very well, don't you? Lily looked radiant, and you'd think Neil had won a million pounds.'

'Poor guy!' Jack made a face. 'Did they go somewhere exotic for the honeymoon?'

'No.' She giggled. 'They had a weekend in the Lake District, and were home by Monday. They're spending the next two weeks doing up their new house.'

Jack shuddered. 'Not exactly romantic.'

'It doesn't *sound* romantic, but it is in a way. They both seem so *happy*, Jack, like it didn't matter where they were, as long as they were with each other.'

He laughed shortly. 'You almost sound envious.'

Perhaps she was. There'd been something about the faces of the newly married couple that had filled her with a sense of longing. She and Jack had looked like that when they'd first met.

When they were getting ready for bed, he said gruffly, 'Don't put your nightdress on. I want to touch you all over.'

Josie had never been able to understand why things had gone wrong, or how they'd gone wrong, but after they'd made love everything seemed right again. He stroked her body, tenderly at first, then more and more feverishly, kissing her nipples, caressing her breasts until she wanted to scream.

'I love you,' he whispered, over and over again. 'I love you.' Then he knelt over her, thrust himself inside her, and Josie's body responded, arching rhythmically against his as they climbed, higher and higher, until everything burst in a scarcely bearable climax.

We should spend time apart more often, was her last thought before she fell asleep.

She felt convinced their marriage had been rejuvenated. Jack was unusually attentive. Not that he'd neglected her, but he'd never bought her flowers before or unexpected gifts of jewellery. He came home one night with a pair of amber earrings in a velvet box. 'To go with that pendant you always wear.'

'Oh, I've always wanted some.' She threw her arms around his neck, delighted.

'I would have got them before if I'd known.'

On Monday he left early for a script conference, and an hour later she found the compact down the side of the settee. It was gold, with a pattern of red enamelled flowers. She opened it – the powder was dark, for a brunette. Josie felt herself grow cold. She shivered, snapped the compact shut, threw it back on the settee and rubbed her hands against her skirt, as if the thing were contaminated.

Charlotte Ward-Pierce was due any minute for coffee. Josie picked up the phone to tell her not to come, just as there was a knock on the door. She was too late.

'Auntie Charlie's come,' Laura sang out from the kitchen where she was drawing a picture of the wedding.

As Josie ran downstairs she told herself she was being silly, too suspicious. The compact might belong to anyone in the mews. Every single woman who lived there had sat on the settee at some time over the last few months. But surely they would have remembered where they'd last had it? Women used their compacts every day. She paused behind the door, her hand on the latch. Bile rose in her throat when she remembered feeling down the side of the settee for Lily's wedding invitation the day before they'd gone to Liverpool.

She remembered smiling, thinking to herself, She might not let us in without it. The invitation had been addressed to 'Mr & Mrs J. Coltrane, and Laura'.

Charlotte's mournful face twisted in a mournful smile when Josie opened the door. Her usually limp hair was arranged in tiny ringlets pinned on top of her head with a diamanté clip. It looked incongruous with her cotton slacks and shirt.

'We're going to a ball tonight,' she explained. 'I hope it won't have dropped by then. I left it too late to book an appointment with the hairdresser, and he was full this afternoon. Neville was cross with me as usual.' Neville Ward-Pierce was a brusque, impatient man, who never hesitated to disparage his wife in public.

'Where are the children?' Tristram and Petronella were on holiday from their preparatory school in South Kensington.

'Elsie's got them. She's taken them for a walk.'

Josie stood to one side, aware she was blocking Charlotte's way. 'Come in.'

She made coffee, gave Laura a glass of milk, filled a plate with chocolate digestive biscuits and admired Laura's picture of the wedding – Lily wouldn't exactly be pleased to know she had one eye bigger than the other.

Charlotte was on the settee, having put the compact on the coffee-table.

'I don't suppose that's yours?' Josie said casually, knowing it couldn't possibly be, otherwise she would have found it when she searched the settee last week.

'No, I've never seen it before.' Charlotte opened the compact. 'It's not my colour, much too dark.'

'Nor mine.'

There was silence. Josie couldn't take her eyes off the compact. She kept telling herself there must be a simple explanation for it, and wished she could think what it was.

Charlotte said, 'You look – what is that phrase you sometimes use? – as if you've lost a pound and found a sixpence. Is there something wrong, Josie?'

She would never be friends with Charlotte the way she was with Lily, yet Charlotte was easier to confide in and had already told intimate things about her own unhappy life. Josie nodded at the compact. 'I found it down the side of the settee, but I know it wasn't there before I went away.'

'It could be Elsie's.' Charlotte's long, gaunt face went red. The cup and saucer rattled in her hand, and she hurriedly put them on the table.

'What is it, Charlotte?' Josie said urgently. 'It's not Elsie's, she doesn't use make-up. Have you remembered whose it is?'

'No, no.' The woman lowered her head and clutched her knees, as if she were trying to roll her long body into a ball. 'I didn't intend to mention this, Josie,' she said in a small voice, 'but on Sunday morning the children got me up about half six wanting their Easter eggs. There was a noise outside. When I looked, Jack was taking the car out the garage. There was a woman in the front seat.'

Josie went over to the window and looked outside, as if half expecting to see the same scene. Her heart was drumming in her throat. 'What was she like?'

'Old,' Charlotte whispered. 'At least forty, very dark, with glossy black hair. She wore tons of make-up.' She picked the compact up, looked at the contents and put it down again.

Mattie Garr! Josie had met Mattie twice, and the description fitted perfectly. 'Perhaps they talked all night,' she said half-heartedly.

'Perhaps.' Charlotte nodded eagerly, as if she hoped this was the case. Her face fell slightly. 'I heard the same noise on

Monday morning. I didn't bother to look, so couldn't swear if it was Jack. But I remember hearing a woman laugh.'

'She turned up late Saturday night,' Jack said easily. 'I'd just got back from Liverpool. We were discussing script changes for the new series. The hours just seemed to fly by. Before we realised where we were, it was morning. I took her home. That's all there was to it.'

'For two nights in a row?' Josie tried not to sound too incredulous.

His face didn't change. 'Well, yes, as a matter of fact. It's easily done when there are important things to talk about.'

She had inspected the bed in the guest room, hoping to find Mattie had slept there, but the sheets were virginally smooth. Then she'd changed the sheets in their room in case they'd made love there. *If* they'd made love. 'Why did Mattie turn up when me and Laura were away? She's never been before.'

'She came *because* you were away,' he said patiently. 'It gave us a chance to talk without being disturbed.'

'Oh, so me and Laura are in the way?' Josie could hardly contain her anger. 'If it was all so innocent, why didn't you mention it? You said the house was quiet, that you felt lonely.'

'Because it didn't seem worth mentioning. And the house *was* quiet most of the time, and I *did* feel lonely.'

For three nights, she slept in the spare room. On the fourth she was woken by Jack's hand gently caressing her beneath the sheets.

'I would never be unfaithful to you, sweetheart,' he said softly. 'I should have told you Mattie had been. Incidentally, she's one of the most unappealing women I've ever met.' His hand curved over her hip and circled her breast. He kissed her neck. 'Why would I want to sleep with someone else when I've got you? Come back to bed, Josie, please.'

Josie went, because she couldn't sleep in the spare room for ever, otherwise their marriage would quickly be beyond repair. She wanted to believe him more than anything on earth. The magic might have gone, but she was still as madly in love with Jack Coltrane as she had ever been.

2

'I used to write that sort of thing,' Jack said boastfully. 'I went into television instead.' He was standing only a few feet away, and Josie could barely hear him above the clamour of other voices and the too-loud music from Maya's gramophone. 'Do not forsake me, oh my darling.' Tex Ritter pleaded.

There must have been at least sixty guests. As well as the residents of Bingham Mews, Maya had invited people from the world of fashion to her New Year's Eve party – magazine editors, photographers, models, male and female.

'You can hardly compare *DiMarco of the Met* with *Look Back in Anger*,' a bearded man Josie had never seen before replied scathingly. 'John Osborne's play was a real breakthrough. There'd never been anything like it before. It started a whole new trend.'

'I wasn't comparing them, was I?' Jack sounded truculent, a sign he'd drunk too much. Josie thought tiredly that these days Jack spent more time drunk than sober. He never got completely plastered, though tonight seemed to be an exception – he must have downed at least five large whiskies. The man had apparently irked him. He gestured angrily with his glass, and the liquid spilled on the sleeve of his maroon corduroy jacket. Jack was envious of John Osborne and Arnold Wesker and the other new young playwrights whose work had blown a blast of fresh air through the staid world of British theatre. They were the sort of plays he wrote himself, he groaned.

'I always said you were before your time.' Josie had tried to comfort him, though she could see little similarity between kitchen-sink drama and Jack's high-minded, rather tedious work.

'Did you see my play, *The Disciples*, on TV?' He glared belligerently at the man.

'Never heard of it.' The man walked away. Jack, staggering slightly, went over to the bar and poured himself another whisky. Maya, in a bright red curly wig, a gold lamé top and tight matching slacks, linked her arm in his and led him to a group in the corner, where Neville Ward-Pierce's penetrating voice drowned all those around him. He was bemoaning the fact that America seemed likely to elect the left-wing Senator Jack Kennedy as its next President.

'I think your husband and mine could well come to blows,' Josie said to Charlotte. They had taken refuge on the uncomfortable white chrome and plastic settee under the window. 'Jack thinks the sun shines out of Senator Kennedy's arse.'

'I quite like him myself.'

'So do I.' Josie's eyes followed the slightly Oriental figure of Maya. 'I'd love to try on wigs, see what I looked like with different colour hair.'

'I quite fancy her outfit, not gold lamé. Crêpe would look nice, black. But Maya's a model. I'd probably look awful.'

'You'd suit that sort of thing,' Josie said truthfully. It would hide her sharp knees and protruding elbows. 'Do I look like a tart in this?' She was wearing a purple Mary Quant mini-dress and showing an awful lot of leg.

'No, you look lovely,' Charlotte said admiringly. 'Neville said if I ever bought a mini-dress he'd divorce me. Do you think we should circulate? After all, it's a party.'

'Nah. You can if you like. I'd sooner stay put.' Where she could keep an eye on her husband.

Maya's lounge, exactly the same shape as every other lounge in Bingham Mews, was sparsely furnished in white and red with a black carpet, already littered with crumbs. Josie looked at the clock. Only an hour before the start of a new decade.

Charlotte left, and her place on the settee was immediately taken by the bearded man who'd been talking to Jack. 'Hi,

I'm Max Bloch, photographer. Who are you and what do you do?'

'I'm Josie Coltrane, wife and mother of one.'

'Boy or girl?'

'Girl, Laura. She'll be six in April.'

'Do you work?'

'Is housework counted? If so, I work.'

He looked at her appraisingly. 'Have you ever thought of taking up modelling? You have very good bone structure. I bet you're very photogenic.'

Josie hooted. 'I'm also size fourteen, far too big to be a model. Look at Maya – she's taller than me and her hips are about six inches smaller.'

They both turned and regarded the statuesque Maya as she swayed elegantly around the room. 'She looks like a beanpole in a wig,' Max said disparagingly. 'I wasn't suggesting you become a fashion model – there's different sorts, you know. I'll give you my card. That's what I do, prepare portfolios for models and actors. If you decide to go ahead, get in touch.'

'Oh, so you're just touting for business.' Josie smiled. 'I bet you've told every woman here she'd make a good model.'

He looked hurt. 'I've done no such thing. I'm very proud of what I do. I regard it as an art form. When I'm taking photographs I feel at one with my subjects. I hope it stays that way, otherwise I shall feel as if I've sold my soul to the devil.' He gestured. 'Like that chap over there.'

'Which chap?'

'The guy pinning back the ear of the girl in the white dress. I can't remember his name.'

Josie glanced across the room to where Jack was talking animatedly to a beautiful blonde in a white mini-dress with legs up to her ears, almost certainly a model.

'Writes some muck for television, but claims to be a great playwright,' Max Bloch continued disgustedly. 'He's sold out. No commitment, I guess. People like him make me want to puke.'

'Perhaps he has a family to support.' Josie felt the blood rush to her head. 'It takes a lot of courage to sell out if you're genuinely committed to what you do. If you're living in one room with a baby, your wife's working to support you and you're putting all your heart and soul into your writing but getting nowhere, then I wouldn't blame anyone for selling out. Anyroad, *DiMarco of the Met* isn't exactly muck. It's quite highly thought of, not just in this country but all over the world.' Numerous other countries had bought the rights.

Max Bloch looked uncomfortable. 'You know the guy?'

Josie smiled icily. 'He's my husband. His name's Jack Coltrane, by the way.'

He left to fetch her a drink, and she wasn't surprised when he didn't come back. She turned to look out of the window, still shaken. It was snowing heavily. The light was on in their house, where Elsie was looking after Laura, who'd pleaded to stay up till twelve o'clock. They'd be watching television. She'd go over in a minute to make sure they were all right. No, she'd leave it until after midnight, till 1960, then she'd wish them a happy new year and make sure Laura went to bed.

She'd surprised herself the way she'd spoken to Max Bloch. Why have I never looked at it in that way before? She wondered if Jack ever regretted that they had met. He had given up his apartment, his friends, then the plays that meant so much, for her, and Laura. She had taken for granted the rich, comfortable life that had cost him so much to provide.

She made up her mind that tomorrow they would have a long talk. She would persuade him to start writing plays again, even if only part time. It might be possible for them to go back to New York, where there was much greater scope for television writers. They had dozens of channels over there.

The party was getting a bit wild, the laughter too piercing, the voices too loud. Nearly everyone had drunk too much. Charlotte returned and reported a man was throwing up outside. She'd been to the bathroom and had found a couple engaged in what she called 'hanky-panky' in the bath, and she'd had to go home to use the lavatory. 'And there are some very peculiar noises coming from the bedrooms. I hope it isn't going to turn into one of *those* sorts of parties.'

'We'll go home if it does.' At a recent party in Bingham Mews the host suggested the men throw their car keys in a bowl.

'What for?' Neville Ward-Pierce demanded suspiciously, concerned for his silver-grey Daimler.

'We pass the bowl around,' the host explained with a wink. 'Whichever keys the bloke picks out gets the wife of the owner.'

'No way, old chap,' Neville said, stiffly indignant. 'Come, Charlotte,' he snapped. 'We're leaving.'

'I wouldn't dream of indulging in such gross behaviour,' a woman gasped in outrage.

Jack Coltrane merely laughed. 'Are you ready, sweetheart? I don't think this is quite us.'

Five couples had stayed, and it had given Josie and Charlotte something to talk about for weeks.

The girl in the white dress looked bored. She kept glancing around, as if hoping someone would rescue her from this drunken man in the maroon jacket. Josie felt sad as she watched the girl wriggle uncomfortably against the wall. She didn't realise it was the great Jack Coltrane she was talking to, one of the most popular men in New York. There, some people would have given their right arm to be in her position.

Maya swayed over to the gramophone and turned it off, then turned the television on. 'It'll be midnight in a minute,' she announced. A silent Big Ben appeared on screen, and within a few seconds the great clock began to chime.

Neville Ward-Pierce came and took Charlotte's hand. Other couples hastily began to seek each other out ready for the first chime of the New Year, a sound that always seemed so significant and full of hope.

Josie and Jack had always greeted the New Year in each other's arms. Perhaps he hadn't realised the time. Josie felt a knot in her stomach as she tried to push her way through the packed room towards her husband.

'Jack,' she called, but he was too engrossed in the blonde to hear, though the room was strangely silent except for the chimes of Big Ben, which struck midnight before she reached him. There was a deafening cheer, and roars of, 'Happy New Year.' 'The sixties, here we come!' a man yelled.

'Happy New Year,' Josie whispered when the same man grabbed and kissed her. At least someone wanted to, if not her husband. *He* was kissing the blonde, and there was something desperate and pathetic about it, something demeaning, as if he were trying to find his lost youth or his lost dreams in the reluctant embrace of a stranger. The girl's eyes were open. Help! they pleaded.

Josie ran downstairs and into the snow that was falling in heavy, wet clumps, just as the party began to sing 'Auld Lang Syne'. She stopped, the key in the door, and looked at the bright upstairs window of Maya's house. Had Jack noticed she'd gone? A sensation of aloneness which she'd had before, but had thought she'd never have again, enveloped her like a cloak. She shivered. Her feet in the thin strappy sandals were wet, and she'd forgotten her stole.

Elsie and Laura had fallen asleep in front of the television, which showed the crowds in Trafalgar Square rowdily welcoming 1960. She managed to carry Laura up to bed, glad she'd changed earlier into her nightclothes.

'Good night, my darling girl.' She placed a visibly ageing Blue Bunny on the pillow and stroked her daughter's smooth forehead. The long, dark lashes quivered in response, and Laura uttered a long, breathy sigh of contentment, before turning over. Josie tucked the eiderdown around her shoulders and switched on the fairy light.

'What's going to happen to us – to you and me?' She sank into the white wicker chair in which she sat when she read Laura a story.

It couldn't go on, not like this, not with Jack drinking so much and them growing further and further apart. She remembered that, earlier, she'd vowed to talk to him, urge him to spend more time writing plays, suggest they return to

New York, say that she hadn't realised the sacrifices he'd made. After tonight it was even more important that she say these things.

She got to her feet with a sigh. 'Good night, luv,' she whispered, closing the door.

In the lounge, Elsie Forrest was just waking up. She jumped when Josie entered the room. 'I didn't hear you come in.'

'Happy New Year.' Josie kissed the rosy, withered cheek of their babysitter.

'The same to you, dear.' She glanced at the television. The revellers in Trafalgar Square had been abandoned for a club in Scotland, where a man in a kilt was singing, 'On the Bonnie Bonnie Banks of Loch Lomond'. 'I've missed everything, haven't I? Oh, well, never mind. Did you have a nice time at the party?' she asked cheerily. 'Where's Jack?'

'Still there. I'll go back meself in a minute. You go to bed, Elsie.' Elsie was staying the night in the spare room.

'I wouldn't say no. I'll make myself a cup of milk to take up. Would you like something?'

'A cup of tea would be lovely. Ta, luv.'

As soon as Elsie left, Josie dialled Lily's number, but there was no reply. She and Neil were probably at the Kavanaghs', and she preferred not to ring there. It would look as if she had no one to talk to on New Year's Eve. Lily was thrilled to bits because she was three months pregnant. Even morning sickness gave her an odd sort of pleasure. 'Twenty-seven is the perfect age to have a baby. We're going to try for Samantha three months after Troy's born.' Everything was so certain with Lily nowadays.

Elsie came in with the tea. 'Here you are, dear. I'm off to bed. I might be gone in the morning by the time you're up, so Happy New Year again.'

''Night, Elsie.'

Josie wandered over to the window. The sounds from the party were subdued. The white curtains had been drawn and smudged bodies moved slowly behind the thin, gauzy material. They must be dancing. Maya's front door opened and a couple came out. The woman put her coat over her head and they ran through the snow to number eleven. Strange, she thought. The Maddisons are usually the last to leave a party.

After a while she supposed she'd better go back, if only to get Jack home before he passed out. She fetched a coat and left it hanging loosely over her shoulders when she went back into the snow. She rang Maya's bell, hoping someone would hear above the strains of 'Some Enchanted Evening' and let her in. The door was opened almost immediately by Neville Ward-Pierce, who was ushering out a clearly embarrassed Charlotte.

'You don't want to go in *there*, Josie,' she said quickly. 'They've already started pairing off, and there's a floor show. I daren't tell you what they're up to.'

'I've never seen anything so depraved since I was in Cairo during the war,' Neville boomed. 'It's utterly repulsive.'

'But Jack's still there,' Josie said hesitantly.

'Jack's in the kitchen, vomiting his heart up.' Neville pursed his lips disapprovingly. 'He'll come home as soon as he realises what's going on.' He slammed the door and took his wife's arm. 'That's the last party *we* go to in Bingham Mews.'

For some reason Josie waited until they'd gone indoors before she rang the bell again, but although she pressed the buzzer for ages and ages no one came.

It was gone six o'clock when Jack came home. Josie, still wide awake, heard him stumble upstairs. He lurched into the room, removed his jacket and trousers and fell on top of the covers, half-dressed. She got up and put on her dressing-gown because she couldn't stand the thought of lying beside him.

She went down and made tea. The central heating had just switched itself on and the house was still cold. She took the tea into the lounge, but found she couldn't sit down. Perhaps it was lack of sleep that made her head feel so fuzzy and thick, as if there were a tight band around her forehead preventing her from thinking, for which she was grateful because she didn't want to think about last night. She drank the tea as she walked to and fro across the room, and found comfort in the scalding liquid coursing down her dry throat. There were dirty dishes in the kitchen, which she washed and dried, hardly aware of what she was doing, just knowing that she had to do something to keep herself busy, not think. Then she polished the walnut table and the six chairs, two of them carvers, rubbing the satiny wood until it shone as it had never shone before.

Elsie came down when Josie was clearing out the cupboard under the sink. 'The paper was dirty,' Josie explained. 'I thought I'd put a new piece in.'

'Yes, dear.' Elsie nodded. Josie could tell by her eyes that the older woman had guessed something was wrong.

'There's tea made.'

'Shall I pour you a cup?'

'Please.'

They sat on the padded benches and chatted about perfunctory things. What would the sixties bring? Elsie wondered. 'At least we're not at war,' she said thankfully, 'not like in nineteen-forty. In nineteen-fifty, we were still on rations, and there weren't enough houses for people to live in. Can you remember the squatters? I reckon we're all better off these days, and things can only improve.'

'Let's hope so.'

She refused Josie's offer to phone for a taxi. 'I'd sooner walk, dear. It's not very far.' It had stopped snowing, and none had stuck to the ground.

Josie finished cleaning the cupboard. She made more tea and took up a cup to Laura, who was disappointed to learn there was no snow. 'I was going to play snowballs with Tristram and Petronella.'

'Happy New Year, luv.' Josie kissed her forehead. 'It's a new decade. Today is the first of January, nineteen-sixty.'

'I'm getting old,' Laura said glumly.

Her mother laughed. 'Is such an old lady in the mood to accompany me to the pictures this afternoon to see *Snow White and the Seven Dwarfs*?'

'Will they sing "Whistle While You Work"?' Laura forgot her age and bounced excitedly on the bed.

'It'll be exactly the same as when you saw it before. Mummy saw the same picture when she was a little girl. I went with Auntie Lily and *her* mummy.'

'Mrs Kavanagh?'

'That's right, luv. You can wear your new blue velvet dress.' It was almost identical to the one Mam had bought in Paddy's market.

'Will Daddy come? He liked Snow White the first time.'

'We'll just have to see. Your dad's got a bit of a cold coming on. He might prefer to spend the day in bed.'

There was no sign of Jack when they got back from the pictures. Laura raced up to the bedroom to tell him about the film. She came down again, her face crestfallen. 'Daddy's not there.'

'Wait here, luv. Perhaps he's in his study.'

Jack was still in his dressing-gown, elbows on the desk, staring at the typewriter which had no paper in. He raised his head when Josie went in. His eyes were swollen and puffy, half-closed, he was badly in need of a shave and his chin was bluish. He looked utterly wretched. She felt a pang of longing for the man he used to be.

'Didn't you hear us come in?' she asked sharply from the door. 'Your daughter would like to see you, even if I wouldn't.'

'I didn't do anything last night, you know.' His voice was as wretched as his appearance. 'I fell asleep on the settee. I kept waking up and dozing off again. There were things going on, I thought I must be dreaming.'

'If Neville Ward-Pierce was right, you must have had some dead peculiar dreams. I think pornographic is the word.'

'I knew you wouldn't believe me.' He rested his head on his fists.

Josie closed the door in case Laura could hear. 'I've only got your word for what went on after midnight, Jack,' she said tightly, 'just like that episode with Mattie Garr three years ago. But I've got the evidence of me own eyes for what went on before. You were as drunk as blazes, and too attached to that blonde to wish me a happy new year. You still haven't.' Her voice broke. 'It really hurt, Jack.'

He raised his head again and said mockingly, 'Happy New Year, sweetheart.'

'Is there any need to say it like that?'

'What other way is there to say it in this house?'

'And is that your fault or mine?'

Jack stretched his legs under the desk and put his hands behind his head. He grinned. 'Mine, I suppose.'

She itched to slap the grin off his face, though she knew it was merely bravado. Her eyes swept the room, looking for something to attack instead of him, and they lighted on his plays, neatly stacked on the top shelf of the bookcase. She went over and swept them to the floor, then turned on him. Her face felt ugly with anger.

'You know, you need your head examined. There's thousands of writers who'd give their eye teeth to be in your shoes, but you? Oh, you've written a few lousy plays, and you're so bloody childish that you've decided to ruin your life, as well as mine and Laura's, just because no one wants them. Grow up, Jack, count your blessings. You're a very lucky man.'

He grinned more widely. 'So, you think my plays are lousy?'

'If you must know, yes.' Josie folded her arms and glared at him. 'They're hectoring and lecturing, not the least bit entertaining.'

'Oh, well, now that the esteemed critic Josephine Coltrane has given my work the thumbs down, I might as well burn it.'

'It wouldn't be a bad idea, except we don't have a fire.'

They stared at each other challengingly across the small room. Then Jack swivelled the chair around until he was looking at the door. 'Have you never wanted to *do* something? Something magnificent that would set people talking, change things.'

'No.'

'Have you never wanted *anything*, Josie?'

'Yes.' She wished there was another chair so she could sit down. 'I wanted a family, a mum and dad, sisters and brothers. I wanted to *belong*. I always felt terribly alone, rootless. But I met you, we got married, we had Laura and the feeling went. Last night it came back again.'

His lips curved in a wistful smile. 'I'd always hoped I'd change things with my plays. They gave me a sense of purpose, a reason for being alive. They were part of me, almost like Laura.'

'Have plays ever changed things? Did Shakespeare?'

He smiled again. 'You're very down to earth all of a sudden. Are you intent on destroying all my dreams today?'

Josie gestured impatiently. 'I think it's time you stopped dreaming, came down to earth and counted your blessings.'

'You've already said that.'

'Well, I've said it again.' She took a deep breath. 'Things can't go on like this, Jack. You're hardly ever sober, we hardly ever talk. If you don't stop behaving like some silly . . .' She paused, searching for words. 'Like some silly prima donna, then I shall leave you.'

The chair swivelled round, and his eyes were like black holes in his puffy face. 'And take Laura?'

'I'm not likely to leave her with a drunk, am I?' His eyes both frightened and repelled her. She recalled having planned to say quite different things today. It wasn't too late to say them, suggest they go back to New York. She took a hesitant, placatory step towards him, but her foot caught on one of the cardboard folders she'd swept off the shelf, and she was shocked by the scorn and disgust she felt as she stared down at the scattered plays. Stupid things, she thought. Fancy mucking up everyone's lives on account of *them*. It's time he grew up and lived in the real world.

Laura burst into the room. 'Why are you so long? Laurel

232

and Hardy are on television.' She threw herself on Jack's knee. 'Happy New Year, Daddy.'

Jack refused anything to eat. He also refused to meet his wife's eyes. 'Black coffee's all I want,' he said shortly to the wall.

'There's loads of Christmas cake left, Daddy. And a big tin of biscuits with only half gone. Would you like a ginger cream, your favourite?'

'No, thank you, darling.' He reached out for his daughter and held her tightly in his arms. 'I love my little girl. Always remember that, won't you?'

Laura looked slightly startled. 'I knew that already, Daddy,' she solemnly replied. 'I love you, too.'

It was pitch dark. Laura had gone to bed and it had started to snow again when Jack announced he was going out. They had spent the hours since the row ignoring each other. Josie was already regretting some of the things she'd said. She shouldn't have criticised his precious plays.

'Where to?' She felt a pang of concern.

'For a drive, to clear my head.' He put his hands to his forehead. 'I can't think straight.'

'Don't have anything more to drink, Jack,' she pleaded. 'It's not safe to drive if you've been drinking. You might have an accident.'

'Would you care?' He looked at her sardonically.

She stamped her foot. 'Of course I'd care. I worry about you all the time when you're driving.'

'Oh, well, that's something, I suppose.'

'You'll need a coat.' She went upstairs to fetch it, but when she came down Jack had gone, and she heard the inside door to the garage slam. Then there was the grating roll as he pulled up the main door. A few minutes later the car backed out, and Jack drove away. The sound of the engine seemed to go on for ever in the stillness of the night.

'What have I done?' Josie whispered to the empty room.

Jack stayed away for almost two days, and during most of the time it snowed. On the first night Josie slept soundly as she hadn't slept a wink the night before. She wasn't surprised when he wasn't in bed when she woke up, or particularly bothered when the spare room proved empty when she looked. He was probably indulging in a long, drawn-out sulk. She regretted telling Laura that he'd be back any minute when she demanded to know where Daddy was, because the child visibly itched with worry as the hours passed and he didn't return.

On the first afternoon the Ward-Pierce children called, and Laura helped to build a snowman. It had black stones for eyes, and Charlotte made something resembling a pipe out of cardboard.

'Have you heard from Daddy?' she demanded the minute she came back.

'Not yet, luv,' Josie said brightly.

Her face fell. 'Mummy, everything in our garage is covered with snow.' She frowned. 'It looks funny, like a Christmas grotto, but there's no Santa Claus.'

'I left the door up so Daddy can drive straight in.' In fact, she hadn't been outside the house all day and had forgotten it was open. It didn't seem worth closing it now.

When darkness fell, and Jack had been gone twenty-four hours, Josie began to worry herself. Laura was fast asleep in the double bed with Blue Bunny clutched in her arms. If Jack had had an accident, surely the police or the hospital would have been in touch. He had his driving licence in his wallet. Maybe he'd holed up with a friend, not that he had many friends these days, or maybe Mattie Garr had offered him shelter from his ogress of a wife. She actually hoped this was the case, and the Austin Healey wasn't buried in a ditch in the depths of the countryside covered in snow, with a dead Jack draped over the steering-wheel. If she rang the police, they'd want to know where he'd gone, and she had no idea. He could have gone north, south, east or west. He might be hundreds of miles away or hundreds of yards.

Why didn't he pick up a phone and let her know he was all

right? *If* he was all right. And if he was, she would never forgive him for putting her and Laura through the mill like this. He'd passed the point of no return, she thought angrily. As soon as he came back, she would leave. But where would she go?

Liverpool, obviously. She felt hungry for the place where she was born. Jack would never see his daughter go short, even if he didn't give a damn about his wife. He would let them have an allowance, then she would rent a nice little house and look for a part-time job. Jack could come and visit whenever he pleased. Life would seem dead peculiar without him, but she welcomed the peace it would bring. She was fed up with the non-stop worry, the guilty feeling that she had ruined his life. It was all her fault that he had become a successful, highly paid writer when the poor man preferred to write lousy plays for nothing at all!

Josie woke up next morning and met the brown eyes of her daughter on the pillow next to hers. 'Daddy's still not home. I've just been to look.' The eyes, normally so shining and full of fun, were wet with tears. 'He's coming back, isn't he, Mummy?'

She inwardly cursed Jack Coltrane with all the invective at her command for causing such misery to a five-year-old child. Reaching out, she took the small figure in her arms and wanted to cry herself when she felt Laura's heart beat anxiously against her own.

'Daddy telephoned,' she lied. 'He called last night, long after you were asleep. The car broke down miles from nowhere in a place called Essex. He had to walk for ages through the snow to find a garage, but they didn't have the parts to fix it. He's staying in a hotel until they arrive. He doesn't know when he'll be back, but there's no more need to worry.'

Laura regarded her gravely. 'Are you sure, Mummy?'

'I wouldn't have imagined all that, luv, would I?'

'You're not just saying it to make me feel better?'

'Ask Daddy yourself when he gets home.'

Throughout the day, Laura inundated her with questions. Where exactly had Daddy phoned from? Had they got a map so Josie could show her the precise spot?

'The road atlas is in the car, luv. It was somewhere round Chelmsford, I think.' She had a feeling Chelmsford was in Essex.

'Is it a nice hotel where he's staying?'

'It's more a pub than a hotel. He said it's nice and warm.'

'And they'll make him something to eat?'

'Of course.' She wondered if Laura was trying to catch her out, expose her lie, and wished she could tell herself a lie and stop worrying.

The day wore on. She made dinner, and forced herself to eat for Laura's sake. For tea they had soup and finished off the Christmas cake. By then it was dark again, and the snow fell relentlessly against the blackness of the sky, obliterating the outline of the houses opposite. The windows were bright blurs in the midst of nowhere. Josie couldn't have felt more isolated in her expensive home if she were living at the North Pole, hundreds of miles from the nearest neighbours.

She made up her mind that, as soon as Laura went to bed, she'd ring Mattie Garr. She'd ring every single person who had anything to do with Jack and ask if they knew where he was. If they didn't know, she'd call the police.

Laura was ready for bed in her nightie and dressing-gown. She lay on the settee with her head on Josie's knee, sucking her thumb, which she hadn't done for years, and idly watching television. The nightie was fleecy white cotton with a pattern of tiny rosebuds. It had long sleeves and a lacy frill at the neck. Josie had bought another at the same time, and they'd cost a mint. That would have kept me and Mam for a few months in Huskisson Street, she recalled thinking in Peter Jones.

She picked up the swathe of black silky hair that was spread like a fan over the blue dressing-gown. It lay like a rope in her hand. Laura gave a little bothered sigh, as if she were half-asleep with her mind on her missing daddy. It was nice to be in a position to buy anything she wanted for her daughter. Mam would have loved doing the same for her. She'd been thinking about Mam a lot over the last two days. Perhaps it was because the house seethed with the same sensation of dread she'd felt when she'd looked across the street and seen the ruins of the Prince Albert. She had known then that something terrible had happened. She had known life would never be the same again.

And life would never be the same if Jack was dead. She would miss him for ever. In the two days since he'd gone, her emotions kept changing by the minute – she loved him, she hated him, she would leave, no, she would stay. Just because *she* had never wanted to write, she reasoned, or paint, or act, or do anything creative, what right had she to judge someone who did? It was impossible for her to comprehend how Jack felt about his plays. When he came back, and he *had* to come back, she would make everything right again. Somehow.

'I love you, darling,' she whispered.

Laura wriggled on her knee. 'I know, Mummy.'

From outside, there came the sound they'd been waiting so long for, the harsh whine of the Austin Healey turning into Bingham Mews, the wheels muffled by the snow.

'Daddy!' Laura raised her head and stared, starry-eyed, at her mother. 'Daddy!'

'Not so fast, luv,' Josie cried when Laura leaped to her feet and raced out of the room. 'Wait till he stops,' she called, when she heard Laura's light footsteps running down the stairs. But the little door to the garage opened, and the car's engine roared, as if in relief at the end of a long journey and the sight of home. There was an unfamiliar bump then the engine was switched off, followed by a silence that went on too long, far, far too long.

Josie tiptoed downstairs, her hands clasped mutely against her breast. 'Please, God, you can't do this to me,' she whispered. 'Say something, Laura. *Please*, God, make Laura say something.'

The first thing she saw was Jack. He was getting out of the car, and his face was a mask of horror. 'I skidded on the snow,' he said in a voice she'd never heard before.

'Back up, back up,' Josie screamed when she saw the body of their daughter jammed between the front of the crookedly parked car and the breeze-block wall. Her head had fallen forward, lying sideways on the bonnet. Blue Bunny was still clutched in her hand, and she was smiling because Daddy had come home.

It was all over. Everything was over – the inquest, the funeral, their marriage. She couldn't live with Jack again. He had murdered their daughter, though the coroner had called it a tragic error which Jack would have to live with for the rest of his life. Only Josie knew that Laura had never run to meet her father like that before. It was only because Jack had disappeared for two whole days that she'd been so anxious to see him, to touch him, to be kissed and cuddled by her dad.

She didn't tell him this, because she loved him too much to cause more suffering. He had suffered enough. Perhaps he blamed her for not closing the garage door, for allowing the snow to drift in and make him skid. He didn't say anything, and neither did she. They hardly spoke to each other in the days that followed the death of their beloved only child.

Josie felt as if her body was a bloody open wound that would never heal. She was sore all over, and her head threatened to explode with unbearable grief. Sometimes it was impossible to believe that it had happened, *impossible*. She would go into Laura's room and expect to find her asleep in the white glossy bed or arranging her dolls in a row so that she could give them a lesson. But the room would be empty, the truth would assault her like a physical blow and she would double up, clutching her stomach, as the awareness sank in that she would never see her daughter again.

Their grief was suffered separately and alone. Josie slept in the spare room. During the day Jack remained in his study, the typewriter silent. He had shrunk inside his clothes, and they hung loosely on his rapidly thinning frame. She never glimpsed him without a drink in his hand, yet he appeared to be stone cold sober. She never asked, and he never said, where he'd been during the time he was away.

The house in Bingham Mews was put on the market to be sold fully furnished. They couldn't live there any more, it held too many bad memories. Jack was returning to New York, Josie to Liverpool. She would go first, and he would wait until the house found a buyer. People had already been to look round, and several had expressed interest.

'According to the estate agent, we'll make a profit.' Jack's thin lips quivered in what might have been a smile. 'It's worth thousands more than we paid. I'll finish off the mortgage and send you what's over.'

'I don't want a penny,' Josie said quickly. It would feel like blood money. That night she tore up the cheque-book for their joint account and threw it away. She had enough money in her bag for the fare to Liverpool. Once there, she'd start again on her own.

'As you wish,' Jack said dully.

Elsie Forrest was distraught. She had loved Laura deeply. 'I felt like her grandma,' she sobbed. 'As if she were partly mine.'

'She loved you, too.' There would be other children for Elsie to love, but not for her, Josie thought bitterly. Laura was her one and only child. She would never have another.

She was grateful Elsie was willing to clear the house of their possessions. 'What about the dishes, the cutlery, all your lovely ornaments and pictures?' Elsie wanted to know.

'I don't give a damn what happens to them,' Josie said listlessly. Her suitcase was already packed with a few clothes, a few photographs.

Charlotte had been a tower of strength. It was Charlotte who telephoned Mrs Kavanagh to relay the tragic news, because Josie couldn't possibly have done it.

'I can't begin to imagine how you must feel, my dear, dear Josie,' Mrs Kavanagh had written. 'Your friend said you're coming back to Liverpool. You know you're welcome to stay with us as long as you wish.'

It was her last day in Bingham Mews. The house had been sold. The final contract would be signed shortly. She said goodbye to Charlotte and promised to write, though she knew she never would. She made the same promise to Elsie, avoiding the woman's kind, worried eyes.

Jack was in his study when she went to bed. Tomorrow they would say goodbye for ever, and she wasn't sure if she could stand it. If only they'd stayed in New York. The 'if onlys' could go right back to the start of time. If only she hadn't worked for Louisa, she wouldn't have gone to America in the first place. If only she hadn't wanted to say goodbye to Tommy, then Mam wouldn't have been in the Prince Albert when the bomb struck.

'Comfort me,' Jack was saying in a muffled voice which was almost a sob. 'Comfort me, sweetheart. Say you forgive me. I already hate myself enough without knowing that you hate me, too.' He began to weep. 'I want to die, Josie. I want to *die.*'

At first Josie thought she was dreaming, that it was part of yet another nightmare, but when she opened her eyes Jack was kneeling beside the bed.

Without hesitation she put her arms around his neck and drew him to her. 'I don't hate you, Jack,' she whispered. 'I know you would never have done anything to hurt our darling Laura.'

'I adored her,' he wept.

'I know, luv.' She patted his back, as if he were a child. 'We both did.'

'I love you, sweetheart.' She had never heard such anguish in a voice before. 'Can't we try and get through this together? Come back with me to New York. *Please*, Josie.'

'No.' She shook her head implacably. It was easy to dispense forgiveness, but she would never cease to blame him for Laura's death. If he hadn't been so childish, so foolish, as to disappear, Laura would be fast asleep in her room now. 'I don't think it would work,' was all she said. Then she herself began to cry, and it was Jack's turn to comfort her, to take her in his arms, stroke her cheek and kiss her eyes and say that she was his lovely girl, his sweetheart, and he was sorry, so sorry, for the way he had behaved, because he loved her more than words could possibly say.

'Remember the night we met?' he said huskily.

'I'll never forget it, Jack.'

He kissed her, and she felt his lips quiver against her own. Incredibly, her body began to respond. Little hot darts of desire coursed through her veins, and she pressed herself against him, while all thoughts of everything fled from her brain, and all she wanted was for Jack to take her, swallow her up, so she would no longer exist.

There was something raw and uninhibited about the way they made love, something desperate and tragic, as if they were the only two people left in a world that was about to explode in one last almighty bang.

Afterwards, they clung to each other silently for a long while. Then Jack took her face in both hands and pressed a final kiss against her trembling lips. 'Goodbye, sweetheart. I won't be around when you leave in the morning.'

'Goodbye, Jack.'

Josie lay against the pillows and watched him leave. The door closed, and she slid under the bedclothes, sobbing uncontrollably. It was a long time before she fell into a restless, jerky sleep. At one point she woke up when she banged her arm against the wall, and a thought drifted through her head – Jack hadn't used anything when they'd made love. But she wasn't likely to conceive, not like that first time in his apartment. Her body felt barren, as juiceless and dead as the plants she'd pulled from Louisa's garden.

She looked at her watch. A quarter past six. This time tonight she would be in Liverpool. For good.

Princes Avenue
1960–1961

I

Josie had been back in Liverpool a week, living with the Kavanaghs, and had no idea what to do with herself. She felt as if her body had seized up, like pipes in winter. She couldn't read, she couldn't watch television and conversation was impossible. Lily came to see her, as did Daisy and Marigold. She could hear them speak, but the meaning went over her head.

She regretted her impulsive decision to tear up her cheque-book, because she had no money. When she telephoned the bank in London to ask for another, the joint account had been closed. Although Jack was the last person she wanted to talk to, she telephoned Bingham Mews, and was perversely disappointed when there was no reply. She called several more times over the next few days, and eventually Elsie Forrest answered.

'Jack's gone, dear.' Elsie's voice was husky with sadness. 'He signed the final contract the other day. I'm just giving the place a final going over. The new people move in tomorrow.'

He'd gone! Her heart turned over, and she knew she had made a terrible mistake. 'Did he leave an address?'

'No, dear. He didn't know where he would be living. He said it might not be New York. He mentioned California.'

'I see. Well, thank you, Elsie.' She rang off before Elsie could ask how she was, how was she feeling, how was she coping.

Everyone thought she was coping extraordinarily well. 'Gosh, I'd be devastated, me,' Lily had said. Or something like that. Only a tiny part of Josie's brain was working, the part that coped with getting dressed, getting washed, getting from one room to another, and now money.

It was ironic because last week she'd had hundreds of pounds at her disposal and now there was only a few pounds left. She was almost grateful to have something important to concentrate on. It meant she'd have to find a job and support herself, which had been her intention all along, she recalled.

'Are you sure it's not too soon, luv?' Mrs Kavanagh said cautiously when Josie brought up the subject of work.

'It will always be too soon, but I need to occupy me mind.'

The older woman looked dubious. 'You're not letting yourself grieve properly, Josie. I haven't heard you cry once. You need to let go, get everything out of your system. Once that's done, you'll find time will heal.'

'I daren't let go,' Josie said simply. 'I'd go mad if I did. I try to pretend it didn't happen. Not that Laura isn't dead, but that she never existed, that I never had her, that I never met Jack. It's seems the easiest way.'

'That won't work, luv. You'll have to grieve some time.'

'It's worked so far.'

She found a job with relative ease, with a builder, Spencer & Sons, in Toxteth, no distance from Huskisson Street where she'd lived with Mam. They wanted someone straight away.

'The missus usually looks after the paperwork.' Sid Spencer had interviewed her in the office, a wooden shed in the corner of the yard where the materials were kept. He was fiftyish, with a tough, kind, weatherbeaten face and an expansive grey moustache. She liked him immediately. 'But now all three of me lads are in with me, and work's growing all the time. Chrissie gets herself in a right ould tizzy. She can only type with two fingers, and me books are in a terrible mess. I don't know what's been paid, or what hasn't, or if a bill was sent out in the first place.' He indicated the desk, piled high with pieces of paper. 'Nothing's been filed for months.'

243

'I'll sort things out for you.' She welcomed something she could concentrate all her attention on. The typewriter was a Remington, relatively modern, and there was a two-bar electric fire and an electric kettle. The shed was warm and cosy, and she could make tea whenever she felt like it. It was far better than a carpeted office, an officious boss breathing down her neck, other women who'd want to talk.

Sid coughed, embarrassed. 'I wasn't expecting someone as posh as you after the job, luv. You look like the secretary to a millionaire. I'm afraid the lavvy's outside. There's only the one, and it's in a disgusting state. I'll get one of the lads to clean it up and put a bolt on the inside.'

'I just want a job, any job,' Josie said quietly. 'And the pay's good.' She probably looked overdressed in the only coat she'd brought with her – camel with a fur collar, which she'd got in the Kings Road, and brown suede boots. Her handbag had cost more than she would be earning in a week.

'Well, if something comes up in a nice, plush office, I'll understand if you leave, luv.'

'I won't leave.'

She put her mind and all her energy into the new job: made new files, giving one to each of the jobs in hand; typed orders, quotations, invoices, the occasional letter, and dealt with calls from customers, mainly wanting to know why someone hadn't turned up as faithfully promised to instal a new bathroom or lay a new floor, or when on earth they would finish the extension started weeks ago – there'd been so sign of a bloody workman in days.

Sorting through the papers, trying to tie quotations to invoices to payments received, Josie discovered that Sid was owed over five hundred pounds. 'And you paid the builders merchants twice for those sheets of plywood you ordered last November.'

Sid was thrilled. 'That's enough to pay your wages for over a year. You're worth your weight in gold, Josie, luv.' He looked at her respectfully. Josie sometimes felt like the employer, not the employee. His three curly-haired sons, Colin, Terry and Little Sid, called her 'miss'.

Chrissie Spencer came to inspect the paragon of a secretary her husband had hired. It was during Josie's second week, just before dinnertime. She was a glamorous woman with dyed blonde hair and a good-natured face, wearing a beaver lamb coat over a smart tweed costume. 'I got done up in me bezzie clothes, so's not to feel at a disadvantage, like,' she grinned. 'Sid ses you turn up looking like a fashion model every day. All he does is go on and on about you. Every time he ses "Josie", I want to scream. D'you fancy a cup of tea, luv? It's bitter outside.'

'I've already had five this morning, but I wouldn't mind another.'

'And where's Mr Coltrane?' Chrissie asked.

'In America. We're separated.'

'Really!' She looked over her shoulder, eyebrows raised. 'You were married to a Yank?'

Josie nodded, dreading that the next question would be about children because she didn't know how to answer. Instead, Chrissie asked, 'D'you take sugar, luv?'

'No, ta.'

She brought the tea. 'Here you are, luv, a nice hot cuppa. Where is it you're living? Sid said you're staying with friends.'

'Childwall, but I'm looking for a place of me own.' She yearned to be alone, ached for it. The Kavanaghs couldn't possibly have been nicer or more sympathetic, but she felt in the way. They turned off the television if something funny was on, and Marigold hadn't brought her children round once since Josie had come to stay. Lily's pregnancy was never mentioned. Everyone was treading on eggshells, all because of her. Josie felt as if she'd cast a blight on their normally happy, easygoing life.

And she wanted to be alone for her own sake, so she wouldn't have to put up a front. She could look as miserable as she felt, get up in the middle of the night, *do* things, make tea when she couldn't sleep, which was most nights, rather than creep around, worried she'd wake someone up.

'You should ask Sid, luv,' Chrissie said helpfully. 'He's just done up this great big house in Princes Avenue for some property company, turned it into flats, like. You never know, one of 'em might do you.'

'I'll ask Sid next time I see him.'

Sid had a key to the house in Princes Avenue. 'Have a look round, luv, it's only five minutes' walk. It's empty, I've still got bits and bobs to do. I'd take you meself, but if I don't get on with Mrs Ancram's kitchen, she'll do her bloody nut.'

Josie went at dinnertime. Princes Avenue was wide and stately, with a line of trees running down the centre. Like Huskisson Street, the houses had been owned by the Liverpool wealthy – importers and exporters, owners of shipping companies and factories. Josie could tell by the different curtains on each floor that most had now been turned into flats.

The house she was looking for was dark red brick, semi-detached, huge, with a wild, overgrown garden that showed signs of once having been carefully cultivated. The massive front door was freshly painted black, with three stained-glass panels in the upper half. There was a row of bells, seven altogether, she counted, with a little blank space beside each for a name. She found the lock stiff and awkward when she tried to turn the key. Once inside, she slipped the latch in case she couldn't get out. Although the February day was dull, the hall and the wide, elegant staircase were speckled with vivid spots of colour from the stained glass. The woodwork was cream, the walls a pale coffee colour. Sid had said the owners intended to carpet the communal areas. 'It won't be let to riff-raff,' he'd said. 'You're just the sort they want. I'll put in a word if you're interested.'

There were doors left and right. Josie opened the one on the right. The flat consisted of two immense rooms, a small kitchen and bathroom. The one opposite was identical. Sid had left the original fireplaces and painted the elaborately moulded ceilings white. On the first and second floors the rooms were just as large, the fireplaces and windows smaller. The walls were the same pale coffee colour as the hall, the woodwork cream.

Her footsteps echoed eerily through the empty, unfurnished rooms, and the higher she went the narrower the stairs became. Steep steps, no wider than a ladder, led to the third floor and a doll's-house door which she had to stoop to get through, to discover an attic that had been given an entirely new floor and dormer window at the back.

'This is for me.' Josie surveyed the long room that ran the length of the house. The peaked ceiling sloped down to walls no more than four feet high. 'I bet this is the cheapest,' she said aloud. There were kitchen units, a cooker and a sink at the front end, and a small square portion had been sectioned off with hardboard at the back. She opened the door and found a shower room, with a lavatory and small sink.

'It wouldn't need a carpet, just a few cheap rugs. I could get a bed and a settee on hire purchase.' She closed her eyes and tried to imagine the room furnished, but felt herself go dizzy. Perhaps it was the empty house, the silence, the echoes, or that she was alone, properly alone, for the first time since she'd come back to Liverpool, but her brain suddenly went into free fall, as if she were in a lift in a New York skyscraper and the mechanism no longer worked. Downwards, downwards, she zoomed, until she could no longer stand. She fell down on all fours. There was an explosion in her brain, and Josie went completely insane.

Laura was dead, Jack had gone!

Josie screamed. Why should she care where she lived when ahead there was only a living death because she had lost her husband and her child? She screamed and beat the floor with her fists. 'Laura, come back!' she groaned, and raised her arms skywards, as if God had the power to restore her daughter to her arms. She beat the floor again when Laura didn't come, because she was dead, and Josie had been at the funeral and

247

seen with her own eyes the tiny coffin being lowered into the ground, leaving her with no reason to go on living. She cursed God, using words, foul words, that had never crossed her lips before, for being so cruel as to have first taken Mam, and now Laura.

Suddenly there were arms around her, and a soft, vaguely familiar voice was murmuring, 'Let it all go, luv. That's right, let it all go. Cry all you like. I'm here now.' Josie pressed herself against the unknown breast and sobbed until her heart felt as if it were breaking, and the voice kept murmuring, 'There, there, luv. Cry all day if you want. It'll do you good. There, there.'

Her chest and ribs were sore, and still Josie cried, while the soft voice continued to make soothing little noises. A hand lightly stroked her hair. Eventually, when she could cry no more, because she felt completely dry, empty, Josie stopped. She was exhausted and, for the first time in weeks, longed for sleep. If a bed had been available, she was sure she could have slept peacefully for hours.

'Better now?' enquired the voice.

Josie realised she was still clinging to the owner of the voice, and that she had no idea who it was. She moved away from the strange arms, and found herself staring into the soft gentle eyes and serene face of Daisy Kavanagh, looking like a Christmas card in white fur earmuffs and a fluffy scarlet coat. She stroked Josie's swollen, tear-stained face. 'Better now, Josie, luv?'

'I don't know,' Josie croaked. 'How did you get in?'

'You left the door unlatched. I called in the yard to invite you to lunch, it's me half-day off, see. A very nice young man told me where you'd be, so I decided to keep you company, like.' She smiled sweetly. 'Mind you, I thought you were being murdered when I first came in.'

'I'm sorry if I gave you a fright.' She felt embarrassed that her outburst had been witnessed, even if it had been by Daisy Kavanagh, so kind and understanding. 'You always seem to be around when I'm in a state.'

'It's only been the twice, luv.' They were sitting cross-legged on the floor now, facing each other in the big empty room. Daisy took both Josie's hands in hers. 'It'll have done you good to get if off your chest, well, some of it. I don't doubt you'll cry again.' She glanced around the room. 'It's nice here. Are you going to take it?'

With an effort Josie switched her mind from the tragedy of the past to the practicality of the present, which had perhaps been Daisy's intention. She sighed. 'If I can afford the rent. I'll need all sorts of furniture.'

'We've got bits of stuff in Machin Street you can have. Eunice is always saying the place is over-furnished.'

'Ta.'

Daisy released her hands and scrambled to her feet. 'Lunch is still on offer, Jose. My treat. We'll go somewhere with a licence so you can have a drink. I reckon a double whisky would do you the world of good.'

Sid Spencer contacted the company that owned the house in Princes Avenue to ask about the rent for the top-floor flat. It was just within Josie's means. 'They're being dead official. You can move in the first of March, but you have to sign a year's lease.'

'That's all right,' Josie said easily.

'It means you can go home for your dinner.' He regarded her with a fatherly eye. 'I don't like the idea of you sitting in this place all day without a break.'

'It's too cold for a walk, and too far to get to Childwall.'

'I know. Princes Avenue is just right.' He looked pleased.

Mrs Kavanagh understood completely that Josie would prefer to be on her own. She came with Lily to see the flat the day the stair carpets were being laid. Josie had signed the lease the day before.

Lily was five months pregnant and beginning to show. She was wearing a voluminous maternity frock, as if she wanted the whole world to know she was expecting. 'It's very pleasant,' she conceded, walking the length of the room, jutting out her stomach as far as it would go, 'but you can't compare it to a house. There's no privacy.'

'Honestly, Lily!' Her mother rolled her eyes impatiently. 'I sometimes wonder if you're dead from the neck up.'

'I don't need privacy, do I?' Josie said with a wry smile. 'I'll be living on me own.'

'It'd be a job lugging a baby up them narrow stairs.'

'*Lily!*' Mrs Kavanagh snapped.

'I meant when I bring Troy to see Josie, that's all.' Lily patted her stomach and looked hurt. 'Can I christen the lavatory, Jose? I'm aching to go.'

'Of course.'

The door to the lavatory closed. Josie looked out of the small window at the front. It was strange, but the other side of Princes Avenue was called Princes Road. She wondered if the postman ever got confused.

'Lily doesn't mean anything, luv, but she was back of the queue when the good Lord handed out tact.'

'I don't take any notice.' The hairs were tingling on Josie's neck. It was the mention of lugging a baby up the stairs that had done it, made something click in her weary brain. She'd been too wrapped up in misery to notice that she hadn't had a period since December, and she knew, more surely than she had ever known anything before, that she was pregnant. It had happened on the last night with Jack, just as Laura had been conceived on the first. Her body shuddered with revulsion. She didn't want this child.

2

'Daisy,' Josie cried hysterically. 'Oh, Daise, hold me hand, there's another contraction coming.'

'There, luv.' Daisy gripped her hand. 'It'll soon pass. It'll soon be all over and done with.'

'I didn't have pains like this when I was having Laura.' Josie gasped as the contraction mounted and swelled, reaching a pitch that was barely tolerable, before gradually fading. She tried to relax, impossible when she was dreading the next pain, knowing it would be worse.

'You didn't have backache with Laura either,' Daisy said in her light, sweet voice. She looked coolly beautiful in a sage green costume and tiny matching hat. 'Or veins in your legs, or swollen feet. Having Laura was as easy as pie, or so you keep saying, but all babies are different, Josie, before they're born and after.'

'Your Lily's terrified of having another baby.' It helped to fill the gaps between the pains with conversation. 'She was going to show everyone how easy it was. Instead, she yelled her head off when the time came.'

'I know, Jose. I was there, unfortunately. It was dead embarrassing. Not only that, she was outraged when Samantha appeared and it should have been Troy. We all thought she was going to tell the midwife there'd been a mistake. Neil was delighted, but he's delighted with everything Lily does.'

'I hope I have a boy, Daise.'

'I know, luv.' Daisy stroked her brow.

It was ten past two in the morning, and they were in Liverpool Maternity Hospital, in a side ward. The main light was off, and a small lamp with a green shade gave off a ghostly glow, making the room, with its cream and green walls and green window-blind, seem dismal and depressing.

The contractions had started six hours ago, eight days before the baby was due. Josie was lying on the settee, reading, when it gave the first sign it was on its way, a very strong sign, but this was only the beginning – the contractions could go on for hours. She made tea and tried to drink it calmly, pretending to admire how the late evening sunshine added a light golden lustre to the attic room, lingering on the pale coffee walls, turning the vase of plastic sunflowers on the table into yellow flames.

The table, like everything except the bed, was second hand, other people's cast-offs. Nothing matched – the chintz-covered settee clashed with the curtains, which clashed with the faded patchwork quilt – but the room looked pretty, almost striking, with the addition of loads of plastic flowers and statues bought for coppers which she'd painted bright red. She'd had more satisfaction from making the room look nice than she'd had from furnishing Bingham Mews when money had been no object, though she often thought wistfully about the television that had been left behind, as well as the twin-tub washing machine and the steam iron. She could have really done with those things now.

The cot beside the bed she would have sooner done without. The white-painted bars made her think of a prison – for herself, not the baby it would shortly hold.

Another contraction started. She gasped and looked at her watch – twenty minutes since the first one. Adding a hairbrush and some make-up to the suitcase that had been packed for days, she caught a bus to the hospital. She was still pretending to be calm. The pregnancy hadn't been easy, and she was glad the time had come. Working for Sid, which she'd done almost to the end, had helped to occupy her mind.

When she reached the hospital she phoned Daisie Kavanagh. Eunice answered and said Daisy was round at Childwall and she would phone her there.

'Don't tell Mrs Kavanagh, will you? Daisy's the one I want. She knows why.'

'I understand, luv. She'll be along in a flash.'

Eunice wished her good luck. Josie hoped she hadn't sounded rude but, much to the chagrin of Lily who regarded it as a betrayal of friendship, she'd grown close to Daisy over the last few months. She was the only person who knew how unwelcome the baby was. Everyone else regarded it as a miracle, a replacement sent by God for her darling Laura, when Josie regarded it as a trespasser, an intruder in her life. It wouldn't be so bad if it was a boy, but a girl . . .

Daisy didn't judge her harsh, muddled emotions, didn't criticise, just seemed to understand.

A nurse popped her head around the door. 'How's she doing?'

'I don't think it will be long now,' Daisy said.

The door closed, busy footsteps sounded in the corridor, babies cried, there was a muffled scream. Someone else was going through the ordeal of giving birth.

'Don't ever have a baby, Daisy,' Josie groaned.

'I nearly did, once.' The soft lips twitched in amusement at the sight of Josie's shocked, astonished face.

'When?' Josie briefly forgot her own discomfiture. 'How? What do you mean by nearly?'

'I had a miscarriage,' Daisy said placidly. 'The father's name was Ralph. He was an assistant librarian where I worked. I knew he had a wife, but I was too much in love to care. I was only twenty, and I suppose you could say he seduced me. I believed him when he swore he loved me. I thought we'd get married one day. I didn't care if it wouldn't be a church wedding because Catholics aren't allowed to marry divorcees.'

'What happened?' It was hard to imagine tranquil Daisy Kavanagh being passionately in love, having sex with a married man.

Daisy smiled a touch sardonically. 'Oh, he dropped me like a hot brick when he discovered I was pregnant. It turned out I was just a girl in a whole line of girls.' Her grip on Josie's hand tightened slightly. 'His poor wife was going out of her mind. She came round to Machin Street to have it out with me. Fortunately, it was the time Ma and Da were moving to Childwall so they were round at the new house. *Un*fortunately, perhaps it was the shock of being jilted, the shock of the wife turning up, but I suddenly had these dreadful pains, just like you're having now, Jose, and my dear little baby was flushed down the lavatory.'

'You mean, while the wife was there?' Josie gasped. There was another muffled scream from outside, followed by a sharp, triumphant shout, then a baby's angry wail.

'Yes, but she was a brick. She held me in her arms,

comforted me, and we called the father every name under the sun.'

'I can't imagine you calling anyone names.'

'Still waters run deep, Jose.' Daisy gave an enigmatic smile. 'Me and Eunice spent many a happy hour planning Ralph's murder, but we were too scared of being caught so we gave up on the idea.'

'Eunice! You mean . . .'

'Yes, I mean Eunice. When the family moved, I stayed in Machin Street and Eunice left Ralph and came to live with me.' She chuckled. 'I know some people, our Lily for one, think there's something odd about it – well, I suppose there is, but it's not what they think. Anyroad, Jose, you are now privy to one of the best kept secrets in the world, and I trust you'll keep it to yourself. I only told you so you'd know how much I'd like to be in your shoes at the moment.'

'Oh, Daisy!' Josie was about to say something else, but another contraction started that seemed to go on for ever, and Daisy called the nurse.

The midwife was black, brusque and efficient. 'It's a girl,' she announced, holding up an ugly, red, baby-shaped object for Josie to see. 'What are you going to call her?'

'I don't know.' Josie ached all over and wanted to be sick. She had intended to call it Liam if it was a boy, but couldn't bring herself to consider girls' names. 'What's your name?'

The midwife frowned unbelievingly. 'Dinah.'

'Then Dinah it is.'

'Me mother's called Shelomith. I bet you wouldn't have latched on to that quite so quick.'

'Oh, I don't know.' Josie closed her eyes. 'I really don't care.'

She had loads of visitors, so different from when she'd had Laura and there'd only been Jack. Mr and Mrs Kavanagh, Marigold and a moidered and extremely cross Lily, who complained that Neil wasn't doing his share with the new baby. She had to get up and feed Samantha twice a night.

'Are you still breast-feeding?' Josie asked.

'Of course I am. Mother's milk is best for baby.' Lily spoke as if she was quoting from a book.

'Then what on earth do you expect Neil to do – grow breasts?'

'He could at least wake up and *talk* to me.'

Chrissie and Sid Spencer arrived with flowers, and presents from Colin, Terry and Little Sid. Daisy came every night. Charlotte Ward-Pierce had kept the Kavanaghs' telephone number, and had called months ago to see how Josie was when she didn't write. Mrs Kavanagh must have rung to tell her about Dinah, because there were cards from her and Neville, and Elsie Forrest.

'I'm so happy for you, Josie,' Elsie wrote. 'It's a miracle, another little daughter, and so soon. How I wish that I could see her. Does Jack know? Has he been in touch?'

Jack knew where the Kavanaghs lived. He could easily have got in touch. But he hadn't. He would never know he had a new daughter, and she wondered how he would feel if he did. She thought about him more than usual the day Elsie's card arrived. The time in New York, the years in Cypress Terrace and Bingham Mews seemed to belong to a different world altogether from the one she lived in now, but she still longed to see him.

The evening visitors poured into the ward, the new fathers stiffly formal in their best suits, a few awkwardly bearing flowers. Josie's attention was drawn to one man who stood out from the rest. He wore a trenchcoat with the belt tightly buckled, and a black trilby perched precariously on the back of his head. He was chewing gum, and his hands were stuffed mutinously in his pockets, as if he wouldn't be seen dead carrying flowers or a bag of fruit. She thought he looked vaguely familiar. Their eyes met when he passed the foot of her bed and they stared at each other. Then the man grinned broadly, and said out of the corner of his mouth, 'Well, if it isn't Josie Flynn!'

'Francie O'Leary!'

He came and sat on the edge of the bed, which was strictly forbidden. Visitors were supposed to use the chairs. 'What are you doing here, luv?'

'What do you think? It's a maternity hospital, Francie.' He was still the handsome rat she remembered from the Saturdays when they'd sorted out the world over a cup of coffee, and she was really pleased to see him. He carried with him the aura of that carefree time when she'd got on well with Aunt Ivy and was going to marry Ben.

He seemed equally pleased to see her. 'Someone told me you lived in America, or was it London?'

'Both, but now I'm back in Liverpool for good.'

'You've had a baby?'

Josie smiled. 'They wouldn't have let me in if I hadn't.'

To her surprise, he picked up her hand and kissed it. 'Congratulations, Jose. Where's the proud father? He's a writer, isn't he?'

'Yes. He's back in America. It . . .' She shrugged. 'It didn't work out. What about you? Are congratulations due?'

His small eyes widened in amusement. 'Jaysus, no, luv. I'm not married. It's our Pauline who's had the baby. She's over there with me Mam and the doting husband.' He winked. 'I'll get an ear-bashing for not fetching in a bunch of grapes.'

'Are you still working in the same place?' she asked conversationally, reluctant to let him go. He'd worked as a clerk for a shipping company on the Dock Road.

He took out his wallet, removed a business card and held it in front of her eyes. 'Francis M. O'Leary, Printer', she read, followed by his address and telephone number. 'Wedding Invitations, Tickets, Letterheads, Business Cards, etc.'

'What does the "M" stand for?' she asked.

'Money, girl,' Francie said with a wicked grin. 'I thought, seeing as we live in a capitalist society, I may as well be a fully paid up member. It means *I* get the benefit of me hard graft, not some cruddy employer. I put the printing machine in the bedroom after our Pauline and Sandra left home. Not doing bad for meself either.'

Daisy had arrived, along with Mrs Kavanagh, who fortunately didn't remember this was the man who had nearly sent her youngest daughter to a convent. Before he left, Francie said nonchalantly that if Josie would like to give him her address, he'd drop in sometimes, and she said she was already looking forward to it.

Mrs Kavanagh wanted to know how Dinah was getting on now that she was five days old.

'Fine.' Josie didn't haunt the nursery like the other mothers, looking through the glass to reassure themselves that *their* baby wasn't crying. Nor did she welcome having the child thrust at her several times a day to breast-feed. She felt no connection, no relationship, to the tiny, pale, fair-haired infant, almost two pounds lighter than Laura, who bore no resemblance to either her mother or her father. In another five days she would be sent home with a baby she still didn't want.

Spencer & Sons were doing their best to hang on to the typist whom Sid claimed kept the firm afloat. Josie said he was being ridiculous – there were dozens of typists around, as good as her or better – though she appreciated a pile of invoices or estimates arriving via Chrissie or one of the lads which she would type on the machine that now stood on her table, something that would never have happened with the insurance company she'd worked for, or Ashbury Buxton in Chelsea. Not many women with a newly born baby were in a position to earn a wage, but she flatly refused to accept the amount she'd had before. 'It's too much. You'll have to pay someone to be in the office and answer the phone.'

Chrissie claimed she missed the office, but not the typewriter. 'I didn't mind answering the phone. It gave me something to do while Sid and the lads were at work.'

Everyone agreed on two pounds less a week, and everyone was happy.

★

Dinah was a fractious baby. She cried if she was wet, if she was dry, if she was hungry, if she was full. She cried for no reason at all as far as her anxious mother could see. Josie nursed her, cursed her and poured gripe water down her throat, because Daisy had consulted a book in the library which suggested she might have three-month colic. If so, it would stop in another five or six weeks.

'I don't think I can stand another week,' Josie groaned, 'let alone five or six. Laura hardly cried at all.'

'That was Laura, this is Dinah,' Daisy said patiently. 'She's such a sweet little thing, so pretty.' She toyed with the white fingers which quickly curled around her own. Dinah gave a little shuddering breath and fell asleep in her arms.

'You seem to have a knack with her.'

Daisy looked Josie full in the face. 'She knows I love her, that's all.' She turned her gentle gaze to the baby. 'I don't half wish she were mine.'

Josie turned away, ashamed. She didn't love her daughter, and doubted if she ever would. Perhaps that's why Dinah cried so much. It wasn't gripe water she needed, but her mother's love.

She'd been half expecting someone to complain about the noise. 'I know it can't be helped, dear,' the smart, middle-aged woman who lived in one of the flats below said when she came upstairs to point out that neither she nor her husband had had a wink of sleep the night before. 'All babies cry, though yours seems to be a champion. We were wondering if you intended to stay, renew your lease. If so, we thought we'd look for somewhere else because I dread to think what it'll be like when she starts teething, and that can go on for months.'

'I *am* moving,' Josie said tiredly. She hadn't had a wink of sleep either, and the woman had woken up Dinah, who'd started to cry, just as she was attempting to get on with some typing. 'I'm looking for a house. Until then, I'm afraid you're going to have to put up with me and me baby. Tara.'

She closed the door, without mentioning she'd had a letter

from the agent who managed the property informing her that the lease strictly forbade children under sixteen and, while he wouldn't evict a mother and baby, he'd had several complaints, and would be obliged if she would find somewhere else as soon as possible.

Josie would have moved the next day had she been able to find a house, where the neighbours could complain until they were blue in the face about a crying baby but there was nothing they could do, and she would have a proper kitchen and hang the nappies out to dry. As things were, she was spending a small fortune in the launderette. And Lily had been right about the stairs. Coming up wasn't so bad, but going down was treacherous. She had to take Dinah all the way to the bottom floor, put her in the pram which she kept in the hall – no doubt someone had complained about *that*, too – then go all the way back for the washing or her shopping bag. Coming home, she did the same thing in reverse. It was worse than Cypress Terrace in a way. Although this room was incomparably nicer, in London Jack had been writing, and there'd been a *point* to all the inconvenience they'd had to put up with.

Francie O'Leary had taken to dropping in at least once a week. He arrived that night with a bottle of wine and cheered her up somewhat. She switched off the light in favour of the white shaded lamp, which made the room look smaller and more cosy. It was raining outside, and a blustery wind kept throwing the rain against the windows. The glass creaked and squeaked in protest. Dinah was fast asleep in the shadows at the other end, and Josie prayed she'd stay that way.

Francie still found it incredible that there was a man alive who had been willing to marry Lily Kavanagh. 'Does she hang him on a crucifix at night to sleep?'

'No.' Josie giggled.

'I visualise him with an arrow through his chest, like a martyr.'

'Don't be silly.' She sipped the wine. Francie always made

her feel young again. He reminded her there was a world outside that could be fun. 'Neil's a perfectly nice, normal young man. He loves Lily to death.'

He grinned. 'That's appropriate. The poor guy signed his death warrant when he married her. She'll nag him into the grave in no time. Eh, what about Ben? I understand he got hitched to a cracking-looking girl. I can't remember her name.'

'Imelda. They've got two children, a boy and a girl.' She hadn't seen Ben since Lily's wedding, since which time things had got worse. Lily said that Imelda was completely unstable, regularly threatening suicide. She was on tablets for her nerves.

'I liked Ben, he was a nice guy. I wouldn't mind getting in touch with him. Have you got his address?'

'No, but I can get it for you. I think he'd appreciate that, Francie.' She wrinkled her nose. 'He's not very happy.'

'Marriage!' Francie snorted. 'I wouldn't get married if they paid me, not even if it were Marilyn Monroe on offer. *Especially* if it were Marilyn Monroe. She's already on her third husband. Marriage is an unnatural state. How can people be expected to get on with each other for a whole lifetime? It'd be okay if you could change partners every few years.'

'So you're going to remain a bachelor gay?' Dinah made a noise, a little hiccup, and Josie turned to watch the cot, praying the bedclothes wouldn't move, indicating that the baby had woken up, hungry for a meal, and poor Francie would have to be surrendered to the rain, which was coming down in buckets, while she breast-fed. She was enjoying their conversation.

'I'd sooner be a bachelor-dead-miserable than be married,' Francie said with an elaborate shudder. 'Talking of Marilyn Monroe, *Some Like It Hot* is on at the Forum. Let's go one night. I've been told it's the gear.'

'Go to the pictures?' Josie looked at him, astounded.

'People do it all the time,' he said airily. 'It's quite a common practice. Some people even do it two or three times a week. In fact, I've known *you* go to the pictures before now, Josie, so don't look so surprised. I distinctly remember you were there when I saw *Samson and Delilah*.'

'You spoiled it,' she pouted. 'It's just that I can't imagine doing anything *normal*, like going to the pictures, for years.' She couldn't imagine reading a book, painting her nails or going shopping for anything that wasn't to do with babies.

'Get someone to babysit, and we'll go next week.'

She'd drunk too much wine, but it was a pleasant, hazy feeling, relaxing. Francie had managed to make her feel vaguely happy. Before getting into bed, she fed Dinah, rubbed her back and raised a satisfactory burp, then changed her nappy. 'Now, look here,' she said sternly. 'Mummy feels exceptionally tired tonight, and she's a little bit drunk, too, so I'd appreciate a good night's sleep, if you don't mind.'

Dinah was an unresponsive child. She didn't gurgle or wave her arms, as Laura used to, but regarded her mother coolly when she was put in the cot. Josie climbed into bed and immediately fell asleep.

It was still dark when she woke up and, apart from the rain which had become a deluge, the room was silent. But she knew what was about to happen. After a few minutes there was a little cry, like a kitten's mewl, followed by another, slightly more urgent. It was as if her brain was connected to her child's, and it recognised when she had awoken and was about to cry.

Josie groaned. She'd been having a lovely sleep, the bed felt exceptionally comfortable and she would have given anything on earth to stay under the warm covers, particularly on such a stormy night.

The cries rose in volume, and she could barely drag her lethargic body out of bed. She swayed dizzily, staggered to the cot, picked up Dinah and carried her back to bed. Halfway through the feed she fell asleep, and woke up to find an irritable Dinah sucking at an empty breast. She transferred her to the other breast, and managed to stay awake until the baby had had her fill. The rain thundered on the roof, and she could have sworn she could hear the slates move.

Josie sighed. She always found these dead-of-night feeds lonely and depressing, sorely missing Jack's warm presence in bed beside her, reminding her that she shouldn't have let him go, not for ever. But she'd been in such a state, sick with grief over Laura. Why, she thought fretfully, hadn't Jack understood she wasn't herself when she said she didn't want to see him again? But he had been sick with grief and guilt himself. The best plan would have been to part for a while, see how she felt, how he felt, in a few months. She considered putting an advert in a newspaper, asking him to contact her, but there were probably hundreds of papers in California, and he might not even be there. Like the time he had disappeared for two days, he could be anywhere. Anyroad, if he wanted to see her again, *he* was in a position to contact *her*.

'I'll burp you and change your nappy in a minute,' she muttered tiredly, leaving Dinah in the bed and covering her with the eiderdown while she went to get a drink of water. It must be the wine – her mouth felt like the bottom of a birdcage.

She drank two glasses thirstily, but on the way back from the sink she felt dizzy again and had to sit on the settee.

It was the slamming of a door that woke her, voices on the stairs. The rain had stopped. Cold December sunshine glimmered through the curtains, and Josie, waking up on the settee, remembered *she'd left Dinah in the bed*.

She might have choked on her vomit, smothered under the eiderdown. Terror gripped Josie like an icy fist. 'No!' she screamed. '*No!*' Somehow she got to the other end of the room. The bottom half of the baby's face was covered with the eiderdown. Josie snatched it away. Dinah lay completely still, eyes closed, very pale.

'*Dinah!*' The tiny body felt cold when she picked it up. She pressed her daughter against her breast, her cheek against the pale one. Dinah stirred and uttered a little sigh, the most welcome sound Josie had ever heard. 'Dinah, oh, darling, I thought you were dead.' She sat on the bed and rocked to and fro, her child clutched in her arms. 'I love you, darling. Mummy loves you more than words can say.' She was trembling, and rocking like a mad woman. 'I love you, I love you,' she said in a hoarse, shaky voice, over and over again.

She moved her arm so that they faced each other, and her eyes met the light blue, almost lavender-coloured eyes of her daughter. There was something about her mouth she'd never noticed before, something determinedly serious, almost wilful, about the small pink lips. 'You're going to be a little madam when you grow up,' Josie said, and could have sworn that Dinah smiled.

'It was bound to happen some time, Jose,' Daisy said that night. 'Having Dinah happened too soon, while you were still grieving for Laura. If the circumstances had been different, it would have been best to wait a year or so before you had another child.'

'I'll never stop grieving for Laura,' Josie said quickly. 'Dinah's just blunted the edges a bit, that's all.'

'I know, luv. But it's not as intense as it used to be, I'll bet. I didn't want to go on living when Ralph jilted me and I lost me baby in the space of a few weeks. It took a while before I realised the world hadn't ended, that life was still there to be lived and I could still enjoy meself, as it were. The world would be a miserable place, Josie, if everyone gave up the ghost when someone dear to them died.'

'I feel terrible.' Josie glanced at the cot, where Dinah was peacefully sleeping. 'I hope she doesn't grow up with the feeling I don't properly love her.'

'You've always loved her, Josie. It just took a while for it to sink in, that's all.'

The sun continued to shine the next day. It was shining at one'clock when Josie's doorbell rang. She hoped it was Lily with Samantha, and they could take the babies for a walk in Princes Park.

A strange, elderly woman was standing on the step. She wore a fur coat and too much jewellery, and her stiffly permed hair was the colour of iron. She's pressed the wrong bell, Josie thought. It's someone else she wants.

'Hello, Josie,' the woman said, however, and there was something terribly sad, terribly lost about the dark eyes in the yellow face when Josie's face showed no sign of recognition.

'I'm afraid—' Josie began, but the woman interrupted with, 'It's Ivy, luv.'

Her last contact with Aunt Ivy had been in the holiday camp, when she'd sent a note more or less telling her to get lost. What was she supposed to say? How was she supposed to act? 'Hello,' she said stiffly. After a long pause, when Aunt Ivy showed no sign of going away, she muttered, 'You'd better come in.'

It was horrible, really horrible, watching the blunt yellow fingers pick up Dinah from the cot and Aunt Ivy stroke the pale cheeks of her great-niece. 'I think that's what she is. And I'm her great-aunt.' Josie prayed Dinah would cry, so she'd have an excuse to snatch her away, but Dinah sat uncomplainingly on Aunt Ivy's knee, letting the horrible woman maul her.

'She's the image of me mam.' Ivy looked up, beaming. 'There's a wedding photo on the mantelpiece in the parlour. Do you remember, luv? I'll bring it round next time I come,' she said when Josie shook her head.

She intended coming again! Not if I can help it, Josie vowed. She wouldn't let her in. No way did she want Aunt Ivy back in her life, the woman who had betrayed her own sister, then her sister's child.

Aunt Ivy sighed. She gently put Dinah in her cot, and glanced at Josie. 'I'm not exactly welcome, am I, luv?'

Josie didn't answer. Aunt Ivy sighed again, and there was that same sad, lost look in her eyes. 'I don't blame you. I let you down more than once. Trouble with me, I've never been much of a judge of character. I turn the good people away, and welcome the bad ones with open arms.'

Still Josie didn't answer. What else could she do but agree?

'Do you mind if I take me coat off, luv? It's hot in here.'

'Of course not.' She mustered every charitable bone in her

264

body and said, 'Would you like a cup of tea?' Anyroad, she longed for one herself.

'I'd love one.' Aunt Ivy removed her coat and came and sat on the settee. She glanced around the room. 'It's nice, this place, but a bit cramped for a baby.'

'I signed the lease before I realised I was pregnant, didn't I?' Josie said shortly. 'I'm looking for a house.'

'Daisy Kavanagh said you'd been given notice to quit.'

'Yes.'

Aunt Ivy raised her yellow hands for the tea. Josie took hers to the table and sat on a wooden chair. Her aunt looked at her almost slyly. Josie remembered the look well from her first years in Machin Street, and her stomach curled again. 'I can help with the house,' Ivy said. Her voice was surprisingly timid.

'You know where there's one to let?' Her spirits rose. 'I can only afford a dead cheap place.'

'No, but there's plenty around that you can buy.'

'Oh, yeah.' She made no effort to keep the sarcasm out of her voice.

'I said I can help.' Aunt Ivy put her tea on the floor and reached for her handbag. 'I've just been to the bank. I told the manager weeks ago that I wanted to take everything out. You've got to give notice with long-term investments – they don't just hand the cash over at the drop of a hat.' She reached into the bag, drew out a cheque and handed it to Josie. 'This is for you and Dinah.'

Josie ignored the cheque. It was pathetic. Ivy was trying to buy her way back into her affections, not that she'd ever truly been there. But Aunt Ivy had always been pathetic. 'I don't want your money, thanks all the same.'

'But it's *your* money,' Ivy said eagerly. 'When Mam died, there was over six hundred pounds in the bank. Half belonged to Mabel, as well as half the house. The way things went, well . . .' a spasm of pain crossed her face '. . . she never got it, did she?'

'No, she didn't.'

It were a bought house, and half of it were mine. And there was money, too, hundreds of pounds . . .

'You know I got married again, don't you, luv?'

'Lily told me, years ago.'

'I knew from the start Alf only married me to get a roof over the head of him and his kids. I didn't mind. I only married him for the company, so I reckon that makes us equal. We don't get on too bad.' She smiled ruefully. 'He was a copper, see, and about to retire, which meant he'd lose his nice police house. Trouble is, Alf's rather keen on the horses, so his pension goes up in smoke, which leaves me the only one working. I'm still in the same place, you know,' she said proudly.

'I thought his grown-up children lived with you?'

'Oh, they do, but they're in and out of jobs by the minute, and more often out than in. I often come home and find one or other of the nice things me dad brought from abroad have disappeared to the pawn shop. I don't mind, not much.' She looked anxiously at Josie, and gave the cheque a little shake. 'Alf knows nothing about this, luv. It'd be gone with the wind if he found out. I've made a will, leaving the house to him and the kids. In the meantime, you and Dinah can have the money. That seems only fair, doesn't it, luv?'

'I suppose it does.' After all, it was *Mam's* money. 'Thank you very much, Aunt Ivy,' Josie said politely, 'though I'm afraid six hundred pounds wouldn't buy a house.'

'For goodness' sake, girl,' Aunt Ivy cried. 'I told you, it's been invested since before the war, moved from one account to another to earn higher interest.' She puffed out her chest conceitedly. 'I even had some shares once in this big electrical company that went bust, but not before I sold the shares at a profit. This cheque's for over five thousand pounds.'

The house was at the end of a row of five, dead in the centre of Woolton, once a little village on its own but now very much part of Liverpool. The tiny houses were invisible from the busy main street less than a hundred yards away. They were reached down a narrow gravel path called Baker's Row, which ran between a shoe shop and a greengrocer's, and had been built almost two centuries before the shops and the main street existed.

Josie's house was the only one not modernised. The others had had their kitchens extended, bathrooms added. They had pretty latticed or bow windows, shutters, wrought-iron gates, glazed front doors. Josie's front door hadn't seen a lick of paint in years, and the wooden gate only had one hinge. The gardens, front and back, were a wilderness of overgrown grass and weeds. Her kitchen still had a deep, brown earthenware sink. The only attempt at modernisation was the washhouse and outside lavatory had been knocked into one and made into a bathroom which was accessed from the kitchen.

When she tried to scrape the wallpaper off the walls, she discovered five thick layers, each pattern more hideous than the one before. Sid Spencer said soaking the paper with warm water would help, and loaned her Little Sid to give a hand.

The house was the cheapest she could find in a place she liked. It had cost fifteen hunded of the five thousand pounds from Aunt Ivy. It would have been easy to buy a place much grander, but Josie wanted to conserve as much as possible. Sadly, she was too far from Spencer & Sons to do their typing, and she needed money to live on. She felt a bit guilty when she bought a television and washing machine, and resolved that as soon as Dinah went to school she would look for a part-time job.

Josie felt very odd, slightly depressed, the day she moved in with the things she had acquired for the attic room. There were times when she was scared she didn't know who she was. The woman she should have been had died with Laura and when Jack had gone away. That woman would never return – only her shell remained.

She would never love another man the way she had loved Jack. She had his child, his little girl, so different from Laura. She loved Dinah, but suspected that Laura would always have first place in her heart.

At twenty-seven, she had many years ahead of her, at least she prayed so for Dinah's sake. But what did those years hold, now that the adventures were all over and the romance had gone?

Baker's Row
1965–1974

I

'Eh, Jose. I wish you'd get a phone.' Lily came puffing into
the house with Gillian on her reins. Lily's plans had gone
madly awry a second time. It had taken three years for her to
pluck up the courage to have another baby, to be blessed with
pretty, roly-poly Gillian instead of Troy. She blamed Neil.

'I can't afford one, can I?'

'I thought you were going to get a job when Dinah went to
school?' Lily said crossly.

'Give us a chance, Lil.' Josie went to put the kettle on.
'She's only been gone a week. Anyroad, I'm waiting to hear
from the accountants round the corner. They want a part-time
shorthand-typist, though I'm useless at figures. Anyroad,' she
shouted, 'why is it suddenly so important that I have a phone?'

'It's always been important.' Lily looked at her irritably. 'I
don't know how anybody can *live* without a phone. Look at
this morning. I had to take our Samantha to school, and she
screamed blue murder. She hates it, not like your Dinah. I
reckon it's because she's more sensitive. Then I had to race
over to me ma's for the letter, bring it here and I'll have to
drive you back to ours to make the phone call. You're a
terrible nuisance, Jose. You've really mucked up me schedule.
Tuesday's the day I clean the fridge and vacuum upstairs.'

'What letter? What phone call? What are you on about?'

Lily took an envelope from her bag. 'Some firm in
California has written to me ma and da' wanting to know

269

where you are. Your whereabouts, they call it. Hang on a mo, I'll read it out.'

'"Dear Mr & Mrs Kavanagh,"' Lily read out a touch pompously, '"I am anxious to trace the whereabouts of Mrs Josephine Coltrane (née Flynn), and have been given to understand you may be able to help. Should this be the case, I would appreciate any information you are able to provide with all possible speed. It may even be that Mrs Coltrane herself is in a position to respond. In the case of a telephoned response, please reverse the charges. I look forward to hearing from you. Yours sincerely, Dick Schneider."'

'It's from Crosby, Buckmaster & Littlebrown – Jaysus, what a mouthful. I wonder if the Crosby's any relation to Bing? Their address is 17 South Park Boulevard, Los Angeles, California, USA. They're lawyers. Fancy a lawyer calling himself Dick. If it were me, I'd call meself Richard in me letters, wouldn't you, Jose?'

Josie's blood had got colder and colder as she listened to the letter. She burst into tears. 'Jack's dead!'

'Don't be morbid, Josie,' Lily said impatiently. 'Anyroad, it beats me why on earth you should give a fig if the bugger's dead or alive. You haven't seen him in years, and who'd have given them our address if he's dead?' The kettle boiled and she went to make the tea. 'Come back to ours and you can phone from there. Though make sure you reverse the charges.'

'But what on earth can it be about, Lil?' Josie cried frantically. Perhaps he was dying, and wanted to see her one last time. Or he just wondered how she was, might even want to come and visit. But if that was the case, there was nothing to stop him from writing to the Kavanaghs himself.

They drank the tea hurriedly, Lily just as eager to know why a firm of Californian lawyers wished to contact her friend as Josie herself was.

Josie sat on the stairs of the Baxters' smart new house in Woolton Park, less than a mile from her own. Lily found the code for the international operator in the book and told her what to dial. 'Don't forget to reverse the charges.'

'You've already said that half a dozen times.' Josie raised her eyebrows. 'I wouldn't mind some privacy,' she said, when Lily looked set to stay.

'I know when I'm not wanted.' She picked up Gillian and flounced into the kitchen. The letter from America on her knee, Josie dialled the operator . . .

Ten minutes later Lily crept into the hall and found Josie in exactly the same position at the bottom of the stairs. 'I didn't realise you'd finished. Why didn't you say? I've made tea. You look a bit sick, Jose. What's happened?'

'He wants a divorce,' Josie whispered dully. 'They said Jack wants a divorce. He's going to marry someone else. Honestly, Lil, I love him so much, I don't think I can bear it.'

They went into the kitchen. Lily did her best to be sympathetic, but she had disliked Jack as much as he had her, and couldn't understand how you could still love someone you hadn't seen for nearly six years.

'I just do,' Josie sobbed. 'I don't know how or why, I just do.'

'It means you can get married again yourself,' Lily said comfortingly.

'Oh, really? Who to? Not only have I no intention of getting married again, but there isn't exactly a horde of would-be husbands beating their way to me door.'

'There's . . .' Lily's face contorted painfully and she virtually spat out the next words. '. . . Francie O'Leary.' It was a sore point that Josie and the first man Lily had ever loved had become such close friends.

'Don't be ridiculous, Lil.' Josie managed to raise a smile. 'I don't think of Francie that way. Anyroad, he's a confirmed bachelor.'

'I wish he'd told me that when we first went out, before he broke me heart, like.'

Josie went back to her own little house, where she could be alone, think, though it was torture to imagine Jack in another

271

woman's arms, marrying another woman, smiling at her, touching her, saying the things he'd said to *her*.

'You're stupid,' she told herself angrily. 'Dead stupid.' She made tea – one of these days, she'd turn into a packet of tea – and carried it out to the deckchair in the garden. It was a lovely warm September day, and she hoped it would stay nice for Dinah's fifth birthday party on Saturday. Best to think about the party instead of Jack.

The narrow garden looked dead pretty. She'd cleared the wild grass and the weeds, grown a new lawn from seed and a neat privet hedge from cuttings off the woman next door. The rose bushes in each corner were from the same source, and this year they'd come on a treat, with big, bulging pink and yellow blooms. Dinah collected the petals and kept them in a bowl in her room. The front garden had been turned into a rockery and the heathers were spreading nicely.

Josie sipped the tea, trying not to think of Jack. Inside the house it was just as pretty. There was still the earthenware sink and the claw-toothed bath. She'd had no improvements made, but the walls were covered with delicately flower patterned paper and all the woodwork was white. She'd gone mad with indoor plants, and Aunt Ivy had let her have one of the lovely, colourful, glass-shaded lamps from Machin Street.

'They're called Tiffany lamps,' she said. 'Me dad brought them from America. One's already gone – to the pawn shop, I presume. I thought I'd give you the other before that goes, too. They have them in George Henry Lee's and they cost the earth.'

Life was so unpredictable and topsy-turvy. Aunt Ivy was a regular visitor nowadays. She adored Dinah, and Dinah, such a strange little girl, regarded Ivy as one of her favourite people.

Josie finished the tea, sighed and went indoors to wash the dishes. She stacked everything on the wooden draining-board, very unhygenic according to Lily, who had stainless steel and couldn't understand why everyone oohed and aahed in admiration over Josie's house, so titchy and run-down, when hers was much nicer – modern, miles bigger and full of G–

plan furniture. She even had an Ercol three-piece, bought when Neil was promoted to under-manager, or it might have been over-manager, at the Post Office.

'And you have so many visitors,' she pouted. 'Hardly anyone comes to ours, except me ma and da'.'

It was probably because Josie didn't expect visitors to remove their shoes before being allowed on the carpets, or frown if they wanted to smoke, or watch them like a hawk in case a drop of tea spilled on the furniture.

On Monday nights, Daisy, Eunice and Francie came and played poker for halfpennies. Josie hoped she wasn't showing her daughter a bad example by letting her join in for a while before she went to bed. Dinah had caught on quickly and usually won. At some time during the week, usually Wednesdays, Josie went with Lily to the pictures or the theatre. The same with Francie. Aunt Ivy was only too willing to babysit. Chrissie and Sid Spencer often popped in on Sunday afternoons to see how she was – two of their lads were now married, and they had three grandchildren. Mrs Kavanagh came frequently, her husband less often now that he was plagued with arthritis and had had to sell the shop.

Josie went upstairs to make the beds, still doing her best not to think about Jack. She had a lovely house, and loads of friends, which was rather surprising as she'd never thought of herself as a sociable person. She'd been careful with the money from Aunt Ivy, and there was still plenty left if she didn't find a job immediately. As she plumped up Dinah's pillow, Josie wondered why, despite this undeniably pleasant, even enjoyable existence, she felt only half alive.

It rained on Saturday morning, but the sky had cleared and the sun was shining by two o'clock when it was time for Dinah's party.

'I hope no one fetches me dolls. I hate dolls,' Dinah had said earlier as they'd wrapped tiny gifts in sheets of newspaper for pass the parcel.

273

'I know, luv.' Josie's present had been, by special request, a xylophone. Dinah could already pick out 'Silent Night'.

'Auntie Ivy's got me a trumpet. Francie said he had a lovely surprise. He's bringing it tonight.' Dinah frowned. 'Samantha and Gillian have got me a doll. Samantha told me, though she wasn't supposed to. It opens its mouth and says "Mama".'

'You mustn't let anyone guess you don't want it, luv,' Josie warned. 'Pretend to be dead pleased.'

'Oh, I will, Mummy,' Dinah assured her seriously. 'It's called being polite.'

Dinah was a very serious little girl. Her conversation, her reasoning, was almost adult. Josie had never discussed where soil came from, how flowers grew, what clouds were made of, why the Queen was the Queen with Laura. Yet she was conscious that there wasn't the same intimacy between her and Dinah as there'd been with her other child. Dinah was too self-contained. She liked her privacy.

Josie often got up in the morning and found her sitting up in bed looking at a picture book, or lying on the floor, her pretty, pale, rather tight little face hidden behind a curtain of creamy hair, doing a jig-saw or some other puzzle and talking to herself. It never crossed her mind to jump into bed with her mam. A few weeks ago Josie had walked into the bathroom when Dinah had been on the lavatory, and her little tight face had got tighter with obvious annoyance. 'You should knock first, Mummy.' Since then she'd fastened the bolt.

Perhaps Josie over-compensated for those first few months when she had resented Dinah so much for taking Laura's place. It was hard to believe, now, that she could have been so stupid, so insensitive as to resent a tiny baby. She must have been unbalanced, sick in the head. Ever since, she had tried to make up by cosseting Dinah too much, fussing over her endlessly, finding it hard to leave the child to her own devices. Sometimes she wondered if she got on Dinah's nerves!

She glanced at the clock. 'It's time you changed into your new frock, luv. People'll be arriving soon.'

'Why didn't Mrs Kavanagh make my frock like always?'

274

'She's had to give up sewing, hasn't she? Poor Mrs Kavanagh can't see that well any more.' It was sad. What with arthritis and glaucoma, the couple she'd regarded as a substitute mam and dad for most of her life had suddenly become very old and frail.

Lily and the girls were the first to arrive, dropped off by Neil on his way to a football match, followed by two little girls from Dinah's class at school. Then Aunt Ivy appeared bearing the trumpet, and Mrs Kavanagh a sewing set. Everyone went into the garden, where deckchairs were provided for the older women and Lily sat on the grass. Josie took the presents into the minuscule dining room where the table was set for tea – the big, rather ugly doll squeaked 'Mama' whenever it was moved. She wasn't looking forward to organising games for five little girls to fill in the time before the birthday tea.

It was difficult, trying to ensure that Gillian, three years younger than the others, wasn't left out, particularly with her mother watching keenly. And stopping Samantha from cheating, something that the same keen-eyed mother didn't notice. Josie prayed the children weren't as bored as she was. She was slightly relieved when Aunt Ivy shouted that there was a knock on the door, seeing it as an opportunity to collapse, exhausted, on the grass.

'I'll go.' Lily returned minutes later with a tall, sad-faced man. Two excessively thin children followed timidly behind, a boy of about twelve, a girl a few years younger. 'Look who's here,' Lily said in a funny voice. 'It's our Ben, with Peter and Colette. They've been home, and me da' sent them here.'

'Ben, is that our Ben?' Mrs Kavanagh tried, unsuccessfully, to struggle out of the deckchair, and for some reason Josie recalled the sprightly woman in the blue coat she'd met in Blackler's bargain basement where she and Mam had gone to look for a tray. 'Ben, son, I haven't seen you in ages.'

Before his mother could get up, Ben did the most surprising thing. Every muscle in his face seemed to collapse, and he strode across the grass, knelt in front of his mother's chair and buried his face in her breast. Mrs Kavanagh gently stroked the fair hair of her youngest son. Lily looked set to burst into tears. Ben's children watched, their faces showing not the slightest flicker of emotion. The five little girls stood awkwardly on the grass, knowing something strange was happening. Josie, shaken by the pathos of the situation, had no idea what to do. Should she take the little ones inside?

It was Aunt Ivy who saved the day. She stood and clapped her hands. 'How about a little walk to the sweetshop?' she cried. 'You two an' all, Peter and Colette. Colette, you take Gillian's hand, she's only a little 'un. Peter, you can keep an eye on the others. Come on. We won't be long,' she sang gaily.

They left. Ben stayed with his head buried in his mother's breast. Josie couldn't tell if he was crying. It seemed ages before he looked up. His dead eyes searched for Josie, and he said in a cracked voice, 'I'm sorry if I've spoiled the party.'

'You haven't—' Josie began, but Lily interrupted.

'That bloody Imelda – what's she done now?'

'Shush, luv,' Mrs Kavanagh chided.

'I will not shush. She's ruining our Ben's life. Did you see the faces of them kids? They look set for a nervous breakdown.'

'Lily, girl, please shush.'

'No, Ma. Why don't you leave her?' Lily demanded angrily of her brother. 'Why put up with it all this while?'

Ben sat on the deckchair Aunt Ivy had vacated. 'I can't leave Imelda, she's sick.'

'No she's not, she's evil,' Lily said flatly.

'Lily!'

'Be quiet, Ma. Anyone with an ounce of spunk would have left years ago. I wouldn't have stood it for a minute, me.'

Josie went to put the kettle on, but could still hear the argument raging on her lawn. She hoped the neighbours weren't listening.

'I can't walk out and leave the children, Lil,' Ben was saying. 'I can't just take them away either. Imelda's their mother. Believe it or not, they love her. Peter's old enough to guess there's something wrong. He used to be frightened, but now he gets protective when she has one of her rages.'

'Rages! Huh!' Lily said contemptuously. 'How did you manage to escape today? Did she write you a pass or something? What time have you got to be back?'

'She took another overdose last night,' Ben said wearily. 'She's in hospital again. I know I should be with her, but I had the children to think of. She'll sleep all day, and I'll fetch her home tomorrow.'

'Oh, no, son!' Mrs Kavanagh's voice quivered like an old woman's.

Lily was unimpressed. 'She never takes enough to finish herself off, does she? Next time she decides to *kill* herself, I hope she lets me know first, and I'll encourage her to take a fatal dose. Good riddance to bad rubbish, I say.'

'Have a heart, Lil. The doctors say it's a cry for help.'

'I'm all heart, Ben,' Lily said virtuously. 'but where Imelda's concerned, it's made of iron.'

There were footsteps down the side of the house and Francie O'Leary appeared. Josie dragged him into the kitchen. 'Don't interrupt. It's a family row.'

'Is that Ben?' Francie said, aghast. 'Jaysus, he looks about eighty. He's only thirty-four, same as me. I wrote to him, years ago, but never got an answer. What's happened to the party? Where are the kids?'

'Gone to the shops with Auntie Ivy.' She closed the door to shut out the row. Lily had started to shriek. 'As you can see, there's been an upset. What are you doing here, anyroad? I wouldn't have thought a children's party was your scene.'

Francie gloomily stuffed his hands in his pockets. 'Anything's my scene these days, Jose. The house seems like a morgue since me mam died. I feel so lonely, I'm thinking of getting married.' He grinned. 'Who should I ask?'

She grinned back, knowing he was only joking and glad he was there to lighten the mood of the day which had suddenly turned so tragic. 'I don't know, Francie. As long as it's not me, because I'd turn you down.'

'I wouldn't dream of asking you and spoiling a perfect friendship!' he said in a shocked voice.

'Mind you, you'd be a good catch, especially since your printing business has taken off.' He now employed six people. She looked at him appraisingly. He was still attractive in a lean, pinched way, and his black outfit – leather jacket, polo-necked sweater, flared trousers, boots – gave him an appealingly sinister air. Since the Beatles had taken Liverpool and the whole world by storm a few years ago, and long hair had become fashionable, Francie had acquired a dashing ponytail.

'You're the first girl I ever fancied.' He leered at her and winked. 'I mean, *really* fancied. I used to be dead envious of Ben.' He went over to the window. Ben was staring at the grass, his arms folded, his long face inscrutable. Mrs Kavanagh was crying, Lily shouting and waving her arms. 'The way things change, eh!' Francie said softly. 'I feel dead sorry for him now.'

The party turned out a success after all. Aunt Ivy came back, having bought the children each a present. 'We found a toy shop,' she smiled. 'I thought it might cheer them two up.' She nodded at Peter and Colette. Peter was earnestly studying a travel chess set, and Colette was nursing a fluffy dog, more suitable for a child half her age. They looked almost happy. 'Before you say anything about the money, Alf would only have cadged it off me for the horses. It's better spent this way.'

Josie had never appreciated Aunt Ivy so much before. She felt sufficiently moved to bestow a kiss on the yellow cheek. 'Ta. I don't know what I'd have done without you today.'

The drama in the garden seemed to be over, though Lily was in a mood for the rest of the afternoon. Josie brought a chair from upstairs and the stool from the bathroom to accommodate the extra guests, and the children sat down to tea. Ben brought his mother inside for a welcome cup of tea, and was astonished to find his old friend Francie skulking in the kitchen.

'It's good to see you, mate.' They shook hands and punched each others' shoulders, and Josie was touched to see the lines of strain on Ben's face melt away. He looked almost like the Ben she used to know.

At six o'clock the mothers of Dinah's two schoolfriends came to collect them, and Aunt Ivy supposed she'd better get back to Alf. Neil arrived, and Lily offered her mother a lift home.

'Ben can take me,' Mrs Kavanagh said. 'You're coming back to ours, aren't you, son?'

'I thought me and Ben could go for a drink later,' Francie said quickly.

'Would you mind having the children, Ma?'

'Of course not, son. I hardly ever see them nowadays.' Mrs Kavanagh seemed drained after the trauma of the day. She patted Ben's arm. 'You have a nice time, now.'

'I'll take you home, then come back. I wonder where I left the car?' Ben looked slightly harassed.

'Don't worry, I can squeeze everyone in. It's only a minute to our house. I'll drop Lily and the girls off, then take your mam and the kids home.' Neil Baxter's earnest, good-natured face glowed with a willingness to help. 'Are you ready, love?'

Lily's eyes flickered from Josie to Francie to Ben, as if she resented leaving them behind. Gillian pulled at her skirt. 'Want beddy-byes, Mummy,' she whined. Lily turned on her heel and left the room without a word.

Dinah thanked her guests nicely for the presents, and Josie went to the door to say goodbye as her house suddenly emptied. 'Why don't you come back later?' she said to Lily. 'It would be like old times, the four of us together. Neil wouldn't mind.'

'I'm a married woman,' Lily said stiffly, 'Not a free agent like you.'

'Thanks for reminding me, Lil.'

'I didn't mean it like that.' Lily's cheeks went pink. 'It's just there's the children to bath and put to bed, Neil's tea to make, the pools to check, the telly to watch, and I always make a cup of cocoa before we go to bed at about eleven.' Her voice was surprisingly harsh. 'Next Saturday will be exactly the same, and the Saturday after that, and so on. I don't know why I was so keen on getting married, Josie. It's more dead bloody boring than working in an office. I sometimes wish I were a lesbian like our Daisy. She has loads more fun than I do.'

Josie hid a smile. She glanced at Neil, waiting patiently for his wife, Gillian in his arms. 'You've got a husband in a million there, Lil. You don't realise how lucky you are.'

'I don't call it lucky to have landed a chap as dull as the proverbial ditchwater,' Lily snapped. 'I should never have married him. I don't love him, and I never will.' She marched away, turned round and marched back again. 'Don't take any notice of me, Josie. It's seeing Francie that's made me feel like this. He looks so gorgeous, so *exciting* in that outfit. Neil wouldn't grow a ponytail if you paid him, and he wouldn't be seen dead in a leather jacket. Yet he's worth ten Francie O'Learys.' She grinned. 'I must remind meself of that when we go to bed.'

Ben and Francie decided to start off the night with a Chinese meal. They left a few hours later to catch a taxi into town, on the assumption they would both be too drunk to drive home. Dinah went to bed with Francie's present, a rubber date stamp and pad that had fascinated her so much when Josie had taken her to the small print works a few weeks previously. The house seemed unnaturally quiet, welcome after the chaos of the day. Aunt Ivy had washed the dishes, everywhere was tidy. It was time to read properly the contents of the fat envelope which had arrived by air mail that morning from Crosby, Buckmaster & Littlebrown in California.

Dick Schneider's letter was couched in friendly tones. His client was pleased to learn she was in agreement to an amicable divorce. Would she kindly read the enclosed papers carefully and sign those places marked with a cross? If she would prefer to take advice from her own lawyer first, then all expenses would be paid. Whatever the case, he would appreciate her treating the matter with some urgency.

Jack was obviously in a hurry to marry his new wife, Josie thought bitterly. Lily had tried to persuade her to ask for alimony, but Josie didn't want a penny.

'Tell them about Dinah,' Lily had urged. 'After all, she's Jack's child every bit as much as yours. He should take some responsibility.' Then, more grudgingly, she added, 'He has a right to know, Jose, particularly after what happened with Laura. And Dinah has rights, too. She's started school, and any minute now she'll want to know why she hasn't got a dad like the other kids. Are you prepared to tell her he doesn't know she exists? It was different before. You didn't know where he was, but now you do, at least this lawyer does. You could send a photograph.'

Dinah had thought Francie was her dad, he was around so much. She didn't seem to mind when told he wasn't, and the subject hadn't come up again. Though Lily was talking sense for once. Dinah would want to know one day, and it would be unfair on her, and Jack, to deny them knowledge of each other.

Josie took a deep breath, signed the forms in the places marked with a cross, then wrote a brief letter informing Jack he had a daughter, Dinah, whose fifth birthday it was that very day. She enclosed a snapshot of their little girl in a bathing costume on Birkdale sands. Dinah, posing stiffly, spade in one hand, bucket in the other, had treated the camera to one of her rare, sweet smiles. Her pale hair was being blown into her eyes. She looked fragile, yet there was a toughness about her stance, an air of confidence, that plump, fun-loving Laura had never had. She put the letter and the photograph in an envelope marked 'Jack Coltrane, Strictly Confidential' and enclosed it with the papers in the large, self-addressed envelope Dick Schneider had sent. She sealed it, and stamped the flap with her fist.

'There!' she said aloud. There might be more forms to sign,

she didn't know, but in a few weeks or months she would be a single woman again, 'on the market', as Lily had put it.

Except she didn't want to be. She sat on the tiny settee and tried not to go through all the 'if onlys'. If only she hadn't done this, said that, gone there. The trouble was, most people needed two chances at life so they could do things right the second time around.

Still, it was too late for a second chance with Jack. She got resolutely to her feet and went upstairs to check on Dinah, who was fast asleep, having stamped the date several times on her new doll's forehead. Downstairs, she watched a play on television, and wondered if Ben and Francie would come back to hers or return for their cars in the morning.

At half eleven, when there'd been no sign of either, she went to bed, and had just read the first page of an Ed McBain thriller when there was a knock on the door. She groaned, slipped into a dressing-gown and went to answer it.

Ben was outside, grinning at her stupidly, looking young, very boyish and extremely drunk. 'I've come for my children.'

'They're at your mother's. Oh, you'd better come in,' she said, too late, as Ben had virtually fallen inside the door.

'Francie said they were. Or was it my car?'

'Your car's around somewhere.' She helped him to his feet. 'I'll make some black coffee, sober you up.' She went into the kitchen. If only she'd had a phone, she would have called a taxi. After he'd had the coffee, she'd get dressed and call one from the box on the main street.

She was running water in the kettle when Ben came lurching in. To her astonishment, he grabbed her by the waist and said hoarsely, 'I don't want coffee, I want you. That's why I came back — not for the kids or the car, but for you.'

For one mad, wild moment she felt a surge of desire. It was so long, too long, since she'd made love, and the pressure of his hands on the curve of her hips reminded her of what she had been missing. But common sense returned, and she moved out of his reach. 'Don't be silly, Ben,' she said shortly.

He dragged her back against him, his hands grasped her

breasts, he groaned. 'I love you, Josie.' He buried his head in her neck. 'Not silly, love you, love you, love you.'

'You're drunk, Ben. You'll feel dead embarrassed tomorrow.' She tried again to move away, but his hands tightened on her breasts. She was trapped. She jerked her elbow sharply back into his stomach, but it had no effect.

'I've never loved anyone but you,' he was saying, almost sobbing against her neck. 'You were my girl, my special girl. We were going to get married. What happened, Jose? Why didn't we?' He turned her round so they were facing each other, and she stared, shocked, at the ravaged face, the haunted eyes. 'What happened, Josie?'

Life, she wanted to say. Life happened. Wrong decisions, right decisions. You said no when you meant yes, or the other way around. Someone else might have married Imelda, another woman might have married Jack Coltrane. Laura might not have been born, Laura might not be dead.

Ben was kissing her, kissing her roughly, hungrily, trying to force her mouth open with his tongue. She resisted and felt his teeth grind against her own. This wasn't the Ben she used to know. She didn't like this Ben at all. His hands were tugging at the belt on her dressing-gown, undoing it, caressing her body, hurting it, through the thin material of her nightie, telling her all the time how much he loved her, missed her, wanted her, that she was on his mind every minute of every day. She was the only woman for him, always had been, always would, and she was so beautiful, so precious.

Now he was touching between her legs, and she felt him shudder powerfully against her. She contemplated screaming. The walls of the house were paper thin. Someone would hear, someone would come, rescue her. The police would be called. But she didn't want to do that, not to this tragic, unhappy man. Not to Ben. Nor did she want to frighten Dinah.

Josie stopped struggling and let herself go limp. She gently clasped his face in her hands and said in a soft voice, 'Are you going to rape me, Ben?'

He froze. He stayed completely still for a long time. Then he removed his hands, stepped back. 'Jesus Christ, Josie. I'm so sorry.' He didn't meet her eyes.

She picked up the kettle. 'Go and sit down, and I'll make us both a cup of coffee.'

The kettle rattled on the ancient gas stove so she didn't hear the front door open and close, and when Josie went into the parlour with two cups of coffee, Ben had gone.

He came early next morning to apologise, extremely shamefaced, highly embarrassed. She'd had a feeling he would. Dinah had gone to Mass with Aunt Ivy. Josie, her head still spinning after the previous day, intended to go later.

'I walked home last night, sobered myself up,' he said on the doorstep. 'This time I really have come to collect my car – if I can remember where I left it.'

'Come in.' She half smiled, and he gave a sigh of relief.

'I thought I'd blotted my copybook for ever. I don't know what came over me last night, Josie. I've never behaved like that before. Mind you, I've never been so drunk either.'

'Let's put it down to a single aberration.' They went into the parlour and he glanced appreciatively around the tiny room.

'I like it here. It's so calm and comfortable, like a fairy-tale house.' His lips twisted slightly. 'A fairy-tale house for a fairy queen. Remember the fairy queen in *The Wizard of Oz*, Jose? We saw it together. You said you'd love a frock like hers.'

'She was a good witch, not a fairy.'

'Was she?' He looked oddly troubled. 'I thought I could remember everything we did with complete clarity.'

'I've seen the film twice since, first with Laura, then Dinah.'

He gave a rueful smile. 'It keeps me going, reliving the times we spent together. Some mornings I wake up and try to imagine it's *you* in bed beside me, that we got married after all. I drive home from work, and think what it would be like if *you* opened the door.'

'Ben,' she said warningly, 'I wouldn't have let you in if I'd known the conversation would turn this way.'

'Sorry, Jose.' He glanced at her curiously. 'But we've both made a complete cock-up of things. You're separated, my marriage isn't exactly what you'd call happy. Aren't you ever sorry *we* didn't get married?'

She shook her head firmly. 'No, Ben.' She had thought about it sometimes, but never with regret.

'I just wondered.'

Aunt Ivy and Dinah could be heard coming in the back way. Ben got up to leave. 'Can I come and see you occasionally? Just to talk?'

'I'd sooner you didn't, Ben.' He might take it as a sign of encouragement.

'Oh, well.' He shook hands formally. 'See you around some time, Jose.'

2

Josie had told Dinah about Laura years ago, when she was still too young to understand, to grasp the concept of death and the passage of time, and the things that had happened before she was born. Josie had thought this the best way, rather than spring the fact of a dead sister later, right out of the blue.

Dinah was eight when she began to plague her mother with questions, about Laura, about Jack. She demanded pictures, descriptions. Why didn't Jack come to see her? Was Laura clever, was she nice, was she pretty?

'Not as clever as you, luv, but every bit as nice, and just as pretty, though in a different way. She was dark, like your dad. You take after my side of the family.'

'I'm like Auntie Ivy's mummy. Was she me grandma?'

'No, luv, she was mine. Your grandma . . . gosh!' It was impossible to imagine Mam being a grandma. 'Your grandma was dead beautiful. Her name was Mabel. She was only twenty-two when she was killed.'

'Did you love Laura better than me?'

Josie gasped. 'Of course not, luv. I loved her exactly the

same way as I love you.' She reached down to stroke the creamy hair, but Dinah shrugged the hand away.

A fire blazed in the black metal fireplace with its fancy tiled surround. The Tiffany lamp was on, casting jewel-coloured shadows on the walls and ceiling of the small room. Dinah lay face down on the mat, drawing. Josie held a Sunday paper on her knee. It was a gloomy December day, but cosy inside. She might put the decorations up later. It was only a week off Christmas.

'What are you drawing, luv?'

'Laura. I remember what she looks like from the photo you showed me. The one she had done at school.'

'Ah, yes.' It had been a state school, but the children had worn uniforms. Laura's tie was crooked, her hair a mess, but she was grinning from ear to ear. She'd been such a happy little girl. The only time Josie could recall her otherwise were those final two days when Jack had disappeared.

Dinah looked over her shoulder. 'Will me dad send a Christmas card from America?'

'I doubt it, Dinah. He never has before.' There'd been no reply to the letter she'd sent three years ago, telling Jack he had a daughter and enclosing her photograph.

'I think that's rude,' she said primly.

'So do I.'

'I don't think me dad is very nice.'

'Oh, he's all right. But I've told you before – he's got another wife now, perhaps more children. I reckon you and me are very far from his mind.'

'He's still rude. If he comes, I won't speak to him.'

'Join the club, luv. I mightn't speak to him meself.' She knew she was talking rubbish. Hardly a day passed when she didn't think of Jack Coltrane. She was still as much in love with him as she had ever been.

Dinah got to her feet. 'Can I ring Samantha? Auntie Lily took her to town yesterday to buy her a dress for Christmas. I bet it's not as nice as mine.'

'Tell Auntie Lily I'll be round tomorrow after work. Say about one o'clock.'

'Okay, Mum.'

Josie had got the job with the accountants, only a minute's walk away but tedious beyond words, typing never-ending columns of figures. She would never get used to figures, but the wages were good and had paid for the installation of a telephone, and the subsequent bills which she tried to keep small. Lily looked after Dinah in the school holidays. It would be nice, she thought wistfully, to have a job you could get your teeth into, something stimulating. But all she could do was type!

She went over to the window. The view was dead miserable – the back of someone's hedge and the path, which ended outside her house so no one ever walked past. Still, it looked pretty in the summer when it was almost like living in the heart of the countryside, instead of busy Woolton. Perhaps it was the weather, or talking about Jack and Laura, but today Josie felt unusually discontented. She wished the house were somewhere else, somewhere busy, where there were cars and people to be seen, noise. She wished everything about her life was different.

With a sigh, she returned to the settee. Dinah's drawing of Laura lay on the floor, and her heart turned over when she picked it up. Dinah had drawn her sister with a great deal of skill, particularly the dark, tousled hair, the pretty mouth, but why had she felt compelled to spoil it with a stark, black, jagged cross, completely obliterating Laura's smiling eyes?

'Oo-er,' Lily said next day when Josie told her about the drawing. 'That's dead peculiar, that is. Did she say why she did it?'

'I thought it best not to mention it.'

'I would have given our Samantha a clock around the ear if she'd done that to a picture of Gillian.'

Josie made a face. 'I doubt if that would have been the best approach, Lil. It would have only made things worse.'

'What things?'

'I dunno, do I? I'm not a psychiatrist. Her feelings for Laura, I suppose. Perhaps I should have talked to her about it,' she said thoughtfully. 'Maybe she left it there deliberately, knowing I'd see it, like. I just put it back where I found it, and didn't say a word.'

'I shouldn't take any notice,' Lily said lightly. 'Kids do ever such peculiar things when they're little. I remember cutting all the buttons off our Stanley's best suit. I've no idea why.'

'I put a bad spell on me Auntie Ivy loads of times, but none of them ever worked.'

'Oh, I don't know. She married Vincent Adams, didn't she?'

'That was before I was born. It was nothing to do with me.'

'Try not to think about the drawing. Maybe she crossed it out because she didn't think it good enough. You're reading too much into it. By the way, Josie, would you mind putting your coffee on a coaster, please? That's what they're there for.'

Christmas passed pleasantly enough. On Boxing Day afternoon, Josie threw a drinks party. Lily had never heard of such a thing before, but came willingly enough with Neil and the girls. Aunt Ivy came early to help prepare the food, and Francie O'Leary brought a new girlfriend, Kathleen, a divorcee with long, dramatic, black hair and an hourglass figure. The Spencers were there. All the Kavanaghs were home for Christmas, and the old people managed to make a joke of the fact that one could hardly see and the other barely walk. Stanley and Freya, Marigold and Jonathan, Robert and Julia — all arrived with their children, so that Josie's tiny house bulged at the seams. Ben was the only Kavanagh absent.

It was the day Daisy and Eunice announced they were getting married.

'To each other?' Lily spluttered.

'No, idiot.' Daisy's laugh tinkled through the house. 'Eunice has been quietly courting for ages. He's a teacher, same as her. I met Manos in Greece last summer, and we've been writing to each other ever since. He proposed over the phone last night.'

There was a chorus of cheers and congratulations. 'I never thought you'd do it, girl,' Stanley whooped.

Mrs Kavanagh was close to tears. 'I'm so happy for you, Daisy, luv. Get married soon, won't you?'

'As soon as humanly possible, Ma.'

The Kavanagh children looked fearfully at each other. Their mother wanted an early wedding while she had the sight left to see.

All the Kavanaghs were back again in Liverpool on St Valentine's Day, when Daisy married Manos Dimantidou. She looked like a Greek goddess, in a simple white dress with a silver cord tied around her slim waist. Manos was a tall, suntanned man, sporting an awesome amount of black, curly hair with a sprinkling of silver in the long sideburns.

'Ah, well, that's the last of the children off our hands,' Mr Kavanagh said at the reception. 'Six down and none to go.'

His wife laughed. 'Now I can die happy. Though the grand children's weddings will soon be starting. Our Marigold's Colin will be twenty next year. He's already courting.'

And Laura would have been fifteen, Josie thought with a pang, old enough to be thinking about boys. She looked for Dinah, and saw her playing with Samantha in the corner of the hotel ballroom. She'd never mentioned the drawing of Laura and, since Christmas, Dinah seemed to have lost interest in both Jack and her sister.

'Hi. We only seem to meet at parties and weddings.' Ben appeared beside her.

'Hi, yourself. You're looking well.' He wasn't nearly as tense as the last time she'd seen him at Dinah's party. 'Is Imelda here?'

'She wouldn't come. Too tired, she claimed. I promised to be home by four, which is a shame. Peter and Colette are having a great time.' He regarded her soberly, and there was a message in his eyes she would have preferred not to see. 'You look beautiful, as usual. I like your frock. You always suited blue. It goes with your eyes.'

'It's only C & A.' It was a suit, not a frock, cornflower blue wool with satin lapels and cuffs on the fitted jacket and a slightly flared skirt.

'I expect you know what I'm thinking.'

That they'd come to the wedding together as man and wife? 'I'd sooner not know, Ben,' she said stiffly. 'We all make choices of our own free will. It's no good looking back and wishing we'd chosen different.'

She walked away, but was sorry for the rest of her life that she'd been rude. Ben remained at the reception until half past six, by which time the newly married couple had left for their honeymoon. The family decided not to tell them yet that when Ben arrived home, Imelda was dead, having taken what turned out to be a final fatal overdose.

'She was expecting Ben back in time to save her,' Lily sneered. 'I'm glad he was late. Good riddance to bad rubbish, I say.'

'You can be awful hard when you like, Lil,' Josie remarked.

'Oh, I'm as hard as nails, me. I believe in putting meself, me kids and me family first, and that means our Ben. I always said he was a soppy lad. He should have given Imelda her cards years ago. There's no way I'd let someone ruin me life the way she did his.'

Imelda had only been buried a month when Mollie Kavanagh fell the full length of the stairs in the house in Childwall. She never regained consciousness and died two minutes before midnight the same night, with her husband and four of her children at her bedside, having been given the Last Sacraments just in time. Stanley and Robert arrived too late to be with the mother they had loved so dearly.

Josie waited anxiously by the phone. Lily had rung earlier to explain what had happened. She longed to be there, to say goodbye to the kind, loving and immensely generous woman who had been such a significant presence in her life, but would have felt in the way.

The telephone went at half past twelve. 'She's gone, Jose,' Lily said in a ragged voice. 'She went half an hour ago. Me poor da's in a terrible state. Our Marigold's taking him home. Oh, Josie! Why don't nice things ever happen? Why is everything always so bloody sad?'

The funeral was held on the first of April. It rained solidly, all day, without a break. Francie O'Leary was one of more than a hundred mourners; Mrs Kavanagh had made many friends over the years. Josie was grateful for his presence beside her during the Requiem Mass and, later, in the house in Childwall in which she'd known so many happy times.

'Can I come and see you tonight?' Francie asked when it was time for him to leave for his printing business, now occupying a small factory in Speke.

'Why the formality? You don't usually ask.' He turned up at all sorts of unlikely hours, and she was always glad to see him. Francie managed to make everything seem more cheerful than it actually was. Tonight he would be more than welcome.

He gave an enigmatic smile. 'Tonight's different.'

It was just gone eight when he arrived, having changed from a formal suit into jeans, a loose Indian shirt and a long, padded, velvet jacket. He'd recently had a perm, and his narrow face was framed in loose, bouncy waves.

'Where's Dinah?' he asked.

'In bed. She went early with a book. She can read ever so well, Francie. At school, they reckon she's bound to pass the eleven plus and go to grammar school.'

'Good.' He settled in a chair and looked at her intently. 'I'm not going to beat around the bush. Will you marry me?'

She smiled. 'No.'

'It's not a joke, Josie. I mean it. I seriously think we should get married. We get on perfectly together, we never row.'

'That's because we're not married.' She still thought he was joking. 'What happened to Kathleen?'

'I ditched her.'

'Poor girl. She was mad about you.'

'Stuff Kathleen. It's us I want to talk about.' He cleared his throat. 'I'm not in love with you, Jose.'

'I'm not in love with you, Francie.'

'Though I fancy you something rotten, always have.'

'I quite fancy you,' she conceded. 'Though you don't suit a perm. You look like a Cavalier.'

'That's a pity.' He gave an amiable, laid-back grin. 'I would have been on the side of the Roundheads. We're both getting on, you know, Jose. I'm thirty-seven, you're thirty-five. Why spend the rest of our lives apart when we can be together? It's a terrible waste. I really am serious, Josie. Honest.'

'Would you like a cup of tea?'

'Don't change the subject. I'll have tea when you've said you'll marry me.'

'Then you'll never drink another cup of tea again, Francie O'Leary,' she cried. 'I wouldn't dream of marrying you. I like you too much.' She looked at him curiously. 'If you really are serious, why ask now, after all this time?'

'Because I want to snap you up before Ben Kavanagh does,' Francie said surprisingly. 'He's crazy about you, Jose. After a decent interval he's bound to propose.'

'Then I shall tell him no, same as you.'

'Are you sure?'

Josie nodded furiously. 'Positive.'

'In that case, I'll have a cup of tea. Strong, two sugars, to steady me nerves.'

'You don't have nerves, Francie.' She went into the kitchen.

'Are you still in love with that husband of yours?' he shouted.

'Ex-husband.' She returned to the parlour. 'Yes, though I know it's hopeless. It's strange, because we weren't exactly happy a lot of the time.' Even in New York, which she looked back on as having been perfect, she'd nevertheless been full of doubts and uncertainties.

He looked at her curiously. 'What's it like, being in love? It's never happened to me.'

'It's . . . it's indescribable, Francie.' She clasped her hands against her breast, smiling, remembering the night she'd met Jack. 'Everything seems different, the whole world. It's agony and ecstasy at the same time.'

'It doesn't sound too healthy to me,' Francie said drily.

She thought about Ivy and Uncle Vince. 'It isn't always.'

The kettle boiled and she went to make the tea. Francie appeared in the kitchen doorway. 'I meant what I said earlier, that we should get married. I don't expect an answer now, but think about it, Jose. Another thing . . .' He winked at her suggestively. 'I reckon we'd be good together in bed.'

Josie thought about it, and decided it wasn't a bad idea. Whenever Francie got a new girlfriend she didn't feel jealous, but she was always worried she would lose him as a friend. He'd become part of her life, like Lily and Aunt Ivy, like Mrs Kavanagh had been. Francie touched a side of her that no one else did. He made the world seem funny and young. They had a good laugh together. Was that enough to make a marriage? Well, she'd never know if she didn't try. And they might grow to love each other one day, you never knew.

'But would you mind if we left it until next year?' she said to him the night she accepted his proposal. 'It's been such an awful year so far. We've known each for half our lives, so another few months won't make much difference. And, if you don't mind, I'd sooner we kept it between ourselves for now.'

'In case you get cold feet?'

Josie chewed her lip. 'I'm not sure, Francie, to be honest. I mean, this isn't exactly a romantic situation we're in, is it? It's almost a business arrangement. *You* might get cold feet. Say you fall madly in love with some girl next week, for instance?'

'I don't think I'm capable of falling in love,' Francie said glumly. He folded his arms over his lavishly embroidered waistcoat, and looked at her challengingly. 'Okay, so we get married next year. In the meantime, what about the bed bit?'

'What *about* the bed bit?'

'Do I have to wait for that until next year, too?'

'Oh, I dunno, Francie. Let me think about it.'

They made love the first time in Francie's new house in Halewood, because it would have been impossible in Baker's Row with Dinah in the next room. He was a fervent, inventive lover, who still managed to make her laugh, even at the height of passion, and Josie felt enjoyably exhausted when it was over. They leaned against the pillows and finished off the wine they'd brought with them to bed. Francie looked even more sinister naked, with the faintly blue bones of his ribs showing through a surprisingly hairy body.

'Now we've broken the ice, we must do this more often,' he said. 'Twice a night would suit me fine.'

'You'll be lucky.' Josie stared around the bare room. 'You could do with some pictures up, Francie. And those curtains are dead dull.' The curtains were a sickly beige, to go with the carpet and the walls.

'It needs a woman's touch.' Francie grinned. He pulled her hand under the bedclothes. 'Like me.'

'Nineteen-seventy,' Lily said gloomily. 'It'll be nineteen-seventy in a few hours. Where have the years gone, Jose?'

'I dunno.' All day, Josie's mind had kept going back to the eve of the last decade. She glanced at her watch. It was just gone six. Ten years ago she was putting on the purple mini-dress ready for Maya's party, waiting for Elsie Forrest to arrive. Laura was running around the house in Bingham Mews, excited that she was being allowed to stay up till midnight. Jack had already started to drink.

'It's been the most miserable Christmas I can ever remember.' Lily's eyes were moist.

'I know, Lil.' Stanley had stayed in Germany, Robert in London. Daisy and Manos had gone to Greece to spend Christmas with his family. There'd been no sign of Ben. It was as if Mrs Kavanagh had been the thread that had held her children together.

Now it was New Year's Eve. Francie had got tickets for a dinner dance, but Josie had felt obliged to spend the evening with Lily, who had been deeply depressed since her mother died. Dinah was in the lounge, watching television with Samantha and Gillian. Neil had gone to the pub, but had promised to be back before Big Ben chimed in the New Year. Francie, being Francie, hadn't minded being forsaken for the woman he most loathed. There were plenty of parties he could go to.

'I mean,' Lily was saying, 'what's it all for? We're born, we get married, we have children, we get old, then we die! It hardly seems worth it, Jose.'

'Not if you put it like that. We're supposed to enjoy ourselves along the way, be happy.'

'Are you happy, Jose?'

Josie shrugged. 'Well, yes. I think I am. A bit.'

'*I'm* not, not the least bit, and it's not just because of Ma. It's, it's . . .' Lily searched for words. 'It's *Neil*.' The name came out like a gasp. 'Oh, I know he's a bloke in a million, you said that once, but . . .' She seemed lost for words again. 'Remember that day in Haylands? It was the day after you'd been with that Griff for the first time. Your face, Jose. I often think about your face that day. It was sort of lit up – radiant, I think you'd call it. And your eyes were so bright, almost as if you'd been crying, except they were such happy eyes, shining.' Lily looked shyly at Josie. 'My face has never looked like that, Jose. Making love with Neil is a bit of an ordeal nowadays, and it's never exactly turned me on. Oh,' she cried, 'I missed so much, marrying him. I should have waited. Look at our Daisy, madly in love at forty.'

'Lily, you would have been unbearable if you'd had to wait to get married until you were forty. You'd have had all of us nervous wrecks by now.'

'I know.' Lily sighed. 'I'm too impatient. I grabbed the first man that asked. Neil's good and decent, but I should have turned him down. He would have been hurt, but not as much as he'll be hurt now.'

Josie looked askance at her friend. 'What do you mean?'

'I'm going to chuck him out, Jose,' Lily said in a shaky voice. 'Ask him to leave. I'll suggest we sell the house, get rid of the mortgage and I'll buy something smaller for me and the girls. I don't want the poor bloke on the streets. Then I'll get a job like you. Anything's better than being stuck in a dead boring marriage for the rest of me days. I always said our Ben was daft, sticking by Imelda. Well, the same rule applies to me. I'm wasting me life with Neil.' Lily glared at her friend, her small face knotted in determination. 'And do you know what else I'm going to do, Jose?'

'What's that, Lil?'

'I'm going to chase Francie O'Leary like he's never been chased before. I'll get him to the altar if it's the last thing I do. I could never understand you still being in love with Jack, until I realised I've been in love with Francie since I was sixteen. I'm going to marry him, Josie, or die in the attempt.'

There was a significance about 1974, but Josie couldn't remember what it was. It wasn't to do with turning forty, which she didn't regard as significant, but something else. A long while ago, 1974 had been mentioned as a year when something would happen. She had racked her brains every day since the year began, but nothing would come.

She got ready for work on a crisp, February morning, making up her nearly forty-year-old face in the dressing-table mirror. Now she worked for the accountants from nine till four, with half an hour for lunch, almost full time. She kept promising herself she would leave, but it was convenient and well paid.

I'm wasting me life, she told herself. Though perhaps I expect too much. There was always a nagging feeling that she was missing out on something.

'Dinah,' she yelled. 'It's half past eight. You should be on your way to school by now, not still in bed.'

There was an answering thump. Josie went downstairs and made herself a bowl of cornflakes. It was no good putting food out for Dinah, she rarely had time in the mornings to eat. A few minutes later her daughter appeared, looking surprisingly neat in her gymslip, blouse and tie, considering the short time she'd had to get dressed.

'Don't want breakfast, Mum.' She disappeared into the bathroom. Water briefly ran, the lavatory flushed. Dinah reappeared. 'Where's me satchel?'

'Don't ask me, luv. It's wherever you left it last night.'

'Where did I do me homework?'

'I can't recall you doing any.'

'I read a book, didn't I?' Dinah looked at her defiantly.

'I didn't realise they set *True Confessions* as homework these days.'

'I read a chapter of *Vanity Fair*, if you must know.'

She must have read it awfully quickly. Josie held back the comment, and found the satchel on the floor beside the settee.

Dinah swung the bag on to her shoulder. 'Ta, Mum. I might be late home from school.'

'Where are you going, luv?' Josie asked anxiously. Dinah was late home most nights. Sometimes it was seven o'clock by the time she put in an appearance.

'Round Charlie Flaherty's house.'

'A boy! Will there be other girls there, Dinah?'

'Oh, Mum. Get with it. Charlie's a girl – Charlotte. We're only going to listen to her record player. Where's me coat?'

'Behind the door, where it always is.'

'Well, it's not there now!'

The navy blue duffel coat was on the floor on the other side of the settee. Dinah picked it up, muttered a curt, 'Tara,' and left the house, only half into the coat.

Josie stood at the window and watched the tall, slim figure of her daughter go running down the path, still struggling with the coat. She sighed. It was a sad fact, but she didn't get on with Dinah. They never really had, but things had gone from bad to worse since she'd started at the local comprehensive school three years ago. She'd failed the eleven-plus, Josie suspected deliberately, out of sheer bloody-mindedness, because everybody, her mother included, had expected her to pass, or it might have been because she didn't fancy the long journey each day to the nearest grammar school. Whatever the reason, Dinah had failed, and now they seemed at daggers drawn most of the time.

She went into the dining room and finished off the cornflakes, then drained the pot of tea. She couldn't help but wonder what Laura might have been like at fourteen. Josie felt sure she wouldn't have spoken to her mother the way Dinah did, so impatiently, so rudely. They would have done things together – gone shopping, to the pictures, had little confidential chats. Perhaps Dinah would have been different if she'd had a father. Well, she *did* have a father, but he'd decided to ignore her existence, which only made it worse. It can't have done the girl much good.

'Oh, well, it's no use sitting here thinking about what might have been. I'll be late for work,' she said to the empty room.

She would have missed it if it hadn't been for Mr Kavanagh, still living with Marigold and bedridden most of the time. He telephoned one Sunday morning in July. 'Do you get *The Sunday Times*, dear?'

'No, The *News of the World*.'

'Well, I should get *The Times* today if I were you. There's an article about that writer you used to work for, Louisa Chalcott. It's very interesting. It's her centenary, you see. She was born a hundred years ago this month.'

1974! Louisa had given her a brown envelope sealed with wax which wasn't to be opened until 1974. Josie thanked Mr Kavanagh, and began to search for the envelope. She couldn't remember where she'd put it. She ransacked the house, waking up an irritable Dinah who liked to lie in on Sundays, and found it at the bottom of the wardrobe drawer, underneath the spare blankets. She knelt on the floor and took the envelope out.

'Oh, gosh!' She recalled the night Louisa had given it to her. She'd just finished the garden, and they were sitting on the bench outside. The sea, the sky, the sand, had looked so beautiful, peaceful.

The envelope looked remarkably new. Josie broke the wax, and withdrew three shiny red exercise books. She flicked through them. Every page was crammed with Louisa's scarcely decipherable scribble. It wasn't poetry. She managed to read a page, thought it might be a highly risqué novel, then realised it was the story of Louisa's life, her autobiography.

'Oh, gosh!' she said again. *Lady Chatterley's Lover* was probably mild by comparison. She noticed a slip of paper had fallen from one of the books. 'This book,' she read, 'is both dedicated and gifted to my dear friend, Miss Josephine Flynn, to do with whatsoever she may please.'

'Well, I'm not likely to throw it away, am I, Louisa?' Josie said aloud. 'All I can do is read it, if I can make sense of your lousy writing, that is.'

'Who are you talking to?' Dinah, in the skimpiest of nighties, was at the bedroom door.

'Meself. I'm just going to get the Sunday paper.'

'What are those?' Dinah asked as Josie returned the books and the slip of paper to the envelope.

'Just something written by an old lady I used to work for. She was a poet. Her name was Louisa Chalcott.'

'Can I have a look?'

'Well,' Josie said doubtfully, 'it's not suitable for young eyes, luv. It's pretty hot stuff, as they say.'

Dinah pouted. 'You don't mind me reading *True Confessions*.'

'I do, actually. And this is *True Confessions* with knobs on. Oh, go on.' She shoved the envelope at her daughter. 'You probably won't be able to make head or tail of her writing. Be careful with it. I'd like to try and read it meself some time.'

The article in *The Sunday Times* repeated much that had been in Louisa's obituary twenty years before. She was before her time, her scandalous lifestyle had caused a furore in turn-of-the-century New York, and even later, in the twenties, when she had given birth to twins but had refused to name the father. The writer went on to say that the twins, Marian Moorcroft and Hilary Mann, now living in Croydon, England, had refused to discuss their mother. Lousia Chalcott's raw, earthy poetry had seen a renaissance of late. The unsuspected power of her work was only now beginning to be recognised, and would shortly be republished in full. There was, however, one choice piece of work the public would never see. According to her agent, Leonard McGill, Miss Chalcott had written her autobiography, but unfortunately it appeared to have been lost.

'"She assured me, several times, in the years prior to her death, that she was writing her life story," Mr McGill told me. "But although I and her daughters made a thorough search, the manuscript has never come to light."'

'Dinah,' Josie said urgently. 'Where's that scrap of paper that fell out the books?'

'Here.' Dinah was reading a red exercise book, mouth open, eyes shocked. 'Shit, Mum. This woman was an *ogre!* A nyphomaniac ogre! She must have been hell to work for.'

'She was, and she wasn't.' Josie searched for somewhere safe to put the paper. 'I might need that if it comes to a battle with the twins. And don't swear, luv. It's not very nice.'

3

Next day, she rang Directory Enquiries during her dinner break to get Leonard McGill's telephone number. She could actually remember his address in Holborn.

'He's at lunch,' she was told. 'Would you like to leave a message?'

'Yes, please. It's about Louisa Chalcott. He'll probably remember me.' They'd spoken over the phone often enough. 'I used to be Josie Flynn. Tell him I've got Louisa's manuscript.'

'Have you really?' remarked the disembodied voice. 'He

will be pleased. He'll return your call the minute he gets in. Can I have your number?'

Josie reeled off the number. 'I'm going back to work, I'm afraid. I won't be home till four o'clock.'

'Oh, dear. I shall have a very agitated gentleman on my hands for the next three hours,' laughed the voice.

The phone was ringing when Josie unlocked the door two minutes after four. The years seemed to fall away when she heard the familiar, cultured tones of Leonard McGill. He courteously asked how she was before mentioning the manuscript, which she could tell he was dying to do. 'So, madam left it with you, did she? The twins will be thrilled. I'm over the moon. I long to read it, find out what that awful woman got up to.'

'Actually, she left it *to* me, not just with me. I didn't realise I had it until yesterday. It was in an envelope which Louisa asked me not to open until nineteen seventy-four.'

There was silence, followed by a strange noise, like water gurgling down a drain, and she realised Leonard McGill was laughing. 'The twins will be as sick as dogs, and I'm even further over the moon. What a turn-up for the books, eh? Dreadful pair, those two. I'm not sure who was worse – the mother, or her frightful daughters.'

'Oh, the daughters,' Josie said promptly. 'At least Louisa was honest.'

'I'll let the press know. Offers of publication are bound to come pouring in. Now,' he said, and she could imagine him mentally rubbing his hands together with glee, 'I hesitate to abandon something so precious to the tender mercies of the Royal Mail, and I can scarcely ask you to bring it all the way to London. I think it best if I came personally to collect it as soon as possible. If I cancel my appointments, I could come tomorrow. Would that suit you?'

'No,' Josie said firmly. The manuscript was *hers*, and she wasn't prepared to let it out of her possession, not yet. 'I tell you what – the firm where I work has just got one of them new photo-copying machines. I'll do a copy tomorrow and post it straight away.'

He was clearly disappointed, but Josie didn't care. She rang off. She was holding something very important, with which Louisa had said she could do 'whatsoever she may please'. Knowing Louisa, she'd had publication in mind, and had obviously wanted Josie to have the benefit of the royalties it would earn, which wouldn't be much, if her previous royalties were anything to go by, but better than nothing. But a principle was involved and, with the twins hovering on the horizon, it seemed important to hold on to the original until an agreement, or a contract, or whatever it was called, was signed.

She sank into a chair, feeling elated. At last something exciting had happened, and it was all due to Louisa.

In the nine years she had worked for Terence Dunnet, a small, reserved man with skin like parchment, half-moon spectacles and very little hair, they had never had a proper conversation. She felt slightly nervous when she asked if he would mind if she used his new copying machine. 'It's quite a few pages, hundreds, but I'll pay for the ink and paper. And I wouldn't do it during working hours, naturally.' She had told Dinah she might be late home, but Dinah said it didn't matter, she'd be even later.

'Well . . .' He looked from her to the gleaming new machine that stood in the corner of the main office. 'I don't suppose it would hurt. I get a discount the more paper that's used.'

'Ta, very much,' she said gratefully.

It was a slow job, and took much longer than expected. She was still hard at work at six o'clock when Terence Dunnet came out of his own office, ready to lock up and go home.

'I'll have to finish tomorrow.' She wiped her brow. It was a hot day, and continual use of the photocopier had turned the room into an oven. 'I'm only two-thirds of the way there.' There was still another exercise book to copy.

'What is this?' He looked with interest as a double page of barely legible scribble emerged from the machine and plopped on to the pile already there.

'It's a book, written by a friend of mine. I'm doing a copy for her agent,' Josie felt bound to explain.

'Has she had anything published before?'

'Yes, but only poetry.'

'*Only* poetry!' He smiled his dry-as-dust smile. 'My wife is something of an amateur poet, Mrs Coltrane. She would be annoyed to hear it referred to that way. What is your friend's name? If she's been published, Muriel may have heard of her.'

'Louisa Chalcott.' Josie herself did her best not to be annoyed. 'And I said "only" poetry, because this is something different, that's all. I wasn't being offensive.'

Terence Dunnet's glasses nearly dropped off his nose. 'This surely cannot be the manuscript that was mentioned in *The Sunday Times*? Louisa Chalcott is one of Muriel's favourite writers, and she gave me the article to read.'

Josie nodded, and explained she'd been Louisa's secretary, and had only known she held the missing manuscript on Sunday.

'How remarkable.' He looked dazed. 'How absolutely remarkable. And it's actually in *my* office! Muriel will be knocked for six when I tell her.' He put his briefcase on the floor, removed his jacket and rolled up his snow-white sleeves. 'It is obviously important that this reaches Miss Chalcott's agent with all possible speed. The last post goes from Whitechapel at eight o'clock. You look exhausted, Mrs Coltrane. Make us both a cup of tea while I finish this off. You know where the large envelopes are kept. Why not get one ready? *I* will make sure the post is caught. And forget about paying for the paper and the ink – a copy of the book when it's published would suffice.' He smiled again. 'Signed by you, of course.'

The twins consulted a solicitor, but according to Leonard McGill had been advised they hadn't a leg to stand on. 'I sent them a copy of Louisa's note,' he told Josie on the phone, 'and they tried to claim it was a forgery. I said if that was the case, the entire book must be a forgery because the writing is identical. By the way, I've had another offer – two and a half thousand pounds. The publishing trade are vying with each other for Louisa's last work. Sex and art.' He chuckled. 'A highly volatile combination.'

Josie gulped. She'd had no idea you got paid for books before they were published – half on signing the contract, the rest when it was published. This was the third offer, five hundred pounds more than the last. 'Will you accept?'

'Will *you* accept, Josie?' Leonard said smoothly. 'It's entirely up to you. As your agent, I would recommend against it. It's early days yet.'

'It makes me feel uncomfortable,' she confessed. 'After all, it's not as if I wrote it.'

'Would you feel uncomfortable had Louisa left you a valuable antique that was up for auction?'

'Probably not.'

'Well, this is no different, my dear.'

By the end of August, the bidding had reached twelve thousand five hundred pounds, and Leonard McGill phoned.

'It's a new company, Hamilton & Ferrers. I know nothing about Ferrers, but Roger Hamilton is a well-known entrepreneur. He's been in oil, plastics, mining, owns a racehorse or two. The company have already published half a dozen works that haven't exactly set the world alight. He hopes to create a stir with *My Carnal Life*. I have tentatively accepted on your behalf.'

'Do you think the title's okay? It's the way Louisa described it more than once.'

'It's perfect, Josie. Oh, Roger Hamilton would like to meet you. I thought if I brought him to Liverpool one day soon, we could sign the contract over dinner and you can hand over the original manuscript at the same time.'

'Can I come?' Dinah demanded.

'You'd feel out of place, luv, with a crowd of old people.'

'You're only forty, Mum. And who's to say this Roger chap mightn't be young? Anyroad, I'd quite enjoy it. And you need someone on your side.'

'It's not a battle,' Josie argued. 'There won't be sides. If there were, Leonard McGill should be on mine. He's me agent.'

'He's also a man. It'll be two men against one woman if I don't come with you.'

'As I said, it's not a battle . . . Oh, all right. I'd like to have you with me. I'll ask Leonard to book a table for four.'

She felt touched that Dinah seemed protective all of a sudden, and bought them a new outfit each for the occasion. They actually ventured into George Henry Lee's, where the prices were normally way beyond her reach. It meant being temporarily overdrawn at the bank.

'Gosh, this brings back memories.' She searched through a rack of elegant suits, possibly a bit warm for early September.

'Memories of what?'

'Of shopping in the Kings Road when money was no object. You should have seen the things I used to buy, Dinah! You know me camel coat with the fur collar? I bought that in the Kings Road. It's older than you are, and still in good condition.'

'I suppose Laura had lovely clothes, too,' Dinah said.

It was a long time since she'd mentioned Laura, and Josie was upset by the bitterness in her voice. She touched the slim, white arm. 'You didn't exactly go short, luv. I always made sure you were as well dressed as Lily's Samantha.'

For once, Dinah didn't shrug her away. 'Are going to buy one of these?'

'No, I'd prefer something not so heavy.'

She settled on a violet shot silk suit with a straight skirt and boxy jacket, with a black lace blouse to go underneath. Dinah refused to be talked out of a brief green linen frock that barely covered her behind.

'You'll have to wear tights,' her mother advised as she

gritted her teeth and wrote the cheque, 'else your thighs will get stuck to the seats if they're leather.'

The dinner was arranged for five days later. That afternoon they went together to the hairdresser's. Dinah was still on holiday from school, and Terence Dunnet willingly gave Josie the time off. He had been dining out on the story of a famous lost manuscript being photocopied in his office, and she had kept him abreast of the various bids. He had offered to read the contract before it was signed. 'As an accountant, I often read through agreements, contracts, that sort of thing. I can check if you're getting a good deal.'

'I'm signing it at dinner, but I trust Leonard McGill – that's the agent – completely. He's entitled to ten per cent, I know that much.'

'Well, if you need help or advice, I'm at your service.'

'Ta.' She was pleased that they had become friends. They'd started to call each other Terence and Josie. His wife, Muriel, had been to see her, wanting to know all about Louisa Chalcott.

'Do I look all right?' she anxiously asked Dinah that night when she was ready to go.

'Gorgeous, Mum. That suit makes your eyes look a lovely dark blue. I wish mine were darker. What colour did me dad have?'

'Brown – still does, I expect. You've got lovely colour eyes, Dinah, there's a touch of lilac in them.' She looked sophisticated, and at the same time very young and fresh, in the green dress. Her fair, rather fine hair, tucked behind a green band, was shoulder length and turned up at the ends. She wore lipstick for the first time, a light coral, and her normally pale cheeks were slightly flushed. She was obviously excited at the thought of the evening ahead.

Relations with Dinah had improved enormously over the last few weeks. It was as if, since the discovery of Louisa's book, she was seeing her mother in a new light, with an interesting past, not just someone who nagged her to get up or wanted to know what time she'd be home. Had she been a

306

different sort of girl, Josie would have told her about Louisa – and all sorts of other things – before, but Dinah had never seemed interested in talking to her mother.

Leonard McGill had booked a table at The George in Lime Street, expensive and discreet. Josie had never set foot in the place before. Dinah insisted they be five minutes late. 'You don't want to look too anxious.'

'I want to look polite, that's all.'

'Let them be waiting for us, not us for them.'

The restaurant was barely half-full. Two men were sitting at a corner table, set slightly apart from the others. Waiters hovered attentively, and there was the subdued clink of dishes, the mouth-watering smell of food. One of the men stood, waved and came towards them.

'Josie! We meet at last. Leonard McGill, how do you do?' He shook hands effusively. 'And this must be Dinah!' He turned back to Josie. 'Why, you were scarcely any older than this when we first spoke on the phone all those years ago. How lovely to see you both. Let me introduce you to Roger.'

Roger Hamilton was equally effusive. Both men were remarkably similar in appearance – early fifties, silver-haired, wearing dark suits and dark ties. Roger Hamilton's clothes were clearly more expensive than those of a mere literary agent, and his face redder, his chin jowly. Josie wondered if the large green stone in his tie clip was a real emerald. She was immediately struck with the feeling that she'd seen him before, and also that she didn't like him much. Behind the smiling eyes she sensed a hardness. This man could be very cruel and ruthless, she suspected, but perhaps that went for all entrepreneurs.

Throughout the meal she felt she was being slightly patronised by both men. 'I suppose this will be your first and only venture into the world of literature,' Roger Hamilton remarked over the main course, delectable roast beef and melt-in-the-mouth vegetables.

'It's not her first.' Dinah spoke up. 'My father used to be a

307

famous television writer, and she used to do his typing. What was it he wrote, Mum?'

'*Di Marco of the Met*, and a few other things.'

'He's in Hollywood now. He writes scripts for films. Mum divorced him because she didn't like living in London. Before that, they lived in New York.'

Under the table, Josie kicked her daughter's ankle, but was glad she'd spoken, even if she'd made half of it up. She was regarded with new respect. They had probably thought they were dealing with an ignorant peasant. She said to the publisher, 'I've a feeling I've seen you before, but can't remember where.'

'On television? I'm often interviewed about this and that. I'm on the book programme shortly, promoting *My Carnal Life*.'

'No.' She shook her head. He hadn't had silver hair. It was more the cut-glass accent she remembered, the rather jerky gestures. 'It'll come to mind eventually.'

The meal ended, more wine was ordered, glasses filled, including one for Dinah who'd drunk lemonade so far. 'To toast the signing,' said Leonard McGill. He produced a sheaf of papers from his briefcase. 'The contract, Josie. Do you have the manuscript with you?'

'Of course.' Terence Dunnet had loaned her a leather document case to carry it in. 'It's here.'

'Fair exchange is no robbery.' He laughed. 'Read through this, my dear. Initial each page at the bottom, and sign on the dotted line at the end.'

'I'm sure there's no need to read it.' Josie began to flick through the pages, conscious of Roger Hamilton watching, almost licking his lips, as he waited for her to sign.

'I have been long awaiting this moment, but I'm afraid nature calls. Please, excuse me.' The agent left the table.

Josie reached inside her handbag for a pen. The man opposite was playing with a knife, turning it over and over in his hand. She stared at the knife, then at his face. 'I've definitely seen you before. Have you ever been to Liverpool?'

'During the war, yes. My regiment stayed overnight before sailing for Cairo.' He smiled charmingly at her. 'But you would have been just a babe in arms then, possibly not even born.'

'You've got a sister called Abigail.'

He dropped the knife. 'How can you possibly know that? She died years ago.' His face went ghostly white, his jaw wobbled. He picked up a glass, drained it, smoothed back the silver hair with a hand that shook.

Josie's eyes never left his face. He'd remembered, too! 'You called me mam a whore,' she said softly. 'You nearly raped me. I wasn't a babe in arms, but I was only six.'

There was silence, and it seemed to go on for ever. A waiter appeared, and went away when everything seemed to be in order. Across the room someone laughed. A cork popped.

'Look, that was a long time ago.' His voice was hoarse, uneven. Saliva oozed from the corners of his mouth. 'We were living on the edge. We did things we wouldn't normally dream of doing. We weren't ourselves.'

'Nothing can excuse what you tried to do.'

He swallowed, recovered slightly, became belligerent. 'If I recall rightly, your mother *was* a whore.'

'*I* wasn't,' said Josie. 'I was six.' She stood, collected her things together, put them in her bag and picked up the document case. 'Goodbye, Mr Hamilton. I think Louisa would have preferred her book to be published by someone else.'

'Look!' He was angry now, so angry that it scared her. 'If this gets out, you won't look whiter than white. Your mother was a prostitute. It's not something to boast about.'

'It's not something to be ashamed of either. But it won't get out, Mr Hamilton. I'm going to put it to the back of me mind again, where it's always been until tonight when I met you.'

'Mum, Mum. You left without me.' Dinah caught her up at the door and grabbed her arm.

'I'd forgotten you were there! Oh, luv!' She could have

wept. 'You shouldn't have heard all that stuff.' Dinah wasn't fourteen until the end of the month.

'Are you all right?'

'No, luv, I'm not. Me legs seem to have disappeared, and me head feels like someone else's. I need a drink – a cup of tea, dead strong.'

They emerged into Lime Street. Dinah linked her arm in Josie's for the very first time. Josie said shakily, 'Let's go to the Adelphi lounge, hang the expense.'

'What was all that about, Mum?'

'I reckon you've already got the gist of it, Dinah.'

'Grandma was a prostitute?' The girl's face was bright with curiosity, and Josie was relieved there was no sign of disgust.

'Yes. Look, once I've got a pot of tea in front of me, I'll tell you the whole thing.'

'Did the dinner go well?' Terence enquired next morning.

'It went abysmally.' Josie made a face. She'd hardly slept, reliving the awful meal, worrying about Louisa's book. 'The publisher chap was dead rude, so I walked out. I'll call Leonard McGill when I get home. He'll have to get someone else.'

'What a dreadful pity. Call him from here if you wish,' he said generously. 'The sooner the better. Muriel can't wait for that book to be in print.'

'Ta, very much. Oh, I've got the contract. I was so mad I stuffed it in me bag without thinking.'

'Ah, do let me see.'

She handed him the contract, then dialled the London number. The friendly receptionist answered as usual. 'What did you do to him, Josie? He's like a bear with a sore head this morning. Hold on a minute, I'll put you through.'

The extension rang. 'Josie! What on earth happened last night? Poor Roger, he claimed you took umbrage over something trivial. I said that wasn't like you.' His voice was strained, as if he was finding it hard to be his courteous self.

'Poor Roger's talking rubbish, but I'd sooner not talk about it if you don't mind. I'd like you to find another publisher.'

'That's easily done, though the advance won't be as large.'

'I don't mind.' Josie was conscious of something very odd happening. Terence Dunnet was doing a war dance in front of her eyes, mouthing, 'No, no, no,' and waving his arms, jumping up and down. To her complete astonishment, he suddenly snatched the phone out of her hand in mid-sentence and slammed it down.

'Sorry to be rude,' he gasped, 'but you don't just need another publisher, Josie, you need another agent. Did you agree to sell the book outright to this Hamilton chap?'

'I didn't agree to anything in particular.' She looked at him, alarmed. 'Is something wrong?'

'There most certainly is,' he said grimly. 'No author in their right mind sells a book outright. If you had signed this, you would have given up all rights to the work. You wouldn't have received a penny in royalties.' He waved the contract. 'It would seem that Hamilton and McGill took advantage of your ignorance, did a deal, signed a private contract of their own. Either that, or a very large backhander was involved.'

She was back to square one, no further than that. At least in the beginning she'd had an agent to negotiate on her behalf. How did you acquire an agent? Terence offered to find out.

'Do you *need* an agent?' Dinah queried that night. 'Why can't you send it to a publisher yourself?'

'Terence said that might be tricky. Leonard McGill had offers from most major publishers, so he'd consider himself entitled to ten per cent. He rang earlier, and wasn't half mad when I told him nicely to get stuffed.' She wasn't prepared to let him have a penny, and still bristled with indignation at how close she'd come to being conned.

'Another agent might find it tricky, too.'

'I know.' Josie sighed. She was beginning to wish Louisa hadn't left her the damned book.

'Mum?'

'Yes, luv?'

'I'm sorry.'

'For goodness' sake, luv.' Josie laughed. 'None of this is your fault.'

'I know, Mum.' Dinah came and sat beside her on the settee. 'It's that stuff you told me last night. I've been thinking about it all day. I've been horrible, haven't I? I was a hateful little girl, and now I'm a hateful big girl.'

'Dinah, luv! You've never been horrible. I must concede you've been a bit awkward from time to time, but horrible and hateful? Never!'

'Yes, I have, Mum.' Dinah seemed to hesitate, before laying her head on her mother's shoulder. 'You didn't have a mum or dad, and today I realised how lucky I was, having you.'

'And I'm lucky, having you.' Josie's heart turned over. Was it possible that after fourteen strained years they might become friends?

'When I was little,' Dinah said in a small voice, 'I used to have this dead funny feeling that you didn't want me, that I was in the way. When I got older I was convinced you kept comparing me to Laura, wishing I was nicer, more like her. I *was* awkward. I did it deliberately, I don't know why.'

'I was *glad* you weren't like Laura,' Josie cried. Guilt almost choked her. Fancy, a tiny baby sensing it was unwanted. 'I preferred to have a little girl different to Laura. It was wonderful, you know,' she said softly, 'to find meself pregnant only a few weeks after Laura died. Like a miracle. I would have been dead lonely without you, what with your dad gone an' all.' It came to her how empty the last years would have been, spent alone. 'Mind you, it was me own fault your dad went, I told you that last night. He didn't want to go, I made him. If we'd known about you, nothing would have made him leave.' Last night, she'd told her daughter just about everything except the murky part Uncle Vince had played in her own and Mam's life. She wasn't quite old enough to know *that* yet!

'And you nearly married Ben Kavanagh!' Dinah wrinkled

her white nose. 'He's a bit of a drip, Mum. I'm surprised he didn't propose again when his wife died.'

'Oh, he did, but I turned him down. He's not a drip, Dinah, just a very sensitive man.'

'Huh! I always thought you'd marry Francie O'Leary. I've always liked him.'

'So has your Auntie Lily.' Josie grinned. 'And now she's got him, hasn't she?'

Directly after that New Year's Eve four years ago, when Lily had claimed it was her intention to chase Francie O'Leary to the ends of the earth, Josie had told him she didn't want to marry him. She didn't add that Lily's need was much greater than hers.

Francie's face was tragic. 'Why ever not, Jose?'

She looked at him in surprise. 'I didn't think you'd care. I mean, we don't love each other.'

'I *don't* care,' Francie wailed. 'That's what's so bloody tragic. I *want* to care, about something, someone. I've got a gene missing, Jose. The gene that makes a person fall in love.'

'Don't be so ridiculous, Francie. You just haven't met the right person yet, that's all.'

'What about the bed bit? I *do* care about that.'

'The bed bit's over and finished with. We're not getting married, and I'm not the sort of woman who sleeps around.'

'Oh, Jose! But we'll still be friends, won't we?'

'The best of friends,' Josie assured him.

A distraught and tearful Neil Baxter left the house by Woolton Park and got a flat in Anfield as close as possible to Liverpool Football Club. Lily was a bit put out when, after an indecently short interval, he started going out with his landlady's daughter, almost twenty years his junior. They got married two years later, as soon as the divorce came through.

In the meantime, Lily ruthlessly set about wooing Francie O'Leary with all the wiles at her disposal. She and Josie developed a code. When Francie came to Baker's Row, Josie would dial Lily's number and let it ring three times. Shortly afterwards, Lily would arrive, as nice as pie, usually with the children who had been trained to call him 'Uncle Francie' and sit on his knee whenever possible. Invitations were printed for Samantha's and Gillian's parties, which required Lily calling on Francie at his place of work, and also for the headed notepaper she suddenly found essential. She threw grown-up parties, and played nothing but Louis Armstrong records, Jellyroll Morton, King Oliver – Francie's all-time favourite music.

One night, Francie arrived at Baker's Row, and collapsed in a chair. 'Lily's proposed,' he said in a strangled voice.

'Are you going to accept?' Josie held her breath. She'd known a proposal was on the cards.

'It's either that, or moving to another country. Or another planet.' He smiled slightly and stretched his legs. She thought he looked a bit smug. 'Actually, Jose, it wouldn't be such a bad thing to have someone like Lily Kavanagh on your side. She's come up with all sorts of ideas for the business, quite good ones. But I won't be nagged,' he said warningly, as if Josie had the power to prevent it. 'I will not be nagged or pissed around or told off in public – in private either, come to that. By the way, Jose, you've never told her about us, have you?'

'Lord, no, Francie.' Lily would have killed her.

And so it came to pass that Lily became Mrs Francis O'Leary, twenty-two years, almost to the day, since she'd been so publicly jilted by him in a noisy pub in Smithdown Road.

'I've been thinking, Mum,' Dinah said three days after the fateful dinner. 'You could publish Louisa's book yourself.'

'Oh, yeah! On Terence Dunnet's photocopying machine?'

'No, get Francie to do it. He does books, at least he does booklets. Marilyn brought one to school one day. It was a history of Liverpool Docks.'

'He won't do it for free, luv.'

'Get a loan from the bank,' Dinah said promptly. 'Francie got a loan when he expanded, I remember him saying once.'

'I'll talk it over with Terence.'

'It's not such a bad idea.' Terence smiled. 'Your daughter has a good business head on her shoulders. This is not a first novel by an unknown author, it's a book that comes with its own advance publicity. It doesn't need to be promoted. A circular sent to every bookshop in the land, a few advertisements in the press, should do it. It's a venture I would very much like to invest in, Josie. Get a quotation from your friend, and I'll draw up a business plan. We mustn't forget postage and packing, and I'm sure there will be other things to take into account.' He rubbed his dry hands together. 'This is getting rather exciting. Wait till I tell Muriel!'

'How many copies would you want, Jose?'

'I haven't a clue, Francie. Thousands, I expect.'

'That's a great help. I'll do two quotes – one for five thousand, another for ten. Once the machine's set up, it's a simple matter to run off more. Have you thought about the cover? The more colours you have, the more expensive it'll be. And would you like it glossy?' He punched the air. 'Actually, Jose, I've never done such a big job before. It's dead exciting.'

Daisy said there was a directory in the reference section of the library listing bookshops in the British Isles. 'It's not supposed to be borrowed, but I'll make an exception, seeing as it's you. Let me have it back as soon as possible, though.'

Terence Dunnet's clients were neglected as Josie spent several days typing the envelopes for the circulars announcing the publication of *My Carnal Life* in November. There was a cut-off section at the bottom for orders.

'Don't forget to send advance copies to the critics,' Mr Kavanagh advised from his sickbed.

'Can I have ten copies for Christmas presents?' enquired Muriel Dunnet.

Lily, heavily pregnant with what she prayed was a son, borrowed a typewriter from Francie's works and typed the manuscript out. She kept ringing Josie every time she reached a particularly juicy bit. 'Louisa went on a cruise once, and she slept with three stewards and the purser.'

'I remember her telling me that.'

'Will you dedicate the book to me after all my hard work?'

'I'll do no such thing. It's already dedicated to me.'

'It's a miserable cover, Mum,' Dinah remarked.

'No, it's not. It's dead tasteful.' The cover was plain grey, with Louisa's name in black and *My Carnal Life* embossed in gold. 'That gold cost an arm and a leg.'

'Another thousand!' Francie gasped. 'That'll be twenty altogether. You're going to have a bestseller on your hands. By the way, Jose, your company needs a name.'

'What company?'

'Your publishing company. Even if it's only a one-off, it needs a name. Coltrane Press would do.'

Josie cogitated overnight. 'Make it Barefoot House Press,' she told Francie next day.

'That's a bit of a mouthful. What's wrong with just Barefoot House?'

'Nothing,' she agreed.

'I'll sue,' Leonard McGill threatened when news of the imminent publication reached him.

'So sue. I'll tell everybody how you tried to rook me.'

'I am Louisa's agent.'

'You *were* Louisa's agent. You're not now.' Josie slammed down the phone.

This is better than sex, she thought one morning, feeling a surge of pleasure when even more envelopes than usual were pushed through the letter box. Well, no, not better. Not even as good. But close. One of the orders was from a shop in Knightsbridge where Laura had ordered books when she'd stayed in London before the war. There was a letter enclosed. 'One of our assistants, Miss Whalley, can actually remember Miss Chalcott coming in. All our staff wish you well with your venture, and look forward to having the book on our shelves.'

Oh, Lord! There was an order from W.H.Smith for 6000 copies. Josie whooped. She quickly got ready for work and rushed to tell Terence.

It was a dreary November morning. The air was wet with drizzle, and banks of ominous black clouds slowly rolled across an already grey sky. But the six people gathered in the glass-partitioned office in the corner of a print works in Speke were oblivious to the weather. Lily and Francie O'Leary, Muriel and Terence Dunnet, and Josie and Dinah Coltrane had something to celebrate. The first pages of *My Carnal Life* had just begun to roll off the press. Francie produced a bottle of champagne. Lily had brought glasses.

'To Louisa.' Francie raised his glass.

'To Louisa.'

That night Lily gave birth to a boy weighing eight pounds six ounces. Francie called Josie from the hospital. 'She wanted to call him Louis, in memory of Louisa, like, but I talked her out of it. I mean, Louis O'Leary is a helluva moniker to wish on a kid. We're calling him Simon instead.'

Some critics thought *My Carnal Life* disgusting, but confessed they couldn't stop turning to the next page. Others said Louisa's life was reflected in her dark, passionate poetry. Or that she had been a feminist before the word had been invented. That she had been a greedy, arrogant, over-sexed woman, who'd known what she'd wanted and hadn't cared who she'd hurt in the process of getting it. But they all agreed she wrote like a dream.

By Christmas, Louisa's book had already been reissued three times. Josie had given several interviews to the press about her part in Louisa's life and the publication of the book. She'd gone all the way to Broadcasting House in London to be interviewed on the wireless.

'Radio, Mum,' corrected Dinah. 'Don't say "wireless", they'll think you've come out of the ark.'

By March, the orders had virtually dried up, the foreign rights had been sold, the interviews were over, the excitement had died down. Terence Dunnet's loan had been repaid with interest and all the bills had been settled, leaving Josie with a reasonable sum in the bank, more than enough to have her house modernised and extended or buy somewhere else, as well as get a car. It was nice to be well off, but life seemed emptier than ever after the last tumultuous months. She still worked for Terence, and the job was much more pleasant since they'd become friends, but it wasn't enough to occupy her mind. She badly missed finding heaps of post on her doormat, the endless phone calls, typing letters late into the night on her *own* behalf. The portable typewriter she'd bought hadn't been used in weeks.

She badly wanted back the turbulence, the excitement. But how?

The manuscripts had started to arrive when Louisa's book had hardly been out a week, poetry mainly. Sometimes only a single poem was sent, or two or three. 'In case you should ever decide to publish an anthology,' the authors wrote. They were addressed to 'The Editor', as if Barefoot House were a huge company with loads of staff.

Josie always sent them back with a polite letter, explaining that Louisa's book had been a one-off and there would be no more. A few novels came which, out of interest, she began to read, but gave up when she realised they were awful. There was a murder mystery from a man in Somerset that was so good she read it right through to the end, returning the manuscript with a flattering letter saying she was sure he would find another publisher for his excellent book.

She came home from work one day and found a large, fat envelope on the mat, obviously delivered by hand. It was from a William Friars of Bootle, she discovered when she read the badly typed covering letter. The more than three hundred pages, entitled *The Blackout Murders*, were just as poorly typed. She made a cup of tea and began to read. She was still reading when Dinah came home from school to find there was no meal made, and she was despatched for fish and chips. Josie read while she ate, and was still reading at midnight. She took the book to bed and read there.

'Phew!' she gasped when she had finished. Her eyes were hurting, her head was aching, but she had never read anything so gripping before. It was a thriller, set during the last war, in which a killer stalks the blacked-out streets and back alleys of Bootle, secreting his hapless victims in the rubble left by the blitz. The hero, Edgar Hood, a sensitive, disturbed young man with a club foot, rejected by the Army and longing to do his bit, has set up his own private detective agency by the time the novel ends.

Josie visualised more books involving the same character – Edgar Hood could be another Hercule Poirot or Lord Peter Wimsey. She went downstairs and made tea, too excited to notice it was almost two o'clock, then found the carbon copy of the letter she'd sent to the man in Somerset who'd written the thriller, not quite as good as *The Blackout Murders*, but still highly readable. She wrote there and then and suggested he kindly send his novel back.

Tomorrow she would hand in her notice, and ask Terence to draw up another business plan. It would be harder this time as the authors would be unknown, but Barefoot House was about to become a proper publishing company of crime fiction. She knew nothing about poetry, and only liked it if it rhymed, but she'd been reading thrillers all her adult life.

Huskisson Street
1974–1984

I

'That was dreadful.' Dinah yawned and threw the manuscript to the floor.

'Be careful, luv. I can see it's beautifully typed.'

'That's the only thing good about it. I could tell who "dun" it by page five. I'll get Bobby to send it back tomorrow.' Dinah read through every piece of work received by Barefoot House, the small but highly respected publishing company located in Liverpool. Sometimes a few pages were enough to judge if it wasn't suitable. The more promising ones she passed over to her mother.

'I'd better get ready. Me and Jeff are going to the Playhouse.' She got to her feet. Dinah hadn't stopped growing until two years ago when she was seventeen, and she was now three inches taller than Josie, slender and graceful in her jeans and T-shirt. 'Actually, Mum . . .' She sat down again. 'There was something I wanted to talk to you about.'

'I'm all ears, luv.' Josie felt sleepy, curled up in a chair in front of the realistic flames of an electric fire.

'I'm thinking of moving to London.'

She was suddenly wide awake. 'London! But why, Dinah? I thought you and Jeff were serious?' She found it difficult to keep track of Dinah's young men, but Jeff had lasted longer than most. He was twenty-four, a quantity surveyor, almost handsome. She quite fancied him for a son-in-law.

Dinah wrinkled her nose. 'Jeff's serious. I don't want to

settle down, Mum, not like Samantha, with a husband and baby at nineteen. There's a whole world out there I've yet to see.'

'I know, luv.' She sighed. She'd felt the same when she was young. 'But what about a job? Unemployment's soaring.'

'I can type, Mum, and I have experience in publishing. In fact . . .' She looked ever so slightly uncomfortable. 'You know that agent, the new one – Evelyn King? Well, she's offered me a job, doing more or less what I do now – reading manuscripts, corresponding with authors, that sort of thing. She even said I can stay in her flat till I find somewhere of me own.'

'When was this?'

'A few months ago.'

Josie smiled. 'So you've been plotting and planning behind me back, have you?' Despite the smile, she was hurt.

'Not exactly, Mum. I didn't take much notice till Jeff asked me to marry him, and I realised it was the last thing I wanted.' Dinah leaned forward in the chair, her blue eyes bright with hope and excitement. 'I haven't *lived*, Mum. At least London's a start. I thought I might go after Christmas. One day I'd like to go to New York, like you.'

'Well, I'll not stand in your way, Dinah.' Josie smiled again. 'Not that you'd let me if I tried. It's your life, and you must do with it exactly as you please.'

'I knew you'd understand.'

Dinah went upstairs, and returned fifteen minutes later in different jeans and T-shirt. She was also wearing a short, fake-fur coat, which seemed a dead funny outfit to wear for the theatre but, then, Josie had worn a few dead funny outfits in her day.

'Tara, Mum.'

'Tara, luv. Have a nice time.'

Josie listened to the footsteps racing swiftly down the stairs. The front door opened, and again Dinah yelled, 'Tara.' The door slammed.

'Tara, luv,' Josie whispered. A lump came to her throat. She felt incredibly sad, as if Dinah had gone for good.

She didn't want her daughter to go to London. Over the last few years, with Lily preoccupied with Francie, Dinah had become her best and closest friend. It was selfish, but Josie wanted her to get married, live in Liverpool and have children so she could visit her, the way Lily visited Samantha and her grandson.

Tea! She urgently needed a cup of tea. The new fitted kitchen was in Maude's room. Ever since she'd bought the house in Huskisson Street, four doors away from where she'd lived with Mam, with exactly the same layout, she couldn't help but think of the girls. Irish Rose's room was Reception where Esther, her secretary, worked, as did the office junior, Bobby, who staggered to the post office twice a day with returned manuscripts.

Fat Liz's room had been split into two – one half Josie's office, the other Dinah's and Richard White's, who was in charge of publicity and circulation. What had been a very large cupboard now housed Eric, who'd been made redundant by the English Electric Company and worked part time, organising the wages, paying the bills and keeping the books in tiptop condition for Terence Dunnet, who did the firm's accounts and read through contracts to make sure they were correct. The more complicated legal work Josie passed on to a solicitor. Lynne and Sophie, the proofreaders, both graduates and married with small children, worked from home.

The kettle boiled. How many times in her life had she stood and watched a kettle boil? Millions. She made tea, furiously stirring the pot, but instead of taking the mug back to the lounge she went up two flights of stairs to the attic, to Mabel's and Josie's room! The house had been renovated throughout before she'd moved in, but there seemed little point having the little black grate and the corner sink removed.

This was where the rubbish was kept – the odds and ends of furniture she didn't want to throw away, the books she'd read but might read again, Dinah's school books which she preferred to keep, despite the fact she hadn't exactly been a star pupil. With her record, she'd been dead lucky to have a job waiting for her in Barefoot House when she left. There was a box of Dinah's toys, the trumpet Aunt Ivy had given her on her fifth birthday on top, its shine long gone.

It had been a shock, Aunt Ivy dying so suddenly without any apparent reason. It turned out her heart had just decided to stop beating one night as she lay beside Alf who, with his children, had stripped the house in Machin Street of everything nice. Josie had been surprised to find herself in tears at the funeral. Perhaps it was because she was gradually losing all links with the past – Mr Kavanagh had died not long before, and Sid and Chrissie Spencer had retired to More-cambe. According to Daisy, who still lived in Machin Street with Manos, Aunt Ivy's house had been sold to pay Alf's debts with the bookies. No one knew where the family had gone.

'Well, Mam,' she said loudly, 'Your daughter's about to be left on her own again. What are you going to do about it, eh?'

Mam didn't answer, and Josie's own heart might well have stopped beating if she had. She switched off the light and closed the door. At the top of the stairs she paused on the plush green carpet and watched the cold December stars blinking down at her through the skylight, the same stars she'd shown Teddy forty years ago.

'This is making me feel even sadder!'

She went down to the bottom floor, pausing in Maude's room on the way for another mug of tea. In Dinah's office she found a manuscript with a yellow sticker, indicating it had been read but Dinah was in two minds as to whether it was any good. She tucked it under her arm to read. A red sticker meant very good, a green one that the work showed promise, and a rare gold one that the novel was a knockout. Black was the death knell for any hopeful author, and their work was returned with a letter of rejection. Dinah was an excellent judge for someone so young. She'd do well with Evelyn

King's literary agency. She knew as much about publishing as Josie, admittedly only on a small scale.

In her own office, Josie sat at her desk and began to read. After a few minutes she gave up, unable to concentrate for thinking about Dinah. Perhaps if she made her daughter a partner, signed half of the company over to her, she might stay. But that would be unfair. She would almost certainly see it as a desperate move on her part but, knowing Dinah, she still wouldn't stay, and it would create tension. Best let her go, with smiles and best wishes for a better, more exciting life in London.

Josie glanced at the shelf of Barefoot House publications: seventy-three books so far. There'd been only five the first year, ten in the second. Now they were putting out twenty-five novels a year, all with the same bright red glossy covers, the author's name in black, the titles embossed in gold.

The Blackout Murders, their first publication, had put Barefoot House on the map. The paperback had sold more than a hundred thousand copies within three months, but William Friars, the author, lately of Bootle, now living in a smart residence in Calderstones, had turned out to be a pain. A retired schoolteacher, he contested every alteration the copy editor made, complained about the covers always being the same, demanded ever-increasing advances which were only just met by the admittedly huge sales.

His latest offering, *Death By Stealth*, was on her desk. It was the first he'd set post-war, and she didn't think it very good. The others, written with a terrible war raging in the background, had had a darkness, a compelling atmosphere of fear. His new book seemed pale by comparison. She had tactfully told him that he would be better off sticking to the war years, but he had lost his temper and demanded an advance that made her wince.

'I have been approached by another publisher,' he said pettishly, 'a firm much bigger than yours, who are prepared to meet my demands.'

Josie wasn't too keen on being blackmailed. 'I'll think about it,' she promised, with a feeling that she would shortly be telling William Friars to get stuffed.

Still, he had contributed to the so far modest success of Barefoot House. Without William Friars, she wouldn't have been able to buy this house, centrally situated in the shadow of the Protestant cathedral, a perfect place to live and run a company under the same roof.

She returned to the spacious first-floor lounge, tall Kate's room. If only Mam could see it, with its pink and cream striped wallpaper and a four-seater settee covered with matching material. The armchairs were pink velvet. Lily had said she should buy Regency furniture, but Josie preferred pine, even if it was out of period. There was a pine bureau, coffee-table, chests, two bookcases, both full. The carpet was a lovely warm brown. She threw herself full length on the settee. Gosh, she'd never thought she'd end up in such a grand house. Mind you, she thought drily, she'd started off in one exactly the same.

Christmas was very quiet. Esther, fifty, unmarried, and living alone, came to dinner, along with a miserable Jeff, who still lived in hopes of persuading Dinah to stay in Liverpool.

On New Year's Eve, Lily and Francie held a family party. Lily, at the remarkable age of forty-two, had produced a second son, Alec, now three, the image of his sinisterly handsome father. Simon was five and blond, like all the Kavanagh boys. Gillian was home from university in Norwich, where she was studying politics. She had brought a boyfriend, a spotty youth called Whizz who got more and more drunk as the night progressed. Samantha came with her husband, Michael, and their three-month-old son. ·

'Gosh, Lil. You're starting a dynasty of your own,' Josie remarked in the kitchen as she helped make more sandwiches when they ran out, Whizz having devoured far more than his share. Except for Lily and Daisy, it was ages since she'd seen another Kavanagh. Ben and his children had apparently disappeared off the face of the earth.

'I know.' Lily was starry-eyed. 'When I think of the way I used to envy you, Jose. You were so beautiful, you still are, and you never went short of boyfriends. Yet look at the way things have turned out! Oh, I know you've got a dead successful company, but it's nothing compared to me.'

For a moment Josie felt tempted to tell her friend that she wouldn't have had the opportunity to establish such a large dynasty if she hadn't given up Francie O'Leary on her behalf. She was also tempted to tell her she was getting much too fat, that it was about time she did some exercises so she didn't look six months pregnant all the time. Francie wasn't the sort of husband who'd take kindly to a wife who let herself go. She succumbed to neither temptation, contenting herself with a tart, 'You say the nicest things, Lil.'

'Why didn't your Dinah and Jeff come? They were invited.'

'Jeff preferred to have Dinah to himself. She's off to London in a few days.' Dinah hadn't realised – no one had except Josie – that she was leaving twenty years to the day that Josie had lost her other daughter.

It would soon be 1980, another decade gone. The years seemed to be leaping by. Josie excused herself and went upstairs. She wished Dinah had come to the party, so she'd have had someone there of her own, instead of being surrounded by Lily's children, husband, grandson, son-in-law and a possible prospective and extremely spotty second son-in-law.

She sat on the bed in Francie's and Lily's room and looked at herself in the mirror. For some reason, she recalled doing the same thing in Aunt Ivy's bedroom when she was sixteen and about to go to the pictures with Ben. It was the first time she'd realised she was beautiful, because she looked so much like Mam. She hadn't changed much since then. Apart from looking thirty years older, she thought wryly. She wore her brown hair in much the same style, loose and bouncy on her shoulders. There were a few strands of grey, hardly noticeable. She still took the same size clothes, but it was undoubtedly a middle-aged woman who stared back at her from the mirror across the room, despite the fact she was too far away to see the wrinkles under her eyes.

'You know, I still fancy you something rotten,' said a voice, and Francie O'Leary came in. He wore tight jeans, a navy V-necked sweater, no shirt. A thick gold chain nestled in the dark hairs on his chest and there was a gold hoop in his left ear. His hair was combed in a fringe on his forehead to disguise his slightly receding hairline, making him look a touch evil, Josie thought, a bit like Old Nick, but dead dishy all the same.

'You're not supposed to say things like that, Francie,' she said reprovingly.

'Can't help it, Jose.' He sat down beside her. 'I still miss the bed bit.'

'Francie!'

He winked. 'Don't you?'

'I wouldn't say if I did.' But she did, she did! If the door could have been locked without anyone noticing, if she had been capable of temporarily throwing her conscience to the wind, she would have welcomed half an hour of the bed bit with Francie.

'Lily's not exactly appealing these days,' he said glumly. 'I keep falling off her belly.'

'Francie! What a horrible thing to say.'

'I'm a horrible person. I've never pretended to be anything else. Lily knew that when she proposed.' He sighed. 'I love the lads. In fact, I'm mad about the lads. But life's a bit tedious nowadays, Jose. All we talk about is carpets and wallpaper and kids' shoes. Did you know that little boys wear their shoes out at a rate of knots? Lily's on about it all the time. I say, "Chuck 'em away, kiddo. Buy more. Money's no object," but she goes on about it all the same. Apparently – and this will fascinate you, Jose – since cobblers became shoe repairers, they charge the earth.' He put his hand on the bed over hers, and said wistfully, 'You used to make me feel young.'

She snatched her hand away. 'You made *me* feel young,

Francie, only because we had nothing that really mattered to talk about. You and Lily have shared responsibilities. Shoes matter.'

'I'm not old enough for responsibility, Jose. I'm only forty-eight.'

'What are you two up to?' a sharp voice demanded.

Francie groaned and got to his feet when his wife came in. 'Nothing, Lil,' he said in a pained voice. 'I was checking to see if Simon and Alec were asleep, and found Josie sitting on the bed all by herself. We were talking, that's all.'

'Well, you can talk downstairs.'

Josie was shocked to see the naked suspicion in Lily's eyes. Did she actually think there might be something going on? If so, it would serve her right, pay her back for the awful thing she'd said earlier, which Josie had found deeply wounding. It was a long time since she and Lily had had a row, but New Year's Eve wasn't exactly a good time to start one. She said coldly, 'I think I'll go home. Dinah might be there, and I'd like to see in the New Year with me family.'

She waved frantically at Dinah's Mini as it turned the corner of Huskisson Street on its way to London. Dinah gave one last wave and the car disappeared. Josie returned to the house, ready to sink into a decline, to be met by a grim-faced Esther emerging from Reception.

'I've just had William Friars on the phone. He refused to wait and speak to you. He's transferring to another publisher, Havers Hill. He said would you kindly send them *Death by Stealth*. He only has a carbon copy.'

'Does that mean they haven't read it?'

'I assume not. Actually . . .' Esther grinned '. . . he didn't say "kindly", he said "tell her" to send the original.'

'I shall do no such thing,' Josie said indignantly. 'Send it back to Friars, Esther. Tell him to send his lousy book to his new publisher himself.' She chuckled. 'They'll do their nut when they read it. It's not a patch on the others. Oh, it'll sell well – he's acquired a loyal following, who will be sadly disappointed. I bet it gets a mauling from the critics.'

Esther returned to Reception when the phone began to ring. 'It's for you, Josie.' She looked impressed. 'New York.'

'I'll take it in my office.' Her heart missed a beat. New York! She picked up the receiver. 'Josie Coltrane.'

'Hi, Josie,' said a friendly American voice. 'Val Morrissey, Brewster & Cronin, publishers. Read one of your books last week on the plane back from good old Blighty, *Miss Middleton's Papers*, a really creepy tale of good and evil in Victorian England. I wondered if we could do a deal?'

She had actually thought it might be Jack. 'What sort of deal, Mr Morrissey?'

'Call me Val. Brewster & Cronin are a bit like Barefoot House – small output, nothing but crime fiction. I wondered, if we took some of yours, would you take some of ours? I've checked – none of your books are published in the States. The same goes for us the other way round. We don't seem to be able to break into the UK market.'

'We've tried to sell in the States, but no luck,' Josie confessed. 'Except for *My Carnal Life*.'

'Those big companies, they've got no imagination,' Val Morrissey said disgustedly. 'It's us little ones who are the innovators.'

Josie agreed wholeheartedly. 'I love American thrillers. Ed McBain is my favourite.'

'Mine's the little lady who wrote *Miss Middleton's Papers*, Julia Hedington. Great book, Josie! We'd like to take it. Can't offer much initially, I'm afraid – five hundred dollars. We'll only be dipping our toe in the water with a couple of thousand copies to begin with, see how the market takes it. If that's agreeable, I'll have a contract in the post by tomorrow.'

'I'll have to ring Julia first.'

Julia Hedington screamed with joy when told an offer had been made for the American rights of her first novel. She was a widow with five school-aged children, who had been writing the book for years, scribbling away in a notebook whenever she had a rare, spare minute.

'It's only five hundred dollars, Julia,' Josie said, alarmed when the screaming became hysterical. 'And Barefoot House takes ten per cent of that.'

'I don't care if it's only five dollars. I don't care if you take a hundred per cent. My book's going to be published in *America*. Oh, Josie, I can hardly believe my luck.'

She called Val Morrissey back. 'The author's delirious. So, if you'd let me have that contract?'

'It'll be on its way tomorrow.' They rang off, promising to send each other a selection of books.

Josie went into the next office, where Richard White was typing away on the latest model electric typewriter which had cost a bomb. Dinah's desk was piled high with manuscripts that had arrived that morning – Barefoot House received about fifty a week and, on average, accepted one every two weeks.

'I've just done a deal with an American publishing company,' she said.

'Goodo.' Richard didn't look up. A calm, bespectacled young man, hard-working and conscientious, she'd rather hoped he and Dinah would hit it off.

'We need more staff.'

'I know. We definitely need someone in place of Dinah.'

'I should have advertised.' She'd kept putting it off. 'Do you know anyone?'

Richard shook his head and continued typing. How on earth could he concentrate on two things at the same time? She concluded he must have two brains.

She sighed. 'I hate interviewing staff.'

'I would, too.'

'I might pick the wrong person.'

'It happens sometimes.'

'Then I'd have to sack them, and I'd hate that more.'

'So would I.'

'I'll put an advert in the *Echo* tonight.'

'That mightn't be a bad idea.'

She made a face at his back. Bloody workaholic.

She missed Dinah, but didn't have time to mope. The contract came from Brewster & Cronin, and she sent it to Terence Dunnet to appraise. She hired a replacement for Dinah. Cathy Connors had moved to Liverpool eighteen months ago when her husband's firm had relocated to Cheshire and she had been forced to resign her job as editor with a publisher in London.

'I'm working for a bank at the moment, producing their house magazine, but quite frankly I find it mind-bogglingly boring. Give me fiction any day. I never thought I'd find a position up North with a genuine publisher.'

'Well, you've found one now,' Josie said contentedly. Cathy would take some of the load off her own shoulders, giving her more time to travel round the country, meeting her writers, taking them to lunch, trying to make them feel as if they were part of a family, not just anonymous assets of a large, impersonal company.

April arrived, and Josie realised that Lily was avoiding her. She was cold and unforthcoming when Josie phoned, and hadn't been to see her once since the New Year's Eve party. Lily was too thick-skinned to have taken offence because she'd left early. It must be something else. She recalled the suspicion in her eyes when she'd come into the bedroom and found her talking to Francie. It wasn't that, surely!

Francie's workforce had grown larger, mainly due to regular orders from Barefoot House. She needed to speak to him, warn him that two of their books would be reissued shortly so that he would be prepared. It could have been done by phone, but she decided to go in person for a change.

It was impossible to carry on a conversation in a glass office with no roof while the presses thundered away. Francie took her outside, into the soft mist of a spring morning, and they sat on a wall and talked.

'It's not exactly an ideal place to consult with me best customer, but I'm afraid it'll just have to do.' He looked a bit down in the mouth, unusual for Francie, who rarely let anything bother him.

She told him about the reissues, and he promised to drop everything as soon as he heard from her. He knew how important it was that orders were met with minimum delay.

'What's the matter?' she asked, when he got to his feet and began to walk up and down, hands in pockets, kicking at stones.

'Your friend's the matter, Lily Kavanagh.'

'I thought she was known as Mrs Francis O'Leary these days?'

'Yeah, and it's Mr O'Leary's bad luck that she is. Honestly, Jose . . .' he sat down again '. . . I wouldn't dream of saying this to another soul, but we've always been completely open with each other. She's a pain in the bloody arse. If you must know, she thinks you and me are having an affair. I wish to God we were. It would be worth the endless nagging.' He leered at her weakly.

'Just because she found us talking in the bedroom?'

'She said there was an "air of intimacy" about us. I said why the hell not? I've known the bloody woman for over thirty years, she's me friend. Lily said she'd prefer it if I weren't, and I told her to get lost. I'm not giving up me friends because she's got a dirty mind.'

'You said some very intimate things that night, Francie.'

'I wish I'd done them, not just said them.'

Lily was her own worst enemy. Josie didn't know what to say.

'I wouldn't mind if I'd done anything wrong,' Francie continued irritably. 'You know, Josie, I swore to meself I'd never get married because I wanted to avoid this type of thing. I'm a laid-back sort of guy, I like to get on with people. I never cause trouble. If people like me ruled the world, there'd never be another war. If it weren't for the lads, I'd do a runner. I can't take much more.'

It was *that* bad! She'd speak to Lily, if she'd let her. Try to talk some sense into her bad-tempered friend.

She kept putting it off. Lily would be taking Simon to school, collecting Alec from playgroup, making dinner, making tea, just sitting down to the television, on the point of going to bed.

In the end it was Lily who rang her, early one morning when Josie was about to go down to her office. 'I've got a lump, Jose,' she whispered fearfully.

'Oh, no, Lil! Where?' Josie cried.

'In me breast.' She began to cry. 'Will you make sure Francie looks after the boys properly when I'm gone? I don't want to ask our Samantha. She's only young, and she's expecting again. Not that I'll see it,' she wept. 'I'll go in that hospice near Ormskirk. I'll not let me family watch me suffer. I'm going to be dead brave, Jose. And don't send flowers to the funeral. I'd sooner the money went to cancer research.'

'Is it much of a lump, luv?'

'Well, actually, I can't find it,' Lily sniffed, 'though I've felt all over. But I had a mammogram last week, and they've written and said to come back this avvy for another. They've found something on the X-ray. Oh, Jose. I don't want to die.'

'You bloody idiot!' Josie gasped with relief. 'That might mean nothing at all, just that the X-ray hasn't come out properly or there's some quite innocent shadows. Even if there is a lump, the chances are it's benign. It's a bit early to be planning your funeral, Lil.' The same thing had happened to Esther only last year. Mind you, Esther had been worried sick when she'd got the letter asking her to go back. She said, more kindly, 'I'm not surprised you're upset, but try not to worry. Would you like me to come with you to the clinic?' She had arranged to drive to Rhyl to take a new author to lunch, but it would have to be changed. Lily came first.

'*Please*, Jose. I don't like worrying Francie.'

Another X-ray and a thorough physical examination revealed Lily's breasts to be completely lumpless. They went to town to celebrate, and got slightly tipsy over a pub lunch. Then they linked arms and went shopping.

'This is just like old times,' Lily said. 'But Liverpool's so different from how it used to be. There's no Owen Owen's any more, where Francie threw me on a bed and sort of proposed. It's Tesco's instead.'

'There's no Blackler's either, or Reece's, where we used to go dancing.'

'The Rialto burnt down,' Lily reminded her.

'Most of the cinemas have closed. And we're two middle-aged women with grown-up children and greying hair.' Josie laughed. 'Everything changes, Lil. Us and Liverpool included. Come on, let's have coffee in St John's Market. That's not half changed, too, since I used to go there with me mam.'

'I'm sorry I haven't been in touch for a while,' Lily said when they were on their second coffee. 'I've been rather busy, what with the boys. I thought . . . Oh, it doesn't matter. I haven't exactly been meself lately.' She crumbled the remains of her scone. 'I think Francie's a bit fed up with me.'

'That's not like Francie,' Josie said carefully. 'He's not the type who easily gets fed up.'

'How would you know?' Lily was immediately suspicious.

'For goodness' sake, Lil. We've both known him since we were sixteen. He doesn't like people making waves. Remember when he walked out of that pub in Smithdown Road?'

Lily pursed her lips. 'There was no reason for that.'

'Yes, there was. You were moaning your head off over just about everything in sight. He couldn't stand it so he left.'

'I'd die if he left again.'

'Then don't make waves,' Josie said simply.

'Who said I was?'

'You, in effect, when you claimed he was fed up. He wouldn't get fed up without a reason.'

'As I said, I haven't been meself.' Lily scowled. 'He drives me mad when he walks away and all I want to do is talk.'

'You mean nag?'

Lily suddenly grinned. 'Probably. Anyroad, I'm going to be

334

as nice as pie to everyone now that I'm not going to die. I was ever so scared, Jose, when that letter came. I'm glad I've got you.' She squeezed Josie's hand. 'Thanks for coming with me.'

'Think nothing of it. Now, let's go try on those frocks we saw in that boutique in Bold Street. You'd really suit the red one. And I'll treat you to a shampoo and set. I could do with a trim meself. Oh, and another thing, this new woman who works for me, Cathy, goes to a gym in the lunch hour. I thought I'd do the same in the evenings. I'm getting a paunch.' She patted her stomach which was as flat as a pancake. 'Why don't you come with me, Lil?'

'I must admit me figure's not what it used to be.'

'Then it's a date. We'll go together, twice a week.'

Dinah was homesick in London, but now she had a flat of her own and was determined to stick it out, become an international executive and travel the world.

'Well, your room's always here for you, luv,' Josie assured her whenever she rang.

'I know, Mum. It's that thought that keeps me going, knowing I've got a real home in Liverpool if things go wrong. Is Barefoot House busy?'

'Incredibly busy.'

Brewster & Cronin had bought the US rights to five books, and she had bought British rights to six of theirs. It meant Barefoot House would soon be producing a book a week. Josie was sometimes in her office until midnight, writing letters, reading manuscripts, making phone calls to New York where the time was five hours behind.

One of her books reached number five in the bestsellers chart, and stayed there for almost two months, an achievement only surpassed by William Friars, whose transfer to Havers Hill she'd read about in *Publishing News*, though there was no mention of when his new novel would be coming out.

My Carnal Life was reprinted for the eighth time. Val Morrissey reported that *Miss Middleton's Papers* was being

335

seriously considered by a Hollywood company, Close-up Productions, for a film. Josie rang Julia Hedington when she knew her children would be home, in case she fainted at the news.

One hot, clammy morning in July, Cathy Connors came into Josie's office holding a manuscript. Josie recognised the look on her face straight away. She'd read something that wasn't merely a run-of-the-mill enjoyable thriller, suitable for publication but unlikely to set pulses racing throughout the land. She'd read a 'breaking new ground' book, as Josie called them, different, exciting, innovative.

'This is marvellous,' she said in a rush. 'I read it last night – all night, in fact. My husband thought I'd fallen asleep downstairs when he woke up at four o'clock and I wasn't in bed. The thing is, Josie, the author's only twenty-one. He lives in Northern Ireland.'

Josie looked at the cover. *My Favourite Murderer*, by Lesley O'Rourke. 'It's a woman,' she said. 'The man's name is spelled differently.'

'Of course! I'm so tired, I can hardly think.'

'I know the feeling. Go home, why don't you? Have some sleep. I don't expect my employees to work all night. I'll read this later. I'd start now, but I'd never get a minute's peace.'

Cathy said she'd slip off at midday. 'You'll enjoy that, Josie.' They smiled at each other. 'I almost envy you, having it to read for the first time.'

'There can't possibly be a better recommendation than that!'

Everyone felt lethargic with the heat, despite the open windows and electric fans. The front door was propped open. Even Richard's typing wasn't at its usual fast pace. The telephone hardly rang; perhaps all over the country people felt the same. Cathy went home, Richard and Bobby went to lunch. Eric was still to arrive. There was only Esther in Reception when Josie went upstairs to take a shower and change her soggy clothes. It was one of the advantages of living over the office.

She emerged from the shower, feeling only slightly fresher and longing for a little nap. The heat was debilitating. Half an hour wouldn't hurt, on the bed in Dinah's room, which was at the back of the house, much quieter. She put on the alarm in case she slept all afternoon.

The high-pitched beep sounded thirty minutes later. Oh, Lord! She felt worse, not just tired but groggy. Her head seemed to be stuck to the pillow, she could hardly lift it. And she'd had a terrible dream, a nightmare, in which Francie had slain Lily with an axe, and Laura had been watching, laughing. Then the dream changed. Mam appeared, crying bitterly, and Josie began to cry with her. 'Stop that!' Aunt Ivy screamed, pinching her wrist. The dream changed again. She was with Jack in the snow-covered garage in Bingham Mews. 'I love you,' Jack whispered. 'I don't want you to go.' But Josie had flown away, soaring up into the night sky until the world below disappeared, and she was alone in the stark, black wilderness, knowing she was destined to stay for ever, that she would never see another human being again.

She rolled off the bed, put on a towelling robe, went downstairs and made tea. Her cheeks were wet with tears. She dried them with her sleeves, blinking because the room looked so weird. The units, the taps, the kettle – all seemed to have two outlines, the real one and another, slightly fainter, behind. She couldn't wait to go down to the office – talk to Esther, ring Lily, do some work – so everything would seem back to normal.

'Is anyone there?'

The voice, a man's, came from downstairs. Josie went on to the landing and peered over the white bannisters. A blurred figure, framed by a halo of dazzling sunlight, was standing in the doorway, clutching a travelling bag. Not many people came to the office without an appointment. It was probably a salesmen, offering stationery at a discount, or office machinery. Esther would see to him. At any other time Josie would have done it herself, but she was wearing a bathrobe. It would

337

give a most unbusinesslike impression, even if only to a salesman.

Esther must have gone to sleep. The man's eyes, probably blinded by the sun, hadn't yet adjusted to the change in light, and he hadn't notice the door marked 'Reception'.

'There'll be someone with you in a minute,' Josie called.

The man stepped inside and shaded his eyes with his hand. He looked up, saw Josie, smiled. 'Hi, sweetheart,' he said.

It was Jack Coltrane.

2

Over the years, Josie had sometimes imagined how she would greet her ex-husband should they meet. Coolly, she had decided, even though the longing to see Jack again was never far away. But she had her pride. He'd made no attempt to contact her. 'Why, hello, Jack,' she would say with a warm, slightly distant smile.

Never had she thought she would burst into tears, race downstairs, throw herself in his arms and hungrily kiss him, as if it were only yesterday they had parted.

'Jack, Jack, Jack.' She kept saying his name over and over between kisses. 'I've just been dreaming about you. Oh!' she wept, 'I felt so sad. I flew away, and you wanted me to stay.'

It really was only like yesterday when he held her face in both hands, kissed the tears, then her trembling lips. He touched her hair, pressed his cheek against her burning forehead. She felt his body shudder. 'I'm sorry,' she said, drawing away, embarrassed. 'I'm feeling a bit . . . weird! You must think I'm mad, throwing myself at you like this. It's been twenty years . . .'

'Hey.' He pulled her back in to his arms. 'I like you weird. I expected to be shown the door. This is a welcome surprise.'

Esther opened the door of Reception, blinked and quickly closed it. Richard and Bobby's voices could be heard outside, returning from lunch.

'Let's go upstairs.' Lord knew what they'd think if they found their employer in her bathrobe with a strange man. She pulled Jack towards the stairs.

Had he come another day, had she not just had the awful dream, felt so distinctly weird, no doubt she would have greeted Jack with the warm but distant smile. Instead, when they reached the landing, out of sight from down below, they kissed again.

'Let me look at you,' Jack said huskily, and undid the knot on her robe. It fell in folds around her feet. His eyes travelled slowly over her body, and she felt every single nerve quiver, turn to liquid, and was filled with desire. 'You're as lovely as ever. I've missed you, sweetheart. You'll never know how much.'

'I do, Jack. I've missed you.' She looked at him properly for the first time. He looked tired, she thought. His face was thin and drawn, and there were tiny crinkles beneath the warm brown eyes, perhaps slightly duller than they used to be. Deep, craggy lines ran from nose to jaw. But his hair was as black and thick as it had always been, and lay in the same careless quiff on his forehead. His skin was brown, from the Californian sun, she assumed. The off-white linen suit he wore over a plain white T-shirt was crumpled, but worn with such casual panache it looked smart. Some men were lucky, she thought enviously. Age served them well. Jack was fifty-one, but as charismatic and attractive as he'd always been, possibly more so.

He reached out and began to caress her breasts, brought her closer, stroked her waist, her buttocks, slid his hand between her legs. Oh, this is mad, she thought wildly. This is quite mad. It's been twenty years . . .

'Come.' She drew him up another flight of stairs, to the bedroom, where she lay on the bed, inviting him. He kissed every part of her body, made her come with his tongue, with his hand.

'Jack!' she said urgently. She badly wanted him inside her.

He laughed joyfully and began to remove his clothes. 'I

can't believe this is happening,' he said incredulously, and the familiarity of his smile, his closeness, the way his hair flopped down in front of his eyes, made Josie gasp. He bent over her, and she stroked the brown skin of his arms, his chest, noting somewhere at the back of her mind that he'd lost a lot of weight, too much.

When he entered her, it was as if a miracle had occurred. This was something she had thought would never happen again. But it had, and it was almost too much to bear. She giddily wondered if it was just another dream, like the one she'd had before, and any minute she would wake up and he wouldn't be there.

But then it was over. She was lying in Jack's arms, and it wasn't a dream. It was real.

'What I'd like now,' he said comfortably, 'is one of your famous cups of tea. I'm still in throes of jet lag.' He gently kissed her lips. 'You're a very demanding woman, Mrs Coltrane.'

'I'll get dressed.'

He watched her find clean pants and bra, and slip into a thin white cotton frock and sandals, then began to put on his own clothes. Two floors down a phone rang, and she realised she had forgotten all about Barefoot House, which could manage perfectly well without her.

'The kitchen's on the floor below.' In Maude's room! She went down, put the kettle on and was waiting for it to boil when she heard his footsteps on the stairs and smiled at him through the open door.

He smiled back, but she wondered why he was walking so stiffly. Why did he have to concentrate so hard, hold so tightly to the bannister, as if he was worried he'd fall? At first she thought it was the jet lag, but a chill ran through her bones when she realised he was drunk. He'd been drunk when he'd arrived, and he was drunk now. Not mildly, not even moderately, but completely, totally inebriated. And he was so used to it, it was so much a part of him that he'd learnt to cope, to converse, to pretend, when he'd probably been drunk for days, for months or it might even be for years.

'What made you come?' she asked over the tea. His hand, holding the cup, was shaking slightly. They were in the lounge, sitting together on the pink and cream settee.

'Two things. Remember Bud Wagner? He was always round at the apartment.'

She shook her head. 'No.' She remembered hardly anyone from those days.

'Well, he remembers you. He runs a literary agency in New York. We've kept in touch, and he sent an article from the trade press about a company – I don't recall the name – buying the US rights to books published in Britain by a firm called Barefoot House. That rang a bell. You'd told me that's where you lived with Louisa Chalcott. When I read that the firm belonged to Josephine Coltrane, I knew it could only be you.'

'What was the other thing?'

His lips twisted ruefully. 'Dinah.'

She remembered, too late, one of the reasons for the cool reception she had planned, the warm, distant smile. He had ignored the letter telling him about Dinah. 'You took your time, Jack.' She tried not to spoil things by sounding cold. 'I wrote to you about Dinah on her fifth birthday. She's twenty in September.'

'I only got it last week, sweetheart. I showed Jessie Mae the article, told her who you were and she gave me the letter. It's Mae with an "e", by the way, she's particular about that.'

She'd actually forgotten he had a wife! If only he'd arrived yesterday, or tomorrow, when she was fully dressed, with a clear head, when she hadn't felt so damn *weird*.

'Coral used to open mail that came from the lawyers about the divorce,' Jack was saying. 'We were living together by then.'

'Who's Coral?'

'My wife. She died two years after we were married. Leukaemia.'

341

'I'm sorry.' It was horrible to hear him say, 'my wife', when it wasn't *her* he was referring to. 'Then who's Jessie Mae?'

'She's my daughter, stepdaughter. She's nineteen, same as Dinah. I have a stepson too, Tyler. He's twenty-one.'

'Really!' Josie muttered. How fortunate for Tyler and Jessie Mae to have had the benefit of a father all these years, she thought cynically, when his real daughter had been deprived.

She seemed to have lost the thread of the conversation. 'You mean Coral, your wife, opened my letter, but didn't show it to you?'

'Yes,' he said simply.

'But it was marked "Strictly Confidential".' She could actually remember writing the words on the envelope.

'All the more reason for her to open it. She would have guessed it was from you, and was worried it might say something that would stop us getting married. She gave it to Jessie Mae, said to let me have it when she thought the time was right.' He put the cup and saucer on the floor, which seemed to require much frowning concentration, then took Josie's hands in his. 'Coral was dying, sweetheart, she wanted a father for her kids. We met on the set of this movie we were making. She was the continuity girl, divorced. Her ex was a bastard, she was terrified he'd get his hands on Jessie Mae and Tyler when she died. We weren't in love, but I was prepared to take on the kids.' His mouth twisted wryly. 'You can guess why.'

She guessed straight away. 'Because of Laura?'

He nodded. 'I wanted to give something back for what I'd taken away.'

It had been a supremely kind, very noble thing to do, but Josie felt herself withdrawing slightly from him. She felt resentment for the woman who had kept her letter, and even more for Jack for understanding why. She'd been the victim of an underhand trick, conned out of the husband she loved. Then she remembered that five years had passed before he had met Coral, five years during which he hadn't thought to get in touch, see how she was. She was about to ask why, tell him she'd tried to contact him in Bingham Mews and he'd already left. But what was the point of raking over the past? She'd told him she never wanted to see him again, and he'd taken her at her word.

'Where is Dinah?' he asked.

'She works in London. I'll ring soon, tell her you're here.'

He gave a nervous grin. 'How is she likely to take it? It's a bit of a bombshell.'

'I don't know,' Josie said truthfully. 'I've never been able to guess how Dinah will react. She's a law unto herself.' She picked up the cups. 'I'll get more tea.'

In the kitchen, she leaned on the sink and took several deep breaths. It was hotter than ever, and the afternoon air felt sticky and humid. Her head was whirling. She almost wished that Jack hadn't come, that she was downstairs in her office dealing with the mundane affairs of Barefoot House.

'I'm getting too old for this sort of trauma,' she muttered.

But then she took in the tea, and there was Jack Coltrane sitting on her settee, and she felt a wave of love that took her breath away. He looked up. 'Have you been happy, sweetheart?'

She paused before answering. 'I haven't been *un*happy, not for most of the time,' she said seriously. 'How about you?'

He shrugged tiredly. 'It's been difficult. Tyler's always been a sweet, laid-back kid, but Jessie Mae was badly damaged by the divorce and Coral's death. She had problems at school.' He shrugged again. 'Poor Jessie Mae, she's had problems more or less every damn where.'

It hardly seemed fair that Jessie Mae's problems should be *his*. 'You said you were working on a film?'

'I'm a script editor. It's reasonably well paid. We've got a neat little house in Venice with a pool. You must come and stay some time, Josie.'

She almost dropped the tea. 'That would be nice.' She put both cups on the coffee-table and went over to the window, where she clutched the curtains to steady herself. What on earth had possessed her to assume he had come back for good?

How long did he plan to stay, she wondered, a few days, a week, a month?

'Where's the bathroom, sweetheart?' He stood, holding himself determinedly erect. 'I need to freshen up.'

'On the floor above, at the back.'

He glanced around the room. 'I had a bag when I came.'

'I'll go and look.' She found the leather holdall at the top of the stairs. Bottles clinked when she picked it up. Aftershave, perhaps? Mouthwash?

Josie returned to the sanctuary of the curtains, and watched a sharp black shadow creep across the street. Soon the house would be in the shade. She wished, more than she had wished anything in her life before that she had never met Jack Coltrane. I ruined his life, she thought bleakly, and he ruined mine. I thought we were meant for each other, but we weren't. And now I'm lost, because I still love him. I'll love him till the day I die.

He returned to the room, having combed his hair and changed the T-shirt for a black one, looking reinvigorated.

'What happened to your plays?' she asked.

'The last time I saw them, they were on the floor of the study in Bingham Mews where you'd thrown them.' His eyes twinkled at her. 'Then you kicked them.' He held out his arms. 'Sweetheart, come here.'

She ran across the room and buried her face in his shoulder. 'Have you written any more?'

'No.' He gave an exaggerated sigh. 'Been too busy, too uninspired, had too many burdens, needed to earn a crust.'

'It's not too late to start again.' She gave him a little shake.

'I might, one day.'

Later, she went down to her office so she could phone Dinah in private. 'Are you sitting down? More importantly, are you alone?'

'I'm sitting down, entirely alone. Evelyn went home early. The heat and the menopause were getting her down, and it didn't help when I handed in me notice this morning. That job came up, the one I told you about with the much bigger agency. I was going to ring you later. Anyroad, what's up?'

Josie told her that her father was there, and about the complications with the letter she had sent all those years ago, finishing with, 'He's dying to see you.'

There was a long pause, then Dinah said, 'I feel as if I should come rushing home, but I don't want to.'

'Then don't.'

Another pause. 'This Coral sounds a selfish bitch, if you ask me,' she cried passionately. 'I don't care if she *is* dead. And Jessie Mae, stupid name, seems just as bad. It's not *fair*, Mum.' Dinah was close to tears. 'He would have come to see me if it weren't for them.' The voice became plaintive. 'He would have, wouldn't he, Mum?'

'Like a shot, luv.'

'I might come, I dunno. How long will he be there?'

'I haven't got round to asking yet.'

That night they went to dinner, and she showed him the house where she had been born and had lived with Mam. 'In the attic. I never told you before, but she was – what do you say in the States? – a hooker.'

He placed an arm around her shoulders and squeezed hard. 'You've come a long way, sweetheart.'

'Only four doors,' she said drily.

They strolled into town, and ate in a little dark pub in North John Street. 'You know,' Jack said when they had finished, 'I never dreamed it would be so *easy*, us being together, talking naturally, like old times. I thought I'd be straining to think of things to say, then saying the wrong thing, and there'd be all sorts of awkward silences. I always got on with you better than anyone. We were best friends as well as lovers.'

He was looking back through rose-coloured glasses. They hadn't got on all that well in Bingham Mews, where he'd been frustrated by success he hadn't wanted. She realised, sadly, that something in him had died. This was the old, easygoing Jack, the charming, twinkling Jack she'd married in New York, but now resigned to the fact he would never be a successful playwright. The need to survive – earn a crust, as he'd put it – had killed any ambition he used to have. It was the way of the world, no doubt full of middle-aged men and women who'd long ago given up their dreams of becoming famous at something or other.

'I think another bottle of vino is called for.' He went over to the bar. It was the fourth bottle he'd ordered. Josie had had two glasses and was toying with her third. His brain seemed surprisingly unaffected by the amount he'd drunk. He was lucid, witty, clear-headed. There was merely that slight stiffness in the way he walked. She decided to say nothing. Criticising his drinking, mild in comparison to now, had caused tension when they'd lived in Bingham Mews.

It was almost dark when they came out of the pub, and they wandered, arm in arm, down to the Pier Head, then caught the bus back to Huskisson Street.

She showed him round the offices downstairs. 'We have only six staff, and one of them's part time, though I'll have to take on some new people soon. Production's increased, everybody's working their socks off at the moment.'

'You've done incredibly well.' He eyed the rows of Barefoot House books in their bright red covers. 'Strange,' he said in an odd voice. 'It was me who wanted to be someone, not you. You once said all you wanted was a family. Now look at us! I'm a third-rate script editor on third-rate movies, and you're a successful businesswoman.'

'Perhaps this . . .' Josie waved a hand at the books '. . . is instead of a family. Anyroad, I've got Dinah. *She's* me family, even if she's the only one.'

'That's nice to know,' a voice said brightly, and Josie turned, startled. Dinah came sauntering into the room. 'I decided to shut up shop and come home.' She stared at them defiantly. She must have got changed since she arrived, as Josie recognised the yellow cotton frock as one she'd left behind when she went to London. Her long legs were bare, and she

346

wore Indian sandals, the sort that fitted between the toes, which Josie had never been able to wear because they were so uncomfortable. The long fair hair was slightly damp, brushed away from her slightly flushed face. She looked exquisitely fresh and lovely.

'Hello, luv! What a nice surprise.' Josie kissed her daughter's cheek. She stayed, holding her hand, concerned that the defiant look was because she and Jack gave the impression of being a couple, and Dinah felt excluded. 'This is your dad.'

Jack didn't move. Oh, but the look on him! Josie could have wept as myriad emotions chased across his handsome, mobile face: astonishment, followed by admiration for the beautiful young woman who was his daughter; anger for some reason Josie couldn't define, perhaps because he'd never been told of her existence until now; sadness, possibly for the same reason; then the soft, gentle, fond look that people gave, usually women, when they set eyes a small baby. 'Hi, Dinah,' was all he said.

'Hello,' Dinah replied. 'The kettle's on, Mum. It'll have boiled by now. Shall I make tea?'

'Please, luv.'

'Like mother, like daughter, the same passion for tea,' Jack commented as Dinah ran lightly upstairs. Then he turned away, his back to her. It was a while before he spoke, and when he did his voice was thick. 'Christ, Josie! When I think of what I've missed. What we've *both* missed. We could have been together all this time, raised Dinah between us. We could have had more children, the family you've always wanted.'

'Don't think like that, Jack,' she said softly. 'It's too late.' Or was it? It was too late for children, but not for them to be together. She had plenty of money. She could turn the attic into a study, he could write full time. Twenty years ago she had made the mistake of sending him away. Now she would ask him to come back. 'Jack,' she said hesitantly.

347

'Yes, sweetheart?' He faced her, and her heart ached when she saw the tears in his eyes.

'Why don't we get married again?'

He smiled his dear, sweet smile. 'We can't, sweetheart. There's all sorts of reasons why we can't.'

'I can't think of a single one.'

'There's Jessie Mae,' he said. 'I can't leave Jessie Mae. She'd go to pieces without me.'

'Bring her to Liverpool. She can live with you, with us, here.'

He slid his arms around her waist and shook his head. 'That wouldn't work, sweetheart. She's Hollywood born and bred, and she would never accept another woman in my life. She'd be impossible to live with.'

They stood in each other's arms, their chins resting on one another's shoulders. It felt so comfortable, Josie thought, so natural. This is where God intended me to be! She remembered thinking the same thing the night they'd met.

'You've given this girl twenty years of your life, Jack,' she said reasonably. 'Isn't it time you had a life yourself?'

'I promised her mother on her deathbed that I'd always care for Jessie Mae. I can't go back on that.'

Not even for me? she almost said, but it would have sounded childish, and she knew that Jack Coltrane would never go back on his word to a dying woman. 'I suppose I'll have to wait until Jessie Mae finds a husband. Will you marry me then?'

She leaned back so that they were face to face, and was cut to the quick when he suddenly pushed her away with a curt, 'No!'

'Why not?' she asked, startled.

'Christ, Josie!' His face was dark with anger. 'Are you always so persistent? Hasn't it entered your head that I might not want to get married again?'

'But you said earlier . . .'

'I was lamenting the years we'd lost, that's all. I've had it with relationships, up to here.' He held a hand to his chin. 'When Jessie Mae gets married I want to live alone, in peace.'

It was too much. It had been such a peculiar day, what with the strange dreams earlier, the heat, Jack coming, being so strangely drunk, having to tell Dinah her father was there, then Dinah herself coming all the way from London and behaving so coolly, upstairs now, making tea. There'd been a brief vision of happiness, imagining living with Jack again, and now the brutal rejection, which wasn't a bit like the Jack she used to know.

Josie burst into tears, wild, racking tears that tore at her body and made her chest want to burst.

'Sweetheart!' Jack threw himself in the chair behind the desk and dragged her on to his knee. 'Oh, my darling girl. I love you so much. I didn't remember how much until earlier when you came running downstairs. You're *part* of me. I love you with all my heart and soul. There is nothing on earth I want more than for us to be married, to spend the rest of our lives in each other's arms. But it's not to be, my love.'

'Why not?' she sobbed. 'I love you just the same. I always have, Jack. I want what you want. I understand if we can't have it right this minute, but surely we can have it in the future?'

His arms tightened around her so that she could hardly breathe. 'I'm no longer the guy you first met,' he said savagely. 'I haven't been in a long time. I'm a physical and emotional wreck. I get depressed. I have terrible black moods. I'm on pills for my nerves.'

'I don't care, I love you. Anyroad, you wouldn't need pills if you were with me. I'd make you better.'

'Josie, I ruined your life once, I don't want to ruin it a second time.' He gestured around the office. 'You've got a great business, a lovely daughter, a nice life. The last thing you want is me fucking everything up for a second time.'

Josie began to cry again. 'This afternoon was wonderful. Oh, Jack, half of our lives are already over. Why can't we spend what's left with each other?' With all his faults, she would sooner have Jack Coltrane than any other man on earth.

He stayed for six days, Dinah left after two, by which time they were getting on reasonably well. They talked mainly about films, which seemed to be a cover for things the more wary Dinah would prefer to avoid for now. She left for London on Wednesday morning, having kissed her mother and shaken Jack's hand. 'I hope we'll meet again one day,' she said politely.

'Well,' Jack said with a grin after she'd gone, 'I suppose a kiss and a "Dad" was too much to expect after only two days.'

'A kiss might be on the cards, but I'm afraid "Dad" is most unlikely. She talked to me about it yesterday. "Jack" is the most you can look forward to.'

'That's better than nothing, which is all I've had so far. Oh, I'm not complaining,' he said hastily, when Josie opened her mouth to say he was expecting too much too soon. 'I feel privileged that such a stunning, autocratic and supremely confident young woman was so nice to me.'

'She's not quite as confident as she appears.' Josie didn't want him getting the wrong impression of their daughter. 'She was a very withdrawn little girl. It was my fault. I didn't want her, Jack. She came too soon after Laura. I think she sensed she wasn't welcome, even though she was only a tiny baby.'

'Ah, Laura!' Jack said the name reverently. They had hardly mentioned their other daughter. 'She would have been twenty-five. I wonder what she would have looked like?'

'I often wonder the same thing,' Josie said softly. 'I reckon she would have been a female version of you and driven the boys wild.'

'Why did we call her Laura?' He looked puzzled. 'I've tried to remember, but I can't. It drives me crazy sometimes.'

'We saw that film together in a little cinema in New York – *Laura*, with Gene Tierney and Dana Andrews. When I was expecting, we decided on Laura for a girl, Patrick if it was a boy.'

'We had a girl, but then we lost her.' Jack's face was tight with pain. 'Since that day I've never driven a car. I'm not surprised you never wanted to see me again.'

'I wanted to see you again within a week. But you'd already gone, to California, according to Elsie Forrest. If it had been New York, I would have tried to find you.'

'Don't say things like that!' he groaned. 'I went through hell over the next few years, and it doesn't help to find I could have been with you – and Dinah.'

'By the way, should Dinah ever bring the subject up, she's named after Dinah Shore, your favourite singer.'

He looked taken aback. 'Did I say I liked Dinah Shore?'

'No, but I couldn't tell her she was called after the midwife because I couldn't be bothered to think of a name meself, could I?'

'Where are we going today?' he asked when they were outside, after she had checked that Barefoot House was working smoothly without her. Cathy reminded her of the manuscript, *My Favourite Murderer*, that she'd been given to read.

'I'll read it this weekend,' Josie promised. 'My friend, well, actually, it's my ex-husband, goes back to California on Saturday morning. I'll be looking for something to do.'

'We're going to New Brighton on the ferry,' she told Jack. The day before, they'd gone to Southport, and she'd showed him the arcade where she'd had tea with Louisa, and where Mr Bernstein's little book shop used to be, now a burger bar. They'd been to Old Swan to look for the house where he used to live, but it was no longer there. 'Tonight I thought we could go and see Lily.'

He made a hideous face. 'Are you two still friends? How's that poor guy she married? Assuming he's not already dead.'

'Neil was dispensed with ages ago. She's got a different husband, Francie, and two lovely little boys, as well as two grown-up daughters.'

The weather had remained hot and humid all week, and

351

New Brighton was packed with day-trippers. There wasn't even the suggestion of a breeze drifting across the crowded beach from the Mersey. They bought fish and chips and ate them in the paper, then an ice-cream cornet with a chocolate ripple. Josie wanted to go to the fairground, but Jack complained he felt queasy. 'I need a drink to settle my stomach.'

'I would have thought a drink would make it worse.'

He smiled. 'You don't know my stomach.'

She agreed that she had little acquaintance with his stomach. In the big, busy pub she found two seats, and her eyes searched for Jack in the hordes waiting at the bar. He was ages getting served. She'd asked for coffee, and wondered why two large glasses of spirits were placed in front of him when at last he caught the bartender's eye. To her dismay, she saw him quickly swallow one in a single gulp while waiting for the coffee. Her heart sank. He was drinking massively more than he'd done in Bingham Mews. She had investigated his bag and discovered two bottles of Jack Daniels. This morning there'd been only one. There was also a bottle of mouthwash, which he must have used to disguise the fact that every time he went to the bathroom he had a drink. Or two.

'Here we are.' He put a glass and the coffee on the table. 'You've got a cookie with yours, on the house.'

'Ta.' She grabbed his hand. 'I love you.'

'I love you, sweetheart.' He kissed the hand that was tightly holding his.

'I wish you could stay.'

'So do I, but it's not possible, I told you . . .'

'I know.' She grimaced. 'Jessie Mae.' One day, though, she would get him back. She was set on it. In the meantime, she could have cheerfully strangled bloody Jessie Mae, particularly when, after only a few minutes, Jack returned to the bar and gave a repeat performance with the two drinks.

'He looks ill,' Lily declared when the two men went to the

352

pub. Francie and Jack had taken to each other instantly, and it had been Francie's idea to go out. 'And he isn't half thin, Jose.'

'The first time you met, you told him he was fat!'

'He looked healthier fat.'

'Francie's no more than skin and bone,' Josie said tartly.

'Yes, but he's healthily thin. Jack's like death warmed up.'

Josie rolled her eyes. 'Talking about skin, why is it you always manage to get under mine?'

'Mind you . . .' Lily winked '. . . he has a *ravaged* sort of look. It's dead sexy.'

'I would prefer it if you didn't describe my ex-husband as sexy, Mrs O'Leary. It's just not done.'

'Is the ex likely to become an ex-ex soon? How do you describe a husband you marry a second time?' Lily regarded Josie with a beady eye. 'He's obviously mad about you. He can't take his eyes off you, in fact. And you're just as bad, I can tell.'

'I dunno, Lil.' Josie sighed. 'I took a leaf out of your book and proposed but, unlike Francie, he turned me down, at least for the time being.' She explained about Coral, Jessie Mae and Tyler. 'Gosh,' she sighed, 'I won't half miss him. I was jogging along quite comfortably before, enjoying me business. He's disturbed me equilibrium, Lil.'

She was determined not to make a show of herself when he left on Saturday morning. They embraced silently behind the big front door, the offices either side eerily empty.

'I'll miss my plane,' Jack said after a while.

'I don't care. I don't know how I'm going to live without you,' she said bleakly.

'You managed very well for twenty years.'

'Not really.' She sniffed, fighting to hold back the tears.

'I'll give you a call as soon as I'm home. I'll call every month. No, every week. Oh, Christ!' He looked at her despairingly. 'I'll call every single day.'

'Once a week will do fine, and I'll call you.'

They kissed passionately. 'We'll see each other at Christmas, won't we?' he said huskily. 'Try and persuade Dinah to come. I'll pack Jessie Mae off to stay with Tyler, so there'll just be us three. Our first family Christmas together.' He reached for her wrists and removed her arms from around his neck. 'Goodbye, sweetheart.'

With that, the door closed and he was gone!

Dinah telephoned a few minutes later. 'Have I timed it right? Has he gone? He called last night, just to say goodbye. He said he had to leave prompt at ten o'clock, which is why I'm ringing at ten past. I thought you'd be dead miserable.'

'I'm as miserable as sin, Dinah,' Josie said shakily. She swallowed hard. 'What did you think of your dad?'

'He's lovely, Mum. I really liked him. I can understand why you fell for him so hard. Oh, but I wish he'd been around when I was little. It would have been great to have had a dad like him.'

'Did he mention staying with him at Christmas?'

'Yes.'

'Will you go?' Josie enquired cautiously.

'Just try and stop me, Mum.'

3

On Monday, Josie threw herself back into work in the hope that it would take her mind off Jack. It worked, to a degree. She read manuscripts while she ate, in the bath, in bed, on trains. There were inevitably times when she was left to her own thoughts, and she would pray that Jessie Mae would soon get married or take up a career, and Jack would be free to spend the rest of his life with her. Until then she would just have to make do with his frequent phone calls – and seeing him at Christmas. Dinah was already looking forward to it, and Josie could hardly wait.

★

My Favourite Murderer was a vivid and telling account of the conflict in Northern Ireland. There was no indication whether the young narrator, a girl, was Catholic or Protestant. She referred to 'our side' or 'the other side'. The murderer was her terrorist father, whom she loved, but she couldn't understand why she should hate other people because of their religion. Should she protect her father, or betray him, when she knew he was guilty of a heinous crime?

'You're right,' Josie said to Cathy Connors. 'It's brilliant. Write to Lesley O'Rourke and offer her a five thousand advance. I think we've got a bestseller on our hands.'

Lesley O'Rourke turned out to be a pseudynom, and the writer refused to reveal her real name or where she lived. They corresponded through a box number. 'If my address is known, then so will my religion,' she wrote to Cathy. 'I'd sooner not appear to be on anyone's side.'

'She's probably protecting her father, too,' Cathy said, showing Josie the letter. 'I bet the book is autobiographical. Shall I slot in publication of the hardback for January? Richard's already preparing next year's catalogue.'

'Yes. I'd like to get it out as soon as possible. It's got something meaningful to say, not that it'll make any difference to Northern Ireland. I don't think anything will.'

William Friars' *Death By Stealth* appeared in hardback in September, and was slated by the critics. Josie tried her best not to be pleased.

Later that month Val Morrissey rang from New York. Close-Up Productions had offered one hundred thousand dollars for the film rights to *Miss Middleton's Papers*. 'So our little enterprise has paid off in spades, eh!' he said triumphantly. 'Now, William Friars' *The Blackout Murders*. I'm not convinced a thriller set in the Liverpool blitz would sell in the States, but I'm intrigued by this guy's uptight private eye. I'd like to give it a go with a couple of thousand copies – see how the cookie crumbles. The usual advance applies.'

'I'll contact both authors. By the way, I bought two plane tickets for Los Angeles this morning. My daughter and I are spending Christmas with my ex-husband. Pity New York's on the other side of the country. We could have met up.'

He guffawed delightedly. 'It so happens *I'm* spending Christmas in Los Angeles – Long Island. Where will you be based?'

'Venice. Is that far?'

'Twenty, thirty miles. Chickenfeed. I'll only be staying a couple of days, but we could meet for a drink.' He expressed envy for what was obviously an amicable divorce. 'My ex-wife and I are still conducting the Third World War.'

Josie rang off and called a dazed Julia Hedington, who seemed less concerned with the money than the fact that well-known actors would be speaking *her* lines. 'Do you know who will be in it?'

'It won't have been cast yet.' She promised to let her know as soon as she heard.

'I hope it's Meryl Streep and Al Pacino. They'd be perfect.'

Josie asked Esther to send Julia a bouquet of roses, and dictated a letter to William Friars. Barefoot House still owned the rights to his earlier work. He replied by return of post, a stiff, condescending letter conveying his willingness to be published in America but expressing dismay at the small advance.

'You'd think he was doing us a favour,' Josie said disgustedly.

The downstairs dining room, so far unused, was converted into an office. Three new desks were ordered, and all the paraphernalia required by a modern business in the eighties. A second secretary arrived to assist the overworked Esther. Another editor was hired, Lynne Goode, happy to transfer from her job with a large London publisher to work for Barefoot House, as well as a young woman straight from university whose first job it was to study rights, because requests for foreign rights, book club rights, audio rights, large print rights, even TV rights, were flooding in.

Sometimes, when everyone downstairs had gone and she was alone, and the deathly silence was broken only by the creaks and groans of the old house, Josie would feel quite literally terrified by what she had created. It was getting too much, too big, too successful. She wouldn't be able to cope. She would shiver, imagining the whole edifice one day tumbling down about her ears.

But next morning the postman would deliver a mountain of post and manuscripts, the staff would arrive, the phone would ring for the first time, and would probably ring a hundred times again before the day was out, and the calls could be from anywhere in the world.

This is mine, she would think with another shiver, this time of pride. All mine. It would never be as good as sex. But it came close.

Christmas at last! The plane tickets were already tucked inside the handbag she was taking, her passport had been renewed and one acquired for Dinah, and her suitcase had been packed for days. Jack said the weather in Los Angeles was magic – brilliantly sunny and warm.

'We'll buy summer clothes there,' she said to Dinah. They phoned each other constantly. 'I'll treat you. American clothes are gorgeous, and dead cheap.'

'Just imagine, sunbathing in December!' Dinah sighed rapturously. 'It's snowing in London at the moment.'

'There's a blizzard blowing in Liverpool.'

'We can swim in Jack's pool!'

'You can, luv. I've never learned. I'll just sit in the sun and watch.'

'Oh, Mum. I can't wait!'

'Me neither.' She was longing to see Jack again and lie in his arms. For weeks now she'd been useless in the office, her stomach on fire with anticipation, her mind miles away in sunny Los Angeles.

Two days before they were due to leave, Josie felt an ominous tickling in her throat. Then her joints began to ache, and she had a throbbing headache. On the day they should have flown to Los Angeles, she was in bed with a virulent attack of flu.

'I'll catch a flight to London tonight,' Jack said instantly when she called and told him in a cracked voice she wouldn't be coming.

'You'll do no such thing. The weather's awful here, and you'll only catch my germs. Dinah's coming to look after me.'

'Are you sure? Are you absolutely positive? I'll be there like a shot if you like.'

'No, we'll come to you as soon as I'm better.'

'If you say so.' He sounded disappointed, and she was always to regret not taking up his offer to come and visit.

'Did Jack say I called on Christmas Day as we had arranged?' Val Morrissey enquired early in January.

'Yes. I'm so sorry I wasn't there. I didn't think to let you know. Jack said he explained what had happened.'

'Are you better now?'

'Still a bit weak, that's all.' Josie smiled at the receiver. 'Jack said you came in for a drink, anyroad.'

'I did indeed. Great guy, your ex. Great constitution, too. He drank me under the table, but it had no effect on him.' There was a pause, and Josie assumed he was about to discuss their mutual business interests, but he continued, 'That girl, Jessie Mae. She's his stepdaughter, right?'

'Right.'

'I hope you don't mind my asking, but how old is she?'

Jessie Mae had recently had a birthday. 'Twenty.'

Val whistled. 'Wow! She looks fourteen, but acts older. Do you think it would be okay if I made a move?'

'What sort of move?' Josie asked mystified. 'Oh, I see. You mean you fancy her?'

'That's a cute way of putting it,' he laughed. 'Yes, I do. It's not often you meet a real old-fashioned girl like that.'

'I'm afraid Jessie Mae and I have never met, but I'm sure Jack would have no objection if you made your move.'

'You'd love her,' Val Morrissey said enthusiastically. 'In that

358

case, I'll send some flowers, and I'm sure I can think up an excuse for going to L.A. in the near future.'

She didn't mention the conversation to Jack, who reported that the guy from New York, whose name he had forgotten, was inundating Jessie Mae with flowers and phone calls. 'She's quite chuffed. What she needs is a father figure, and this guy's still on the right side of forty. I'm sure Coral would have approved.'

Josie didn't say that *she* approved wholeheartedly. If Val Morrissey married Jessie Mae, Jack would have no excuse when she badgered him to marry her. And badger him she would, even if it meant going to Los Angeles and *dragging* him to the altar.

The reviews for *My Favourite Murderer* were glowing. One critic wrote, 'The saying is that "small is beautiful". Barefoot House, the diminutive publishing company based in Liverpool, seems to prove this point with every book they produce, but never more so than with Lesley O'Rourke's compelling tale of violence in Northern Ireland.'

Three companies made offers for the film rights, and vied with each other, increasing their offers until the final bid had reached half a million pounds.

Lily arrived just as Josie was reading the letter. She had phoned that morning to ask if they could lunch together. 'Please, say yes, it's rather important. I need someone to talk to.'

Josie showed her the letter. 'Just look at this! It makes me go all funny. Half a million *pounds*.'

'Very impressive,' Lily said dully. She sank in the chair in front of her friend's desk.

'What's up? You don't exactly *sound* impressed.'

'I'm pregnant.'

Josie gasped. 'You can't possibly be. You're forty-six. You've made a mistake, Lil. It's probably the menopause. You can have the same symptoms.'

Lily gestured impatiently. 'It's been confirmed. I'm bloody

pregnant. Five months gone, if you must know. I mean, I'm a grandmother twice over, Jose. I'm not exactly thrilled at the idea of providing a new aunt or uncle for me grandkids. And I've just got the boys off me hands – Simon's at school, and Alec's at playgroup. I'll feel daft, buying nappies and stuff at my age.'

'What does Francie have to say?'

'Oh, *him!* Well, you know Francie. Nothing seems to shake him. The thing is, it's all his bloody fault.'

'What did he do?'

'What the hell d'you think he did to make me pregnant?'

'Maybe he thought you were still on the Pill,' Josie said reasonably. '*I* did.'

Lily scowled. 'I came off the Pill months ago, didn't I? There didn't seem much point. Me and Francie aren't exactly Romeo and Juliet these days. I don't know what got into him the night this happened.' She pointed to her bulging stomach, which bulged no more than it had done six months ago – the visits to the gym hadn't lasted long. 'He must have been drunk.'

'Did Francie know you weren't taking the Pill?'

'I didn't tell him, no, but you'd think he'd have noticed the box wasn't on the kitchen window-sill any more.'

The telephone rang. Josie went and told Esther to get someone else to deal with it. She returned to her office. 'Come on, Lil, let's go to lunch and get a bit pissed. It'll do you good.'

'I'm not supposed to drink,' Lily said sulkily. She got to her feet, a bulky, shapeless figure with dull, listless eyes. Josie felt sad, remembering the bright-eyed young woman she'd accompanied to Haylands Holiday Camp.

Lily aimed a kick at the chair. 'Oh, I suppose I'll just have to have it, won't I? But I'm not looking forward to it, I'll tell that for free.'

Neither was Josie nor, she suspected, was Francie or any other people likely to have anything to do with Lily over the next few months. She'd made a huge meal out of her four other pregnancies, and was likely to turn this one into a banquet.

Lily had always been house-proud, but now it became an obsession. Not a speck of dust was allowed to rest for a second in the house in Halewood. Windows and mirrors were polished daily, the bathroom cleaned, carpets vacuumed, towels changed, clothes washed.

'I thought you had a squeegee mop,' Josie said when she called one day in the lunch hour and found Lily on her hands and knees scrubbing the kitchen floor.

'It doesn't get in the corners,' Lily puffed.

'And what are the dishes doing in the sink when you've got a dishwasher?'

'I don't trust the thing to get them properly clean.'

'I suppose you'll be doing the washing by hand next,' Josie said laconically.

'What do you mean by that?' Lily struggled to her feet and wiped her brow. She opened the kitchen door and dumped the bucket outside.

'Come off it, Lil. You're not fooling me. You're deliberately wearing yourself out to make everyone suffer, particularly poor Francie. There's no need for any of this.' She nodded at the sink and the wet floor. 'If you're so concerned about being clean, pay someone else to do it.'

'Do you seriously think I'd let another woman clean my house?' Lily glared at her, enraged.

'I don't see why not. Another woman cleans mine – two, actually. They come on Saturday morning and clean the offices at the same time.'

'That's different.'

'No, it's not, Lil.' Josie led her friend into the spotless living room and sat her down. 'Stop making such a martyr of yourself. It's driving all of us doolally.'

Lily got to her feet. 'I'll make some tea.'

Josie pushed her down again. 'I'll make it. Do you want me to collect Alec from playgroup?'

361

'No, ta. Our Samantha's getting him. Those flowers in the window are crooked.' She made to get up. Josie shoved her back.

'I'll do it. Now, you stay there while I make the tea. When I come back, if I find you've moved an inch I'll biff you.'

While she waited for the kettle to boil, she put the dirty dishes in the dishwasher. In a perverse way Lily was enjoying being overworked and miserable. Francie claimed to be at his wits' end. 'The only thing I can do to please her is allow meself to be endlessly nagged. She snaps at the lads, even when they try to help. One of these days, so help me, I'll kill the bloody woman, baby an' all.'

Lily rowed with both her sisters. 'Our Daisy had the cheek to tell me I was *lucky* to be having a baby at my age. Just because *she* couldn't have one, it doesn't mean *I* have to be glad. I said to her, I said, "You don't know what it's like to bear a child, Daise. You're talking through the back of your neck." Now she's taken umbrage. Not that *I* care,' she finished haughtily.

And Marigold had the nerve to admonish Lily for chastising her own boys. '"I beg your pardon," I said to her, "I *beg* your pardon. Just who do you think you are? These are *my* children, and I'll talk to them however I please. If you don't like it, you can lump it somewhere else." So she did!' Lily gave a fiendish grin. 'I don't give a damn. Some sisters *they* are.'

Even Samantha found reasons for giving her mother a wide berth, and Gillian, at university, no doubt forewarned, found something else to do during the Easter holidays rather than return to Liverpool. Francie was suddenly inundated with orders, all urgent, and had to work late. Only the two little boys were left but, then, they had no choice, and Josie. She came every lunchtime and most evenings to sit with her friend because she had the miraculous knack of coping with Lily's tantrums, of never taking offence, of giving as good as she got and somehow managing to love Lily, despite her numerous faults.

★

362

Lily's blood pressure rose alarmingly at eight months, her ankles swelled, her head ached. The doctor, who came every day, ordered her to rest. Only Lily could make resting an ordeal for everyone around. She was bored. 'I can never get to grips with a novel, you know that,' she said when Josie brought her a pile of books to read. She didn't like magazines, they were too bitty, she announced when Josie brought them instead. Daytime television was nothing but rubbish. She couldn't sew, she couldn't knit or embroider. 'I'd write a letter, but who is there to write to?'

'There's your Stanley and Robert,' Josie said helpfully.

For some reason they wouldn't do. 'I'd write to our Ben if I knew where he lived. I wonder where he went, Jose?'

'I don't know, Lil.' Ben hadn't been heard from in years.

'Give us his address and I'll write to Jack.'

'My Jack?' Josie's jaw dropped. 'Jack Coltrane?'

'How many Jacks do we know?'

'All right, Lil. I'm sure Jack will be pleased.' Jack would probably faint with shock.

Jack phoned a week later. 'I've had this very odd letter from your pregnant pal, Lily. Is she okay?'

'As okay as she'll ever be. What did she have to say?'

'In a nutshell, that you're a walking saint, and we should get married again immediately. She goes on in a muddled way about life being short and it shouldn't be wasted. It's rather touching in a way.'

Josie said nothing, and Jack went on, 'I suppose she's right, about life being short and stuff, though I don't go along with the walking saint bit. Saints don't throw a guy's plays on the floor and kick them.'

'I'm sorry,' she said abjectly.

'Too late, I'm afraid.' She imagined him grinning, and was surprised when his voice suddenly became harsh. 'Josie, you're a beautiful, vital woman. You should have married again years ago.'

363

She cradled the receiver in both hands. 'You weren't here to marry, Jack.'

'Forget about me, damn you!' he yelled. 'I made a lousy husband the first time, and I'd make a worse one now. You must meet a whole heap of eligible men when you're running that business – marry one of them, for Chrissake.' There was a pause, then a noise that might have been a sob. 'Sweetheart, my sweetheart,' he groaned, 'I love you too much to marry you. You deserve something better than an old, washed-up has-been like me. I've had it, Josie. I'm finished, over the hill. Forget me, my dearest love, and find someone else.'

'Jack!' she cried, but the line had gone dead, and when she tried to ring back she got the engaged tone, and continued to do so the next day and the day after. A week later the receiver was still off the hook. In desperation she rang Val Morrissey in New York to ask if there was anything wrong. He might know. He'd been seeing a lot of Jessie Mae.

'Didn't Jack tell you?' he gurgled happily. 'Jessie Mae and I flew to Las Vegas last weekend and got married. I've written to you, expressing my everlasting gratitude. We wouldn't have met if it hadn't been for you. You won't have got the letter yet.'

She was conscious of her heart beating rapidly in her chest. 'Did Jack go?'

'No, but Jessie Mae came to me with his warmest love.'

'So he should be at home?'

'I don't see why not. He didn't say he was going away.'

If it hadn't been for Lily, she would have flown to Los Angeles there and then. As soon as the baby's born, she vowed, we'll go, me and Dinah. They'd hoped to go at Easter, but Dinah had changed jobs again to become an assistant editor with a leading publisher, and was unable to take time off. Josie had no intention of giving up so lightly on Jack Coltrane, not this time.

'Did Jack get my letter?' Lily enquired. It was the last night Josie would spend with her pregnant friend in the house in

Halewood. The baby wasn't due until the fourteenth of May, two weeks off, but Lily was going into hospital the next day so that her blood pressure could be regularly monitored. It was still too high.

'Yes, luv. He was very pleased.'

'I hope he takes my advice. I'd like to see you happy, Jose.'

'I'm already quite happy.'

'Happier, then.'

Josie didn't say that the letter had probably arrived at the worst possible time for Jack — and for herself. Jessie Mae had just married and Lily rambling on about life being short, time being wasted, had unsettled him. He'd said things that, without the letter, it might never have entered his head to say. She changed the subject. 'I've brought you a prezzie — two prezzies, actually.'

'Goodie! I love prezzies. What are they?'

'Open them and see.' Josie handed her a George Henry Lee's bag. 'One's so you'll look dead gorgeous when you've had the baby. The other's so you'll smell like a dream.'

'Oh, Jose. It's lovely.' Lily held up a filmy pink nightie, thickly trimmed with ivory lace. 'And Opium! I *love* Opium. It's me favourite.' She sprayed behind her ears, and heady, exotic musk perfumed the air.

'That's why I bought it.'

They were sitting together on the settee and Lily grabbed her hand. 'You've been the best friend in the world, Jose,' she said in the clear, sweet voice she rarely used. 'No one could have had a better friend than you. You've always been there for me, ever since we were six.'

'And you for me, Lil.'

'No.' Lily shook her head. 'No, I haven't. I've always been too selfish to think of anyone but meself. But everything's going to change after I've had the baby. These last few weeks, I've had nothing to do but think.' She sighed massively. 'Poor Francie, I couldn't wait to get me hands on him, but I've led him a terrible life. Yet he's a husband in a million. Neil was, too.' Her face softened. 'And me kids! They're lovely kids,

Josie. I'm never going to snap at them again. Our Marigold was right to tell me off, and I was horrible to our Daisy. I'll write to them from hospital and say how sorry I am. I'm going to turn over a new leaf, Jose.'

Josie had heard all this before and didn't believe a word of it. 'You're all right as you are, Lil,' she lied.

'Light the candle and I'll try and relax. Do you mind nipping upstairs first, make sure the lads have settled down? They're both a bit upset about me going to hospital. Oh, and switch on the landing light. It's getting dark.'

The boys were fast asleep in their bunk beds. The walls were full of *Star Wars* posters, and Simon was clutching a plastic Darth Vader to his chest. The younger Alec slept with a teddy in his arms, his feet protruding from under the duvet. She covered them, suddenly feeling tearful at the sight of the perfect childish feet, the still pearly toes. It was many years since she'd done the same thing for her little girls.

When she went downstairs, Lily had already lit the candle and drawn the curtains. 'I don't find it all that relaxing,' she said. 'The doctor suggested it, said it might calm me mind, but I keep wondering where the draughts come from that make it flicker. It reminds me of when we had candles during the war, in that cellar we used as a shelter.'

'Aunt Ivy had an oil lamp. Phew, it didn't half stink. I only used the shelter once. There was a spider.' Josie shuddered. 'It was *huge.*'

Lily set off on a long, winding journey of memories. 'Remember the fairy glen, Jose? . . . Remember when you had a crush on Humphrey Bogart? . . . Remember that boyfriend I had, Jimmy something? Or was it Tommy? . . . Oh, and the pictures we used to see! I'm sure they were funnier in those days, and the men were much more handsome – except for Humphrey Bogart!' Remember this, remember that, when this happened, when that.

'Remember Haylands. Oh, we had a glorious time, didn't we, Jose?'

'Wonderful.' Josie felt hypnotised by the flickering candle.

366

She couldn't take her eyes off it. The scenes, the memories, seemed unnaturally real. She could smell the flowers in the fairy glen, the salty sea air at Haylands, the cigarette fumes in the picture-houses they'd gone to, the choking tang of yellow fog that used to hang heavily over the Liverpool streets, sometimes for days.

Lily's voice was getting sleepy. 'Remember the time I came to Bingham Mews? I met Neil going home on the train. Laura was such a sweet little girl, Jose. You must be very proud of her, having such a responsible . . . job . . . in . . . London.' Lily's head fell on her chest. She was asleep.

'Laura's dead, Lil. Dinah's in London,' Josie murmured under her breath. She longed for a cup of tea, but felt too indolent to move, still fascinated by the dancing flame which cast agitated shadows over the room. She tried to think of reasons to make herself get up, but if tea wouldn't do it, nothing would.

I'll ring Jack! She blew out the candle, and was on her feet in an instant, swaying dizzily because she'd risen too quickly. It was half past ten, but only half past two in Los Angeles. In the hall, she dialled the number with stiff fingers, and felt a surge of relief when she heard the dialling tone, which meant the receiver had been replaced. A woman answered after three rings. 'Hi! Shit, I can't read the number. Sorry about that. Hi, again.'

'I'd like to speak to Jack, please. Jack Coltrane.' She was too relieved to wonder why a woman was answering the phone.

'Sorry, honey. He doesn't live here any more. I'm Lonnie Geldhart from the realtors. This property is up for sale.'

'Where has he gone?' Josie cried franticically. 'Do you have his new address?'

'No, honey. I've never even met the guy.'

'But when the house is sold, you'll be sending him the proceeds. Oh, please, I have to know.'

'Gee, honey. I'd love to help,' the woman said sympathetically, 'but the money's being split between his kids – Tyler and Jessie Mae, I think their names are. I can give you their addresses if you like.'

'It's all right, I know where Jessie Mae is. Thank you for your help.'

'Any time, hon. I hope you manage to find the guy.'

Josie replaced the receiver. 'You've done it again – disappeared,' she whispered. 'Val Morrissey said he didn't know where you were.' She stamped her foot, forgetting the sleeping children upstairs and their pregnant mother on the other side of the wall. 'You *bastard*, Jack Coltrane!'

Francie entered the house through the back door. Josie was in the kitchen, on her third cup of tea. 'Been working late,' he said brazenly.

'You've been drinking.' Josie curled a caustic lip. 'Don't deny it, Francie. I can smell it on your breath.'

'Only a couple of beers after work, Jose. How's her ladyship?'

'Asleep, not that you'd care.'

'I *do* care, quite deeply, as a matter of fact, but caring does me no good, Jose.' He grinned. 'The other day she called me a rapist.'

'You probably are, amongst other things.'

'Apparently, I raped me own wife, though she was perfectly willing at the time. I thought the bloody woman was on the Pill, else I wouldn't have touched her. I'll feel like a pervert every time I look at the new baby, even when it's twenty-one.'

'You'll be pleased to know she's turning over a new leaf when she's had the baby.'

They smiled at each other. 'In a pig's ear, she will,' Francie said.

Josie rinsed her cup. 'I'm dead on me feet. I'm going home.'

'Ta, Jose.'

'What for?'

'For everything.' He kissed her forehead and gave her a

brief hug. 'You're a cracking girl, you know. I'm dead lucky Lily's got a friend like you. You've kept me sane over the last few months.'

'I'm hardly a girl, Francie. I'll be forty-seven next week.'

He winked suggestively. 'You'll always be a girl to me.'

'Oh, shurrup, you.' She gave him a shove. 'Tara, Francie. I'll go and see Lily in the hospital tomorrow.'

She was climbing into her car when she heard the scream, and she paused, unsure where it had come from. Then Francie opened the front door. 'It's Lily,' he shouted. 'The baby's coming. I'm taking her to the hospital straight away.'

The scream had woken the little boys. They came creeping downstairs, looking scared, just as Francie's car screeched away. 'What's the matter with Mummy?' Simon asked worriedly. A wide-eyed Alec sucked his thumb.

'She's had to go to hospital a bit early. By this time tomorrow you'll have a lovely little sister or brother. Won't that be the gear?'

'When will Mummy be home?'

'In a few days. Come on.' Josie held out her hands and they each took one. 'Shall I make you some warm milk?' It would be better if they didn't return to bed immediately, with Lily's scream still ringing in their ears. 'Would you like a biccy?'

'Yes, please, Auntie Josie,' they said together.

They sat together on the settee, their small bodies tucked against hers. She had got on well with all Lily's children.

'Will the new baby make Mummy scream again?'

'No, Simon.'

'It'll be a nuisance. Mummy said it will be a nuisance.'

'She didn't mean it.' She stroked Simon's pale hair, and wished Lily were there so she could give her a piece of her mind. What a thing to say! She thought how beautiful the love was that young children had for their mothers, who could do or say the vilest things yet the love persisted – unconditional, loyal, totally committed. 'The children love her,' Ben had said once of Imelda. And she had loved Mam, oh, so much, so much.

'Back to bed,' she sang out when the milk had gone. 'It's school and playgroup in the morning.'

Simon was obviously a worrier. 'Who'll take us if Daddy's not here?'

'Daddy will almost certainly be back by then. If not, I'll take you meself.'

Alec lisped, 'We making cakes tomorrow, with currants.'

'Shall I take one to the hospital for Mummy?' Josie offered.

'*Please*,' Alec said eagerly. 'And one for the new baby, too.'

After they had been tucked up in bed, Josie wandered round the house, trying not to think of Jack, failing utterly, thinking about him, cursing him, loathing him, loving him. I'll find you, she vowed. You're not getting away from me again.

She was about to make tea, but felt the urge for something stronger, so searched for bottles. There was beer in the fridge, but she hated beer. She found a bottle of gin in the sideboard, and wondered how much the legal limit was for when she drove home. A double – she'd risk a double, mixed with orange squash.

The hours crept by. She drank more gin, lay on the settee and tried to sleep, couldn't, got up, had another gin, thought about Lily, thought about Jack, thought she heard a burglar, but it was next door's cat scratching at the door, no doubt attracted by the light. She gave it milk and let it out again – Lily would have a fit if she knew, she hated cats.

Four o'clock! A child started to cry. She went upstairs. Alec, in the bottom bunk, was sobbing hopelessly.

'What's the matter, luv?' She held the small, shaking body in her arms. 'Have you had a bad dream?'

'Feel sad, Auntie Josie.' He could hardly speak. 'Feel dead miserable. Want my mummy.'

Simon turned over. 'Shurrup,' he muttered.

Alec quickly fell asleep, and Josie sat at the top of the stairs in case he woke again. Gosh, it was creepy, so quiet and so still. Alec's wretched crying had disturbed her. She longed to be in her own house in her own bed. Hurry up, Lil, and have your baby, she urged.

The phone went just after half four. She raced downstairs and picked it up before it woke the boys. 'Francie!'

'Hello, Jose.' His voice was curiously calm.

'How's Lily?'

'Dead, Jose. Lily's dead. She went into a fit or something, then she haemorrhaged, then she died. The baby's dead, too. It was a little girl. We were going to call her Josephine, after you.' He laughed. 'I can't believe I'm saying this. Lily's *dead*.'

4

They had put Lily in the pink nightgown trimmed with ivory lace that Josie had bought. Her lips were painted a delicate pink, her hair brushed away from the forehead made smooth by death and arranged in waves on the white satin pillow of the best coffin money could buy, which would have pleased her no end. Her hands were crossed over her breast. She looked peaceful, serene, as she had never done in life. It was hard to imagine a cross word had ever emerged from the pink mouth, Josie thought in the funeral parlour as she gazed down at the still, silent figure of her friend. She still couldn't believe Lily was dead. She half expected her to sit up and bark, 'Who d'you think you're staring at? Is that all you've got to do, Josie Flynn?'

The crematorium chapel was half-full − Lily's children, her husband, her brothers and sisters, a few nieces and nephews, their husbands and wives. Josie was the only person not a relative. Lily had had few friends. Dinah hadn't come. The new job was making her paranoid about taking time off.

At first, Josie didn't recognise the tall, tanned, athletic man in the front pew, blond, fiftyish, in an expensive grey suit. Then she realised it was Ben. Ben Kavanagh!

So all the Kavanaghs had turned up for the funeral of their

baby sister. Were they looking at each other, wondering whose turn it would be next? Their ma and da had gone, now Lily, the youngest. For which Kavanagh would the next funeral be held?

Daisy and Marigold felt guilty. They shouldn't have taken offence and neglected their sister while she was pregnant. They should have made allowances. After all, Lily hadn't been herself.

'She realised it was her fault.' Josie told them. 'She was going to write from hospital and apologise.'

'Well, she might have,' Marigold said with a dry smile.

'It would have been a first,' muttered Daisy.

It was strange. No one seemed all that upset, as if they, like Josie, couldn't believe Lily was dead. She had been so noisy, had made her presence so forcefully felt, that it didn't seem possible she had been silenced for ever.

Francie grieved for his lost wife, but felt no guilt for having found her a pain to live with, a fact that couldn't be challenged just because she was dead. He arranged for the most lavish of funerals, because it was what Lily would have demanded had she known she was going to die. 'I keep hearing this nagging voice in me head telling me what to do,' he confided to Josie. '"I want roses on me coffin, red ones, shaped like a cross. Make sure you wear a clean shirt and a black tie for me funeral. And don't drink too much afterwards, Francie O'Leary. Don't forget, I've got me eye on you."'

She would always be grateful to Francie for making life seem not quite as tragic as it really was.

Everyone went back to Marigold's house in Calderstones for a drink and something to eat. Marigold's children were grown up, long married, and numerous grandchildren cluttered the rooms.

Josie grabbed a sandwich and a glass of wine, and hid in a corner. Perhaps because Lily wasn't there, for the first time she felt out of place within the hubbub of this large family.

'I wanted a word with you.' Daisy approached, elegant in

floating black chiffon. 'It's rather sad, I'm afraid. In a few weeks, Manos and I are leaving Liverpool to live in Greece.'

'Oh, Daisy!' Josie cried. 'You've always been a permanent fixture in me life, almost as much as Lily.'

'I know, and you in mine.' Daisy smiled tremulously. 'It was our Lily going that did it. Stanley and Robert live so far away, and I had no idea where Ben was. Marigold's wrapped up in her family. There seemed no reason left to stay, and Manos has this huge extended family in Crete. I miss being part of a family.'

Josie kissed her on both cheeks. 'I hope you and Manos will be very happy in Crete. Twice in me life you've come to me rescue when I've been at rock bottom. I'll never forget that, Daise.'

'Promise you'll come and stay some time, Josie. You'll always be welcome. You're one of Manos's favourite people.'

'I promise.' Josie nodded vigorously, knowing she almost certainly wouldn't. It was just that partings were much easier if you promised to see each other again.

'I've been trying to escape from our Stanley for ages.' Ben arrived in her corner. 'You look great but, then, you always do. Have you sold your soul to the devil in return for permanent youth?'

Josie opened her mouth to laugh, but quickly closed it. Lily wouldn't approve of people laughing at her funeral. 'You can talk! You look wonderful, like a Nordic god.'

'I've taken up tennis. I'm rather good at it. I'm champion of the local club.' He grimaced. '*Senior* champion, in the section for the over forty-fives.'

'Where exactly is the local club?' she asked curiously. 'It's something all of us have wanted to know for a long time.'

'Isle of Wight. Come on, let's find somewhere quieter to talk.' He took her arm and led her into the garden. It was full of children, but there was a bench right at the bottom, half hidden by an apple tree iced with pink blossom. 'After Imelda died,' Ben said when they were seated, 'I felt I wanted a change of scene, for myself and the children. We drifted

373

round the country for a while and I worked as a supply teacher. I kept meaning to write to say where I was, but never got round to it.' He shrugged. 'I was pretty mixed up for a while. Then I got a job with an aeronautic design company on the Isle of Wight. We settled down, and it seemed too late to let people know, so I never bothered.'

'Who told you about Lily?'

'Read it in the *Echo*,' he said surprisingly. 'About this time last year, I felt dead homesick. Colette was already married and living in Dorset – I'm a grandfather of twins, by the way – and Peter discovered the social conscience I used to have meself. He's in Cuba, working on a farm. I decided to look for a job in Liverpool, come home. I've been getting the paper ever since.'

'It'll be nice to have you back.' She meant it sincerely. A Kavanagh coming, a Kavanagh going, and one gone for ever!

'I can't wait to be back,' he said, 'though I was expecting a right earful from our Lily when I showed me face. Instead, I feel gutted. I thought the Grim Reaper would have to drag Lily to her grave kicking and screaming when she was a hundred.'

Josie was glad of the buzz of activity in Barefoot House when she returned next day. William Friars had called when she was away. Havers Hill had decided not to publish *Death By Stealth* in paperback because of its initial mauling by the critics and the subsequent small sales.

'He said he would graciously allow us to publish it.' Cathy grinned. 'I said I'd talk to you.'

'Write and tell him to get stuffed,' Josie said curtly. 'I didn't want the book in the first place. Tell him if he'd like to write another set in the war, we might take it.'

'With pleasure. Have you had any further thoughts about that suggestion Richard made?'

'I haven't had time to think for weeks.' Barefoot House seemed to have reached a plateau. There was only a limited amount of good crime fiction available. She didn't want standards to drop by accepting work she might once have rejected, and Richard had come up with the idea that they extend their range to another genre of novel – science fiction, romance, war or historical, books for children. 'I don't know, Cathy. I don't think I want to become a millionaire. I'm content with things as they are.'

Cathy left, looking disappointed. Josie chewed her lip and worried that she was letting down her staff by being too unadventurous. She should be looking for ways to go forward, not be content with standing still. Mind you, it would be *her* taking the risk, not Cathy, Richard or the others, and she wasn't in the mood just now.

She scanned the post. There was a letter from Brewster & Cronin in New York, marked 'Personal'. Val Morrissey had hired a private detective to trace Jack's whereabouts, but had had no luck so far. 'I'm worried about Jack myself,' he wrote. 'After all, the guy's my father-in-law of sorts. I really liked him the few times we met. I'll not give up until every avenue has been exhausted.'

There was no mention of Jessie Mae being worried about her stepfather. Josie opened the top drawer of her desk and took out the photo Val had sent in January. She was glad to have a face to put to his familiar voice. He was smaller than she had imagined, going slightly bald, very ordinary and rather nice. He was smiling happily at the camera but, then, this had been his wedding day. Yet the bride wasn't smiling. Jessie Mae's plump, pretty face was expressionless. She didn't glare at the camera, she didn't smile, merely stared. She didn't look happy, she didn't look sad, or excited, or even faintly pleased that she had just married a relatively wealthy man who was crazy about her. Josie didn't think she had ever seen such dead eyes before. 'Jessie Mae's had problems,' Jack had said.

Well, at least his real daughter was upset. Dinah was hurt and angry that the father she had only just met had vanished from her life again. 'I can't have meant much to him, can I?' she said bitterly whenever she called to ask if Jack had been found.

At six o'clock, Ben came to take Josie to dinner. He was staying the week with Marigold. 'You didn't say yesterday you had your own business. Our Marigold told me this morning. Who'd have thought it, eh? I've actually read two of your books.'

'Don't sound so surprised,' she said indignantly. 'Did you think I was too thick to start a business?'

'I never considered you even vaguely thick, Jose. You didn't seem the type, that's all.'

'I suppose it was born of necessity.' She glanced around the office, at the rows and rows of bright red books. 'I was in a rut, and the thing just grew and grew.'

Ben had come in his car – the latest model BMW, she noticed. The job on the Isle of Wight must pay well. They drove into the countryside and ate in a little seventeenth-century pub near Ormskirk, with beams and an inglenook fireplace. Over chicken and chips, she told him about Richard's suggestion. 'But I'm not as entrepreneurial as I look. Barefoot House became a success despite me. It happened so gradually I hardly noticed. If I'd known I'd end up handling things like film rights and TV rights, I'd have probably backed off.'

'I doubt it,' he said comfortably. 'Anyroad, most businesses start from nothing. Didn't Marks & Spencer grow from a stall selling candles? Or was that Harrods? Great oak trees from little acorns grow, so it's said. Would you like to finish off this wine, Jose? I've already had two glasses, and I'm driving.'

He emptied the bottle into her glass. It had been an enjoyable, relaxing evening. They had talked, without a hint of strain, about when they had been children living in Machin Street, the things they'd done together, the times they'd had, about Lily and the tantrums she used to throw. He seemed to have got over the passion he'd once had for her, and she was glad. He had spoken about Imelda, how painful the marriage had been, how he and the children had suffered from her moods.

'It would have been so easy to blame her, hate her, but the

poor woman couldn't help it. She was sick. If she'd had a physical illness, everyone would been sympathetic, but people have no patience with the mentally ill.'

She was reminded of how kind he'd always been, how understanding. 'Imelda was lucky to have had someone like you.'

'It wasn't easy,' he muttered. 'There were times when I felt at the end of me tether. I'm the sort who likes a quiet life.'

Mrs Kavanagh had remarked once, 'Our Ben will make some girl a good husband, but not a very exciting one.'

'He's a soppy lad, our Ben,' Lily had said.

He took out his wallet and picked up the bill. Josie watched his face as, frowning slightly, he counted out the money. It was a sensitive face and, despite all he'd suffered, the green eyes were guileless and innocent, like a child's. He was a good man, through and through.

'If you can spare the time before you go back, perhaps I could treat *you* to dinner,' she said impulsively.

His face lit up. 'I've always got time to spare for you, Jose. Not tomorrow, I'm seeing Francie. The night after?'

'It's a date.'

Josie woke suddenly with the eerie feeling that she'd just been sharply prodded in the ribs. The room was pitch dark, and the electric alarm clock showed thirteen minutes past three. She reached out a shaking hand to switch on the bedside lamp, terrified that another hand would grab it. She would never get used to sleeping alone in the big old house.

'Who's there?' she enquired timidly.

No answer. Josie gritted her teeth and sat up. The bedroom was empty. She rubbed her left side, where there was the definite sensation of having been poked. Lily had had the irritating habit of poking people if she thought they weren't listening, or had said something she didn't like, a habit Josie had suffered from more than most. It had driven Francie to the verge of murder, as his ribs were unnaturally exposed.

It dawned on Josie that Lily was dead. *Lily was dead?* She

would never see her friend again. 'Lil,' she wailed. 'I want you back.' She began to cry for the first time since Francie had called from the hospital to say Lily and the baby had died. The tears flowed for the girl who had been her best friend since they were six, whose death she'd been unable to grasp. Until now, when she'd been poked awake by an unseen finger.

'You bitch, Lily Kavanagh,' she whispered through the tears. 'You did that on purpose.' She'd like to bet that, all over the country, various Kavanaghs and a somnolent Francie O'Leary had been awoken by a red-faced, bad-tempered Lily, waving her arms and stamping her feet because no one had acknowledged the fact that she was dead. No one had cried. No one had mourned, only her daughters and her two little boys.

'You've left a great big hole in me life, Lil, and I'll always miss you.' Josie snuggled back under the bedclothes. 'But if you do that again, I'll bloody kill you.'

Two months later, on the first of July, Ben Kavanagh returned to Liverpool, having procured a job with a chemical company over the water in Birkenhead. He bought the top half of a large Victorian house in Princes Park which had been converted into two flats.

The evening after his furniture had arrived from the Isle of Wight, Josie helped arrange it in the big, elegant rooms.

'You've got excellent taste,' she said as she straightened the cushions of the comfortable three-piece, upholstered in coarse, oatmeal wool. The carpet was new, mustard tweed.

'I got most of the stuff from Habitat. I like the modern look – plain colours, no curly-wurly bits on the furniture, white walls.' He was stacking books in alphabetical order on a natural wood bookcase.

'Shall I hang the curtains?'

'Please. I put the fittings up last night. The rings are already in.'

The navy blue curtains took only a few minutes to slide on the pole. She found a screwdriver and secured the pole at each end, then took the screwdriver and another set of curtains, brick red, upstairs to hang in the bedroom. Here the carpet was grey. The bed had a slatted base, a polished plank for a headboard and was covered with a grey duvet. A wardrobe and six-drawer chest were equally unadorned.

She hung the curtains, secured the pole and sat on the bed to admire her handiwork. A bit spartan, but what you'd expect of a man. Well, some men. Jack's apartment in New York had looked as if he were about to hold a jumble sale.

Ben came in. 'I'll hang me clothes up tonight. They're still in boxes.'

'What else shall I do? What about ornaments?'

'Don't believe in them. I prefer the cool, uncluttered look.' He sat beside her on the bed.

'That chest looks very bare. It needs something.'

'It'll have a bowl for my small change, and that's all.'

'What about a little vase on the window-sill? I've got things in me attic you can have.'

He grinned. 'They can stay in your attic, thanks all the same. Ornaments need dusting. I can live without them very well.'

'You've always been so sensible and organised,' she said admiringly.

'It doesn't seem to have got me anywhere.' He laughed shortly. 'So far, my life has been extraordinarily chaotic. My wife killed herself, and I've spent years living in places I didn't want to live.'

'Well, you can settle down now.' She patted his knee. 'You're home.'

He put his hand over hers before she could remove it. 'I'm looking forward to it, Jose. But I'd look forward to it even more if I were settling down with you.'

'Ben!' She tried to remove her hand but he wouldn't let go. Instead, he took her other hand, placed her arms around his neck, and drew her towards him.

'I won't kiss you,' he whispered. 'I want you to listen, that's all. I still love you. I know you don't love me, and I won't come out with all that guff about me having enough love for both of us.' He drew in a deep breath, and let it out slowly.

'You just said I was sensible, and it makes perfect sense for us to be together. I don't want a commitment, I'm not going to propose. Instead, I'd like us to conduct a little experiment, which is what I do all the time in my job. When you feel ready, if you ever do, I'd like us to be lovers, not just friends. Let's see how we get on, you and me, together, as a couple.' He released her so suddenly, she almost lost her balance. 'I'm not being very sensible now, am I?' he groaned. 'That was totally impetuous, and I've probably alienated you for ever.'

Josie didn't speak. She went over to the window which overlooked the back of the house. A very old man was mowing the grass in the garden next door, and a woman about the same age, presumably his wife, was fetching in washing. She wondered what it would be like to have been married to the same person for forty or fifty years. Had she married Ben, they would have clocked up their silver wedding anniversary by now. Their children might be married, they might have grandchildren. She would never have experienced the ecstatic highs and the tragic lows there'd been with Jack Coltrane.

There was still no trace of Jack. It could be another twenty years before he resurfaced. But Ben was here, loving her still, loving her for a whole lifetime. He had always made her feel safe and secure, even when she was a child. But he hadn't understood her need for adventure, even if it was only a few months at Haylands, because he wasn't adventurous himself. But Josie was forty-seven, and Barefoot House provided all the excitement she needed. Jack Coltrane had never made her feel remotely safe or secure, but Ben would.

'Ben.' She turned. He was still sitting on the bed, watching her, and the love in his eyes made her heart melt. 'Oh, Ben!' She sat beside him, laid her head on his shoulder. 'I don't deserve you. You make me feel a desperately horrible woman.'

'You're the woman I want.' He kissed her lips, softly,

gently, and she laughed. 'You were always a good kisser. You haven't changed.'

Nothing much had changed. He undid her blouse, caressed her breasts, kissed them, and Josie found it pleasant, slightly arousing, but that was all. She felt more aroused by his own mounting passion, which was catching, and the tenderness of his touch, the lovely things he said between kisses. He made her feel a uniquely special person, the most beautiful woman who had ever lived. She felt cherished and very fortunate that a man like Ben regarded her body, possessing it, as equivalent to finding the Holy Grail.

They reached orgasm together. 'Darling,' Ben panted. 'Oh, darling, that was wonderful.' He folded her in his arms, and she was conscious of his pounding heart, his body shuddering against hers. 'Was it all right for you?' he said anxiously.

'More than all right, silly.' It had been sweet and enjoyable. She would quite like to do it again.

5

Josie was founder and managing director of Barefoot House, but didn't want to appear an autocrat so she called a staff meeting. Everyone crowded into her office, and she asked for their views on the company branching out to include another genre of novel.

'What do you think? It's ages and ages since Richard suggested it, but I've had a lot of things on my mind lately, personal things.'

'Why don't we do westerns?' This came from Bobby, the post-boy, who Josie was surprised to see there as he hadn't been invited. But he was a cheeky character, blissfully unaware of his place in the office hierarchy. 'They're me fave.'

To her surprise, there was a rumble of agreement. 'Westerns are like thrillers, always popular,' someone murmured.

Josie thought westerns old hat, but didn't say so. It was

quickly turning into one of those times when she felt inferior to her staff, who were mostly far more experienced and knowledgable about publishing than she was herself. She folded her arms on the desk and tried to look cool and in charge of the situation.

'Josie, do you know Dorothy Venables?' asked Lynne Goode, who had come to Barefoot House almost a year ago.

'I've heard of her, naturally.' Dorothy Venables wrote women's sagas that sold by the cartload. Her name was always near the top of the year's bestselling writers.

'I was going to talk to you about this anyway. She had a three-book contract with my old company,' Lynne explained. 'I was her editor. It was the only thing I regretted about leaving, parting with Dottie. We still keep in touch. She's uneasy about signing a new contract since they've been taken over by this big, soulless American company. It's the reason I left myself. I think I could persuade her to come to us.'

There was an even louder rumble from the assembled staff, this time of excitement. 'I can't believe you have *that* much influence, Lynne,' Cathy Connors said jealously.

'No one can influence Dottie. She's more than capable of thinking for herself.' Lynne smiled. 'I've told her about Barefoot House. She's a right-on feminist, though you'd never tell by her books. She likes the idea of being published by a woman.'

'Would she want a massive advance?' Josie enquired.

'Probably, but you'd get every penny back, and more.'

Josie swallowed nervously. Women's sagas! Dorothy Venables! Was she getting in too deeply? Would she be able to cope? She was aware of a dozen pairs of eyes, watching her intently, and felt a sudden thrill of excitement. *Dorothy Venables!* 'Sound her out,' she said to Lynne. 'If she's willing, I'm willing, as long as she doesn't want an advance that will bankrupt us.' She grinned. 'Or even if she does.'

Dorothy Venables telephoned an hour later. She spoke quickly and aggressively in a hoarse, gruff voice, with a strong North Country accent. 'I've read about you, and I like the sound of you,' she growled. 'Come from a working-class background meself. We drank our tea from jam jars in my part of Yorkshire.'

Josie was unable to match such depths of poverty. She promised to draw up a contract. The advance agreed on was less than expected. Lynne said later it was only half what she had received for her previous novel.

'She realised a figure like that might cause problems. She's very kind underneath all that bluster. I'm sure you two will become great friends.'

'Dorothy Venables!' she crowed that night.

'Never heard of her,' Ben said.

'She's published all over the world in umpteen different languages. It's like signing up the Queen. I'm going down to London next week to take her to lunch. Lynne, one of me editors, is coming with me. They're old friends. I sent Bobby out to buy some of her books. I want to read the lot before we meet. Gosh, Ben. Sometimes I can't believe this is happening.' She still felt nervous and strung out. She was lying on the pink and white settee, her legs draped over his knee, and she smiled up at him. 'I'm glad you're here to talk to.'

He laid his hand flat on her stomach. 'Pleased to be of service, ma'am.'

Since Dinah had gone, she had missed having someone there with whom to discuss the events of the day. Ben was particularly soothing to be with. They had been together three months, and he was a perfect companion, utterly reliable. She would have trusted him with her life. If Ben said he would telephone at six, or arrive at seven, he would keep his promise to the dot. He looked up timetables for her, met her off trains, made sure her car was serviced and filled with petrol, kept an eye on when insurance premiums were due, found things she had lost. He even brought her tea in bed each morning, and generally looked after her in a way no one had ever done before. She felt dearly loved and very precious.

They were virtually living together in Huskisson Street,

though he hadn't properly moved in. He returned to his flat in Princes Park to change his clothes, do his washing, keep the place dusted and tidied. He wanted to move in permanently, but Josie had put him off. 'Not just yet, let's leave it a while,' she had said gently.

'Hmm. That's nice.' She sighed dreamily when he began to rub his hand in a circle on her abdomen. Closing her eyes, she immediately began to worry that she was using him. At the back of her mind there was a feeling that the relationship wouldn't last, which was why she hadn't wanted him to move in, give up his home. He knew she didn't love him, not in the way he loved her, but it still felt wrong.

Dorothy Venables turned up in a leather jacket and well-worn jeans. She was in her fifties, thin and lanky with dark, burning eyes and a badly scarred chin. She looked as tough as old boots. A cigarette dangled from her narrow, unpainted lips. Having been forewarned by Lynne, Josie had booked a table in a restaurant that didn't have a dress code.

Books were one of the few subjects not mentioned throughout the meal. Dottie – Josie had been told to call her Dottie – smoked between courses, slagged off the government, the aristocracy, royalty, the stock exchange, banks, building societies and any other bastions of the establishment that came to mind, using the sort of language that never appeared in her novels. Unmarried, her most scathing criticism was directed at men, most of whom she unreservedly loathed. Josie found it incredible that such tender love stories could have been nurtured in so cynical a mind. Even so, she liked down-to-earth Dottie Venables very much. Lynne was right. Josie just knew they would become great friends.

Josie and Lynne had come by train, and would make their own way home. Lynne went to see her mother in Brent, and Josie to the West End to do some shopping, then to Holborn to meet Dinah after work.

Her daughter emerged from the high-rise office building

carrying a briefcase, looking anxious and flustered. 'I don't like leaving so early,' she said.

'Early!' Josie looked at her watch. 'It's twenty-five to six.' She thought Dinah looked rather pale and much too thin.

'Yes, but everyone works all the hours God sends, Mum. I felt dead conspicuous, being the first to leave. I hope no one noticed, else it'll be a black mark against me.'

'People should live to work, Dinah, not work to live.' Josie took her arm and ushered her inside the first reasonable-looking restaurant they came to. 'I'm sure not everyone works as hard as you say,' she said when they were seated, 'otherwise they'd have no home life.'

'Well, no, not everyone,' Dinah conceded, 'but I'm the youngest assistant editor there, and the only one who didn't go to university. I have to put in more effort than the others if I'm to get anywhere.'

'And where exactly is it that you want to get, luv?'

'I've told you before – to the top,' Dinah said promptly. 'Some of the senior editors fly all over the world, meeting writers. I'd like to work in the States one day, become an executive, edit a top magazine. I want to get *on*, Mum.'

'Well, while you're getting on, I wish you'd eat properly. You look as if you haven't had a decent meal in ages.'

'I'm too busy to eat,' Dinah muttered.

'I suppose you'll be too busy to come home for your birthday.' Dinah would be twenty-one in a fortnight's time. It was a long while since she'd been to Liverpool. 'We can have a party,' Josie said coaxingly.

'I can't see me managing it, Mum.'

Josie would have liked to discuss the matter more, but Dinah rushed the meal. She pointed to the briefcase and said she had stacks of work to do at home.

The journey back seemed to take for ever, and Josie worried about Dinah the whole way. There'd been a hardness about her daughter that she hadn't liked, yet beneath the hardness had been an air of vulnerability that touched her mother to the core. And she was admirable in her way. She could have had a cushy, secure job at Barefoot House, but preferred to make her own way in the publishing world. Josie sighed. Perhaps she was old-fashioned, but she felt a young woman of twenty should be out and about having a good time, not working herself to death in an office, skipping meals.

Ben had been primed as to when the train would arrive, and was waiting at Lime Street station. 'I've had some great news,' he said joyfully. 'I had a letter today from Cuba. Our Peter's coming home for Christmas. I haven't seen him in over two years.'

Twelve people sat down to dinner that Christmas in Huskisson Street: Josie and Ben; a very tense Dinah; Peter Kavanagh, now a lovely bronzed young man, the image of Imelda; Francie O'Leary and his two little boys; Esther, Josie's secretary, still alone; and Colette, Ben's daughter, with her husband, Jeremy, and their twin daughters, Amy and Zoe. They were staying in Ben's flat.

'Bloody hell!' Josie swore, as she struggled with pans of vegetables and a giant turkey in the steaming kitchen. 'I can't believe I wanted a big family. I would have had this lark every sodding year.'

'Need a hand?' Francie poked his head around the door.

'No, that's the problem. You're not the first to offer help, but I don't know what to give people to *do!* Colette's set the table, Ben's organising the drinks.'

'Can I peel a potato or something?' He sidled into the room.

'I did them last night, idiot. Can you see the white dish I was going to put the sprouts in?'

'Is this it?'

'I think so. I need one like it for the carrots.'

'What's wrong with your Dinah? I think this might be the carrot dish.'

'Ta, Francie. She's working too hard, that's what.' She suddenly noticed Francie's bizarre outfit. 'Why have you come to Christmas dinner at my house wearing a nightshirt?'

'It's the latest fashion, Jose.' He did a little twirl. The long white shirt almost reached the knees of his black velvet trousers. 'Hey, I knew you and Ben were seeing each other, but I didn't realise you were such a close item. I'm dead envious. If I'd known he was going to make a move, I'd have proposed to you at Lily's funeral.'

'Oh, Francie. You only say things like that to shock. If you're not careful, I'll find someone else to print me books.'

'I let you go once, I'm determined not to let it happen again.'

She snorted. 'It's a bit late. Anyroad, Mr O'Leary, it was the other way around. It was *me* that let *you* go.'

'Whatever.' He waved his hand. 'Seriously, Jose, Ben's a decent guy, but I hope you're not going to marry him or anything daft like that. He'll bore you rigid after a while. Here, let me help you with that.' Together, they lifted the sizzling turkey out of the oven. 'Me, now, I'm a different proposition altogether, but you already know that. And we were great together when we did the bed bit.'

'Shush!'

There were footsteps outside and Ben appeared. 'I thought you might need some help. Will dinner be long? It's chaos back there. The twins are starving, Simon and Alec are squabbling over something out of a cracker, Esther's worried dinner might be so late she'll miss the Queen's broadcast, and our Peter and Dinah are having a flaming row about Fidel Castro.'

'I think I might treat meself to a holiday,' Dinah said somewhat surprisingly over breakfast on Boxing Day. Ben had left early for Princes Park to see Colette, and Peter, who was staying in Josie's spare room, had risen at some unearthly hour to go for a walk. 'I've enough money saved. I've never been abroad. We never managed to get to Los Angeles, did we?'

'No, luv.' Josie sighed. 'But what about work? You can't just take time off without telling anyone.'

'Oh, I'll give my boss a ring,' Dinah said carelessly, which was even more surprising.

'Would you like me to come with you?' Josie offered. 'Cathy Connors and her husband have gone to the Seychelles for Christmas. She said the weather's perfect this time of year.'

Dinah blushed. 'Actually, Mum, I'm going to Cuba.'

'Cuba!' Josie's face burst into a delighted smile. 'With Peter Kavanagh?'

'Yes, but there's nothing in it. He said it's a wonderful place, and I said I didn't believe him. It's a dictatorship, however benign. He invited me to come and look for meself. I'm only going for a fortnight.'

Josie couldn't have been more pleased. 'I hope you have a lovely time.'

'I doubt it,' Dinah said darkly. 'Peter's a dead irritating guy. He has these really peculiar opinions. All we do is argue.'

A fortnight passed, and Dinah didn't come back from Cuba. She wrote to say she had telephoned the company she worked for to say that she'd left, and had no idea when she would be home. She'd got a job in a hospital and was learning to speak Spanish. Peter had turned out okay after all, and they were sharing a flat. The Americans were shits, the way they treated the Cubans. Would Josie mind driving down to London and collecting her belongings from the flat? She'd given the landlord a month's notice. The dishes were hers, the pots and pans were the landlord's. In the oven there was a lovely casserole dish which she didn't want left behind.

'Why the hell should she give a damn about a casserole dish when she's in Cuba?' Josie wanted to know. 'Your son has a lot to answer for, Ben Kavanagh.'

'You don't mind, do you?' Ben said anxiously.

'Of course not. He's a lovely lad. Though I wish he lived a bit nearer.' Josie smiled wistfully.

'So do I. I wonder if our children ever miss us as much as we miss them?'

'I doubt it.'

★

As soon as it became known that Dorothy Venables had transferred to Barefoot House, the company was deluged with women's sagas. Josie engaged two more editors, an assistant for Richard in Publicity, and another secretary, by which time space had become a problem. There were too many desks in too few rooms. She could have afforded to move into a spacious office block in town, but preferred the more intimate accommodation of Huskisson Street. She solved the problem by giving up her lovely lounge and elegant dining room for offices, and moving up a floor. The attic was ruthlessly emptied, decorated and turned into a bedroom, and Josie slept with Ben in a room identical to the one she'd lived in with Mam, just four doors and more than forty years away.

The following year, Josie and Ben went to the Odeon in Leicester Square to attend the premiere of *Miss Middleton's Papers*. Great Britain was at war in the Falklands, but war was far from the minds of the expensively dressed guests that night as they strolled across the red carpet into the cinema.

Ben looked dead handsome in the evening suit hired for the occasion. 'Distinguished,' Josie declared. 'I feel quite proud to have you as me escort.' Her own frock was a blue crêpe sheath with long sleeves – she felt convinced the tops of her arms were getting fat. She hoped it looked worth the extravagent amount of money it had cost.

She found the evening very pretentious, the way people fell upon each other and called each other 'darling'. She rather traitorously wished Francie O'Leary were there instead of Ben, because he'd have poked fun at everyone and made her laugh. Ben was very much in awe of the well-known faces, very reverential when people spoke to them. There were times when she wouldn't have minded swopping Ben for Francie. Just for a week or two!

In another month she would be fifty. Fifty! She looked at Ben, aghast. 'I can't believe it! I've been alive half a century. It doesn't feel nearly that long.'

He suggested she throw a big party, invite her staff and all their friends, but Josie demurred. 'I'm not sure I want me staff to know I'm fifty.'

'Have a little dinner party, then. Get caterers in. We'll ask Francie and his latest woman, our Marigold and her husband, that peculiar friend of yours, Dorothy. How many's that?'

Josie counted on her fingers. 'Seven with us, but Daisy and Manos are due home shortly for a few weeks, and I'd like to ask Terence Dunnet, me accountant, and his wife, Muriel. I hardly see them these days.'

'That's eleven. Twelve would make a perfect number. We need another man to partner Dorothy.'

'She'd prefer a woman.'

Ben's eyebrows raised in surprise. 'I didn't know she was that way inclined.'

'She's not. She prefers women's company, that's all. Men are only allowed to do their duty in her bed.'

'Ugh!' He pulled a face. 'Some things are beyond the call of duty. Anyroad, Jose, dinner for twelve. I'll pay, it'll be half me present.'

'What's the other half?' she asked greedily.

Ben went over and switched off the television, which she found slightly irritating as she'd been waiting with the sound turned down for *EastEnders*. 'I thought you'd like a ring,' he said. 'A wedding ring.'

If it had been Francie, she would have said, 'Turn the bloody television back on, and we'll talk about wedding rings when *EastEnders* has finished.' But you could never say things like that to Ben. Even when they were little, she'd had to be careful because his feelings were so easily hurt. Oh, God! She still felt annoyed that he'd proposed just as one of her favourite programmes was about to begin. She remembered he was still waiting to know if she'd like a wedding ring.

'I'd sooner continue as we are,' she said lamely.

'In other words, you don't want to' marry me?' His voice was icy.

'I never said that.'

'We're not married and you want to continue as we are. *Ergo*, you don't want to marry me.'

'What does *ergo* mean? We didn't do Latin at St Joseph's junior and infants school.'

'It means therefore, and don't be so sarcastic.'

'Then don't argue with me in Latin,' she said furiously. She had been looking forward to a relaxing evening watching television, and wasn't in the mood for a fight. 'Things are fine as they are. Why change them? Why rock the boat?'

'As far as I'm concerned, things will never be fine until you're my wife.' He folded his arms stubbornly.

'Too bad, Ben.' There was something about his face, the way his lips were drawn in an angry line, almost prim, that brought back memories of the only other row they'd had. 'You know what this reminds me of? That time I wanted to go to Haylands and you decided to put your foot down for some reason I never understood. Just because I wasn't prepared to do your bidding on one, small, unimportant thing, you were equally prepared to ruin everything. Any minute now you'll threaten to leave if I don't marry you, and ruin everything again.' He was easygoing to a fault, but seemed to find it necessary once in a while to put up a hoop for her to jump through. She hadn't jumped the last time, and she had no intention of jumping now.

'Darling!' Suddenly, he was on his knees in front of her, holding her hands. 'I want you to be *mine*. I'm terrified you'll meet someone else during one of the times you go flitting off all over the country. I want you to have my ring on your finger when you take strange men to lunch. I want you to be Mrs Kavanagh, not Coltrane.' His voice broke, and he sounded just like the young man who'd pleaded with her on a bench in the fairy glen. 'I love you, Josie. I love you so very much.'

'Oh, Ben.' She put her cheek against his. He was so sweet, so nice, comfortable to live with, a truly decent man, entitled to some happiness. If they married, the comfortable life would continue. She imagined the years stretching ahead, serene and contented, as they no doubt would have passed had she married him in the first place. 'All right,' she said in a small voice. 'We'll get married.' She had jumped through the hoop after all.

His face broke into a delighted smile. 'When?' he demanded. 'I know, let's do it on your birthday.'

'Not quite so soon,' she said quickly. She was about to say, 'Let's leave it till next year,' but remembered it was what she'd once said to Francie because she'd felt so uncertain. 'In a few months,' she said to Ben. 'I'd like time to get used to the idea.'

'We'll announce it at the dinner,' Ben said jubilantly. 'I'll buy you an engagement ring instead.'

It was three days before her birthday. Ben was down in London at a conference and was coming back tomorrow. The caterers would be arriving at six o'clock on the day and would take over the kitchen. Dinner would be served at half seven. Josie had wasted a lot of time deciding which floral centrepiece she preferred. Dorothy Venables was coming up from London and would stay for two days. The obvious person to make up twelve guests was Lynne Goode, another friend, though she'd been asked not to breathe a word to Cathy Connors who might feel hurt at being left out.

Daisy and Manos were already in Liverpool, and looking forward to the evening. Francie still hadn't decided which of his women to bring. 'If *you* can't be me partner, Jose, then I'm bloody stuck.' Josie hadn't told him about the engagement, knowing he'd laugh like a drain. In bed that night, she sighed wistfully and wished he were bringing Lily. She'd have hurt everyone's feelings, but she'd sooner Lily were coming than anyone.

She was fast asleep when the telephone rang, and immediately felt fearful. It wasn't quite three o'clock, and a call at such an unearthly hour could only be bad news. She gingerly picked up the receiver. 'Hello.'

'Josie, it's Val Morrissey. Sorry, I've just realised it's some ungodly hour in the morning over there. I'm a bit drunk, if the truth be known. I should have left it till tomorrow.'

'Val!' Josie was wide awake, knowing there could be only one reason why he should call at such a time. She swung her legs on to the floor, and sat tensely on the edge of the bed.

'I've found him, Josie. I've found Jack Coltrane. Me and a few guys were watching this video after office hours. I'll leave you to guess what sort. His name was on the credits. I rang the film company. He's still works for them, and they gave me the name of his hotel. The manager confirmed he's a permanent guest.'

'Where is this hotel?' She could hardly speak.

'Miami. I'm not sure what to do, Josie. I don't want to go down there, scare him off.'

'Don't do anything, Val. *I'll* go. I'll go tomorrow – today. As soon as there's a flight.'

'Not by yourself, Josie. Not Miami. Look, when you arrive, check in the Hotel Inter-Continental. It's in downtown Miami, not far from Jack's place. I'll reserve two rooms. Try and let me know your schedule, and we'll meet up there. Okay?'

'Okay,' she agreed. 'See you, Val. And thanks.'

She dialled Directory Enquiries for the number of Manchester airport, then called and made a reservation. She would have to change planes at Orlando, Florida, she was told. Her hand shook as she wrote down the times. A taxi – she needed to book a taxi for six o'clock in order to check in on time. There was the number of a reliable firm in the telephone book downstairs. She went down in her nightie, made the booking, put the kettle on, waited for it to boil, remembered her birthday dinner, remembered Ben!

The kettle boiled. Josie took the tea into the living room, opened the bureau and quickly scribbled letters of apology to all her dinner guests. It had had to be cancelled due to 'unforeseen circumstances', she wrote, and worried that the words sounded too stiff and formal. She put the letters in

Esther's tray in Reception with a note asking her to have them sent by first-class post the minute she came in.

Now Ben! What on earth should she tell him? Even if she didn't find Jack, she knew it was over between her and Ben. She had forgotten him too quickly when the call had come from Val. What did you say to someone whose heart you were about to break a second time?

'My dearest Ben,' she wrote, then paused and chewed the pen. Time was getting on. She needed to get dressed, pack a few things. Her eyes lighted on the little blue box in a pigeonhole of the bureau. The engagement ring Ben had bought that she'd intended to wear for the first time at the dinner! She'd never had one before. She opened the box, and the diamond solitaire winked back at her. Oh, Ben! She wanted to weep for the little boy, wrestling on the floor with his brother, scarlet with embarrassment as he carried her satchel home from school. The young man she'd sat with in restaurants all over Liverpool while they'd argued about politics with Lily and Francie. She'd missed him so much when she'd gone to Haylands, but had quickly been distracted by Griff.

Josie could think of nothing to put in the letter that didn't sound cruel. 'I'm so sorry,' she wrote, 'but I've gone to Miami to meet Jack Coltrane.' She had to get across to him that it was over, just in case he was there when she came back, hurt, disillusioned, but still living in hopes that they had a future together. 'I've always loved you, Ben, but never enough,' she added. How to finish? After gnawing her lip for several seconds, she signed the letter simply, 'Josie.'

The Last Post
1984–1989

I

It was hot in Miami. The streets reminded her of New York, choked with impatiently honking traffic, pavements teaming with people. She caught a taxi from the airport to the hotel, and sat numbly in the back, feeling as if she wasn't really there. Her body felt as heavy as lead, her head like a balloon. She ached for a long, cold drink, then a lie-down, somewhere cool and quiet. She stared through the window, scarcely taking in the colourful sights, and wondered why she'd come. To see a man who had shown no interest in seeing her, a man who had gone out of his way to avoid her, who had advised her to marry someone else? She must be mad.

This is the last time, she vowed. I'll never do it again. If Jack tells me to get lost, I'll put him out of me mind for ever, get on with me life. I'm fifty today, or it might be tomorrow. It could have been yesterday. She had flown through several time zones and had no idea what day it was.

The foyer of the Hotel Inter-Continental contained a huge sculpture by Henry Moore. Josie checked in at reception, and was told she was in room 33 on the third floor. 'A Mr Morrissey in thirty-two has asked to be advised when you arrive. Is it okay to tell him you're here?'

'Yes, of course.'

Val Morrissey was waiting when she got out of the lift. He tipped the bell-hop and took her bag. 'You look shattered. It's

395

nice to meet you after all this time, but I wish the circumstances were different.'

'So do I.'

They kissed affectionately. Their relationship had been conducted entirely by phone, but she looked upon him as a friend. He seemed less brash and sure of himself in the flesh. He showed her to her room. 'It's lovely,' she remarked. It was large, airy, very modern. The bed looked inviting. Josie looked at her watch – a quarter to nine. 'You'll think me stupid, but I don't know if it's night or morning. It never seemed to get dark on the plane.'

'It's morning. Jack will be at the studios by now. I went round to his hotel yesterday. The manager said he's been there two years, and he really likes the guy. The only trouble he has is getting rid of the bottles.'

'Nothing much has changed, then?'

Val shrugged. 'Doesn't seem like it.'

'This film company he works for . . .' She struggled for words. 'You know, I can't see Jack getting involved in porn.'

'It's only soft porn, Josie,' Val said quickly. 'The sort you can rent in any video store. There's nothing illegal about it. Me and the guys in the office wouldn't know where to get the hard stuff. I drove out to the studios yesterday, managed to get talking to a guy in reception. Jack does the scripts, helps with the sound system. He's popular there, too. Rumour is he used to be a well-known playwright till he hit the sauce.'

'He had a play produced off-Broadway,' Josie said proudly. 'It got wonderful reviews. And he wrote one of the best crime series ever seen on British television.' She sat on the bed, and Val regarded her worriedly.

'You look all in. Why don't you rest? I'll do some sightseeing, buy Jessie Mae and Melanie gifts from Miami.'

'How are Jessie Mae and Melanie?' she asked politely.

'I told you Jess was pregnant again, didn't I? We're hoping for a boy this time. She's fine. Having Melanie did her the world of good. She smiles a lot these days.' He made a rueful face. 'She didn't smile all that much when we first got married.'

'I'm glad she's so much happier.'

'We're both happy, Josie, and it's all due to you.'

She hoped he would be returning the favour. He had found Jack, but whether there would be a happy ending was yet to be seen.

He came into the hotel lobby, only slightly unsteady on his feet. The cream linen suit looked like the same one he'd worn in Liverpool, and the T-shirt underneath was white, unironed but clean. He badly needed a shave. There were streaks of grey in the black hair that hung over his eyes. He looked ill, very ill, with dull eyes and a face ravaged by deep, craggy lines.

Josie and Val Morrissey had been waiting for almost an hour in the lobby, sitting side by side on a shabby settee. She got to her feet, and felt the same thrilling sensation course through her veins as the night thirty years before when she'd first seen him in a New York coffee-bar. She went to meet him, stopping a few paces away. 'Hello, Jack.'

'Sweetheart.' He said it without surprise, as if they'd only seen each other yesterday. Then he smiled the smile that would never cease to charm her. 'I knew you'd find me, Jose. I guessed one day you'd track me down.'

'Did you want to be found, darling?'

'I think so.' His head drooped. 'I'm awfully tired, Jose.'

'Then come home with me.'

She bought a house in Mosely Drive, a four-bedroomed bungalow overlooking Sefton Park, not far from the fairy glen. It had belonged to a retired colonel who had called it 'The Last Post'. Josie thought it a silly name and took the sign down. The house had a number, it didn't need a name, though over the years circulars continued to arrive addressed to 'The Occupier, The Last Post'. The decoration inside was ultra-conventional – cream paint everywhere, anaemic flowered wallpaper. She had the walls stripped and painted dusky jewelled colours – deep rose pink, turquoise, amethyst, garnet red, topaz – with curtains to match made from lustrous silks. Much of the furniture was bought from a warehouse in London that imported from all over the world – a wicker bedroom suite, a cane three-piece, an Indian carved table and matching chairs, embroidered rugs and wall hangings. Japanese lanterns hung in every room, and there was always a joss stick burning somewhere, so that the house smelled of musk, orange blossom, sandalwood.

The lounge was at the back, with French windows opening on to the large, somewhat bizarre garden, filled by the retired colonel with statues and tubs, trellises and arches, a fountain and a fish pond, and steps up and down to various levels. It was a cross between a jungle and a maze, with strange plants with curious blooms and prickly leaves that emitted sweet, heady scents.

As the house was painted and furnished, Lily's voice was constantly in her ear. 'Why on earth d'you want to buy *that*, Jose? I couldn't live in the same house with such a peculiar colour/picture/chair.'

It *was* unusual, she had to admit, like one of those Arabian palaces in the Sinbad and Aladdin films she'd seen with Ben when she was little. Jack's study was a restful green, with the latest word processor installed on the desk and a comfortable settee to rest on while he waited for the Muse to strike.

'It's lovely, sweetheart,' he said when everything was done and she showed him round for the first time. 'Exotic, that's the word.'

Until then they'd been living in Huskisson Street, and she had been making him better. When she'd found him in Miami he'd been close to a physical breakdown. Now he was her lover, her child, her patient. She made him rest and fed him, but she couldn't stop him from drinking, and didn't try.

There were times when he tried to stop himself. She could tell when they occurred. He would be scratchy and bad-tempered. He would forget things that had happened the day before, things she'd said. After a while he would break out in a sweat and his face would glisten, as if he had a fever. His hands would shake. 'I think I'll have a drink,' he would say, and go over to the pine sideboard where she openly kept the whisky and brandy – the drinks she knew he liked best – pour himself a large glass and immediately be all right again.

He needed drink to keep going as much as he needed oxygen to breathe. He never had hangovers. He had a drink instead. As he seemed able to function normally after drinking an amount that would have made Josie senseless for a week, she reckoned it was sensible to leave him alone. He knew about Alcoholics Anonymous. If he wanted to go, he would. At the same time, she knew it was killing him. She went to the library, and read with mounting horror the various ways alcohol could kill. It could stop the liver working, damage the heart, cause all sorts of cancers. She thought angrily that he wasn't being fair on her. She had him back, and she wanted to keep him, but she realised there was nothing she could do.

They had been in the new house a week when Dinah and Peter came home from Cuba. Dinah had come especially to see her dad.

'In case you disappear again.' She hugged Jack tearfully. Josie had never known her normally withdrawn daughter be so demonstrative. Perhaps being in love had done it, broken down an emotional barrier. She and Peter were obviously crazy about each other, though they weren't married. Josie would have liked her daughter to become a Kavanagh. There was a chance they might stay in England. Peter had an interview with a trade union in London in a few days' time.

'I'll never go away again,' Jack said. Was it just her imagination, but did he look sad when he said that? She was concerned that he regarded the house as a prison. He'd been very low in Miami, allowing himself to be bundled on a plane, virtually kidnapped. After the glamour of Miami and Los Angeles and the hubbub of New York, how on earth could she expect him to settle in a bungalow, no matter how exotically it was decorated, in a quiet suburb of Liverpool?

It must have been her imagination, the sad look. Not long afterwards Jack declared he hadn't felt so fit in a long time. His eyes had begun to sparkle with the old, irresistible warmth. All of a sudden life in Mosely Drive became almost as good as it had been in New York thirty years ago.

Josie was working mornings only at Barefoot House. After much consideration, she had made Richard Assistant Managing Director. Cathy Connors was more experienced, but she and Lynne Goode didn't get on, and giving her the job would have created waves. Anyroad, Richard had been there from the start, when they'd only been producing a few books a year. He knew as much about the company as Josie.

One dull October day when she and Jack planned to go shopping in town, then to the cinema, followed by dinner, she came home at one o'clock, and the music was audible when she turned into Mosely Drive, even though the car windows were closed. I wouldn't like to live next door to *them*, she thought, and was horrified to discover her own house was the culprit. It was Irish music, the sort she loved – but possibly the neighbours didn't.

In her lounge, two young men were playing the fiddle with an awesome brilliance, and a girl was shaking a tambourine and singing 'The Isle of Innisfree' in a clear, sweet voice.

'Hi, sweetheart.' Jack gave her a hug, and yelled, 'This is Mona, Liam and Dave. I met them at the pub. They're singing at another pub tonight in Dingle. I thought we'd go.' The young people nodded at Josie, but didn't stop playing. She noticed a man, much older, sitting in an armchair, tapping his feet to the music. 'Oh, and this is Greg. He played at the Cavern when it first opened, New Orleans jazz. The group still play occasional gigs.' Greg smiled and nodded.

'Out of interest, will Greg be using our house to rehearse in, as well as Mona, Liam and Dave?' Josie enquired.

'They're not rehearsing, sweetheart. This is by special request, it's my favourite.'

'I see.' She went into the kitchen and put the kettle on, not sure whether to be annoyed or not. The music stopped, and suddenly it was, 'What did you think, Jack?' 'Would you like us to play something else, Jack?'

His head appeared around the door. 'What's your favourite Irish song, sweetheart?'

'"Molly Malone",' she said automatically, and minutes later the fiddles began to play, and Mona began to sing, '"In Dublin's fair city, where the girls are so pretty . . ."'

And Josie began to cry, because it was so much like New York and never, in her wildest dreams, had she imagined she would have those days back again. But it seemed she had.

By Christmas, Jack was at the centre of a network of friends. The house seemed to have become a meeting place for people of all ages, and the phone never stopped ringing. Nine times out of ten it was for him, inviting him to a party, a gig, for a drink, for a meal, to a concert or a play – and the wife, of course. They had tickets for this, tickets for that, and would Jack and the missus like to come? They had friends over from the States, or Australia, or some other country, and would very much like them to meet Jack. Oh, and Josie, too. Their brother or sister was up from London, and had been told about Jack Coltrane. Could Jack pop over for a drink and a chat? And don't hesitate to bring Josie if she'd like to come.

Josie always went. Life had become almost surreal, she was never without a sense of *déjà vu*, or the feeling it was all a dream and one day she'd wake up and Jack would be gone, and she would be living somewhere other than their little palace on Mosely Drive. She felt very much in Jack's shadow, but didn't care. With the same glow of pride she'd had thirty years before, she watched people fussing over him, wanting his opinion on everything under the sun. She noticed the way women tried to grab his attention, flirt, but it didn't bother her. He was *hers*. Everyone assumed they were married, and she supposed they still were in the eyes of God. Jack seemed to have forgotten they were divorced, and always referred to her as his wife, so she called him her husband because in her heart she'd always felt he was.

She and Jack shared history. They'd had two children and one had died, and only she knew he was a hopeless drunk.

Dottie Venables came to stay, having driven from London in her battered Mini. She wore her leather jacket and jeans, and had brought a few bare necessities in a plastic bag. She was immediately bowled over by Jack and he by her. They told each other dirty jokes, tore the government to pieces, went to the pub together when Josie was at her desk in Barefoot House, and matched each other, drink for drink.

Francie arrived on one of the nights she was there. He brought his new girlfriend, Anthea, who would never see fifty again. Francie was already best mates with Jack. They had the same taste in music, and went to football matches together. Josie had never known such an hilarious evening. They swopped outrageous stories. Dottie told them about the time she'd slept with an orang-utan.

'Not a real one?' Josie gasped, worried the conversation was taking an unhealthy turn.

'Of course not. I met him at a party. I didn't realise he looked like an orang-utan till I woke up next morning. I told him to get lost, go swing from a tree, and he wanted to know if my chin had been gnawed by rats.'

'I remember a party once,' Jack said. 'I fell asleep on the couch, and when I woke up it had turned into an orgy. I thought it was a dream and went to sleep again.' He laughed. 'My one and only orgy, and I slept the whole way through.'

He was describing the party they'd gone to at Maya's on New Year's Eve, Josie realised.

'I've always fancied an orgy,' Francie said longingly. 'But they don't seem to have them in Liverpool.'

'You're very lucky,' Dottie said. She nestled in a chair, a glass of whisky in one hand, a cigarette in the other. Francie and Anthea had gone, Jack was in his study, writing an article. It was a new venture. He'd already sold two on the theme of an American's impression of Britain in the eighties. 'You've got a bloke I'd sell me soul for. A great improvement on the other one, the stuffed shirt.'

'Ben?'

'Yeah, Ben. Not your type, not like Jack. Mind you, he's everyone's type.' The leathery face creased in a suggestive smile. 'I could eat the bugger.'

Josie frowned. 'Do you mean he's like a chameleon? He's all things to all men sort of thing?'

'I don't mean any such thing.' Dottie paused. 'Oh, I don't know. Perhaps he *is* all things to all men. It's not that Jack changes, but men see him as the person they want as their best friend, and women the romantic lover they've always desired. I've never envied a woman before because she was married, but I envy you being married to Jack Coltrane.'

'He drinks far too much, Dottie. You must have noticed.' Dottie was one of the few people she felt she could open up to. 'I worry about it all the time. I should stop him, but I don't know how.'

'Leave him be,' Dottie said brusquely. 'It's his body, not yours. You might find Jack the reformed alcoholic an entirely different kettle of fish to Jack the drunk. The drink keeps him going, it's fuel for his engine. Without it, the engine will pack up and die.'

'He's going to die, anyroad, at the rate he drinks.'

'Let him die his own way.' Dottie waved her cigarette. 'These are shortening me life, but I've no intention of stopping. I enjoy them too much, I need them. I'd sooner go to an early grave then give up me fags.'

There'd been no sign of Ben since she'd come back from Miami, not surprising under the circumstances. When Jack had first wondered why Peter's father didn't come to visit when he lived less than a mile away, Josie told him they had

403

lived together for three years. 'You advised me to marry someone else, remember?' she said virtuously. 'Well, me and Ben didn't quite go that far.'

On Saturday Ben had been invited to Mosely Drive for tea, because now the two families had a grandson between them and they couldn't go on not meeting for the rest of their lives. Josie wasn't looking forward to it.

Peter had got the job in London with the trade union, just as Dinah discovered she was pregnant. It was May again when Josie and Jack went to London to be with their daughter when she had Oliver, nine pounds six ounces, and the most beautiful baby boy Josie had ever seen.

'Pleased to meet you, luv,' she whispered to the fat, lobster-coloured ball that was her first grandchild. 'You'll have lots more, won't you?' she said to Dinah, who was sitting proudly up in bed, despite having had three stitches. Peter looked exhausted, as if it had been he who'd given birth.

'I'm not sure whether to have another two or three. What do you think, Pete?'

'I couldn't stand another one,' Peter groaned.

'Come on, Pete.' Jack slapped him on the back. 'I'll treat you to a cup of tea.'

The men left, and Dinah said, 'Mum?'

'Yes, luv?' Josie was examining the tiny fingers, the pink toes. 'He's perfect,' she breathed.

'Mum, you've no idea how much it's meant to me, you and Dad being around when I was having Oliver. For the first time in me life I feel part of a proper family.' Dinah's eyes were unnaturally bright.

'I know exactly how much it's meant, luv,' Josie said softly. 'I feel the same. I've got you, your dad, a grandson, Peter.' She sighed blissfully. 'It's a long time since I felt so happy.' Jack had probably made an excuse to go to the Gents to swig half the contents of the little flask he carried in his hip pocket. But, then, you couldn't have everything.

It was an awkward meal. Ben turned out to be the first person in the world to hate Jack Coltrane on sight. He hardly spoke, and then only to mutter a reply to something said to him. Josie found herself paying an awful lot of attention to Oliver, now a month old and already smiling broadly. 'Isn't he gorgeous?' she said several times.

'Yes,' Ben would grudgingly agree.

Jack didn't seem to notice anything amiss. He drank glass after glass of wine and regaled them with bits of gossip from his time spent in the film industry.

For some reason Ben's normally good-natured face got darker and darker. As soon as the meal finished he pushed back his chair and declared he had to go. 'Perhaps you and Dinah could bring Oliver to see me while you're home?' he said stiffly to his son. He clearly had no intention of returning to Mosely Drive.

Josie went with him to his car. 'Thank you for coming.'

'Thanks for asking.' He unlocked the door, opened it, then angrily turned on her. 'I don't take kindly to being dumped for such a . . . a *blaggard*,' he snapped, almost choking on the words. 'And I've never known anyone down so much wine with a meal. Is he an alcoholic?'

'Mind your own business,' Josie said coldly.

'Then I take it that he is.'

'Take it any way you like.' She went back into the house and slammed the door.

That night they had dinner in a new vegetarian restaurant in town, where one of Jack's friends had an exhibition of paintings – one of the garish offerings already hung in their hall. Before long their table was packed, and Jack was at the centre of an admiring audience.

'Is it always like this?' Dinah enquired.

'Always, luv. Here, give us Oliver, so you can eat your pudding in peace.'

'It makes me feel quite proud he's my father. It's like having Robert Redford for a dad, or Paul Newman. I'm sure everyone's dead envious.'

'It's a nice feeling, isn't it?' No one asked Josie what she did.

They didn't know she owned one of the most successful small publishers in the country. She was Jack Coltrane's wife, which was enough as far as they were concerned.

'Christ, Josie, that guy's a dork,' Jack said disgustedly when they were in bed. 'Why didn't you and he get hitched?'

Because he's a dork, Josie wanted to say, but held her tongue. It was unfair to make fun of a nice, decent man like Ben. 'It just never seemed the right time.'

'He's still in love with you. His eyes followed you everywhere. And he hates me.' He spoke matter-of-factly, with a certain amount of satisfaction. 'Come here!' He folded her in his arms. 'Whose woman are you?'

'Yours, Jack,' she whispered.

'What was the dork like in bed?'

'Not very good,' she said truthfully. 'He never turned me on, not like you.' She stroked his face. 'There's never been anyone like you. Kiss me, Jack, quickly. I can't wait.'

On Monday Ben came to Barefoot House to apologise. 'I'm sorry about the way I behaved,' he said stiffly. 'It got to me, I suppose, seeing you and him together.' His lips pursed. 'I won't pretend to like him, because I don't. He's not worthy of you.'

'And you are?'

He went red. 'I didn't mean it like that. If you were going to leave me, I wish it had been for someone . . . different.'

'We're together because we love each other, Ben,' Josie said gently, and immediately wished she hadn't because he looked as if he was about to burst into tears.

'I realise that.' He nodded. 'I've just got to learn to live with it, that's all.'

Another May, Josie's fifty-fourth birthday, and the day Dinah had a second son, Christopher, two ounces heavier than Oliver. 'Though I only had two stitches this time,' she said happily when Josie went to see her in hospital. During the birth she'd stayed in their small house in Crouch End looking after Oliver, who would be three next week.

'Another two babies, and you mightn't need stitches at all. The more grandchildren the better, as far as I'm concerned.' She already haunted Mothercare, buying toys and clothes for Oliver. The dark-eyed, dark-haired baby in her arms reminded her very much of Laura, though she didn't say so. She tearfully kissed the sleepy face.

Dinah wrinkled her nose. 'Two's my lot, I'm afraid. Peter thinks it's wrong to over-populate the world. There's hardly enough food for the people there are now, though I intend to try and change his mind. I'd like to have another two babies – a daughter would be nice, for a change, like.'

'I'll get your dad to work on him.' Peter took far more notice of Jack than he did of his own father. They shared the same radical views. Ben, once the champion of the Peasants' Revolt, had become very pro-establishment over the years, whereas Jack remained a die-hard Socialist.

Dinah looked worried. 'Is Dad okay? I wish he was here.'

'He wanted to come, I told you, but he was feeling tired. He'll be sixty next year, Dinah. He's slowing down.'

'He drinks too much, doesn't he, Mum? You can't help but notice, though I've never seen him pissed.' Dinah pleated and unpleated the sheet between her fingers. Her eyes were scared. 'I wish you'd make him stop.'

'Nothing on earth can stop your dad drinking, Dinah. I've reached the age when I realise it's no use trying to change people. They are what they are, and there's nothing you can do about it.'

When Josie got back to Mosely Drive it was almost dark, and Jack appeared to be out. Their little Arabian palace was unnaturally quiet, unusually cold. The bell mobile in the living room was tinkling eerily – she must do something about the draught from the French windows. There was a musty smell, as if the place had been empty for weeks. For some reason she shivered. This was a house that was rarely still, and silence sat uneasily on the warmly coloured rooms with their foreign furniture and exotic ornaments.

She switched on lights, and went into the kitchen to put the kettle on. In the lounge, she turned on the gas fire with real flames. 'That's better,' she muttered. 'More like home.'

Where was Jack? She searched for a note to tell her where he'd gone. When she'd called from London to say what time she would be home, he'd promised to have a pot of tea waiting. He'd been in the study when she'd phoned.

With a feeling of alarm she went into the hall and opened the study door – and a great black hole seemed to open in front of her. Jack was lying on the settee, and she knew straight away that he was dead. His face was sickly pale, his lips curved in the slightest of smiles. He had rested his head on a green satin pillow,one hand cupping his chin, the other hanging limply. His body, from head to toe, seemed to be covered in a grey veil, like the finest of cobwebs. A half-empty bottle of whisky was on the desk.

'*Jack!*' She screamed, and the veil disappeared. Jack opened his eyes, and said blearily, 'Hi, sweetheart. I must have dropped off. Hey, guess what, I've started a play.'

'You bugger!' She sank, shaking, into a chair, her hand pressed to her crazily beating heart. 'I thought you were dead!'

'I'm very much alive, Josie. Well, almost. I've got pins and needles in my legs.' He tried to stand, laughed and fell back. 'They'll go in a minute.'

Perhaps it was because she had thought him dead, or that she had been away for ten whole days, but Josie was suddenly struck by how old he looked, and so very frail. She hadn't realised that his hair had turned quite so grey, or that he had a slight stoop, or that the flesh on his neck was hanging loosely. Had his wrists always been so thin, with the bones protruding sharply, like little white doorknobs? His eyes, though, his eyes were just the same – warm, brown, smiling at her from the face more heavily lined than she remembered.

He made another attempt to get up, and Josie said, 'Stay there, darling. The kettle's just boiled. I'll make some tea.'

She put milk in cups, two sugars for Jack, none for her, and spread a plate with chocolate biscuits. She'd make a proper meal in a minute, something quick from the freezer. In the lounge the bell mobile tinkled, and she thought again about the draught, but all the while there was a buzzing in her head, a feeling of dread in her bones, because she knew, somehow she just knew, that Jack was dying. She had seen it in his face, as if death were lurking somewhere near, waiting to pounce. There'd been a feeling in the air when she came in, a haunted quietness, like the calm before the storm. If she hadn't arrived when she did, she felt convinced that death would have taken from her the man she loved.

He was passing blood. She found it on his clothes, but he flatly refused to see a doctor. 'I don't want to know what's wrong,' he said, so airily that she wanted to thump him.

'You might only need a few tablets.'

He smiled sweetly. 'I don't think so, sweetheart.'

She stamped her foot. 'Since when have you been such an expert on medical matters?'

'I'm an expert when it comes to treatment for myself. No doctors, no tablets. And kindly don't mention the words "hospital" or "operations" in my presence. I'm having no truck with either.'

Josie rang Dottie and told her about Jack's intransigence.

'I don't blame him,' Dottie said gruffly. 'It's his body. I said that to you once before. It's up to him how it's treated.'

'That's stupid,' Josie wept. She told her about the blood on his clothes. 'What can it mean?'

'Do you want me to be brutally honest?'

Josie hesitated. 'Yes, please.'

'It might be something quite innocent, but Jack's drunk so much for so long that his insides have probably rotted. It could be cancer.'

'Oh, God, *no!*'

'It's probably why he won't see a doctor. He doesn't want all that radiotherapy rubbish. In fact,' Dottie said thoughtfully, 'we talked about it once. We both agreed we'd sooner die than have treatment that can drag on for years. Relatives suffer as much as the patient. I said I'd like to meet me maker with a fag in my hand, and Jack said he wanted to go holding a glass of Jack Daniels.'

He was visibly getting weaker and weaker, day by day. He ate scarcely anything. They didn't go out much. Francie came round on Saturday afternoons with half a dozen cans of beer, and they watched football on television.

It had happened, like every major event in her life, in the twinkling of an eye. Josie had gone to London to see a new life being born, and returned to find another life being slowly snuffed out.

'*Make* him go to the doctor, Mum,' Dinah raged on the phone.

'I can't, luv. He refuses to budge.'

'Then get the doctor to come to *him*.'

'I did, and your dad refused to see him. He went into his study and played New Orleans jazz at top blast.'

'Is he depressed?' Dinah asked curiously.

'No, he's perfectly happy. There's people dropping in to see him all day long. He's busy writing his play, and drinking like a fish, which is probably why he doesn't have any pain. It's almost as if . . .' Josie paused.

'As if what, Mum?'

'As if he *doesn't care*.' She suppressed a sob.

'But, Mum,' Dinah cried despairingly, 'he's always been so full of life. Why on earth should he not care?'

'I don't know, Dinah. I wish I did.'

They had begun to talk openly about death. 'No Requiem Mass, no priests, no prayers, no hymns,' he said lightly. 'If there must be music, I want Louis Armstrong, Jerryroll Morton and Ella Fitzgerald singing "Every Time We Say Goodbye".'

'Fuck off,' Josie said.

He looked at her, pretending to be shocked. 'I've never heard you use that word before.'

'I never have. How dare you sit there, dictating the music for your funeral? Have you got no thought for me?' She burst into tears. 'I haven't the remotest idea how I'll live without you.'

'You'll get over me in time, Jose,' he said, so complacently that she nearly threw her book at him. 'Everyone gets over everything in time.'

'Have you got over Laura? *I* haven't. A day never goes by when I don't think about her.'

His thin face paled. 'That day is indelibly etched in my mind. It will be a relief to escape. I don't believe in an afterlife but, you never know, sweetheart, if there's a heaven, I might meet our little girl.'

'Oh, *God*, Jack. I don't think I can take any more of this.'

By now, he was housebound. Every part of him was gradually breaking down. His legs wouldn't carry him far, his hands could barely grasp a cup. He felt the cold acutely, even though it was a fine, warm summer. His study was a hothouse, where he worked feverishly on his play, still able to type. 'It's the best thing I've ever done,' he gloated. You would never guess from his voice, from his laugh or the warm brown smiling eyes that he was a dying man.

'Can I read it?' Josie asked.

'No, you cannot. I'll not forget the way you treated my other plays. You kicked them, if I remember rightly.'

'I won't kick this one,' she promised.

'You're not touching this play until it's in a sealed envelope.' He grinned. 'Then you can post it. Now go away. I'm in a hurry to finish.'

His meaning was obvious. Josie went into the kitchen and threw a cup at the wall.

She had forgotten she was supposed to be running a busy publishing company, but Barefoot House seemed to be coping quite well without her. Dottie Venables produced a charming saga every year, and each one sold in its hundreds of thousands; William Friars's Bootle thrillers continued to be

411

hits, particularly in the States, where he had a large cult following. The anonymous young Irish writer who called herself Lesley O'Rourke never wrote another book, but *My Favourite Murderer* continued to sell well in the shops. There were other new writers that she'd never met. One of these days I must catch up on them, she thought, and remembered what would have to happen before she did.

The play was done. It was called *The Last Post*. 'You called it after the house?' Josie was startled. 'What's it about?'

'Mind your own business.'

'Am I allowed to know where you're sending it?'

'I can't keep that a secret, it's on the envelope. It's going to Max Stafford-Clark at the Royal Court. I met him once. Tomorrow I shall run off a copy and send it to another theatre, and another the day after, and the day after that. This play is going to every theatre in the country.'

Josie hurried to the post office with the large brown envelope under her arm. She would have given everything she possessed in return for Jack's play being accepted before he died.

She rang Francie. 'Can you do me a letterhead, just one sheet?'

'It must be for a very important letter, Jose.'

'It is.' She explained what it was for. 'I'll send you the particulars – I got them from the London phone directory. I'll type the letter meself.'

'I'll get it done today, Jose.'

'There's no need to rush.' There had to be a decent interval between the play's arrival and acceptance by the theatre. She prayed Jack would last that long.

Dinah rang. 'Mum, I'm pregnant,' she said in a small voice.

'Good heavens, Dinah.' Josie sat down quickly. 'I'm thrilled to bits, but Christopher's only four months old. You're going to have two babies on your hands. I thought you didn't want to over-populate the world?'

'One of the reasons the world is over-populated is that

some women think they can't become pregnant if they're breast-feeding and not having periods.'

'You mean they can?'

'I'm living proof. Not that I mind, but Peter's a bit fed up. Anyroad, that's only half me news. The other half is we're getting married.'

Josie's hand tightened on the receiver. If only they'd thought of it before, when Jack . . . 'That's marvellous, luv. I wish your dad was well enough to be there.'

'I wouldn't dream of getting married in London. We've booked the register office in Brougham Terrace for half past two on the fourteenth of September, two weeks on Friday. Can you put us up? If Dad can give me away, it'll be the best wedding *ever!*'

2

Only close friends and relatives had been invited to the actual ceremony – Ben, obviously, Colette, Jeremy, and the twins, Marigold and Jonathan, Dottie Venables, Richard White from Barefoot House who'd once worked with Dinah, Francie O'Leary and his sons, Lily's two girls and Oliver, in new shorts and his first proper shirt. Josie would carry Christopher.

Every single person they knew was coming to the reception, which would be held in Mosely Drive – Josie's staff, Jack's friends and their neighbours either side so they wouldn't complain about the noise. Josie didn't bother to count the numbers. She ordered enough food and drink for a hundred and fifty, hoping there'd be enough and that the weather would be fine so people could go in the garden. If everyone had to stay inside, they wouldn't be able to breathe.

The Irish group were coming, as were Greg and his jazz band. Francie was bringing his sixties records, and Josie made sure there was a spare stylus for the turntable on the music centre.

She had never known a week like it before in her life. The

air tingled with bitter-sweet excitement. Her husband was dying, her daughter was getting married and she never seemed to be without a lump in her throat. The phone scarcely stopped ringing; people kept dropping in with wedding presents. She had Jack try on his suits and discovered they were all too big, so a tailor was persuaded to come round and measure for alterations. He took away the mid-grey flannel she liked best, and promised to have it ready by Friday morning. He was so nice and helpful that she invited him to the wedding.

There was a posy to order for Dinah, buttonholes for the guests, flowers for the house, bedrooms to get ready. She still hadn't bought herself an outfit. A problem cropped up at Barefoot House and she told them she didn't want to know. The firm could go bankrupt for all she cared. This coming Friday represented a full stop in her life, and she didn't give a damn what happened afterwards.

Dinah arrived with Oliver and Christopher on Tuesday, Dottie on Wednesday to 'give a hand'. Peter wasn't coming till Thursday evening.

'Did you give him that letter to post?' Josie said to Dinah anxiously. 'It's got to have a London postmark.'

'He's posting it Thursday morning.'

Josie gazed out of the window, where Jack was sitting on a bench with Oliver. Her heart turned over. There was hardly anything left of him. His face was calm, as if he were at peace with himself. With each day that passed she sensed he was growing further and further away, from her, from everyone, that he was holding himself together until Friday.

She took Dinah and the children to the fairy glen. 'I used to bring you in a great big pram when you were Christopher's age,' she told her daughter. The baby was fast asleep in his carrycot on wheels, which would have been dead useful when she'd lived in Princes Avenue. Oliver chased the ducks, and Josie showed Dinah the bench where she'd had the argument with Ben, and where Daisy Kavanagh had been sitting the morning she'd rescued her from a great dilemma.

'What sort of dilemma?' Dinah wanted to know.

'I can't remember now,' her mother lied. It had been all to do with Uncle Vince, and Josie found it hard to believe she was still the same person who'd lived in Machin Street with the man who had been both her uncle and her father. Or the little girl from Huskisson Street whose mam was on the game. She hardly ever thought about Mam these days, yet there'd been a time when she'd thought of her every day.

'Mum, what's wrong? You look as if you're going to cry.'

'I dunno, luv. It's the passing of time, growing old. It's all so terribly *sad*. Oh,' she cried angrily, 'I wish people didn't have to die!'

'But then there'd be no space for babies to be born.' Dinah sounded very practical. 'One of these days Peter and I will die, by which time our children will have had children. Even this one in here.' She patted her stomach. 'It's the way of the world, Mum.'

'There's still no reason why it has to be so bloody *sad*.'

She went shopping alone and bought a dress of ivory sculptured velvet, very fine. The material clung to her hips, swirling around her ankles in soft folds. Her own wedding outfit had been pink velvet, she remembered, and she'd got it in a thrift shop. When Dinah's wedding was over, she would put this dress away and never wear it again, nor the delicate, high-heeled, strappy shoes and the hat that was like a large flower, the petals framing her face. She was buying everything especially for Jack.

'You'll look more like the bride than the real one,' Dottie commented when Josie got home and showed her everything.

'Dinah won't mind.' Dinah had decided on a plain blue suit that would 'do again'. 'What will you be wearing, Dottie?' She was praying that one of the country's bestselling novelists didn't intend to turn up to the wedding in her customary leather jacket and jeans.

Dottie must have guessed her thoughts. She hooted raucously. 'I won't let you down, Jose. There's a smart check suit hanging in the wardrobe.' She winked. 'I got it in Harrods. By the way, has Lynne told you not to expect a book from me next year?'

'No, but I've deliberately cut meself off from Barefoot House all week.' That could have been the problem they'd wanted to discuss the other day. Josie didn't care if Dottie never wrote another book again.

'Don't you want to know why?' Dottie pretended to look hurt.

'Of course, Dottie. Why can't I expect a book from you next year?'

'Because I'm trekking round the world, that's why.' The small eyes twinkled wickedly.

'Trekking!' Josie giggled. 'In a pith helmet and khaki shorts?'

'Forget about the helmet, but I've already got the shorts. And, no, I'm not really trekking, but I'm going to visit the most out-of-the-way places where there's no chance of being murdered or kidnapped, so Barefoot House doesn't have to worry about paying a ransom.' Dottie sighed rapturously. 'I intend to cross America by Greyhound bus, travel through Canada by train, learn to play the didgeridoo in Australia. I'm fifty-five, Josie, same as you, and I've never seen an iceberg in the flesh, walked through a jungle, crossed a desert on a camel, sailed down the Nile. Before I get too old I want to do every single one of those things, and a few more I haven't mentioned.'

Josie said it sounded marvellous, and she was looking forward to lots of postcards, though she was unable to imagine a time beyond Friday.

She woke at half six on the day Dinah was to marry Peter Kavanagh. The glimmer of light showing between the curtains looked ominously dull. When she got out of bed to look out of the window, her worst suspicious were confirmed. It was raining, not heavily but a steady drizzle, and dark clouds rolled across the leaden sky.

'What's it like?' Jack was struggling to sit up.

'Horrible!'

'It's only early. There's plenty of time for it to improve.'

Josie got back into bed and curled up against him. 'How do you feel?'

'Great.'

'Are you sure you're up to going to the register office?'

He looked at her, amused. 'I just said I felt great. I mean it, Jose. This is a day I never in my wildest dreams thought would happen. My daughter is getting married and I'm giving her away.' He kissed the top of her head. 'Thank you for the last five years, sweetheart.'

'Thank *you*, Jack. They've been wonderful.'

They stayed leaning against the pillows for quite a while, neither speaking. Questions chased each other through Josie's head. How many more times will I do this? How many more times will I hear him call me 'sweetheart'? They were questions to which she didn't want an answer.

The post came. There was a letter for Jack with a London postmark. Josie had typed the envelope herself a few days before. He was in the bathroom, no doubt having the first drink of the day. For some reason he had always shut himself away for the early morning drinks. She knocked on the door and sang out, 'Letter for you. I'll put it on your desk.'

By nine o'clock the sun was struggling to come out. By ten it was a shimmering golden ball, and the clouds had miraculously disappeared. The garden was like a fairy tale, engulfed in a mist of steam as everything began to dry in the heat. Dinah's posy and the buttonholes were delivered, along with a great heap of russet chrysanthemums. Josie mustered every vase she possessed and arranged them around the house. The caterers were bringing the buffet while the wedding was in progress – the woman next door would let them in. Jack still hadn't opened his letter.

She went with Dinah for a shampoo and set, and Dottie looked after the children – nothing on earth could persuade Dottie inside a hairdresser's. Peter had stayed the night with his father. It had been Josie's idea. 'It's unlucky for the groom to see the bride before the wedding,' she stated. Dinah thought the idea daft. They'd been living together for years and had two children and another on the way. 'Don't tempt fate, luv,' Josie warned.

'Oh, *Mum*,' Dinah said impatiently, but nevertheless agreed.

They returned from the hairdresser's to find the tailor had delivered Jack's suit. Jack was in the shower, and emerged shortly afterwards, wearing the trousers and a new white shirt, a leather belt around his much too narrow waist. He looked ten years younger, and fitter than he'd done in weeks. There was colour in his cheeks, and he held himself sternly erect. 'Which tie, do you think?' He held up three.

'Let Dinah choose, it's her wedding.'

Dinah frowned at the ties. 'The light grey one, Dad.' She went to give Christopher his midday feed.

'She called me "Dad".' Jack's smile was sweet and grateful. 'Your hair looks nice.'

'I thought I'd have it tucked behind me ears for a change. It'll look better with me hat.'

'When am I going to see this incredible hat?'

'Later, when I'm completely ready. Who was that letter from?' she asked casually.

'I haven't opened it yet. Probably an acknowledgement from one of the theatres for my play.'

Josie looked at her watch and screamed. A quarter past one! 'I'd better get changed.'

She took particular care with her make-up, outlining her eyes with black kohl, which she hadn't done in years, smoothing pale gold shadow on her lids, giving the lashes several coats of mascara. She lightly powdered her face, stroked her cheeks with blusher, painted her lips a shade similar to the chrysanthemums that filled the house. There were new tights, very pale, bought specially to go with the ivory dress. No need for a slip as the dress was lined. The cold material was icy when she put it on, making her shiver. The strappy shoes felt uncomfortable straight away, but she didn't care because they went perfectly with the dress. She searched through her jewellery box for Louisa's amber pendant, and the earrings Jack had given her to match. Finally, the hat, which cast shadows over her face, making her look enigmatic and aloof, like Greta Garbo.

She was ready, and her full-length reflection stared back at her from the wardrobe mirror. I *am* beautiful, she thought, but I will never be as beautiful again as I am today.

Jack was in his study. There was no sign of the letter that she was so anxious for him to open. 'How do I look?' She gave a little twirl.

He caught his breath, and the expression of tender, naked love on his face made her heart turn over. His lips trembled slightly when he smiled. 'Was that a Liverpool accent I just heard?'

She remembered the way his dark eyes had smiled into hers when he'd asked the same question on the steps of Best Cellar. 'Yes,' she replied now, as she had done then.

'Please, can I kiss you? I haven't kissed a girl from Liverpool in years.' He took her in his arms, ever so gently.

'I can't remember what I said then.' She rested her cheek against his. 'It's thirty-five years since the night we met.'

'I asked your name and where you came from. You said you were Josie Flynn from Penny Lane. I decided there and then to change your name.'

She didn't think that was true. 'Have I ever told you I'd been watching you for ages?' Watching the handsome, animated young man across the tables of the basement coffee-bar in New York.

'Hmm. We only met because I'd forgotten my coat.'

And if he hadn't! Oh, what would have happened then? Things couldn't possibly have turned out more tragically if they'd both married someone else. Yet there was nowhere else on earth she'd sooner be at this moment than in the arms of Jack Coltrane.

He seemed to have found a mysterious inner strength. His voice in the register office was steady when he gave his daughter to Peter Kavanagh. He firmly held Josie's arm for the photographs, kissed Dinah, shook hands with Peter and Ben, shared a joke with Dottie and Francie.

They went back to Mosely Drive. Guests had already started to arrive. Champagne was opened, toasts were drunk, food began to rapidly disappear. Mona, Liam and Dave played Irish songs and encouraged everyone to join in the choruses. Greg and his group of grey-haired musicians belted out 'Side walk Blues', 'Beale Street Blues', 'Snake Rag' . . . Francie put on his Beatles records, Dottie did an imitation of Mrs Thatcher, the tailor, whose name was Maurice Cohen, sang a haunting Yiddish ballad, and quite a few people cried.

The day wore on. Josie had removed her hat and shoes, Dinah had combed her hair loose and changed from the blue suit into something lilac and filmy. She looked heartbreakingly lovely.

Dusk began to fall, music continued to play, the children went to bed, and everyone lit the hundreds of candles which had been placed inside the house and in the garden, and it was like walking through stars.

But none of the stars shone as brightly as Jack. Josie couldn't take her eyes off the man she had married. He seemed almost to float among the guests, a glass in his hand, everyone anxious to have a word with him, just catch his eye. Perhaps she had drunk too much, perhaps time was going backwards, but the more she watched, the younger he seemed to be, as if a miracle was happening.

'He's okay.' Ben appeared at her side, slightly tipsy. He nodded towards Jack. 'He's okay.'

'I know, Ben.' She linked his arm in hers. 'Can we be friends?'

'Always, Jose. Always.'

Midnight. People started to leave. They shook Jack's hand, pressed his shoulder, even hugged him, as if the men knew this was the last time they would see this very special person they regarded as their best friend and the women the lover they had always dreamed of.

Francie put on a Frank Sinatra record, and the vibrant, tender voice began to sing 'Smoke Gets In Your Eyes'. The few people left were in the living room, where the French windows opened on to a carpet of candles, fluttering low now. Gradually, the flames began to go out, one by one by one.

Dinah and Peter were dancing, wrapped tightly in each other's arms. Oh, she was so pleased their daughter was happy. Then Jack held out his hand, and Josie drifted into his arms. She could hardly think. There was too much emotion in the room, and she couldn't bear it.

'I don't want to leave you, sweetheart,' Jack whispered.

'My darling, I don't want you to go.' Over his shoulder she could see the last remaining candle flicker out, and the garden was plunged into darkness. 'They asked me how I knew, our true love was true,' Frank Sinatra sang.

Jack was beginning to flag. It must have come over him very suddenly. She could feel his body heavy against hers. She was virtually holding him up. 'Go to bed,' she urged softly. 'I'll join you in a minute.'

'That mightn't be a bad idea.' He jerked himself upright, one final effort to get through his daughter's wedding day. The music finished, Jack said goodnight.

'Goodnight, mate.' Francie pumped his hand. He was nodding for some reason, nodding over and over.

Dottie kissed him. 'Sleep well, Jack.'

Ben shook his hand, Peter gave his father-in-law a hug, Dinah flung her arms around his neck. 'Night, Dad.'

Jack touched her chin. He said something Josie couldn't hear, then left the room.

Dinah's eyes were bright with tears. 'He called me Laura,' she said.

'Do you mind?' Josie asked anxiously.

'No.' Dinah shook her head. 'That's what the drinking's always been about, isn't it? He killed Laura and he's never got over it.'

'Probably, luv.' For some reason she thought about the

other children there might have been had she and Jack had stayed together. She said her own goodnights, and apologised if it looked rude but she'd like to be with Jack.

He was already in bed when she went in. She noticed he'd managed to put the grey flannel suit neatly on a chair. 'Nice try, sweetheart,' he said.

'What?'

'Nice try, with the play, that is.' He chuckled. 'The Royal Court wrote last Monday and turned the play down. A few days later they write on a completely different letterhead, saying they'd be pleased to put it on.'

'I'm sorry.' Josie removed her clothes and slipped, naked, into bed. She pressed herself against him. One of these days she'd read his play for herself. 'Are you mad at me?'

'I'm mad about you, sweetheart, always have been.' He yawned. 'I think I'll sleep now. Have you enjoyed the day?'

'It's been wonderful, Jack.'

He was already asleep. Josie woke up during the night, and he was making love to her with all the energy of a young man. His brown eyes were smiling warmly into hers, his hair flopped on his forehead. She could feeling herself coming, coming . . . Oh, this was the best she had ever known, exquisite. Her body was on fire, and Jack was pouring himself into her, loving her . . .

It must have been a dream because when she woke Jack was barely conscious, and he never got out of bed again.

Over the next few days he slipped in and out of reality. Now and then he could carry on a perfectly lucid conversation, then his eyes would close and nothing could rouse him.

'Ben would make a good husband,' he said one day. He even managed a rusty laugh. 'He'll cut your meat up for you when you get old. Francie would make you laugh. Did you know you're the first girl who turned him on?'

'He told you?'

But he had drifted away. Next time he woke up, hours later, he asked for Laura. 'She's not here, darling. Shall I fetch Dinah?'

He had gone again. Josie called the doctor when he began to have hallucinations and a sedative was injected. 'It's a pity we didn't meet before,' the doctor, an elderly man, said drily. 'I would have told him how much my late wife and I used to enjoy that television series of his. What was it called?'

'*DiMarco of the Met.*'

'That's right. We could never get our little son to bed the night it was on.' He promised to come again that night.

'He should have injected a triple whisky,' Dottie said. Like Dinah and Peter, Dottie had stayed in Mosely Drive. Francie and Ben came every day. People kept telephoning. 'He's stone cold sober for the first time in years.'

'What can I do?' Josie cried frantically.

'Nothing. Just pray the end will be quick.' Dottie wasn't inclined to beat about the bush.

Jack Coltrane died when his daughter was with him, and his son-in-law was holding his hand. It was ten past two in the morning. Josie was snatching a few hours' sleep on the settee in the study when Dinah woke her. 'He's gone, Mum. It was very peaceful. One minute he was breathing, then suddenly it stopped.'

They embraced each other, then Josie went into the bedroom. She pressed Peter's shoulder. He kissed her and left the room, and she was left with Jack. She knelt beside the bed, laid her head on his chest and wept.

Somehow she got through the days before the funeral. Jack had wanted to be cremated, and the service was in the same chapel as Lily's had been held. There was no Mass, no hymns, no prayers, no priests, just people taking turns to say a few words about their friend. The rather rusty strains of Louis Armstrong, Jellyroll Morten and King Oliver drifted from the loudspeaker, but Josie hadn't mentioned he'd wanted Ella Fitzgerald because listening to 'Every Time We Say Goodbye' just wasn't on. She would have broken down, along with everybody else.

She didn't look when the curtains closed on the coffin and it slid into the flames. Jack had dismissed the idea of flowers, so there were no wreaths to admire when they emerged into the pale sunshine of a mid-September day. Everyone stood around awkwardly, talking in subdued voices. Dinah said, 'Do you mind if Peter and I go, Mum? I'm worried about leaving the children with the woman next door. Francie or Ben will give you a lift home.' She squeezed Josie's hand. 'I'll have tea made.'

'I've invited a few people back.' Only a few. It would be such a contrast to last week's wedding.

She shook dozens of hands, thanked people for coming, her voice cold with grief. Would she ever feel normal again?

Nearly everyone had gone, just a few old friends left. Marigold and Jonathan kissed her and said goodbye, then Terence and Muriel Dunnet, both now very old, Cathy Connors and Lynne Goode from Barefoot House, Richard White, all terribly sad.

Josie was left with Dottie and the two men who had featured so largely in her life – Ben Kavanagh and Francie O'Leary. They walked over to their cars, unlocked the doors, looked at her expectantly, waiting for her to choose.

Dottie said, 'See you back at the house, Jose.' She took it for granted that Josie wouldn't want a lift in the decrepit Mini with rusting doors and an engine that sounded a bit like its owner's gruff voice.

There's nothing left for me! Josie thought despairingly, as she glanced from Ben to Francie, from Francie to Ben. Then, from nowhere, came a vision of leafy jungles, hot arid deserts, trains and buses to far-away places, strangers speaking languages she didn't understand.

She caught her breath. Dottie was about to slam the door of the Mini. 'Dottie,' she called.

'Yes, Jose?'

'Can I come with you?'